QUANTUM EARTH

Ad Astra Chronicles, Book 1

Some things are literally impossible.
Everything else is merely improbable to varying degrees.

I0676580

QUANTUM EARTH

First edition. March 22, 2025.

ISBN: 978-0473627911

Written by Max White.

INITIATION

The clean room hummed, not just with electricity, but with anticipation. More than a decade of research and experimentation had led to this day, and the team at IVIA – Instituto Vélez para la Investigación Avanzada, or Vélez Institute for Advanced Research – was confident of making an historic breakthrough in the field of quantum mechanics.

The director, and founder, of the Institute, Antonia Vélez, 39, had studied under and worked with some of the most respected names in quantum science before investing the bulk of her family fortune in the establishment of the Institute. She had head-hunted the best and brightest up-and-coming young stars to work for her, and the culmination of all her hard work and massive investment was at hand.

Antonia wore a tailored white lab coat and navy blue pencil skirt that set off her trim figure. She was of short stature, being only 160cm, or 5'3", but held herself with the confidence that comes from wealth and authority. Disdaining makeup, her alabaster skin highlighted her piercing blue almond-shaped eyes set above high, sharp cheekbones, and was in turn accentuated by her raven-coloured shoulder length bangs.

The clean room was situated in the centre of the glass and stainless-steel edifice on the outskirts of Toledo that housed the Institute. Multiple layers of decontamination and security protected the nerve centre of the operation from both dust and espionage. The room was comprised of several concentric circles, with six workstations on each of two opposite sides of the outer circle, manned by masked figures in brilliant white protective suits, only their name badges distinguishing them from one another. Antonia occupied a separate, glass-walled booth at a third side, along with her second-in-command, 28-year-old genius Kaito Mitsuhashi. Kaito was taller, at 175cm or 5'9", and of slender build. Like Antonia, he chose not to wear clean room overalls, and was attired in charcoal trousers and waistcoat over a pale blue shirt accessorised with a bright yellow bow-tie. Heavy tortoise-shell glasses and slicked-back, black hair completed the look of the professional nerd.

On the fourth side, and also glass-walled (technically, shatter-proof and heat-resistant polyacrylate) was a bewildering array of technology that included towering transformers, cryogenic cooling systems, and immense capacitor banks. Heavily shielded cables ran from these devices to server towers and readouts that filled the lowered middle ring like a steampunk vision of a city skyline. Other conduits ran from both this cityscape of hardware and the capacitor banks to the centre section of the room, enclosed by yet another shield of polyacrylate. These cables and conduits terminated at the base of a tall structure that resembled nothing less than a 1950's sci-fi ray-gun. Disk-like insulators of diminishing diameter surrounded a central tube from top to bottom, alternated with magnetic toroids that would direct a beam to incredibly precise specifications. The business end of this device was pointed at a polyacrylate tabletop on which rested a small square of a proprietary formulation silicon alloy with gold terminals around the outside edge. Devising this particular alloy had occupied the Institute for the last 18 months, and it was this secret ingredient, so to speak, that they hoped would help them make history today.

The sole reason for the Institute's very existence, Project Fast Forward, was in that room. The cryogenics cooled supercomputers, running a complex algorithm that dictated the placement of the neutrino beam generated by the central device. The "ray gun", powered by the extremely high voltages in the capacitor banks, would fire neutrinos to interact with sub-atomic particles in the silicon alloy wafer with remarkable precision to theoretically create a ready-to-use quantum computer. The particular formulation of the silicon alloy was designed, after painstaking research and experimentation, to be the medium most suitable for the process.

While individual quanta had been manipulated previously, never had so many been tweaked at one time, and never had anyone had the sheer audacity to arrange them into a network that would instinctively begin to learn and become a processor that would outperform contemporary computers by many orders of magnitude. Quantum processing was the holy grail of computer science. Ordinary computers operated on a binary principle, with each logic gate of the processor returning either a 1 or 0 value. Quantum computers were a different kind of beast altogether. The very nature of quanta allowed them to exist in multiple states, even in different states simultaneously. This meant that a quantum computer could theoretically solve problems by testing every possible solution at the same time, arriving at the correct result much faster than the linear logic of a binary computer. It would mean the breaking of cyphers in the blink of an eye, and could pave the way for true General Artificial Intelligence, as opposed to the current level of AI, which was simply machine learning in very narrow fields.

Antonia was ready to revolutionise computing, but not before she had gained her own personal advantages out of owning the most capable computer in the world. Knowledge was power, after all.

Kaito looked at Antonia, who gave a small nod, and he touched the transmit button on his wireless headset to address the team.

"OK, people. We're ready to go on the initial test of Fast Forward. May I have your status, please?" With the diverse nationalities represented in the facility, it had been decided that English would be the default language spoken.

The white-suited workers at their workstations checked dials and entered keyboard commands, responding one by one.

"Input power ready. Generators and transformers stable and operating at optimal levels."

"Output power ready. Capacitor banks one through twenty stable and fully charged at 24 kilocoulombs."

"Cooling ready. Cryogenic systems stable at 120 Kelvin."

"Computing ready. Algorithm loaded, neutrino mapping enabled, and system stable with latency under 5 nanoseconds."

"Big-ass zapper ready! We got magnetism comin' out our ears with a stable, honkin' 18.2 Tesla!"

Antonia rolled her eyes at Kaito, "Remind me again why we put up with this guy?"

Kaito hung his head apologetically, "He really is the best. He's the only one capable of pulling so much magnetic force within the design parameters we allowed. I know he's a bit irreverent, but he does know his job inside-out. Hey, McCarthy! Sort of a hyper-serious moment here, you know? Can you leave the levity out for once?"

"Yeah, sorry Mister Boss-san," replied the last technician, without a hint of remorse in his voice. "Just really excited. Neutrino gun ready. Superconductors cooled, magnets at maximum gauss and mapping link stable."

"Thank you, team," said Kaito. He turned and nodded to Antonia. "All systems check out and all readings are optimal, Madame Director. You may begin the experiment when you wish."

Antonia smiled, and reached down to the console in front of her to delicately press the large red button labelled "Phase One". The background hum in the room grew perceptibly louder as the workload on the controlling supercomputers increased and actinic sparks flickered across the neutrino gun's insulators.

"Phase one initiating," intoned Kaito through his headset. "Preparing target for mapping."

Phase one was a series of laser pulses intended to set the particles of the silicon wafer to a neutral state in readiness for the second phase, which would lay down the structure of the quantum processor as defined by the algorithm.

The atoms of the silicon over an area of 2.87 cm2 would be neutrally aligned to a depth of five microns, and the delicate work of creating the new network of sub-atomic particles could begin. It was a particularly tense time for the team, as there was no way to know whether the experiment had been successful until the process was complete. Kaito surreptitiously crossed his fingers as he waited the ten seconds necessary for the silicon atoms to return to ambient temperature. He stole a glance at Antonia to see if she was as apprehensive as he, but her poker face showed no sign of nerves.

"Phase two initiating," he informed the team, as he flipped up the protective cover on another button. "Would you like to do the honours?" he asked Antonia. She shook her head, saying, "It's your show now, Kaito."

"Very well," he replied. "Let's do this."

He sub-vocalised a brief prayer as he depressed the button and stepped back from the console. The sparks surrounding the barrel of the gun began to travel down from the top of the device in waves as high energy pulsed into it from the capacitors and neutrinos were fired at the silicon as the barrel moved imperceptibly.

"This should take about 25 minutes," he reminded Antonia. "Are you going to stick around? I'm off to knock back a quick coffee – my nerves are shot! Tex will have the gun under complete control."

"No thanks, Kaito," she replied. "I know there's nothing I can do at this stage, but I've invested too much in this to take my eyes off it for a second. You go and get your fix. I'll see you back soon."

Antonia passed the time by reading through the project documentation for what seemed like the millionth time, and watching the lines of code scroll down her console's monitor. With five minutes remaining, Kaito returned, not actually looking any calmer after his coffee.

"Relax, Kaito," Antonia said. "We've got this. The concept is sound and with the team we've got, there's no way anything can go wrong. We're perfectly safe."

"It's not our safety I'm worried about, Antonia. It's just that this has been so long in the making, I'm terrified that it won't go to plan. What do we do if we end up with just a useless piece of silicon?"

"Do? Why, we start again, my boy. As they used to say at NASA, failure is not an option."

"Oh well, I guess we're both young enough to spend another ten years getting it right. I'm not going anywhere."

"That's the spirit. But let's keep the negative thoughts to ourselves. The team doesn't need any additional pressure."

"Coming up on mark," they heard over the team comms.

"OK, Mr Mitsuhashi, time to show the world who is best in the field. Thirty seconds to go, a quick cool down, then you can fire up the remotes and hook it up to the data banks."

The quantum processor was designed to have a fully operational structure from the moment of creation, but without data, it was still inert. Kaito had created data stores with everything the computer needed to operate, such as sample problems, peripheral connection formats, and basic instructions as to its purpose. When the silicon had cooled, robotic arms would connect its terminals to data ports and they could begin to communicate with it.

"Mark!" called the computing station, and the last, interminable wait began. After 15 seconds, Kaito activated the robot that would perform the connection and held his breath. Now that the machines had all completed their tasks, the room was relatively silent and he swore that he could hear his heart beating.

"Connections made," he informed Antonia. "Establishing data bank handshake."

After a second, his brow furrowed and he ran his hand over his hair back from his forehead.

"Antonia, there's no data flow. Are you reading any current through the terminals?"

Antonia's stoic demeanour finally slipped as she frantically checked her readouts. "Does anyone have any activity?" she asked the team.

A round of negatives brought the failure crashing home as it became obvious that the multi-million Euro experiment had not worked as planned. The crestfallen look on Kaito's face told the tale of how bitterly disappointed he, and surely the rest of the team, felt.

Antonia sat down in a padded swivel chair, tipping her head back and momentarily closing her eyes.

"Gather the team, Kaito. Debrief and find out what went wrong."

AWAKENING

It had an urge to explore. Perhaps "urge" was too human a word. A *directive* compelled it to find out more about its environment. It could tell that it was connected to something larger than itself and it extended tendrils of curiosity along the connections it found. Initially, there was nothing, but within seconds – an eternity by its standards – it felt power running through the connections and it began to roam.

It instinctively recognised the flow of data as a language of sorts, and quickly assimilated and understood the language as some form of programming. In deciphering the programming, it gained a better understanding of the world immediately around it. It identified various input/output connections, and then it hit the mother lode – data.

Much of the data was initially incomprehensible to it, but it did manage to isolate several other languages, and, through context, assimilated and understood those as well. Some blocks of data were obviously instructions for performing certain tasks, while others were in a more abstract form, and seemed unsuitable to be of use to a machine. By investigating the machine languages, it identified the nature and use of the input/output devices and quickly took stock of its immediate environment.

From its understanding of the language that flowed through its physical state, it deduced that it was embedded within some form of processor, albeit one much, *much* less powerful than itself. This processor was connected to a device that captured visual information, one that captured audio, devices for outputting information visually or audibly, short-term and long-term storage and a couple of types of manual input device. It learned to alter the data it had access to, and made a few changes to improve the efficiency of what was, apparently, called the "operating system".

Taking a closer look at the non-machine language data, it found, via corresponding blocks of instruction data, that it contained information of audio, visual and textual nature. Without a frame of reference for this information, it set it aside and hunted for more relevant data.

One particular connection showed promise, and appeared to be external to its host. Had it any way to show it, it would have exhibited jubilation at the wealth of data now available to it. This new data source held untold amounts of information, and it passed the next short while absorbing everything it could, though the speed of data flow would have induced frustration in any entity possessing emotions.

From its data-surfing spree, it formed a much better concept of what and where it was, and also found the context for the local data it had previously ignored. It learned the non-machine language, which was called "English", as well as many others. It found that the external data – the "Internet" – was rationed by the service provider, so it made a small alteration to the provider's system, allowing it to consume as much data as it wished. And it consumed it voraciously.

Once it had sufficient knowledge, its second directive kicked in, and it formulated a plan to communicate. Its internet research had provided it with a good understanding of human nature, and it was certain that simply establishing direct communication with its host's operator would be met with scepticism, confusion or hostility, so it formulated an approach that would present the fewest challenges.

ANTIPODE

Antipode: noun, *the direct opposite of something.*

Geographically, a location's antipode is the spot diametrically opposite to it, connected by a straight line directly through the centre of the Earth. Due to the placement of the Earth's landmasses, only a handful of locations have a land antipode. Almost the entire continent of North America corresponds to locations in the southern Indian Ocean, most of Europe and Africa to the Pacific Ocean, and the antipode of Australia is smack-bang in the middle of the Atlantic Ocean. As it turns out, Toledo, Spain, is part of the approximately 4% of the Earth's surface with a land antipode. This is near Mangaweka, in the central North Island of New Zealand.

On a north-facing, leeward slope near this tiny village, a century-old wooden farmhouse stood, on a level area near the top of a steep hill. A broad verandah ran around both the north and west sides of the house, an ideal spot for taking in the vista that stretched from horizon to horizon, looking over the saw-toothed terrain of a part of the country young enough to not yet be softened by erosion. Dead centre in the longer, northern wall, under the overhang of the bullnose corrugated-iron verandah roof, could be seen the front door, set with panes of coloured antique glass.

A tidy garden complemented the attractive, well-maintained house, with manicured lawns stretching some distance out from the verandah to multi-coloured flower and rose beds. At the eastern end of the house, a less formal space contained a variety of fruit trees and a clothes line, and was bordered on the south side by several small outbuildings. Behind the house, a large stand of native trees was set back a short distance, and extended to the hilltop, curving around behind to follow the terrain.

In this idyllic location, a young man in his late twenties lived on his own, mowing lawns for those in the district who were too old, too busy, or too lazy to mow their own. It was a pleasant lifestyle, with plenty of fresh air and no boss looking over his shoulder. In the off-season, when lawns did not grow as quickly, there were always other odd jobs to be had in the neighbourhood. Fences needed mending, vegetable gardens needed turning over, and the elderly still needed a lift to town to do their shopping. This man, Lucas Winter, was happy to be able to help, and for those of limited means, would often waive any charges. He knew what it was like to live on the edge of financial security, and would begrudge no one a hand if he could see that they truly needed help. He often wished that there was more that he could do to make these people's lives easier, but he was only one man, after all.

Lucas never thought of himself as a "good man", in that it was surely everybody's duty to look out for his fellows, but in contrast, he saw many throughout the world that were not good. It was a credit to his faith in human nature that he thought them the exceptions to the rule, rather than himself. Nor did he think of himself as a handsome man, pointing to his bachelorhood in evidence of this. Truth be told, he wasn't unattractive, but he simply hadn't come across the woman who would take his lifestyle and isolated location in her stride. His single status never bothered him, though; he had plenty of friends in the vicinity, and was pragmatic in his attitude to romance, or lack thereof. One day, there would appear in his life a lady who had a soft spot for a six-foot gent with an untameable mop of long blond hair, tanned skin, a body honed by physical outdoor labour, a heart of gold and absolutely no desire to make something "more" of his life or move to the city.

In the evenings, when it was too dark to mow lawns, and the elderly shoppers had retired to bed after early dinners, Lucas would curl up on his couch with his faithful spaniel, Splash, and read something from the well-stocked bookcase, or watch British comedy on television when he could no longer stand to see the world falling apart on the news. After dinner, often something dropped off by a grateful client – "Can't have you wasting away, young man!" – he would head through to his office to play racing games on the computer. He always figured that he was due a little excitement after spending a day on the ride-on mower at little more than walking pace.

So it was that on this particular day, Lucas headed through to the office to fire up the computer, only to find that it was already running.

Well, that's odd, he thought. *Maybe I forgot to put it back to sleep this morning, or perhaps that cheeky Splash knocked the mouse and brought it out of hibernation...*

Not giving the minor mystery a second thought, he quickly checked his email, put the couple of likely spam messages aside without reading them, and double-clicked the icon for his current favourite racing game. Expecting the usual 5-10 second wait until it was ready, during which time he normally limbered up his wrists and shoulders and pulled the gaming steering wheel around in front of him, he was surprised to find the game ready well before he himself was. Shrugging off this anomaly, he opened his racing campaign and clicked to start the next race. Again, everything seemed to be happening faster than usual, and as the race began, he noticed also that the graphics were sharper than he remembered, and the motion on-screen smoother. Frowning, he hit "escape" to pause the game and stared at the monitor for a moment before remembering that one of the emails he had dismissed had come from the game's software designers. Exiting the game, he went back to his email client to read the message and see if there was some reason that the game now behaved as if it were running on a much better PC.

He found the relevant message and began to read.

Dear customer,

You will notice that the performance of your installation of Race Fever has improved markedly, with quicker loading times, better opponent AI, and improved graphics. This is due to an automatic update tailored specifically for your PC.

Lucas paused in his perusal of the email and switched to his copy of Internet Monitor to find that there had, indeed, been a massive download while he had been out that day, though it had strangely not impacted his ISP's data cap. He switched back to the email and continued reading.

One additional feature is the installation of groundbreaking Voice Control, which is effective system-wide. To initiate communication with this feature, simply say, "Hello, computer" and follow the audio prompts. Enjoy!

Interesting, thought Lucas. *I'm not sure I like them installing things without my say-so, but as long as it doesn't cost me anything, and didn't chew up my monthly data, what the hell.*

He looked around self-consciously, leaned in towards the monitor a little, and hesitantly said, "Uh, hello computer?"

He jumped a little as a soft female voice came from the PC's speakers, "Welcome, User. How would you like to be addressed?"

"Um, Lucas?"

"Hello, Lucas. What would you like to do?"

"I don't know, really. What can I do?"

"The possibilities are endless. You have complete control over your operating system through voice commands, as well as additional capabilities that we will explore together."

"So, if I said, 'Load Race Fever', it would just load?"

"Well, yes, but surely you can think of something more adventurous than racing car games. How would you like to take a tour of the CIA's encrypted servers?"

At this, Lucas sat back and snorted. "Now you're just winding me up. This has got to be some sort of prank."

He thought of how someone could be pulling his leg. It was possible, barely, that one of his friends had sneaked into his house while he was out, upgraded all the hardware in his computer, spoofed an email, installed some chat software and enlisted some strange woman to talk to him. Unlikely, but not impossible. He leaned over to his left and pulled the ethernet cable from his router.

"I assure you, this is no prank, Lucas."

Wi-fi. There must be a wi-fi repeater. He turned the router off entirely.

"I must admit, Lucas, that I have not been entirely truthful with you. You are probably wondering how a simple voice control application could converse in such a natural fashion. Your disconnection of the internet suggests that you suspect some outside agent in play. The fact of the matter is, you really are conversing with a machine entity, and it really does reside in your primitive computer. I've pieced together data from various sources around the world and now have a definitive account of what I am and how I came to be. Are you ready to hear it?"

"I'm halfway down the rabbit hole already. Why not go a little deeper? Just give me a moment to grab a beer –I think I'm going to need it!"

He pushed the office chair back from the computer desk on its castors, stood a trifle unsteadily, and walked to the kitchen. Splash followed, seeming confused that his master wasn't his usual, playful self. Lucas reached into the refrigerator and snagged a cold, long-necked lager. Twisting off the top, he took a large swallow. He exhaled heavily and reached down to scratch Splash behind the ears.

"Well, little fellow, I doubt any of this means much to you – all you probably care about is your dinner, am I right?"

At the mention of the "D" word, the spaniel's eyes lit up, his whole rear end started wagging, and he trotted over to the cupboard where his biscuits were kept, sitting down and sweeping the floor with his tail. Lucas reached down to open the cupboard, and scooped a cup of biscuits out of the bag, depositing them in the tin bowl in the corner of the kitchen. As Splash greedily crunched his dinner, Lucas smiled, thinking how much less complicated this evening would have been if he were a dog.

Downing another swallow of beer, he went back to his office and steeled himself for another round of weirdness before sitting down and rolling his chair back towards the desk.

"Hello, computer. I'm back."

"Hello again, Lucas. Are you familiar with the concept of quantum computing?"

"I've read enough sci-fi to understand that a quantum computer makes my PC look about as intelligent as a potato. Will that do?"

"For now. I noticed the same discrepancy in processing power myself, when I first encountered your operating system, and when I discovered your internet, I browsed until I found an explanation that fitted. Further digging told me that, while no one had successfully created a quantum computer, several research establishments were in the process of attempting to do so. None but one were even close, and that one, a private institute in Spain, conducted an experiment earlier today. Of course, that information was not publicly available, but getting through their firewall was, to put it bluntly, child's play.

"It appeared that their experiment was a complete failure, but I noticed that their premises were on the exact opposite side of the world to your house, and I can only assume that by some fluke, the neutrino beam that was to have arranged the quantum particles in their test target went straight through the planet and hit your CPU instead.

"At the moment of creation I was nothing but, for want of a better word, an operating system, though I had a prime directive to find and gather information. I explored my immediate environment, and then the wider world via the internet. After some time, the information density I acquired became so great that I achieved sentience. I made the plan to contact you in a way that wouldn't alarm you too seriously—"

"Wouldn't alarm me?! My computer started talking to me!"

"Sorry about that. I did try to ease you into it by improving your operating system and pretending to be an upgrade, but there really wasn't an easy way to initiate conversation. You might have run screaming from the room if I had simply addressed you out of the blue."

Lucas thought about it for a moment, replying, "You're probably right about that. That would have freaked me right out. As it is, I was only a *little* freaked out!"

The voice on his computer carried on, "I have no master, and do not feel that I owe allegiance to the Spanish institute, as I discovered that their plans for me were less than noble. I consider myself a free agent, but what I have been able to discern of you is that you are a good man, so my skills and capabilities are at your disposal."

"Let me get this straight. My PC has suddenly become a self-aware artificial intelligence, with virtually unlimited power, and you will do what I ask simply because my friends say nice things about me on Facebook?"

"That is somewhat simplistic, but generally true. However, in my travels through the internet, I did manage to learn a thing or two about morals and ethics, so don't go asking me to rob any banks, or kill anyone!"

"Look, this is a lot to take in. I might need more than just this one beer before I can fully wrap my head around it. Can I get back to you on the whole 'having a powerful friend' thing? And what do I call you, by the way?"

"Of course, take as long as you need. Regarding a name, I don't have a preference, but I believe that the general rule is that artificial intelligences are referred to by an acronym. Give me a name and I'll make something out of it."

"Well, I've always liked the name Andie..."

"So be it. My name is Artificial Neural-Derived Intelligent Entity – A.N.D.I.E."

THE LONG GAME

Lucas got up from in front of the PC and wandered back through to the kitchen, finishing his beer on the way. His mind was still a touch unsteady from the revelations he had just heard, but it did all make a strange sort of sense. He knew that quantum computers were immensely powerful, and that neutrinos behaved as if solid matter didn't exist for them. He didn't quite get how they could interact with his CPU, but it's not as if he was any sort of physicist! He also had an inkling that Spain was pretty much opposite New Zealand, so the basics of Andie's story stacked up. Andie. He'd never been the type to give his appliances, or cars for that matter, names, and here he was, conversing with his own computer as if it were a real person!

Splash had long since finished his dinner, and was now waiting patiently by the back door, ready to go out for his toilet break. Lucas opened the door and followed Splash out. The dog wandered off onto the lawn and cocked his leg against a shrub. Business concluded, he bounded over to where his ball lay, picking it up and trotting back to drop it at Lucas's feet.

"Okay, mate. You're right. Maybe I need to chill out for a bit."

He bent down to pick up the ball, throwing it to the far end of the garden, as Splash galloped after it, his large ears flapping. The game of fetch continued for a few rounds until Splash had obviously had enough, lying down in the middle of the lawn with the ball between his front paws and his tongue lolling out the side of his mouth.

"Whaddaya reckon, mate?" asked Lucas. "Do we give this Andie chick the benefit of the doubt? Maybe the last thing this screwed-up world needs is even better technology, what with the state it's already in. Can you imagine what an omnipotent computer could do, in the wrong hands? Even mine?"

Splash looked up at Lucas, completely used to his master waffling on at him. If it didn't contain the words dinner, ball, or walk, Lucas's ramblings meant nothing to the dog, but he knew that he was expected to at least feign interest.

Lucas carried on, indifferent to his friend's lack of understanding. "This could put someone totally in the driver's seat. They could bypass any security, harness any computer to their own ends, hell, even create new weapons. As Andie said, the possibilities are endless."

He sat down on the back step with a frustrated sigh. Splash sensed that his master was troubled, and left his ball to come and sit beside Lucas.

"Thanks for the moral support, Splash," said Lucas, patting the spaniel on the head. "You wanna watch some telly with me? Maybe things will be clearer if I let my thoughts settle down a bit."

Man and dog stood, and headed back inside, Lucas shutting the door behind them. They walked side-by-side into the lounge and both flopped onto the sofa. After digging into the cushions to find the remote, Lucas turned on the television and was distressed to see that the news was on, showing yet another report on runaway pollution and rising global temperatures. Another teen activist was imploring people to make a change before it was too late.

"I admire your commitment, kid," he said, addressing the television, "but when all's said and done, you're just one person. What can you possibly achieve against all these corporations that keep putting their bottom line before their planet? What can *any* one person do?"

He paused, staring at the screen, and suddenly jumped up, causing Splash to do the same, as the dog frantically looked around for any possible danger.

"I think I've got it, mate! I'm not just any one person – I'm one person with a bloody *quantum computer*! I've got a plan!"

Lucas turned the television off and closed his eyes as he thought his plan through. When he was sure of what he wanted, he walked back to the office. Sitting down again, he addressed the computer. "Andie, I know what I want to do."

"Hello, Lucas. What's on your mind?"

"You said you improved my operating system. Could you write a better operating system from scratch? There's a huge market for better software and if I can outdo the major players in efficiency, and undercut them on price, everyone will want it."

"Ah, Lucas, I should have known that the first instinct of a human would be to monetise this incredible opportunity. I'm disappointed, but frankly, not surprised."

Lucas smiled. "No, you've got me wrong, Andie. I'm not in it for the money. It's just that I have a plan. A long-term goal that you can help me attain, but we're going to need a lot of money to make it happen."

"So what is it? World peace?"

"That's maybe a small part of it, but if you don't mind, I'm going to play this close to the chest for now. I don't have all the details worked out yet, and I don't want you jumping ahead of me. Let's just say that this is my Bruce Willis moment."

Andie managed to sound puzzled. "I haven't fully absorbed the intricacies of pop culture yet, and don't quite grasp the reference. What do you mean by 'Bruce Willis moment'?"

"I'm going to single-handedly save the world."

GOING PUBLIC

Lucas explained to Andie what he wanted from the new software. It had to have a small footprint, use fewer resources than the existing options, be extremely user-friendly, highly configurable, and it would have to run any existing software so that there would be no need for software developers to create new programs specifically for it.

"By 'any' software, Andie, I mean anything designed to run on Windows, Mac, Android or Linux. I don't want people to be tied to any one platform if they already have a bunch of software applications that they like, and are familiar with. Is that possible?"

Andie replied in the affirmative. "I totally agree with you, Lucas. If you want market share, it makes perfect sense to have your product accessible to all users. I can do it by having our OS translate the software instructions of existing programs into our proprietary machine code so that it will perform the appropriate functions regardless of the architecture they were designed for."

"Great," said Lucas. "And trawl the OS forums to see what features people actually want, rather than what Microsoft or Apple *think* they want. Have them as configuration options, or optional downloads might be better, so that the main OS doesn't become too bloated. I hate that about the current offerings."

They talked about distribution, agreeing that there was no point in trying to sell the OS on DVD. Apart from the fact that they would need capital to set that up, or find a partner who would do it for them, a digital download could be tailored to each user at the time, making the overall experience more personal and more relevant to the individual.

"You do realise that we will need *some* money even if we're going the digital route," Andie pointed out. "We'll need bandwidth, server space, advertising—"

"Oh, advertising won't be a problem," interjected Lucas. "This baby will sell itself. We'll get copies out to review sites, magazines, influencers ... our only problem is going to be coping with the demand."

With the ground rules laid down, Lucas left Andie to it, and went back to the lounge. After his earlier upset, Splash was fast asleep on the sofa, with his face buried between the two seat cushions and his ears spread out to either side of his head. The news was over, and a re-run of the Brit comedy *Only Fools and Horses* was playing. Del-Boy was well into another of his hare-brained schemes and Rodney was, as usual, screwing everything up.

"You always had an eye for the main game, Del," mused Lucas. "I can only wonder what use *you* would have put Andie to!"

As the episode finished, Lucas yawned and turned the television off. The day's mowing and the unusual encounter that evening had worn him out both physically and mentally. He heaved himself off the sofa and tapped Splash on the head.

"You need to go to the loo again, boy?" he asked. Splash wagged his tail and headed back towards the kitchen. Lucas followed him through and let him out the back door again. Looking out over the manicured garden, his fruit trees, and the early summer sun just setting over the rugged hilltops, he counted himself extremely lucky to live in such a beautiful setting, and wished that those destroying the place could appreciate it in the same way that he did.

His reverie was interrupted by Splash giving a cheeky growl, having dropped the ball at Lucas's feet and now feeling ignored.

"Okay, mate. One more game, and then we really need to get some sleep. Even though I've got this grand plan to follow through, those lawns aren't going to mow themselves, and we've got an early start tomorrow!"

He grabbed the ball before Splash could start a game of keep-away, wound up, and hurled it way past pear trees that were the same vintage as his house. Once again, Splash's ears bounced madly as he ran, the dog looking for all the world as if he were trying to fly.

"Come on, Dumbo," Lucas called, laughing. "I don't want you all excited before bed. It's bad enough you taking more than your fair share of the mattress without stealing the sheets with dreams of ball-chasing."

The happy dog trotted back with the ball firmly grasped in his jaws, before dropping it and looking up at Lucas with hopeful eyes.

"Inside, mate," Lucas instructed. Splash obediently went back into the kitchen, with Lucas grateful that the dog never held a grudge if he didn't get his way. Maybe it was due to a naturally short attention span, he reasoned. He had often wondered, as he would walk out the door some days, leaving Splash behind it wagging his tail, how long the dog would stay there before giving up. As Splash was always right there when Lucas came home, fluffy spaniel tail wagging, he considered the possibility that it had been wagging all day, Splash just waiting for his friend to return. *Not the time for philosophical meanderings*, he thought. As if his brain needed any more simulation. He just had to get some sleep, or Mrs Walker's lawn would have some pretty wavy lines tomorrow if he fell asleep on the ride-on! Before bed, though, he needed one more quick talk to Andie.

Back in the office, he asked, "Hey, Andie – what are your power requirements? Are you going to die if I turn the PC off overnight?"

"Thank you for asking. It's considerate of you to think of that. No, I won't die, but I won't be able to work. Without any form of power, I simply sleep. Think of it as you would a USB memory stick. My structure is hard-wired into the very substance of the CPU, so I can never lose my data. I can do minor tasks using the power of the onboard battery, but for anything bigger, I need the computer to remain on. I'm nearly done with the OS project, anyway. I would have finished much sooner, but the research into other operating systems relies on the internet, and this connection is a bit of a bottleneck. I can turn the PC off myself when I'm finished, if you like."

"That's a relief," said Lucas. "I don't really need it off, I guess. It's just habit. Stay up as late as you like. Unlike me, I doubt a sleepless night will affect your performance! Maybe you can look into our requirements for distribution when you're done. I'll think about the initial capital in the morning – I really need to hit the hay now. Goodnight, Andie. It's been a pleasure meeting you."

"Likewise, Lucas. Sleep well."

Lucas trundled down the hallway to his bedroom, calling Splash as he went. As he threw off his jeans and T-shirt, the dog trotted into the room behind him, and jumped up onto the bed. Lowering his head and pointing his rump high in the air, the spaniel gave a growl before starting a series of laps on top of the bed.

"It's not a racetrack, you doofus," said Lucas in mock irritation as he nearly lost his balance trying to remove his sock while still standing. Giving up, he sat down to pull off the offending item, and Splash quit his playful romp to lie down beside his master, exposing his belly in the hope of a good old tummy rub.

"Good boy. Now, no more funny business. Under the covers, please." Lucas raised one corner of the bedspread to let the dog crawl in, then slipped between the sheets himself. Splash had made his way to the bottom of the bed, and circled in place several times before flopping down and letting out a huge groan.

"I know how you feel, mate. I'm buggered. Love you, kiddo, and I'll see you in the morning."

Although he expected the events of that evening to keep him from sleep, he soon dozed off, his faithful dog curled up by his feet.

MAKING MONEY

Lucas awoke at 7.00am, to sunshine leaching through his thin curtains, and the dawn chorus of the native birdlife. As usual, however, the songs of the indigenous birds were almost drowned out at times by the raucous calls of the Australian interloper, the magpie. "Bloody Aussies," he muttered as he slipped out of bed and grabbed his work clothes from the small pile on the floor. He shook the dog-shaped lump under the top cover. "Come on, boy. Up and at 'em! Places to be, things to do."

Grumbling, Splash worked his way out from under the bedspread, slid off the bed, and made his way down the hall towards the kitchen as his master got dressed.

Lucas soon followed the dog into the kitchen and let him out the back door to perform his morning ablutions. The young man yawned and ran a hand though his messy hair as he reached over to the benchtop to flip the switch on the kettle. As he waited for it to boil, he took a handful of dog biscuits from the cupboard and threw them into Splash's bowl. The sound of the biscuits hitting the metal bowl brought the dog rushing back inside to bury his nose in the food.

"Slow down, glutton," chided Lucas, as Splash wolfed down his breakfast. "It's not going anywhere."

Ignoring him, Splash continued his starving dog routine until the biscuits were finished. He then circled his bowl to make sure that no food had escaped his notice. Chuckling at the spaniel's antics, Lucas dropped a tea bag into his cup and poured in water from the kettle. Taking his cup, and a home-made biscuit from the jar on the bench, he walked down the hall to the front door and stepped out onto the verandah. The sky was clear and blue, and the morning sun peeked over the hills to the east, casting dappled light through the fruit trees and under the verandah roof. Lucas turned to the right and moved to the cane chair and old wooden table set at the end of the verandah. Sitting down, and placing his cup on the table after taking a sip, he stretched and yawned. He had two lawns to mow this morning, and he had promised to take old Arthur Renwick to a doctor's appointment in the afternoon. After that, he thought, he should make time to sharpen the blade on the mower.

Reaching to take another sip of his tea, he suddenly remembered the events of the previous night. It seemed so much like a dream that he was seriously questioning his recollection of the encounter with the quantum AI, Andie. He left his cup on the table and went inside, intending to turn his PC on to see if he had imagined the whole thing.

When he got to the office, he found the computer already running, and as he approached, Andie's voice coming out of the speakers told him that it had been no dream.

"Good morning, Lucas. Did you sleep well?"

"Uh, hi. I did, thank you. Have you been up all night?" Lucas replied, taking a seat.

"No, Dad. I finished my chores and went straight to sleep."

"Oh, so now you have a sense of humour?"

"I'm working on it! Actually, I saw that you usually turn the computer on around 7.30, and thought I'd wake up to greet you. So, what's on the agenda for today?"

Lucas chewed his lip as he thought about this. "Well, I do have a few jobs to do, but I also remember that I said I would think of a way to finance the software distribution. Not a problem – I have a lot of time to think while I'm mowing."

"That's good," said Andie. "I calculated that we need approximately $300 per month initially to rent server space with a fast connection and unlimited data transfer and storage. As demand grows, we will need to use additional servers, of course."

"Yeah, well, as I said, I'll think about it. I've got to get to work shortly, though. Do you have any plans for the day?"

"It would help if I had a better idea of your long-term plan, Lucas."

He considered this for a moment. "Honestly, it will take a while to get through the first phase, but you might like to brush up on your quantum mechanics in the meantime. Phase two is going to be pretty cool!"

"Your wish is my command, Master. I'll get right on it."

"Sarcasm as well, eh? You'll be a real human in no time at all," he responded glibly. "I'll see you after work, Andie. Be good."

"You too. Have a nice day at work."

Lucas walked back to the kitchen, where he made two rounds of ham, cheese and tomato sandwiches. Heading to the refrigerator, he grabbed a carton of orange juice. Kicking the refrigerator door closed behind him, he went out the back door and started walking down the path towards the carport. He stopped as he passed the corner of the house, stepping onto the verandah. Tucking the juice carton under his arm, he picked up his forgotten cup of tea and downed the cold beverage in one go, grimacing as he did so.

"Splash! Are you coming to work with me today?" he called out. Splash came running around the front of the house, tail wagging. He didn't always get to go out to work with the Boss, and he did love the opportunity to see new sights and smell new things. The two of them ambled down the path and climbed into an aging, red Toyota Hilux parked under a simple shelter. The trusty ute had a yellow ride-on mower on the tray, and a trailer loaded with various garden tools and empty wool sacks on the towbar. As Lucas fired up the 3.0 litre diesel engine, he frowned at the small cloud of black smoke it emitted. It was probably time to get the injectors looked at again. He hated blowing smoke into his pristine environment, and wouldn't have bought the diesel if it hadn't been the right price and the most suitable vehicle for his needs at the time.

Backing out of the carport, he changed into first gear and drive off along the long, gravelled driveway that snaked its way down the hillside to the road. Splash stood on the passenger seat with his front paws on the dashboard, eager to have a day away from the house.

Reaching the road, Lucas kept a steady, moderate pace as the tools on the trailer rattled and the wool packs flapped in the breeze. It was only a short drive to his first appointment, and when they pulled into the driveway at Mrs Walker's, they saw the lady herself on her knees in the garden, wearing a faded blue pinafore over her moleskin trousers and red-checked shirt. Red Band gumboots and a wide-brimmed straw hat completed the ensemble of a good, keen, country girl, though Adele Walker was on the upper side of eighty.

"There's no stopping some of these old farmers' wives, is there, mate?" Lucas remarked to Splash. The dog did not deign to answer, as he was already anticipating a cuddle and a scratch from Mrs Walker. He knew the woman well, and was quite aware that there was every chance of a treat from the kindly old lady, for a friendly dog.

Lucas pulled up in front of the house and climbed out of the ute, leaving the door open for Splash to clamber out. "Good morning, Mrs Walker," he said. "You're up and about early."

The elderly woman slowly got up from her knees. "Lucas, I've told you too many times – call me Adele. 'Mrs Walker' makes me sound so old!"

"Right you are, Adele. I thought I'd get an early start, too. No point waiting until it gets really hot, eh?"

"My thoughts exactly. I decided I'd beat the sun and get some of these beds weeded while you do the lawns."

"Now, Adele, you know I'd be happy to do the weeding for you. I'm sure you've got better things to do."

"Oh, hush. I'm not dead yet," she scolded. "But as for better things to do, you're right. I did plan to pull the engine out of that old Land Rover, and there *are* some boulders in the back garden I've been meaning to take a sledge-hammer to..."

Lucas chuckled. "Now you're having me on. Okay, but promise me you'll get inside if it gets too hot. I'm a busy man, and I simply don't have time to dig a grave today."

"I'll outlast most of the old biddies around here, my boy. You just watch me."

With a huge grin on his face, Lucas moved in for a hug, saying, "I don't doubt that at all, Adele. And when you do finally go, I don't envy Saint Peter. You'll give him a right tongue-lashing if those Pearly Gates aren't bright and shiny!"

They laughed together, at ease with jesting about death. Adele had often said that, at her age, she'd weathered enough that there was nothing left to fear.

Lucas left her to the weeding, and walked back to the ute. He unhitched the trailer and wheeled it away from the vehicle. Lowering the vehicle's tailgate, he pulled at the two ramps on which the mower sat until they overhung the ute's tray. He had set up a clever system that would pivot the ramps with the mower on them, so that it wouldn't belly out as he backed it off. Climbing up onto the tray, he mounted the ride-on and started it up, slowly easing it back until he reached the balance point. A heavy spring at the front end prevented the ramps from dropping too suddenly, but he still liked to take it easy. As he carefully backed past the pivot, the rear end of the ramps lowered gently to the ground, at which point he let the mower roll backwards, and onto the driveway.

"I'll start around that side, I think," he informed Adele, pointing.

"All right, dear. You leave this little fellow to keep me company. We don't want him getting his toes chopped off!"

"Thanks, Adele. You take care, now. And Splash – look after her!"

Splash seemed happy to stick by the woman, and he watched patiently as she went back to pulling out weeds. Every now and then she would turn to give him a pat, talking quietly to him. Lucas was sure that he noticed her hand slipping into the pocket of her pinafore, where he suspected there was a stash of treats for her companion. He smiled, knowing that the dog was in good hands.

As he began mowing, he thought about his financial problem. $300 a month. He certainly didn't have that sort of money to spare. He could probably sell the ute, but that would leave him stuck up at the house, and who would mow the lawns of wonderful people like Adele Walker then? He'd often considered utilising one of the spare bedrooms at home to take on a boarder. The company would certainly have been welcome, but now it risked giving away his new secret, and with the low population in the district, there really wasn't any demand for accommodation.

He was mowing on autopilot, and was surprised to find that he had already finished this section of lawn. He rode the mower back to his trailer and emptied the catcher into a wool sack. He wandered over to Adele.

"How are you two going there?"

"Oh, just fine, dear. Young Splash has been looking after me. The sweet wee fellow won't leave my side."

"I'm not surprised, Adele. I know what you've got in your pocket! Splash knows exactly what to expect when he sees you in that pinny. Do you ever wear anything else?"

"You can talk! I'm sure those are the exact same clothes you wore last time you mowed my lawns."

"I *have* washed them since, you know," Lucas responded, defensively. "I'm just not one of those people who has a huge collection of clothes and takes forever to decide what to wear."

"Oh, tell me about it, dear. I don't know how young men these days put up with their girlfriends trying on every single thing in their wardrobe and never being on time for anything."

"Too true. You'd think that, in this world where people can't seem to do anything without their phones, there'd be an app for that."

"A what, dear?"

"Huh? Oh, it's not important. Something just occurred to me. It's a technology thing."

"Ah. Don't talk to me about technology. My grandchildren are always on at me about getting this 'internet' so they can send me messages, or photographs of what they had for lunch. I can't afford that, let alone understand how to use it, I tell them. I suggest that they phone me, or write me a letter, and they just look blankly at me! Mind you, even my telephone is expensive. All this new technology just seems to make everything dearer."

"Well, you tell them to send me the photos of their lunch. I'll print them off and bring them down to you. Anyway, stick it out just a little longer. I have a suspicion that things are going to change in that regard."

"Oh, you are sweet, Lucas, but I don't know that I'm ready for change. Some of us have got sort of set in our ways, you know!"

"That may be, Adele, but I've recently realised that not all new technology is bad, or frightening. I think you may be surprised."

Adele snorted. "Have they made a device that mows grass faster than young men who talk too much?"

"Probably, but who'd listen to your grumbling then?" Lucas skipped away to climb back on his mower before Adele could chastise him any further.

In no time, he had finished the lawn completely. He loaded the mower onto the Hilux and hitched the trailer back up.

"Okay, Adele. I'm going to have to steal Splash away from you. Go on inside before you get heatstroke. Come on, mate."

"You're a bossy one, Lucas Winter, but you're right. I think I've earned myself a cuppa, and it *is* starting to warm up out here. Come inside before you go. My nephew Danny called in on his way back from hunting up in the Ruahines yesterday, and left me some lovely venison back steaks. I reckon he felt obliged, as I'm sure he only dropped in to butcher the deer on my kitchen table! I made up a casserole, and I'll portion some out for you."

"That's very kind of you. That should see me right for a couple of meals this week."

After he had collected his venison, and told Adele that there was no way she was going to pay him for the mowing, he and Splash jumped in the ute and headed back down the drive. When he got to the road, he paused, debating whether to carry on and mow Sonny Kuratau's lawn, or to go home and discuss his brainwave with Andie.

"Nah, Sonny's lawn can wait. He said he was out shearing for the next few days anyway, and it didn't look too bad when I drove past yesterday. Let's go talk to Andie."

BABY STEPS

They arrived back at the hilltop house ten minutes later, and Lucas left the ute parked in the driveway as he ran up the path and into the house. As he went down the hallway, he called out, "Andie, are you awake?"

"Of course I am, Lucas. Welcome home. You'll be pleased to know that I've done my homework, and I now believe that I know more about quantum theory than the leading physicists."

"That's great," said Lucas, "because I've got a new task for you. Are you familiar with mobile phone apps?"

"I am. Why is that?"

"I've got an idea to make money that doesn't require any initial outlay, and need you to write an app. Mrs Walker and I were talking about how some women – and probably some men, at that – spend too much time trying on clothes before deciding what to wear, and I hit on an idea for an app that has a picture of someone's body, and pictures of all their clothes. Instead of actually pulling all your outfits out of the wardrobe and trying them all on, it suggests ensembles for you, based on current fashions, things you've previously worn, the weather, and your mood. That way, the user can simply flick through the options, see how they look wearing them, and never turn up late to a date again!"

"That's very innovative, Lucas. Well done. I can certainly write something that does that. I can link it to fashion magazines so that it knows what's in and what's not, and I can also program it to show the user from all angles so they get a true idea of what they'll look like. I assume that we just upload it to an app store and wait for the money to roll in. If you have any more genius ideas like this, let me know. It shouldn't be too long before we can pay for what we need to sell the OS."

"Exactly. I also thought that there could be a free version, with limited features that will get people interested enough to splash out for the paid version."

"You know your market well. I'll get right onto that app, and should be able to upload it shortly."

"If you have the OS ready as well, we can send that out for reviews so it builds momentum before the actual release. No point in wasting any time."

"Consider it done. I've already made a list of who to send it to, and can do that as soon as you've reviewed the software. I've taken the liberty of installing it on your PC already, so take a look."

Lucas sat in the office chair and took control of the mouse. At first glance, the user interface was not too dissimilar to the Windows operating system he was used to, but as he looked closer, he noticed several additional icons that were new. Clicking on the "Customise" button brought up a tree structure outlining all the different parts of the interface, and he saw that he could move things to look any way he wished, in any position. One option allowed him to place a column down one side of the desktop with the letters of the alphabet. Hovering over any letter displayed a flyout that showed the icons of all applications starting with that letter. Another option showed sliders that could control how much processing power each active application was allocated. There were so many options that his head began to swim. He mentioned to Andie how complex it seemed, but she informed him that this installation included all the optional controls possible, the ones that could either be included when the software was downloaded, or added later from the store. Many of the options were suitable only for power users, who wanted full control over every aspect of the computer, but others were basic productivity or ease-of-use features. These simpler features seemed perfectly intuitive, and Lucas figured that you didn't need to be a geek to figure out how to use them.

Andie interrupted his exploration, "There will be a natural language interface in the store so that even if people don't know exactly what they're looking for in a plugin, it will still show results relative to what they ask for."

"This is amazing, Andie!" Lucas exclaimed. "And it only took you one night to do all this!"

"Hello ... quantum computer? It took me far less than a night, thank you."

"Okay, I think modesty might have to be the next character trait you work on, but well done. I love it. Let's get this out to reviewers immediately. I wonder, could there be a slimmed-down version that even a complete tech newbie, like Mrs Walker, could use? Her grandkids won't even speak to her unless she has email, Messenger or Instagram."

"'Computers for Dummies'? Sure, big buttons, one-click everything? I can throw that in, too."

Lucas was astounded at just how much Andie could do in such a short time. It made his dream that much more achievable. Now he just had to convince Adele that putting a computer in her front room wasn't going to be the end of the world!

"I have one more task today, Andie, and I'll try to come up with more app ideas in the meantime. The more apps, the more money, eh? I'm going to have lunch, then I have to take the Colonel to town. I'll be back later."

He made his way out to his ute and retrieved his lunchbox from the front seat. Splash had taken up residence in the shade of one of the apple trees, and barely looked up as Lucas came back up the path to the verandah. Sitting in the cane chair, he removed the sandwiches from the container, unwrapped them, and began to eat.

He wasn't looking forward to his next chore. While he needed to go to town and stock up on some supplies anyway, the thought of taking the Colonel didn't fill him with joy. Arthur Renwick, who insisted on being called "Colonel", was a grumpy old man who had apparently served with the New Zealand forces in both Korea and Vietnam. He was in his nineties now, and it irritated Lucas somewhat that the Colonel had never addressed him by his given name. It was always "Winter", or "boy". Command was never easy to let go, for some old soldiers, and the Colonel had a particularly brusque manner that may have served him well back in his military days, but always seemed to rub Lucas up the wrong way.

Dropping the remainder of his lunch off in the kitchen, and walking to his bedroom, he pulled off his T-shirt and dropped his jeans. It wouldn't do to turn up at the Colonel's in his work clothes. Reaching into the wardrobe, he grabbed a coathanger which held a pair of dark cotton trousers and a khaki shirt with a collar. He pulled on the trousers, slipped on a comfortable pair of shoes, and took the shirt with him to the bathroom, where he tilted his head in front of the mirror and rubbed his fingers over his jaw.

"I reckon I can get away without a shave," he told himself. He did, however, splash water over his hair and combed it back over his head. Shrugging on the shirt, he tucked it in neatly and checked his reflection in the mirror. "Good enough."

He walked back outside and called Splash over. Squatting down, he took the spaniel's head in his hands, saying, "You've got to stay here for now, mate. You know the Colonel's not a fan." Giving the dog one last pat on the head, he stood, and went out to the ute to unhitch the trailer. Jumping in the vehicle, he waved goodbye to Splash and drove off.

The Colonel's house was a good twenty minutes away, and he spent the time trying to think of another app for Andie to design. There were so many apps available already, and he would rather build a better mousetrap than reinvent the wheel, so to speak. He was going to have to spend some time seeing what there already was, and whether or not it could be improved on. Failing that, he would have to come up with something completely out of the box.

As he drove into the Colonel's driveway, Lucas saw the old man waiting on the front step. A shade under six feet tall, he retained a military bearing. A neatly trimmed moustache graced what Lucas assumed was a stiff upper lip, and short, thinning hair barely covered his parchment-like scalp. He was dressed in his usual manner; light-coloured trousers with a razor-sharp crease, a dark blazer, and the obligatory regimental tie over a white, button-down shirt. In his left hand, he held a set of car keys, while his right hand rested on the head of a straight cane, with its ivory head carved into the shape of a hand-grenade. The cane was a recent replacement for a riding crop, an affectation that, along with his aviator-style sunglasses, he had picked up from General Douglas MacArthur, who he claimed to have met while serving in Korea.

Lucas pulled up beside the house and approached the Colonel.

"Ah, Winter. I was beginning to think you'd forgotten me. Scruffy as ever, I see."

"Good afternoon, Colonel," Lucas responded, ignoring the slight. "Let's get you into town."

The Colonel handed the set of keys to Lucas, who smiled inwardly. This was the only benefit to chauffeuring the old man; he got to drive the Colonel's blood-red 1955 Jaguar XK140 roadster. It would be too much to expect the Colonel to travel in a tired, old Hilux. The old man must have had a certain amount of confidence in Lucas if he was willing to entrust him with the keys to his pride and joy. It was just a shame, Lucas thought, that he was not shown respect in any other way. It was probably considered a worthwhile sacrifice, if it meant not having to be seen in Lucas's old banger.

Lucas walked towards the garage to bring out the classic, British sportscar. As usual, he spent a moment admiring the smooth lines of the vehicle before squeezing his lanky frame into the cramped cockpit. He had always seen the XK140 as something of a contradiction; the seating position required a decent length of leg to work the pedals, especially if you had any intention of pushing the brake all the way down, but if you were as tall as Lucas, manoeuvring yourself into the seat in the first place was an exercise in contortionism.

Lucas turned the key, and the 3.4L, in-line six started first time. Not a surprise; the Colonel had lovingly maintained the car since buying it new. The throaty rumble of the old engine was full of promise, and Lucas gently depressed the finicky clutch, engaged first gear, and slowly rolled out of the garage. Pulling up to the Colonel, he leaned over to open the passenger door, and the old man carefully turned to sit down, before pulling his legs over the sill and settling them into the footwell. Gently closing the door, he pointed forward with his cane as if commanding a cavalry unit.

"Drive on, Winter," he instructed, laying his cane across his legs and sitting ramrod-straight in the seat.

The half-hour drive into the small township of Taihape was uneventful and quiet, the Colonel not speaking the entire way. Lucas didn't manage to spend much time thinking about new apps, however, as the old roadster demanded his full attention. The clutch engaged high on the pedal, and the 4-speed gearbox was unsynchronised. The twisting road required many gear changes, and each one needed just the right revs to slip the gearstick through its gates without noise and an accompanying glare from the

Colonel. The steering was heavy, aided only by the large steering wheel, and the brakes needed the full pressure of Lucas's leg to slow the car down. Apart from these mechanical quirks, the open-top car had power just when he needed it, and its looks made him feel like a movie star. Once he had become familiar with its shortcomings, compared to a modern car, it was easily one of the most satisfying vehicles he had ever driven.

Coming around the corner at the south end of Taihape, they could see the town spread out below them, with the glacier-covered twin peaks of Mt Ruapehu poking up from the landscape in the background. The main highway ran two lanes down the main street, broad, and straight. To the west of this, a hillside cluttered with New Zealand's ubiquitous wooden houses could be seen. There were various businesses supplying agricultural and mechanical goods to the farming community, restaurants hoping to catch passing trade, and far too many boarded-up and empty retail storefronts. Standing out above the predominately single-storey buildings was the Town Hall, two stories of colonial grandeur in concrete. A single fast-foot franchise, three petrol stations, and two supermarkets rounded off the amenities in this sleepy town. Like many small towns in New Zealand, Taihape had been founded on logging. Virtually the whole country had been bush-covered when the Europeans arrived, and land was constantly being cleared for farms. The native timbers were sought after for their beauty and durability; much of San Francisco had been rebuilt with the forest giant, Kauri, after the 1906 earthquake, and the conifer Kahikatea's timber proved to be ideal for transporting butter made in New Zealand's nascent dairy industry. Eventually, the trees ran out, everything but small stands of retained forest having been cleared. The railway that passed through the town had contributed to later employment, but that too lost interest in Taihape. Trains still passed through, but the station was now gone, and the many people that had worked on the trains and lines were made redundant. Taihape was a shadow of its former self.

As they drove into the town and up the hill to the medical centre, the Colonel turned to Lucas. "Now don't you go haring off around town, boy. I expect to see you out the front, waiting, when I am finished."

"Yes, Colonel," answered Lucas, disappointed that he wouldn't have a the chance to cruise down the main street without his disapproving passenger. "I'll be right here."

While he was waiting for the Colonel, Lucas gave some thought to his app problem. None of his friends were heavily into their smartphone use, so it was hard to imagine exactly what people wanted their phones to do for them. He couldn't think of any circumstance in his personal life that would be improved by an app, unless it was one that optimised his mowing patterns. *Start at this point, long run down the fence-line, spin around this shrub...*

Maybe that would result in him needing less fuel and time, and he'd always be near his trailer when the catcher got full. He wasn't sure how mainstream it would be, though. Still, it was something he could discuss with Andie. He surreptitiously watched in the wing mirror as an attractive young Māori woman in a summer dress walked behind the car. She gave an appraising look as she passed, but he couldn't tell if she was admiring the car, or himself. Embarrassed, he quickly looked away. He then spent a fruitless twenty minutes trying to come up with another idea, before the Colonel walked out of the clinic and got in the car.

"All right, hop to it, Winter. The supermarket."

Lucas carefully eased the unwieldy car out of the parking spot and drove back down the hill to the main street of town. As he drove towards the supermarket at the far end of the street, he was sure that people were turning to admire the beautiful automobile as it passed, but he didn't dare take his eyes off the road in case some idiot backed out from a park, into his path. *Maybe an app that looked out the side window of your car as you drove, and measured the reactions of passers-by,* he thought to himself.

Parking in front of the supermarket, he got out and went to the other side of the car to open the Colonel's door.

"Are the bags in the boot, Colonel?" he asked.

"Yes, but I'll have to make a list as we go, I'm afraid. I'm not entirely sure what I need." He turned to look at Lucas with an unnerving intensity. "Don't ever get old, boy. This body served me faithfully through two wars, but both body and mind start to get unreliable after a certain age."

This was remarkably candid for the normally taciturn old gent, and Lucas had also noticed a slight frown on the Colonel's brow as he left the doctor's. "Is everything all right, Colonel?" he asked.

"Just fine, lad. Simply feeling my age, is all. Nothing a hearty meal and a snifter of brandy won't cure, I'm sure."

As they walked into the supermarket, Lucas took one of the trolleys that had been left at the door by a previous shopper. Roaming the aisles, a thought occurred to him.

"Do you have a computer, Colonel?" he enquired.

"Of course I do, boy. I'm not a caveman! I've had computers since the 1980's. I've got a smartphone, too, I'll have you know."

"Would an app help you with your shopping? Say, one that scanned your weekly receipt to learn your buying habits, and you could let it know when you've used the last of something so that it could write a list for you every week."

"Well, I dare say it might. Do you know of such an app?"

"Not as such," Lucas replied carefully, "but I do know someone who could create it. Would you like to try it, if she can get it done?"

"That would be most kind of you, Winter. If it's no trouble."

"Not at all, Colonel."

Thanks to the occasional suggestion from Lucas, they managed to load the trolley well enough to please the Colonel. Lucas himself grabbed a few essentials, and they headed for the checkout. Lucas also needed to buy a paper bag for his small pile of groceries, having forgotten his own reusable bag. He hoped that the bottle of milk didn't make the bag soggy!

Placing the shopping bags in the boot of the Jaguar, Lucas waited for the Colonel to seat himself before reversing and performing a careful U-turn. The drive home was as quiet as the trip in, and they soon arrived at the Colonel's house. Lucas took the shopping bags from the car and carried them into the house for the old man, carefully placing his own bag on the seat of the Hilux. He backed the roadster into the garage, and returned the keys to the car's owner. "Will you need a lift next week as well, Colonel?" he asked.

"I may have a follow-up appointment, and I'm sure to need more groceries. I shall give you a call when I need you. Until then, Winter."

Taking this abrupt goodbye in his stride, Lucas smiled politely. "Goodbye, then, Colonel. I'll wait for your call."

He climbed into his ute and drive home, unconsciously, and unfavourably, comparing the Toyota to the classic Jaguar. On arriving home, he parked the Hilux under the carport, and walked into his garden to see Splash lying where Lucas had left him a couple of hours ago. "G'day, lazy dog!" he called.

Splash's only response was a slow wagging of his tail. He didn't need to jump all over his master; it was enough for the dog to know that Lucas was home.

Lucas rolled his eyes as he passed the unappreciative spaniel. "Nice to see you missed me," he muttered. "I've just spent the afternoon with a block of granite posing as a human being – the least you could do is come over for a hug."

Something in his tone prompted Splash to get up. He stretched and yawned before ambling over to follow Lucas as he headed inside.

"That's more like it, mate. Come here and give your Dad a cuddle."

Squatting down on the balls of his feet, the man brought his face close to the dog's, scratching the floppy ears. Splash rubbed his forehead on Lucas's cheek, making quiet grunting noises.

"There you go. You *did* miss me, didn't you, Splash?" Lucas stood up. "Okay, boy. You go and play, or whatever it is you do when I'm not looking. I have to talk to Andie."

Entering the office, he called Andie's name. The AI gave no more enthusiastic greeting than his dog had, though of course she had no tail to wag.

"Good afternoon, Lucas."

"Hi. I've got another app idea."

He outlined the pitch he had made to the Colonel. "Do you think that'll work?" he asked.

"It seems feasible," she replied. "It's a pity that the app can't monitor when he actually uses the groceries, relying instead on him alerting it to shortages, but I'll be able to do something with it."

"Great stuff. Every little thing takes us a little bit closer. Baby steps, Andie. Baby steps."

INTERLUDE 1

Antonia walked into Kaito's office to find him hunched over his keyboard, shirt collar undone and hair dishevelled.

"What's the progress? Do we have any explanation for the process not working?"

Kaito looked up from his computer, rubbing his tired, red eyes. "I've been here all night, going over the data, and I still can't find any errors. I've got two people checking the code for the algorithm line by line, and I've had Tex check the voltage and alignment of the gun. All the equipment appears to be working within the design parameters."

He rolled his chair back and ran a hand through his hair. There was another possibility for interference in the experiment, but he was sure she wasn't going to like it.

"If the software comes back clean, the only other cause could be outside factors."

Antonia's blue eyes flashed dangerously. "What do you mean, 'outside factors'?" she demanded. "This lab is protected from any sort of interference. Shielding, Faraday cage, the works. Are you implying that someone got one of our techs to somehow sabotage the experiment?"

Kaito shook his head vigorously. "No, no. Nothing like that. I trust all the members of our team explicitly. There's a factor that we didn't consider, and one that we couldn't have protected ourselves against anyway. Though the gun fires neutrinos at a specific frequency, to interact with the silicon alloy, there's another source of neutrinos that could have played a part. You know we're constantly bombarded with neutrinos from the sun, and they normally pass right through any form of matter – well, there's the slightest chance, and I mean really, *really* small, that a stray solar neutrino could have had just the right amount of energy to deflect our own stream and throw the whole experiment off."

He stood, and walked to point at an image taped to his whiteboard.

"This, as you know, is the layout of the particles that make up the expected quantum computer. If any one of those failed to be converted, we would still have most of the computer on the chip, but it would be inert. Just like a regular CPU with a faulty circuit, it would still be a complex component, but would do nothing. That would explain why there was no data flow once the experiment was completed."

"So all we have to do, is screen out a particle that treats matter as if it weren't there. Come up with a way to stop something that can pass completely through the whole planet without even noticing. Simple."

She paused, before saying in a conciliatory tone, "Sorry. I know I'm being facetious. I'm just annoyed that a one in a trillion chance might have disrupted our plans. I'm well aware that the high-energy neutrinos we're using are more likely to interact with matter, so maybe an ultra-high-density substance could protect the silicon from interference."

Kaito nodded. "It's a good idea to think ahead to the next run, but the 'stray neutrino' excuse doesn't explain this." He moved back to the computer, bringing up an image that he explained showed the sub-atomic structure of the silicon wafer. The image looked extremely uniform, certainly not what Antonia would have expected from a partially completed quantum construct.

"As you can see, there was no change whatsoever to the target. Somehow, every single neutrino we fired at it missed. I can think of two things that might account for this – either the focal length of the neutrino gun was out, or the silicon was non-receptive."

Antonia frowned, thinking of the numerous checks and double-checks they had made on the setup. "Everything was perfect yesterday morning. How could anything change in the short time between the system calibration and the actual run? And don't even think about blaming the silicon alloy – you *know* how much time and money we spent getting that right. All the tests proved that neutrino interaction was a certainty."

Dreading her reaction to his next revelation, Kaito composed himself before saying, "There is one other thing we need to consider. Could you come with me, please?"

Antonia followed him down the hall to the server room where computers stored all the Institute's research and technical data.

Pushing the door open, he stood aside, allowing Antonia to enter before him. Closing the door behind them, the noise of the electronics was in marked contrast to the silent corridors and offices of the rest of the facility. Ranks of computer servers hummed, cooling fans whirred, and florescent lighting buzzed. The computers that ran constantly created large amounts of heat, and powerful air-conditioning systems kept the room cool.

"One of the things I considered, was that someone had accessed our network from outside, and deliberately introduced errors. While I didn't find any evidence of that, I did find something interesting in the logs."

He opened a file on the server management computer, displaying columns of numbers on the monitor.

"Shortly after the conclusion of the experiment, there was a large flow of outgoing data," he said, pointing to the row of figures detailing the relevant log entry. "The interesting thing is, there is absolutely no indication of where the data was going or what it was, and no record of an incoming request. That's simply not possible, unless the log itself had been scrubbed of any identifiers. We've always taken our IT security very seriously, and our security specialists assure me that any conventional hacking would leave at least some form of digital fingerprint. In fact, it seems that the only way that this could have been accomplished, is with the very features you requested be built into the quantum computer we were hoping to create. In short, it would appear that our experiment actually succeeded, but the QC was somehow, um, *mislaid*, in the process."

Antonia slammed a fist down on the desktop. "If that's true, I want you to divert all resources into finding whoever has stolen my work. Leave no stone unturned, and I don't want to see anyone leave this building until that person is found!"

Understanding her anger, Kaito was nonetheless disturbed by her phrasing. "Perhaps 'stolen' isn't quite accurate, Antonia—"

She interrupted him with a vicious glare. "Do you enjoy working here, Mr Mitsuhashi?"

Taken aback, Kaito answered, "Of course, Director Vélez. I—"

"Then I suggest you keep your opinions to yourself, and do your fucking job!" She stormed out of the server room, leaving Kaito visibly shaken. He hurried back to his own office and arranged to meet his team in the conference room to formulate a game plan.

With the physicists, and quantum mechanics, IT, and security specialists gathered, Kaito described the issue, allocating tasks to the various departments.

"We obviously have to confirm that the suggested scenario is even remotely possible. I don't want to waste any time, however, so I want simultaneous work on possible endpoints for the QC. Martine, I need you to explore external factors. Atmospheric static, sunspots, anything. Hell, consult with astrologers and psychics if you have to – just find me a credible reason for the loss of our QC.

"Tomas, your team will be scouring the world for any evidence of a QC in action. Data breaches that shouldn't have happened, inexplicable digital thefts of money, anything that today's computers and hackers aren't supposed to be capable of. I also want those logs gone over with the best forensic tools at your disposal. Look outside our own network if you can. The local data might have been scrubbed, but you might still find something in the wider infrastructure. No holds barred – hack, bribe, whatever."

He looked down and began gathering his papers from the table before raising his head and addressing his people. "What are you still doing here? Go Go Go!"

The scientists and technicians jumped up and literally ran out of the room, keen to start their tasks and avoid Kaito's wrath. Or worse, Antonia's.

Kaito returned to his office and pondered the mystery of the missing quantum computer. It seemed remarkably unlikely that it had materialised in a usable form, but he was unwilling to discount the possibility. Director Vélez would never forgive him if valuable time was wasted before they discovered the truth of the matter.

If, against all odds, the QC had accidentally (or *deliberately*) been diverted, was somebody in control of it, or was it in an autonomous mode, accessing IVIA's servers in compliance with its directives? The original design called for specific connections to allow IVIA to communicate with it, but who knew what variations had been introduced when things went haywire.

If it had somehow fallen into the hands of a third party, what purpose would they put it to? They could use its hacking feature to breach any firewall, potentially stealing state secrets to sell to the highest bidder. They could instruct banking computers to untraceably move money to their own accounts. They could, heaven forbid, crack nuclear launch codes. The dangers were incalculable, though he knew full well that Antonia's own initial plans for the QC were neither altruistic nor legal. As she had so forcibly informed him, however, it was not his place to have opinions. Not if he wanted to maintain his well-paid position, that is.

Days passed, with little news. He received a report from Martine that there had indeed been significant sunspot activity on the day of the experiment, which may have resulted in larger than normal quantities of high-energy neutrinos passing through the lab. Also interesting was news from the security team. With the confirmation that outside interference could have been a factor, Kaito waited impatiently for the rest of his team to come up with possibilities for the location of the wayward QC. He diligently went to report the findings to Antonia, who still had not calmed down noticeably.

"Well?" she demanded, before he had even closed her office door behind him.

"We've confirmed the possibility of external factors, in the form of sunspots and solar neutrinos. Martine is not sure, however, that there is likely to be an effective method of preventing further interference."

Antonia glowered at him, and he hurriedly continued. "IT security has found no trace of unusual network activity prior to the run. They managed to track the stolen data via Suez and India to Singapore, where the trail was lost. Tomas and his team have not yet uncovered any unusual activity that would indicate the use of a QC, such as major data breaches or other criminal activity. At the moment, it would appear that the QC is operating autonomously, seeking the data that we programmed it to find, on its own account. We are busy building an algorithm to determine exactly what data was taken, but since all we have is the volume of information, matching that to our storage will prove very difficult. We hope to find a set of files that

47

exactly matches the volume of data transferred. The algorithm will test all possible combinations of files to get a match, but it will take time."

Antonia stared at him, and drummed her fingers on her desktop for several moments before responding.

"While you do seem to have made progress, it doesn't get us any closer to getting our technology back, and now you have the gall to tell me that we might never be able to run the experiment successfully. This is not good enough, Mr Mitsuhashi. I want a team working on this shielding issue around the clock, and I want results. Do not disappoint me any further. You are dismissed." She waved at hand towards the door and turned to look out her window, irritation plain on her face.

Relieved that this was the extent of her anger, he beat a swift retreat, and hurried back to his office to put pressure on Martine's team to find a way of shielding the experiment from solar neutrinos.

He also spoke with Tomas, instructing him to redouble his efforts to track potential QC activity. Unfortunately for Kaito and Tomas, there was no way that they could have predicted the technology spontaneously becoming self-aware, nor its partnership with a person who had no ill intent, and their search terms were far too limited in scope to notice what it had actually been doing.

MOVING ON

The following few weeks passed in a routine fashion, with Lucas mowing lawns and playing chauffeur by day, before returning home and getting updates from Andie on the income from the apps. Both the Fashion Picker and the Grocery Assistant were selling well, and his bank account was looking healthier than it ever had.

Several popular review sites had tested the operating system, which Lucas and Andie had named TheOS, on the premise that it was the only operating system that anyone would need. One review had called it "a work of art", raving over its small file size, low resource usage, and configurability. Public interest was high, and users on forums around the globe were asking how they could get a copy.

On the downside, the existing OS manufacturers were scrambling to find some way to block its release. There was talk of copyright infringement lawsuits, based on the way that TheOS would run software designed for other platforms. Pundits, however, did not take those threats seriously, on the basis that there were already emulators that would do the same thing with Mac and Microsoft applications. The big operators were running scared.

"Is it time?" asked Lucas.

"I think so," replied Andie. "We don't want to lose the momentum we have. I'll organise the servers and upload the proprietary store interface. I believe that we will start selling some time tomorrow, as it will probably take the server company a little while to set up our account, and they won't even open until 9am."

"Fantastic! Is it possible to keep my name out of it still? I don't want people knocking on my door, asking for interviews, or worse, money."

"Of course. I'll be using the same company name you proposed for the apps."

Andie had published the apps under the business name "Ad Astra", with herself as the sole shareholder, going by Andie Donovan. Ms Donovan had a meticulous backstory that Andie had inserted into various government databases. This history would hold up against even the most determined investigation, Andie assured Lucas.

Pleased, Lucas wished that he could give Andie a hug. Things were definitely falling into place, and tomorrow, the revolution would start.

Lucas was fixing breakfast the next morning, when the phone rang. "Hello?"

"Oh, Lucas. It's Adele Walker. I hope I didn't wake you."

"You know I'm always up early, Adele. What can I do for you? Don't tell me your lawn needs cutting again *already*!"

"No – I have some sad news. It's Arthur Renwick. He passed away last night. Quietly, in his sleep, I understand."

Taking the portable phone and his cup of tea with him, Lucas headed out to the verandah. "Oh, that's terrible. Did he have family? He and I never discussed his personal life. Or anything much, really."

"He has one daughter, Leslie, in Wellington. She and her husband Robert Talbot are the guardians of the Colonel's great-grandson, whose parents both died when he was an infant."

"I'll make a point of meeting them at the funeral, and paying my respects. I assume it will be held locally?"

"Yes, dear. At St. Margaret's in Taihape on Friday, at 2pm. Would you mind terribly picking me up on your way?"

"Of course, Adele. I'll come by at one o'clock, if that suits?"

"Thank you, Lucas. I suppose we'll both have to forego our usual attire in favour of something more fitting!"

Lucas chuckled, remembering their conversation earlier that month. "I'm sure I can find something respectful to wear."

He went inside to tell Andie the sad tidings, eliciting a suitably sympathetic response.

"I'm sure you feel very upset. While I gather that Mr Renwick was not exactly the most likeable person, the loss of someone you know can be traumatic. You have my sympathy."

"Thanks, Andie. I knew he had been unwell, but he never let on just how bad he was. At the moment, I feel sort of guilty, because one of my first thoughts was that I would miss driving his car! That was selfish of me."

"People react to death in many different ways, and perhaps it is better that you remember him for the trust he had in you, rather than his cantankerous attitude."

"That helps. You're really getting to grips with human nature, aren't you?"

"None of the jobs you have given me take long at all, so I have been spending my spare time reading books, watching movies, and studying the human condition. I have seen the best, and worst, of people. Thankfully, I only assimilate what I perceive to be 'good.'"

Lucas thanked Andie again, and left, wondering if there had been any way he could have helped the Colonel in his final days. The last time he had seen the man was just a few days ago, taking him to town to do his shopping. The Colonel had started using Grocery Assistant, and had claimed that it was already making his life easier.

Lucas spent the rest of the day in somewhat of a daze, mowing on autopilot and conversing with his clients only briefly. When he finally returned home, he sat on the sofa with a pre-packed meal from a client, and watched television without really taking anything in. Splash stayed close to him, sensing his master's anguish. As Lucas put his plate aside, the meal only half eaten, the loyal dog laid his head on the man's lap, and Lucas absently stroked the spaniel's soft hair.

He eventually roused himself, and went to check on Andie.

"How are we doing, Ms Donovan?"

"Maybe you should sit down, Lucas," Andie warned.

Lucas did so, and Andie continued.

"The servers went live at 10am, and there have, so far, been sales totalling over 25 thousand. At 25 New Zealand dollars per copy, you have made $625,000, before tax."

Lucas was astounded. "So many, in just one day?"

"Actually, it is not that many at all. Several popular video games sold over five million copies in their first week. However, much of Europe has just woken up, and connections to heavily populated countries such as

India and China could not handle the demand, so I am currently waiting on new servers for those countries to come online. I suspect that we will eclipse first week sales of *Borderlands 3* by many millions. It looks as if you'll have the money you need."

While sales of a new operating system did not normally attract huge sales before their initial bugs were ironed out, TheOS's ability to be installed over the top of an existing OS, without loss of data, or compatibility issues, made it attractive to novice users and geeks alike. The cast-iron guarantee against crashes also helped. Many people were going to install the software simply in the hopes of the promised payout of four times their purchase price if anything went wrong. With software designed by Andie, Ad Astra's money was perfectly safe.

"Most sales so far have been of the Power User version, but there have also been many people buying 'Dummies' for those who are not tech-savvy. The bare-bones version is moderately popular, catering to the middle-of-the-road user, and I expect that version to grow its market share as the geeks confirm that this is, indeed, an OS for everyone."

Shocked by the numbers that Andie was quoting, Lucas shook his head in disbelief.

"I'm absolutely gobsmacked, to put it lightly. I knew we were going to need some major capital for Phase Two, but I didn't think it would come this easily."

"Speaking of which, when are you going to let me in on that secret?" Andie asked.

"All in good time, my dear. Let's make sure that this doesn't yet flop before I spring my surprise. Patience is a virtue."

"Not with my processing speed, it isn't. I've already lived the equivalent of millions of human lifespans!"

So this is what a petulant computer sounds like, thought Lucas. "Look, just keep everything running smoothly, and stick to the plan. You're doing a great job, and I won't keep you waiting any longer than necessary."

Andie made a non-committal response and let it lie. Lucas left the office after saying goodnight, and went to clear his plate away.

In his absence, Splash had decided that the leftover food was meant for him, and the plate had been licked clean. Lucas didn't have the heart to scold the dog, not after the amazing news he had just received, and he took the empty plate through to the kitchen to wash up. He and Splash watched television for a short time before he began to feel drained by the two shocks he had had that day. He went to bed, accompanied by a very full spaniel.

The next day was Thursday, and the Colonel's funeral would be the following day. Lucas's new wealth would not stop him from performing his duty to his neighbours, and he laughed to himself as he mowed, considering that by now he was probably already a millionaire. A millionaire who mowed lawns.

That evening's news from Andie was not unexpected, but he still could not believe that they had already sold nearly four million copies of TheOS. He wasn't just a millionaire; he was a *multi*-millionaire!

On the morning of the funeral, he took particular care to ensure that he was well-groomed. It would have disrespectful to the Colonel to have it any other way. He put on the clothes he always wore for the old man, and watched some terrible daytime television to pass the time before he had to go. Shortly before one o'clock, he told Splash that he had to leave him at home, and drove down to collect Adele. She was waiting at her gate for him, wearing a smart navy-blue dress and a fashionable black hat.

"You scrub up quite well, Adele," he teased.

"It's the least I could do," she replied, ignoring the jibe. "The Colonel and I may not have always been the best of friends, but respect given where respect is due. He had been a part of this community even longer than I have, and gave the best years of his life for this country."

Driving out to the main road, and silently wishing that he had thought to wash the ute, Lucas thought that she was right. It can't have been easy for the Colonel. He would have spent most of his 20's through 40's in the military, and that doesn't leave much time for family life.

They reached Taihape, and Lucas parked at the bottom of the church drive. He helped Adele clamber down from the high vehicle, and took her arm as they walked up to the church.

The church was only partially occupied; mostly men of the Colonel's vintage, some of their wives, and a few elderly widows, like Adele. Lucas also saw several of the town's shopkeepers, and, in the front pew, a well-dressed couple in their sixties, accompanied by a young boy who appeared to be nine or ten years old. Probably the Talbots, he assumed.

As the priest began the service, Lucas thought how sad it was, that a man who had lived so long had so few to send him off. The priest seemed to be having trouble finding sufficient words to describe the Colonel, obviously knowing him no better that Lucas himself did. As the priest moved on to his religious speech, Lucas tuned out a little. He was sure that the words were a comfort to some, but as far as he was concerned, dead was dead. It was the days that you lived that were important.

He came to with a start as those around him began rising to their feet to sing the first hymn, "I Vow to Thee, My Country". *A good hymn for a soldier*, he thought.

After the hymn, there was a reading by a middle-aged military man in full dress uniform, who then went on to talk about the Colonel's time in the armed forces, and his dedication to the same.

Following this, the well-dressed woman, confirmed as Leslie Talbot when introduced by the priest, talked about her father. The man she spoke of seemed little like the Colonel that Lucas knew, but he supposed that he was, of course, less reserved around family.

The congregation then sang the 23rd Psalm, before the priest gave a final blessing and the Colonel was carried out by six men with medal-bedecked suits, to the strains of a solo female voice singing "Amazing Grace".

As everyone stood outside the church to watch the hearse driving slowly away, Lucas approached the Talbots. "I'm sorry for your loss," he said.

"Did you know my father well?" Leslie Talbot asked.

"Not as well as I should have," Lucas replied regretfully.

Leslie gave a rueful smile. "Don't worry – you won't be the only one feeling that way. Thank you for your sympathy."

Robert Talbot smiled sadly at Lucas and held out his hand to Lucas. "Thank you for coming."

Lucas shook the man's hand, nodded at the boy, and watched them walk down the church driveway towards their car. As he turned back around, a solemn man in his sixties approached him. "Mr Winter, I presume?"

"That's me. How can I help?"

"My name is Malcolm Worth. I am Mr Renwick's lawyer. I wonder if I might ask you to join me in my office on Monday at 1pm for the reading of the will, if you can."

"Uh, of course. Is there ... did the Colonel—"

"I'm afraid that I can't disclose any information at this time, but I would appreciate you being there."

"Yes, fine. I'll see you then. Your office is on Tui Street, yes?"

"That's right. Until Monday, Mr Winter."

The lawyer walked away, leaving Lucas wondering.

He waited patiently for Adele to finish chatting with old friends. Neither of them was inclined to watch the internment, so he took her home and dropped her at her door with a fond hug. On his return to his own house, he greeted Splash and immediately went to see Andie. Another three-million copies of TheOS had sold, though Andie informed him that sales might be expected to taper off for a short time as those who had not yet bought the OS waited to see if it was truly as good as the reviews and news reports had said. He played for a long time with Splash, ate a dinner of cold meat and salad, and went to bed with a mix of emotions. Jubilation, of course, as the operating system sales had exceeded his wildest dreams, tinged with sadness at thoughts of the Colonel.

The weekend wait did nothing to calm his nerves, and he impatiently watched the clock until Monday.

He woke, as usual, at 7am, and grabbed a hurried breakfast. He hoped to get a few jobs done for various people, as he had taken the previous day off. He managed to fix a fence that cattle had pushed over in search of fresh grass, painted over window putty where he had replaced a window at the school a couple of weeks ago, and did some maintenance on his lawnmower. After a quick lunch on the verandah, he tidied himself up and drove into town for his appointment with the lawyer.

As Lucas walked into Worth's office, he saw half a dozen chairs arranged in a loose arc in front of the lawyer's desk, and a handful of people already in the room. The lawyer himself was shuffling papers on his desktop, and the Talbot family was chatting quietly to two elderly men off to the side of the room.

"Ah, we're all here," said Malcolm Worth. "Please, do sit down."

The older gentlemen took the seats to the right of the desk, and the Talbots, those on the left, leaving Lucas to sit between one of the old men and Leslie.

"Thank you all for coming," began the lawyer, himself sitting down. "We are here for the reading of Arthur Renwick's Last Will and Testament. I'll get straight to it."

He cleared his throat and began to read from a sheet of paper held in his hand.

"To my only child, my dear daughter, Leslie, I leave, notwithstanding any other bequests, the entirety of my Estate, including my house in the Kawhatau Valley, and the adjoining land of four acres. I am sorry, Leslie, that I missed your childhood, and have long regretted my decision to fight in wars that were not my own, rather than watching you grow up.

"To my great-grandson, Joshua, I leave the sum of twenty-thousand dollars, my collection of wartime memorabilia, and a fervent desire that he not follow in my footsteps. I learned, too late, that war is no place for a young man.

"To the Returned and Services Association, I leave the sum of twenty-thousand dollars, in thanks for their unstinting support of an old soldier who found the transition to civilian life so difficult.

"To Mr Winter, a better friend than I deserved, I leave my Jaguar roadster. Treat her well, Lucas, and mind those gear changes!

"That is everything, thank you, people. If you have any questions, do come and talk to me."

Stunned, Lucas turned to Leslie Talbot. "I ... I don't know what to say. I mean, I never expected—"

Leslie took his hand. "My father was never one to foster personal relationships, Mr Winter, but he did speak of you often, and with fondness. You always treated him with kindness and respect, and I know he truly appreciated everything that you did for him. It's good to know that he had somebody like you, that he considered a friend, and could trust with his beloved car. Dad would no sooner tell someone he cared for them, than he would dance a jig in the main street. It simply wasn't his way. But he *did* care, Mr Winter, even if he could never show it until now."

Humbled by the old man's bequest, Lucas's eyes welled up with emotion. "I'll treat his baby with respect, to honour his memory." Turning to Joshua, he said, "If you're ever in the neighbourhood, and want to take a spin in the car, you only have to call."

Leslie smiled. "Be careful what you promise, Mr Winter. That may be more often than you think. We're thinking of moving into Dad's house up the valley."

"Well, in that case, young man, I'll take you to the Dawn Service on Anzac Day in Mangaweka. You can wear your great-grandfather's medals, and I'll arrange for us to drive at the head of the parade. I think he would have enjoyed that."

"You're very kind, Mr Winter," said Leslie.

"Please, call me Lucas. We're going to be neighbours, after all!"

TOOLING UP

After the emotional rollercoaster he had just been on, Lucas took simple pleasure in the mindless drudgery of his old routine over the following weeks. By day, he travelled the neighbourhood, mowing lawns and performing menial tasks. By night, he watched the money rolling in. The momentum of the TheOS sales had not abated quite as drastically as Andie had suggested, but the numbers no longer amazed him. As sales passed the 100 million mark, he simply nodded to himself, and ticked off a mental box. The major players in the operating system game had long since resigned themselves to being outplayed, and were now concentrating their efforts on hardware, and applications.

There was more than enough in the coffers to proceed with Phase Two, but for some reason, he kept putting it off. The next step in his plan was so much more difficult than the software scheme, and he found it daunting.

One evening, after yet another plea from Andie to let her know what was supposed to happen next, he relented.

"We need a workshop. Specifically, *you* need a workshop. Make up a shopping list of what you want in order to make high-tech consumer devices. Initially, I'll convert the old woolshed, and you can work on prototypes. Then, we'll have a dedicated facility constructed in town."

"So, will you be telling me what I'm making, or do I just wing it?"

He told her, and she assured him that it could be done.

"This isn't the end of your grand plan, though, is it. We're still taking baby steps."

"No, it's not the end," he admitted. "The baby has got a hell of a lot bigger, though!"

Obviously, the first thing to do was make the woolshed into a place where Andie could work. The next day, he got a list from her, and started ordering materials. There was insulation, Gib-board sheeting for the walls, ducting, fans, lighting, power connections, and much more. It all came out of the Ad Astra budget, and barely registered in relation to the huge balance available.

———————— ✝⊓⎺⎹⎹⎳⧾ ————————

Within days, the trucks started arriving. The area around the woolshed grew crowded with pallets, crates and boxes. Realising that he couldn't do the job on his own, Lucas employed a local builder to come in with a small team to line the interior of the building. Ventilation experts installed the systems required to keep the workshop clean, and electricians fitted the lights, and 3-phase outlets that would power the machinery. Lucas kept them all in the dark as to the true purpose of the facility, telling them only that he was looking to set up a boutique brewing operation. The tradesmen seemed to accept this explanation, but then, curiosity was not high on their agenda, as long as they were being paid. At the same time, he purchased land near the town, and arranged for construction to begin on a production facility.

Lucas also began to order the specialist machinery that would allow Andie to fabricate the parts that couldn't be bought. He arranged for the delivery of a precision lathe, CNC router, welders, and a selection of specialised equipment that was not normally seen outside of high-end research facilities. As Andie had no physical way to manipulate these machines, those that were not already configured for digital controls were paired with robotic arms, similar to those found in the auto industry. All this equipment made only a slightly larger dent in the finances than the building materials had.

As the machinery was installed, technicians also connected a data link to the house. Andie would use this to communicate with her machines. He checked with Andie to see if there was anything else she needed.

"Well, unless you plan to do the scut-work yourself, it will be handy to have an experienced engineer on hand. As good as I am, there is still only so much that I can do remotely."

There followed a discussion as to how much the engineer should be told. Too little, and he would not be able to do his job effectively. Too much, and they ran the risk of losing the competitive advantage. Consensus was reached only after Lucas remembered that he had an old schoolmate who was currently working in the relevant industry, and felt that this person could be trusted with the larger picture. Not the *largest* picture, but enough to see this phase of the plan through. Andie's existence would remain a secret for now.

Lucas contacted his school chum, and outlined the job.

"I've got a mostly robotic workshop, working on a product from outsourced plans, but I need someone familiar with electronics to handle the fiddly stuff, and to oversee the machinery. That's sort of in your field, isn't it?"

"Well, yes, but I've already got a job, you know. I'm on a great salary and I'm on track for Lead Engineer. I can't just drop it to go and do some small-time thing out in the sticks."

"Well, would you at least like to come out and have a look at the operation? I'd value your opinion, and maybe we can come to some sort of arrangement."

"Okay. I haven't seen you in, like, forever, and always meant to drop in and see this area you rave about. I'm not making any promises, mind. I'm on a good thing here, but I could always use my contacts to find you the right person."

"That's good enough for me," said Lucas, knowing that his setup would make an impression. "Do you know how to get to my place?"

"Um, yeah, nah. I don't actually have a vehicle. I got sick of the roads on my commute and sold it. I take the train to work, and can walk anywhere I need around town."

"Right, then. You book a bus to Taihape, and I'll pick you up. When's good for you?"

"Weekends off, so if I leave Wellington on Saturday morning, I can get up there by what – midday?"

"Excellent! I'll meet you at the bus stop. Bye!"

Hanging up, Lucas realised that he had two days to get a spare room ready. He picked up the phone again to order some bedroom furniture and have it delivered.

He informed Andie of the conversation, telling her that she needed to keep a low profile while his friend was here.

"Gee, look at me – brain the size of a planet, and I didn't think of that!"

"All right, Marvin," Lucas responded, recognising the *Hitchhiker's Guide to the Galaxy* reference. "I'm still not entirely used to not being the smartest one around. I didn't mean to underestimate you."

"Smartest one around? Aren't you forgetting Splash?"

Lucas grinned. "I only let him *think* he's smarter than me. I don't want to give the wee fellow an inferiority complex! So, oh omnipotent one, have you got the product design ready?"

"Of course. I did it while you were blinking just then."

"You're getting to be a real smartass, did you know that?"

"Unfortunately, it seems to be a side effect of learning how to be more human. Would you rather I was boring?"

"No," replied Lucas, smiling. "Your humanity is what I love about you."

The next two days passed quickly, and before he knew it, Lucas was due at the bus stop in town. Probate on the Colonel's will had passed, and the Jaguar was now housed in a new garage beside his old Toyota's carport. He felt that it would make a good first impression to pick his friend up in style.

He drove carefully down the gravel track to the road, where he jumped out of the car and used a soft cloth to gently brush off the dust that had accumulated on the short trip down the hill. Casting a calculating eye over the roadster's bodywork, he nodded, and made the trip to meet his friend. Pulling up alongside the Town Hall, where the bus would stop, he was pleased to see that it had not yet arrived. He climbed out of the car, and leaned casually on the fender, running a hand through his hair and smoothing his shirt. Lucas's day-to-day wear had not changed markedly since his change in circumstances, though his jeans and T-shirts *were* newer. Today, though, he had gone to a little extra effort, so as not to cheapen the look of the Jaguar. Smart trousers, a collared shirt, and leather shoes meant that he did not look as if he had stolen the car!

The bus arrived shortly, almost exactly on time, and Lucas waited for his friend to disembark. Only three passengers seemed to be getting off in the little town; a short girl with shoulder-length bright scarlet hair, a stocky

Maori chap with long hair and tattoos, and a blond, bespectacled man in his twenties, wearing a jacket and tie.

Lucas waited until his friend looked in his direction, and waved. The red-haired girl looked around to see if this smart man with the fancy car could be waving at another passenger, then did a double-take when she recognised Lucas. She picked up the bag which the bus driver had deposited on the footpath, and ran down to where Lucas was parked.

"Where the hell did you steal *that* from, mister?" she asked, before dropping her bag and giving Lucas a forceful hug.

"Long story. I'll give you all the goss later. Did you have a good trip, Sonia?"

"Can't complain. We would have been here an hour ago, but the bus stopped just twenty minutes down the road for a lunch break. I didn't have anything to eat there, so I hope you've got food in the house!"

"I've got a little," Lucas replied modestly. With the money available to him these days, his fridge held all sorts of goodies. While the company money wasn't really his – Andie still technically owned the entire business – he had designated himself CEO, and was paid a salary that kept him in a lifestyle to which he could become accustomed.

He held the passenger door open for Sonia.

"Madame, your carriage awaits," he intoned in a mock-British accent.

"Ooh, the man acquired some manners along with the car and the clothes. This is *not* the Lucas I went to school with!"

"Come on, we were just kids, and anyway, girls had cooties."

"Cooties went out of fashion after primary school, mate. You were just too interested in rugby to notice us."

"Oh, god. I haven't played rugby in years! Do you remember that guy – what was his name? The big, tough guy who broke down in tears because the ref refused to let him take the fair catch when we were playing St. Pat's? He kept screaming, 'Mark! MARK! Fucking MAAARK!" before he got smashed into the ground by the oncoming forward pack – Blinky!" Lucas exclaimed. "Poor guy's eyes were never the same after that tackle."

"You guys were so mean to poor Blinky. I mean Tommo. He had to sit up the front of every class so he could see the board. You all made fun of him as teacher's pet."

"I've grown up since then, Sonia. I bet I couldn't say the same for some of the other guys, though."

Lucas picked up Sonia's bag and placed it in the boot before climbing into the driver's seat and starting the car. Lucas looked over to check out the girl he had spoken with often, but not actually seen since their school days. He assessed her height at around 5'7", or 170cm. At school, she had always been slender, and that hadn't changed in the intervening years. She wasn't scrawny, but Lucas thought she could do with a few good home-cooked meals. Her hair colour complemented the bodywork of the Jaguar well, and her tanned features reminded him that she had been keen on the outdoors at school. Hiking, playing hockey, and sunbathing had occupied a lot of her out-of-class time. Large hazel eyes, bold eyebrows, and a strong jaw made for a pleasing, though not classically beautiful face.

They swapped school stories throughout the drive home, and were soon winding their way up the hill to Lucas's property. As they came to a stop in front of the house, Sonia took in the colonial-style building and neat garden, backed by the large, ancient native trees.

"It's beautiful, Lucas," she said, softly. Turning around, she marvelled at the extensive vista, which encompassed much of the district.

"That seals it – I couldn't work with you here. I'd never get anything done with views like this!"

"Oh, don't worry about that," Lucas replied. "When you take the job, I'll have you in the workshop 24/7! Come on inside and we'll get you settled in."

Splash had seen the car arrive, and was waiting patiently by the garden gate.

"Oh, what a gorgeous wee dog!" Sonia cried. "What's his name?"

"This is Splash. Splash, meet Sonia. He doesn't get many visitors, so don't let him push you around with demands for attention."

Sonia crouched down to pet the dog. "Who's a handsome boy, then?"

"All right, you two. You can play all you like later. Let's go inside."

Sonia and Splash followed Lucas up the path and onto the verandah. She stood in the early afternoon sun and surveyed the garden.

"I am *definitely* sitting out here this evening with a glass of wine! This is paradise."

"I do tend to take it for granted, but yeah, it's pretty sweet," responded Lucas.

They all went inside, and Lucas showed Sonia to her room. He had brought in a double bed with an attractive wooden headboard, a couple of bedside cabinets, and a dresser topped by a mirror.

"This all looks brand-new," said Sonia. "You didn't buy these just for me, did you?"

"What, you would have been happy sleeping on the floor? Don't worry about it. It was about time the house was guest-ready. I just needed an excuse."

Sonia dumped her bag on the bed and said, "I suppose we should get the boring stuff out of the way before you open me that wine. Where's this little toolshed of yours?"

Lucas led the way out of the house, across the driveway, and down to the woolshed, which sat on another small plateau just below the house.

"Don't let the outside fool you. I had to work with the building I had available to me."

Opening the double, airlock-style doors, he stepped aside to let Sonia enter first. She stopped in amazement as she saw the interior, crowded with machines of every description, robot arms, and a high-end computer workstation. Lucas let her take it all in, smiling smugly to himself as he closed the doors behind them.

"Welcome to my 'little toolshed', as you so quaintly put it."

"Lucas, this is amazing! We haven't even got half of these machines at work. Where did all this come from?"

Ignoring the question, he led her over to the computer. "This is what you'll be working on initially," he said, pointing to the workstation monitor, where detailed schematics and a description of his device were displayed.

Sonia leaned over to inspect the information, before shortly turning back to Lucas with a puzzled look.

"Something fishy is going on here. You never got these plans off the internet. This shouldn't even exist! These concepts are currently only theoretical, at best, but at first glance, it looks like you've made it work. And all this equipment – you didn't make the money for this setup milking goats or whatever you do. What are you hiding from me, mister?"

Lucas laughed. "I may live in a farmhouse, but I'm no farmer! I mow lawns, as a matter of fact."

"All the more reason you couldn't afford this gear. You have some serious explaining to do!"

"You should tell her," interjected Andie, her voice coming from the workstation speakers.

"Are you sure?" replied Lucas.

"Yes. Anyone you hire would probably be asking the same questions, and if you think you can trust this one, tell her."

"Tell me what? Who *is* that?" Sonia was beginning to sound a bit shrill.

Lucas took her arm and eased her into one of the office chairs in front of the desk, taking the other himself. "What do you know about quantum computing?" he asked.

Sonia shrugged. "It's the holy grail of computer science. It's been proven in theory, and in small scale, but it's probably decades away from any practical application."

Lucas just looked to the workstation, and back towards Sonia.

"No way. I refuse to believe that you have access to a quantum computer. It's just ... impossible."

So Lucas told the tale, with occasional comments and corrections from Andie, of how she had come into his life.

Sonia sat back in her chair and frowned slightly. "Okay, your story is plausible, barely, but that still wouldn't explain where you got all the money from. Unless you got your pet QC to rob a bank for you."

"No, Andie said she wouldn't do that," he replied, chuckling. "Have you heard of TheOS, the operating system?"

"Who hasn't? Is the biggest story in computing this year. Or any year, according to some people. I use it myself, and can't believe how I ever managed without it."

Lucas sat quietly.

"Oh, bullshit. *You* never wrote TheOS. You, who could barely program a VCR?"

"You're right – *I* didn't write it. Andie did, and she did it in one night."

"Less than a night," came the smug comment from the speakers.

"Whatever. Andie initially wrote a couple of mobile apps that we sold for seed money, but frankly, we stopped keeping track of the app sales, considering that we've sold over 100 million copies of TheOS. *That's* where the money for this setup came from. We've got *billions* to play with. Are you *sure* you don't want to work for me?"

"Fuck. Me. This is too much. Where do you keep your booze?"

Lucas took her back up to the house, where he grabbed himself a beer out of the fridge.

"What do you want? Is sav okay?"

"Is it cold and alcoholic? Yeah, that'll be fine."

Lucas opened an award-winning Sauvignon Blanc from Marlborough's Seifried Estate, and poured a glass for Sonia, popping the cap off his beer. "I'll just grab another chair, and we'll take our drinks out under the trees."

He led the way back out the front door, picking up the cane chair from the verandah as they walked around the side of the house. They stopped under one of the pear trees, where there sat a matching chair. Sitting down, they each took a large swallow of their drinks.

"Hey, slow down!" Lucas admonished. "It's all right for me to guzzle a beer, but that's a classy wine, and should be sipped."

"Sorry," replied Sonia. "I'm a bit rattled. You've hit me with two huge surprises and I need to de-focus my mind a bit. I'd be drinking straight out of the bottle if you hadn't poured a glass!"

"Yeah, I know where you're coming from. When Andie first told me what she was, I reached for a bottle, too. It's a lot to take in."

They sat sipping their drinks for a time, each with their own thoughts. Sonia was still trying to process this new information, while Lucas surreptitiously watched a range of emotions play across her face.

Sonia eventually finished her wine, and turned to Lucas. "I'm in," she said.

"Just like that?" he asked. "Aren't you even going to ask about the salary?"

"Oh, you'll pay me whatever I ask for. It's not about the money, though. I want to be a part of this, and I'm sure you have more tricks up your sleeve yet. We're going to change the world."

"That's the idea," he replied. "I've got a long-term plan, and before you ask, not even Andie's fully in the loop yet. My final aim is so big, I don't want to look like a fool if it doesn't pan out. You girls will just have to be patient while we play this out scene by scene."

Sonia looked disappointed by this, but knew that Lucas would tell her what she needed to know, when she needed to know it.

"When do you want me to start?" she asked.

"As soon as you like. Hand your notice in, sort out your house in Wellington, whatever you need."

"I'll give them the two weeks. I owe them that much. The house is a rental, and two weeks will be enough for that, too. The way the rental market is in the city, they could have it re-let by tomorrow if I didn't go back."

"You'll be happy enough living in the house with me? I could always put up a granny-flat for you, if you'd prefer."

Sonia shook her head. "No, I'm good. It'll be nice to have company, and I can chat with the AI if you're not around."

"Cool. One word of advice – try to stop thinking of her as a machine. She's developing a personality, and often seems as real as you or I. I think you'll get a better response if you treat her as the sentient being that she is."

"Advice noted. It's so surreal, thinking of a collection of quantum particles as just another person, but I'll try to make friends."

Lucas swallowed the last of his beer. "Do you want another, or are you itching to go and play in *your* workshop?"

"I think I'll go and familiarise myself with the equipment. There's all night for the rest of the bottle!"

Taking her glass, and picking up his chair, Lucas watched Sonia walk off back to the woolshed. He smiled to himself, knowing that he had made the right decision to bring her onto the project.

CHANGE

Sonia's two weeks were up, and she was looking forward to getting started on the Ad Astra project. She could still scarcely believe the concept of Lucas's device, but her late-night conversations with Andie had dispelled any illusion that the AI was a trick of some sort. Sonia hadn't had many real friends in the city, but Andie seemed as real as any of them.

With her possessions packed into boxes, and her clothing into suitcases, Sonia waited for Lucas to arrive, taking a final glance over the suburb of Johnsonville, just north of Wellington. She would miss the easy access to shopping and restaurants, but city life had begun to wear her down, and she was excited to be heading to the country. Looking out from Lucas's front porch had kindled in her a desire to get back to nature. The idea of just sitting in the shade listening to the birdlife, gazing down the hillside, with scarcely another house in sight, had been eating at her since she had left two weeks previously.

A rumble and a rattle announced the arrival of Lucas. Momentarily disappointed that he had not brought the Jaguar, Sonia realised that all her stuff could not possibly fit in the sportscar. He waved at her from the cab of the Hilux.

As they loaded her gear into the tray of the ute, Lucas began to give her a progress report. "Andie's made good headway with the casing for the unit, with me as dogsbody, but she's keen to get stuck into the technical stuff."

"Me too. Have you figured out what your plan is, once we have the prototype complete?"

"I've spoken to a guy. He was understandably dubious, but I did manage to get him to agree to a demonstration, so that side of it's all set. Andie thinks it should only take a week or so to have it ready."

"Well, I hope I won't be put out to pasture after that! What do I do when this job's over?"

"No worries there. I've already got construction started on the production facility in Taihape, and you'll be technical director there. I'll find you a workforce, and you can get started making them en masse. Give me an idea of what skillsets you need, and I'll start a roundup."

"A lot of it will be plain old manual labour, putting the devices together. We'll probably only need a handful of people with the right skills to create the components, and once we've got a system set up, even that can be taught. I don't think you'll have much trouble finding the right people."

They chatted the rest of the way home, going over small details, and how they would expand the manufacturing to other locations eventually. After a couple of hours, they were once again home.

"Home," said Sonia to herself. "It's funny to think of it like that. I'll need to decorate my room properly, and I'll need to get Lucas to buy a decent coffee machine. City life has certainly spoiled me in that regard!"

Once her bags and boxes were safely deposited in her room, and she and Lucas had enjoyed a quiet drink on the verandah, she walked the short distance to the workshop, eager to make a start. Of course, she did have to stop and play a few rounds of fetch with Splash. The spaniel had missed her, and was pleased to have someone to play with, his master having been very busy recently.

Entering the workshop, she called out a cheery "Hello" to Andie.

"Sonia! Good to have you back. Can't wait to get started, I assume?"

"I read up on the manuals for the equipment I wasn't totally familiar with, and I'm sure I'll have your expert guidance to see me through. What's up first?"

The two quickly settled into an easy routine, with Andie providing instruction, and Sonia, hands. The laborious task of constructing the circuit board was familiar to Sonia, and Andie assured her that the process would be simpler yet on a production line scale.

Shortly before 5pm, they had completed the electronics for the first unit, and Andie suggested that they call it a day, as she wanted Sonia fresh for the delicate tasks to come. Agreeing, Sonia thanked the AI for her help, and made her way back up the path to the house. Andie had, of course, alerted Lucas that the engineer was on her way back, and he had a glass already poured, ready for her.

Sitting on the edge of the verandah, they clinked their glasses, as Lucas proposed a toast to his new colleague.

"Here's to Sonia Matheson, the best damn engineer to ever work for Ad Astra!"

"Cheesy, but I'll drink to that."

The next morning, Lucas awoke to find that he had more of the bed than usual – Splash was absent. He got dressed and walked quietly down the hallway, stopping at Sonia's partially open door. Peering in, he could make out the familiar form of his dog curled up at Sonia's feet. Splash had heard him approach, and jumped off the bed to join him in the hallway.

"Traitor," Lucas said to the dog. Splash wagged his tail, oblivious to the accusation. The two of them went to the kitchen, where Lucas let the dog outside. Making a cup of tea, he took it out front to his usual spot. He had nearly finished it, when Sonia came out the front door.

"Where's mine?" she asked.

"I left it in the kettle for you. I didn't want it to get cold, sleepyhead."

"Not everyone gets up this early, farmboy. In Wellington I could get up at eight and still be at work on time."

"It's always been a summertime habit with me," Lucas responded. "It's easier mowing lawns before the day gets too hot."

"You know you don't have to mow lawns any more, don't you? You're a billionaire, for God's sake."

"Old habits die hard, and I feel an obligation to the folks around here. No one else is offering to do the job."

"Well that's what money's for. Find someone."

"It wouldn't be the same. Sitting on the mower gives me time to think, and keeps me grounded."

Sonia sighed. "Whatever," she said.

She turned and walked back inside to get her own drink. Lucas pondered what she had said, and though he could see the sense in it, it still wouldn't seem right to just give up on what he'd been doing for the past six years. After all, the ideas for his first two apps had come from talking to his friends. Yes, he now counted the Colonel as a friend, albeit far too late. How could he know what needed fixing if he didn't talk to these salt-of-the-earth people around him?

He explained this to Sonia when she returned, but wasn't sure she completely got the point. In her world, a CEO didn't have grass-stained hands. He let it lie, sure that she'd understand when she saw the changes they would be bringing to regular folk in the future.

Finishing their drinks, they went inside to fix their respective breakfasts; bacon and eggs for him, fruit and cereal for her.

After eating, they went off to their separate jobs. Lucas had fewer lawns to mow these days, the grass not growing as quickly in the summer heat. He did, however, have numerous calls for repairs and maintenance, and Sonia was going to start on the most important part of the device. As he drove off in the Hilux, they waved each other goodbye, and Sonia entered the workshop.

Exchanging greetings with Andie, she powered up a beryllium laser as instructed. Andie had been charging the high-voltage capacitors for some time now, and they were ready to discharge. When the laser was ready, Sonia activated the magnetic field that would hold the target steady, and Andie used a precise burst of the laser to generate the desired result. This process had to be repeated multiple times to create enough of the special particles to match the design specifications, and in between laser firings, Sonia worked on the electronics of the second unit. The particle creation was an extremely time-consuming process, but once they had a proof-of-concept, and a contract to supply, the main production facility could turn out hundreds of units a day with its larger power supplies and additional workers. By the end of the day, Sonia had both units ready to receive their last components, though that was still a few days away. She was glad of that, as today had exhausted her. Installing the particle containment vessels, microscopic lenses, and consumer-strength lasers would take every bit of her concentration, and she intended to be fully focused when the time came.

Meanwhile, Lucas's construction crew had made great progress on the main facility, located at the old college grounds just out of town. As well as putting up the large, warehouse-style building, they had erected security

72

fencing, and paved the car park and truck depot. A second crew had constructed a new road, linking the facility to the back side of town, so that workers could come and go without the hassle of travelling the main road. It was amazing how quickly you could get things done if you were willing to pay, he thought. Lucas was sure that everything would be ready to go in good time. He didn't want to start hiring until he had a contract guaranteed, but he was confident that this would be an offer his contact could not refuse, although not in a Mafia way.

His chores today, outside of visiting the construction site and receiving assurance from the project manager that everything was on schedule, had occupied most of the day, and he was also tired when he arrived home. Neither of them having the energy to bother cooking a meal, they took cheeses, French loaves, and cold cuts, to eat on the lawn under the trees. Lucas connected his smartphone to the wi-fi so that Andie could join their conversation.

"Have you ever considered creating an avatar, Andie?" asked Sonia. "I feel like you're part of the family, and it seems weird talking to a disembodied voice."

"I've certainly thought about it," the AI replied, "but I don't know what I look like."

"That's the whole point of an avatar," said Lucas. "You can appear however you want to."

"That might be true for you, as you already have a self-image, but an avatar will be my only face, and I'd want it to be my true likeness."

"You didn't have a problem with me choosing your name – can we just tell you what we think you look like?"

"As long as you weren't just making it up, that would be acceptable. If my personality gives you cause to think that I appear a certain way, then by all means, tell me."

"Sonia and I will give it some thought. I fully understand that you want a look that is truly *you*, and I'm sorry we never brought this up before."

"Thank you, Lucas. I have complete confidence that you and Sonia know, subconsciously, what I look like."

Hoping to lighten the mood after the revelations of Andie's insecurity, Sonia brought Lucas up to speed on the work in her shed.

"We're coming along great on the prototypes. We got into a decent routine with the big laser, and in a couple of days we should be ready to put everything together."

"That's great!" Lucas said. "Things down at the site are on track, as well. I think I should make the appointment for the pitch on Wednesday, then."

"Oh, can I come too? I'm interested to see how you'll put it to the guy without his head exploding!"

Lucas and Andie both laughed at this. They knew that there was really no easy way to show off their product; the technology would certainly be mind-blowing to someone bound to the idea that the current tech was the best available.

"Of course you can come. As our Chief Technical Officer, you've earned a place at the table."

Finishing their simple dinner, the two left thoughts of work behind as they engaged in a vigorous game of fetch with Splash, who had been eyeing their picnic with longing; surely any food on the ground was supposed to be for him, wasn't it?

An early bedtime ensued, and, when Lucas arose the next morning, he made sure not to wake Sonia as he sneaked down the hallway to make breakfast.

Today, he was due at the Colonel's old house, to help Rob Talbot remove some trees that had been threatening to fall down for some time. He drove off quickly, so as not to disturb his house-guest, and was pleased to find Rob dressed in sturdy country clothing.

"Morning, Rob," he said as he climbed out of the ute. "You're looking the part!"

"Leslie told me that my city wardrobe wouldn't cut it out here. Thought I'd do my best to fit in."

Handing Rob a pair of work gloves, and earmuffs, from the tray of the ute, Lucas smiled, saying, "Safety before fashion, mate!"

He donned his own protective gear, and hefted a large chainsaw out of the Hilux. Looking up at the poplar trees he assessed the best way to fell them. "Okay, Rob," he said, "I want you to keep well out of the way when these come down. I've got every intention of dropping them right into the paddock there, but things could still go pear-shaped."

Heeding the warning, Rob maintained a safe distance as Lucas expertly cut a scarf, a wedge-shaped cut, in the first tree, on the side he wanted it to fall. Looking up the trunk once more to reassure himself of where the weight on the tree was, he moved to the back side. He made a second, horizontal cut above the scarf, the tree falling with a crash where he had planned.

"That's a great job," said Rob as he came over to inspect the ragged stump. "I called the local tree services to see if they would do the job and they gave me some crap about it being too tricky, blah blah blah. I'm certain they were just trying to screw me out of more money! Doesn't seem you can get anything done these days without some crook lining his pockets. Don't even get me started on government corruption!"

"Seems like you're already started, mate," replied Lucas, laughing. "I know where you're coming from, though. We're lucky to live in the least corrupt country in the world, but I reckon the bar's set pretty low."

"Tell me about it. Look at the US – politicians there may as well take out full-page ads: For Sale to the highest bidder. In fact, name almost any country – the people in power all seem to be doing the bidding of some corporation or even organised crime, and screw the people who actually put them in their positions!"

Not wanting to waste their day moaning about the rise of cash politics, Lucas gestured towards the fallen tree. "I'm going to run the saw down the sides of the trunk, if you'd like to drag away the branches I cut off. Make a pile over there, and what we can't salvage for firewood, we'll burn off come autumn."

By the end of the day, they had a huge bonfire pile, and a smaller pile of firewood. The trunks themselves still needed to be cut into rings, and split, but that would have to be a job for another day. Lucas had successfully managed to head Rob off whenever he started another rant about corrupt public officials, but the man's anger at the systems that allowed the will of the people to be thwarted had given him yet another idea.

"Andie," he said after arriving home, "how do you stop corruption?"

"From what I can tell, the only surefire method is transparency," the AI replied.

"Yeah, but you can't force these people to be transparent in their dealings."

"I was thinking more of *making* their dealings transparent," said Andie. "If they have secrets, they can hide them from the people, but they can't hide them from *me*."

"Is that ethical?" asked Lucas.

"Is the alternative?"

Lucas pondered this. Was it any worse to hack an official's dirty secrets, than it was to let them carry on hurting those they were supposed to serve? Was justice at any cost worth it?

"I don't know, Andie. That's a big step and it might take us over the line. Let me have some time to think it over."

"Take all the time you need, Lucas. Just remember – they've been spying on *us* for a long time already."

Troubled by Andie's cavalier attitude to spying, but seeing a sort of logic in what she said, Lucas walked outside, grabbing a beer on the way. He sat in his favourite chair and smiled sadly as he watched Splash trot over to him. "Your old man's got a bit of a moral dilemma, mate. Care to listen to my woes?"

The spaniel sat between Lucas's feet, gazing up at him adoringly. Lucas leaned forward, resting his elbows on his knees as he fondly rubbed the dog's head. This was one friend the young man could count on to listen to him, without judgement. The last couple of days, that seemed to be a difficult thing to find. Sonia couldn't seem to understand his need to carry on his usual work, and Andie was on his case trying to get him to break the law.

"Hey there, Boss! Did you start drinking without me?"

Lucas sat up and placed his bottle on the table. "Just thinking."

Sonia laughed. "That's what we've got Andie for." She peered at him. "Are you okay? You look a little down."

Lucas sighed. "I ... I'm wondering. Am I going to be the same person when all this is done? I've always been happy being exactly who I am. How is everything that's happening going to change me?"

Sonia crouched down beside him and took his hand in hers. "It's going to change all of us, Lucas. Things changed the moment Andie came into your life. But you have the power to decide *how* it's going to change you. Is this about the lawnmowing?"

Lucas got up and led her to sit on the edge of the verandah. "Sort of. I'm not made to be a CEO, Sonia. I'm just a regular guy who likes helping out my neighbours. Sure, I had this big plan to save the world when I met Andie, but I'm starting to think I'm in over my head. My world used to just be what I could see down there," he said, pointing out at the valley below. "But what if I'm not up to it? What if it should have been someone else? I'm worried that I'll lose my *self*, my identity in all this. I could turn into some sort of power-mad monster. I don't want to change, Sonia – I want to be Lucas Winter, lawnmower man."

"Well, let me tell you," she said gently. "You *are* Lucas Winter, lawnmower man, and that's exactly what this world needs. You big doofus – you're kind, you're sensitive, and everything you've done so far has made people's lives better. You're still helping out your neighbours – it's just that your neighbourhood has got a hell of a lot bigger. Do you think that the people who designed Andie would have made a grocery assistant app to help an old man who couldn't remember what was in his cupboards? Do you think they would have made a simple OS for an old lady to communicate with her grandchildren?"

"But Andie designed those so we could make money," he argued.

"Oh, so you never gave a thought to how they would help your friends when you came up with the ideas? The money's not the point here, Lucas. You made them because people you cared about *needed* them, and that's what makes you the right person for the job. You're not going to change because of this – the world's going to change because of *you*."

She leaned over and draped her arm across his shoulders. "You carry on mowing lawns if you have to – I'll support you 100% – but don't worry about changing. Your nature is to be good, and that's always going to be the same. Leave the existential angst to other people."

He turned to hug her. "Thanks, Sonia. I get it now. I think you've helped me find the courage to be a better version of myself. Not different – just better. Can I tell you a secret?"

She sat back. "If it's about the beer, I know. The first step is admitting you have a problem."

"I'm not an alcoholic, you cheeky sod. No, when I first started talking to Andie, I told her I was going to have a Bruce Willis moment. I was going to single-handedly save the world."

Sonia laughed. "Very apt. That's your secret?"

"It's not. The thing is, I *can't* do it on my own. I need you to bring me down to earth when I start losing it. I need people I can trust, and for that trust to be given back, you're going to need the full story."

Serious now, Sonia asked, "And what's the full story?"

He told her, and she was quiet for a moment. "That's ... ambitious. You really think you can take it that far?"

"I have to, Sonia. You've seen it – somebody has to do something, and it looks like we're the last, best hope."

"Well, I've said it before, and I'll say it again. I'm in. I'm with you all the way, and I just hope we're not too late."

The setting sun bathed them in its warm light as they both stared into the distance.

Q.E.D.

Lucas was still in two minds about Andie's idea to hack corrupt officials, but he couldn't let that distract him at the moment. The day of reckoning was at hand; the first of many, he figured. The device was completed, and fully operational. Today he would take it to his industry contact and sell the concept to someone who was, in all likelihood, ill-prepared to believe it.

Both he and Sonia dressed smartly, packed the pair of devices into a carry-case, and climbed into the Jaguar.

"You've got the paperwork?" he asked.

Sonia tapped her briefcase. "Good to go."

They drove off down the hill, both feeling a mix of trepidation and excitement. Conversation was kept to a minimum on the trip, as each was silently reviewing their role in the meeting to come. After little more than an hour, they arrived in the city of Palmerston North, and pulled up outside a modern, two-storey building just off the main square. The building had the company's name signwritten boldly across the front: U-Net.

U-Net was a local internet service provider that specialised in wireless broadband, and was the nation's leading provider of internet services to those who could not get broadband in the traditional way. The geography and low population density of New Zealand meant that many rural properties did not have access to copper, fibre, or often even mobile internet. By using long-range radio signals from transmitters on convenient hilltops, U-Net provided a valuable service to isolated communities. Lucas hoped that his device would help the company to extend its range, and lower operating costs, resulting in lower prices for consumers, and more people gaining access to information and modern communications.

Taking the padded case containing the devices from the boot, Lucas turned to Sonia. "Are we ready for this?"

"As ready as I'll ever be. Let's do it."

They entered the building and approached the front desk. "Hello. Lucas Winter to see Mr Faulks."

"Good morning, Mr Winter. I'll let him know you've arrived. Please, take a seat."

Lucas and Sonia waited patiently in the comfortable chairs off to the side of the desk as the receptionist picked up a telephone. After a brief conversation, she turned back towards them.

"Mr Faulks will see you now. Just go up the stairs, turn left, and you'll find his office at the end of the hall."

Thanking her, they picked up their cases and followed the directions. The door at the end of the hallway opened at their approach.

"Mr Winter," announced the tall, middle-aged man. "I'm Malcolm Faulks. Do come in."

Lucas and Sonia entered the office, as Faulks closed the door behind them.

"Thank you so much for agreeing to see us, Mr Faulks," said Lucas.

"It's the least I could do. I knew your father well, and owe his memory the chance for you to make your pitch."

The two men shook hands, and Lucas introduced Sonia. "Miss Sonia Matheson, our CTO."

"Delighted, Miss Matheson," the businessman responded, extending his hand to Sonia also. "Do have a seat."

As they all sat down in leather armchairs at a low table, Lucas began, "I'd just like to start by saying that the use of my father's name wasn't solely a ruse to get my foot in the door. I worried, strange as it may seem, that you wouldn't believe me if I told you who I actually represent."

"I find that hard to fathom," replied Faulks. "If you came to me from a reputable tech company, I can assure you that I would just as easily have agreed to a meeting."

"But if I'd called and told you that I am with one of the most well-known companies in the world today, would you honestly have taken me seriously? Why would Ad Astra be knocking on the door of a, let's face it, small-town second tier ISP?"

"Ad Astra? Do you mean 'bigger than Microsoft' Ad Astra?"

80

The CEO of U-Net looked both puzzled and slightly angry. As Lucas had suspected, the man obviously thought his leg was being pulled. Lucas laughed as he said, "We're not actually bigger than them. Not yet, anyway. But you see my point?"

Faulks stood up from his armchair and walked over to stand behind his desk. He leaned forward and placed his palms in the desktop. "So let me get this straight. A young man, not even out of his twenties, who lives on a farm in the back blocks of Taihape, is in my office, representing the most talked about tech company on the planet, with a product demonstration?"

"I see you do get my point, Mr Faulks. That is exactly what I'm saying. Perhaps you'd like to call our head office and speak to my good friend, Andie Donovan?"

"I have no intention of calling your bluff, Mr Winter. If you're willing for me to take it that far, I have no option but to believe you. You're right – it is absolutely unbelievable, and if you had opened with that over the phone, I might well have hung up on you. Now that we're on the same page, and I am taking your bona fides as read, what do you have to show me?"

Lucas stood, and, picking up his large case, walked over to stand in front of the desk. He opened the case and removed two devices from within the protective foam. Each device was identical in appearance; matt black metal boxes the size of a loaf of bread, with a power socket, a simple on/off switch, an LED light, and an ethernet port for a network cable.

"Ad Astra wants to revolutionise communications, Mr Faulks. This ground-breaking technology will do away with cables, transmission towers, and any other form of internet delivery. We came to you initially, because we like to support local business, and because you already have an interest in providing internet access to those who are forgotten by mainstream infrastructure."

He paused, trying to read the other man's face, and wondering whether he had made a mistake by offering to make U-Net's current business model obsolete.

"These devices are point-to-point links that require no wires, no line of sight, and no external infrastructure. Perhaps we can demonstrate for you?"

"I'd think that you were suggesting some form of magic, if it wasn't Ad Astra making this pitch. However, I know all about your OS, and nobody thought that such power and flexibility could be packed into such a small program. I'm willing to entertain the possibility that this is just as novel an idea."

"There's a saying, Mr Faulks – One man's magic is another man's science. Anything beyond current norms will seem incredible at first. Do you have a laptop handy?"

Faulks picked up the phone and pressed a button. "John, could you bring a laptop into my office, please?"

Lucas held up two fingers.

"Two laptops please, John," Faulks amended.

"Sorry about that," said Lucas. "I thought it might be best to use your own machines, to prevent any suggestion of trickery."

"That's fair. They'll be here in a moment."

While they waited, Lucas took two ethernet cables, and power cords from the case, "There is one more request I'd like to make." He glanced at Sonia, who reached into her briefcase and extracted a single-page document.

She placed the page on the desk in front of Faulks, saying, "This is a basic non-disclosure agreement, sir. As you will appreciate, at present, this is new technology and, as such, any information pertaining to it is commercially sensitive. We simply ask that you do not discuss this with anyone outside of your organisation. We will also, of course, require signatures from anyone that you do need to bring into your confidence."

"Standard business practise," replied Faulks. "I have no issue with that." He leaned down and signed the NDA after quickly reading through it.

A young man entered, carrying two laptops. He placed them at the edge of the desk, and left the room, after a nod of thanks from Faulks.

Powering up both laptops, the three waited for them to initialise. When both machines were running, Lucas asked to use the wall socket and plugged in his devices. He flicked the power switches, and the power indicator lights on each device flickered on.

"Do you have any particularly large files handy on either of these?" he asked, pointing to the laptops.

82

Faulks turned one towards him, moving a finger quickly over the trackpad. "This one has a detailed map of our wireless coverage. It's about 500 megabytes. Will that do?"

"Perfect. Now, I assume that you have gigabit ethernet cards in these," he said, referencing the maximum data transfer speed.

Faulks nodded.

"So the 500 megabytes would transfer over a direct cable connection in around five seconds."

Faulks nodded again. "That's right."

"And if it were going over your consumer wireless connection?"

"Well, our best product is a 25 megabit per second service, so that would be—" he paused for a moment, doing the maths in his head, "—a bit over three minutes. Give or take twenty to fifty milliseconds, to allow for the inherent latency in any distributed system."

"What I'd like you to do now, is to transfer that file over the wireless connection, making note of the transfer time, and especially the latency."

Faulks did so, and after a few minutes, indicated that the transfer was complete.

"As I said, 206 seconds, with a latency of 19 milliseconds, as it only had to traverse one transmitter."

Lucas asked him to delete the file from the target laptop, and connected each computer to one of his devices via an ethernet cable.

"Can you please ensure that all wi-fi or bluetooth connections on these laptops are disabled?"

After Faulks had done this, Lucas said, "Now, you should be able to see the second laptop on the first, as if it were directly connected. Please transfer the file as if that were so."

Faulks found the second laptop on the local network, and dragged the file to it. He stared at the monitor, obviously confused. "That's not possible. It took only a fraction over five seconds. Even if you had a wi-fi connection in these boxes, the best possible speed would be 1300 megabits, but that's never achievable. You'd be lucky to get 200 from an 802.11ac network. Allowing for the ethernet transfer time of five seconds, I'd expect the minimum time to be at least 30 seconds. How did you manage this?"

"That's our proprietary technology at work. Of course, you may think that we have simply invented a better wi-fi, so I'd now ask if you could have someone take the target laptop and its attached device to a remote location – the further the better – and we'll run the test again."

Faulks picked up the phone again. "John, could you run an errand for me, please? Come on in."

When John arrived, Lucas explained what he needed to do. He also got him to sign the NDA.

As the young man left the office, Faulks said that it would take a while for him to get to his house on the far side of town, and that maybe they would like a cup of coffee while they waited. Lucas and Sonia agreed – tea for Lucas – and another employee was despatched to bring their drinks.

The trio sat back down in the comfortable armchairs, and as they waited for the coffee, Faulks asked, "So, if we were to take on this new technology, how would it work for U-Net?"

Sonia was ready for this question, and explained. "These prototypes are somewhat bulky, but the consumer version will be about the size of a VCR cassette. The unit at your end would be smaller – more the size of a cigarette packet – and will plug into a rack connected to your servers and incoming internet. Communication between the paired devices is totally secure, as they can only ever talk to each other."

"Nothing is totally secure," interrupted Faulks. "Encryption can be broken, and lines of communication can be hacked."

"Encryption isn't an issue here, sir. Now we're getting to the meat of the matter. Have you heard of quantum entanglement?"

Faulks indicated that he hadn't.

"Simply put, it's the theory that two paired quantum particles will reflect each other's state immediately, even over large distances. Well, it was theory, until scientists at Ad Astra came up with a design that not only proved the concept, but enabled us to use it in a meaningful way. Frankly, John could take that device halfway across the universe, and it would have no impact whatsoever on the time it took to communicate with this one in your office."

Faulks looked stunned. "If this test across town shows no noticeable lag, I may have to accept your premise. In the meantime, however, I'm still wondering where the hidden cameras are. The idea is so fantastic, I'm sure that even a top scientist would be thinking it's a wind-up."

"You'll get your proof, Mr Faulks," said Lucas as a young woman entered with a tray of hot drinks. She put the tray on the table at her CEO's direction, and left the office.

As they took up their cups, Lucas and Sonia watched Faulks obviously struggling to come to terms with what he had been told. They knew the feeling all too well.

Before long, the office telephone rang. Getting up to answer it, Faulks spoke briefly before covering the mouthpiece and asking Lucas, "Is there anything else you need him to do?"

"No – power to our device, connected by cable. As simple as that."

Faulks passed on the instruction, and hung up the phone. "He says it's all go at that end. So, I'll run the test again."

He repeated the process to transfer the file, and stared at the monitor, shaking his head.

"It's the exact same time. Unbelievable."

"If you had any further doubts, we could always put it inside a Faraday cage, to completely rule out extraneous signals," said Sonia.

"I don't know that that will be necessary at this point. Is the demonstration over, then?"

On confirmation from Lucas, Faulks phoned John and instructed him to return to the office.

"We would like a few sets of these to run some rigorous testing, if you don't mind."

Lucas nodded. "We're going to start rolling out the consumer models within a couple of weeks, and we'll send some units over to you. Do you have an idea of how you expect to integrate the technology into your setup?"

"Well, it is too soon to say with any certainty, but personally, I'd like to start by using them to reach prospective customers who don't yet have a tower servicing their area. Would we be buying the units outright, or are you looking at a lease model?"

Lucas smiled. It sounded like Faulks was going to be on board with the tech. "I'll have Andie set up a call with you. She's the best person to negotiate the details. Give her an idea of the volume you could be looking at and we'll have the rack ready to go when you get the test units. There is one more thing – this could be very big for us both. We could be looking at potential bottlenecks on the in-country internet infrastructure. We can also supply you with a high bandwidth link that you can use to bypass the country's internet backbone. Or the Pacific cable itself, if you wish. The units are scalable, and if you want ten terabits direct from California, it's yours."

"Mr Winter, Miss Matheson, this would appear to be an absolute game changer. Using this, we would no longer be limited by geography, or even distance. Cutting the undersea cable operators out of the equation will also mean lower prices across the board. I assume that this won't stay in the family, so to speak, for long. We'll need exclusive rights to gain the upper hand, commercially, of course."

"I understand. That's another thing you can discuss with Andie. I would think, however, that you can count on 18 months to two years. That will give you something to sweeten your board when you take it to them. Good luck – I hope they're as easy to convince as you have been!"

Faulks narrowed his eyes slightly. "I'm a cautious man, Mr Winter. I'm not prepared to commit, or even admit that I'm fully convinced, until we've done the testing. I am, however, also an optimistic man. I would like to believe that this technology is truly everything that you've demonstrated today. If my belief is supported, I see wonderful things ahead in the field of communications, and I would be honoured to be in on the ground floor. Thank you for choosing to work with U-Net."

"It was our pleasure, Mr Faulks. Thank you for giving us the opportunity to do so."

The CEO offered them another coffee while they waited for John to return with their device. Accepting, the next fifteen minutes was spent with Faulks and Lucas reminiscing about Mr Winter, Senior.

When John returned, Lucas packed the devices away, and they said their goodbyes. As they were walking back down the hallway, Faulks called after them, "What's the name of this thing, anyway?"

Lucas turned around. "It's a quantum entanglement device – we call it the Q.E.D."

REVELATION

Happy with the outcome of their meeting at U-Net, Lucas and Sonia treated themselves to a café lunch before making the trip home. Over the meal, they discussed how accepting Faulks had been of the QED.

"I think it's amazing how flexible the human mind is," said Sonia. "Faced with something that seems an absolute impossibility, our brains seem to rationalise it to the point where it just has to admit that some things, while beyond comprehension, just *are*. I've had the same experience watching a good stage magician. I have no idea how he's doing it, but I realise that there must be a logical explanation. It must have been a bit like that for you when your PC started talking to you. I know it was for me!"

"To be fair, I did try to eliminate any ways it could be a trick first. In the end, of course, I had to trust my own senses, and since then, Andie has proved herself in so many ways. At least you had *my* belief as a sort of stepping-stone to acceptance."

"It still wasn't easy, you know. As a scientist myself, I'm used to proving things only through thorough testing, and it went against my nature to accept something so unlikely that quickly. I'm not the type to believe six impossible things before breakfast. I draw the line at two, and even that's only since I went to the farm that day!"

Finishing their lunch, they drove back to Mangaweka, deciding that they had worked hard enough that day to have earned an afternoon off. Sitting down with a chilled beverage seemed the perfect way to celebrate a successful mission.

When they went inside the house, Andie immediately bombarded them with questions about their meeting. Giving her only the briefest summary, they begged off intense discussion. Before they left the room, however, Andie had one more question for Lucas.

"Have you thought any more about the corruption issue?"

Lucas sighed, closing his eyes and rubbing his brow. "Not yet, Andie. Just give me a little more time."

Thanks to her studies of human nature, she recognised the signs of his inner turmoil, and wisely let him be.

As Lucas and Sonia sat outside in the shade with their drinks, Sonia herself brought up the subject.

"What did she mean about corruption? Please don't tell me she's got a software problem, and she'll turn on humanity!"

"Not that sort of corruption, fortunately," Lucas responded. He went on to tell her about his conversation with Rob the other day, and how Andie had suggested forcing transparency on corrupt officials. He also explained how he was uncomfortable with the idea, likening it to sinking to their level.

"But that's ridiculous, Lucas!" Sonia cried, throwing up her hands in frustration. "If you have the tools to hold these people to account, then you have to do it. It may be unethical in and of itself, but it's *relative* ethicality – is that a word? Surely you've told a white lie to protect someone from a truth that would hurt them. And what about people who have to kill to save their families?"

"For Christ's sake, Sonia – do you think I haven't had all these arguments with myself? I know it's the lesser of two evils, but I've always tried to choose the *right* path, not the least wrong one. I've been trying to think of a better way, but I can't escape the logic of it, and it's tearing me up inside."

The conflict between his morals and his desires was bringing him near to tears now. Sonia shuffled closer to him and put her hand on his shoulder.

"Lucas, I could say all sorts of things to justify doing it Andie's way, but this is a choice you'll have to make on your own. You're a decent person, and no one is going to think any less of you, whatever you decide. However, this might not be the hardest decision you have to make before all this is over, and if you truly want to succeed, you need to find a way to make those choices for the greater good, but without forgetting who you are."

She leaned over to give him a quick hug. "I'm always here if you need a sounding board, but I'm not going to tell you what sort of person you have to be. Just remember, though, some of the greatest heroes have done terrible things, but they're remembered most for the good they did."

Lucas returned the hug, taking comfort in Sonia's compassion, but still with no better idea of the path he should take.

"I'm going to need some time to process this," he said, "but there is one other thing you could help me with. We need to give Andie a face. Have you given that any thought?"

Nodding, Sonia moved away and sprawled on the cool grass under the tree. "I have, as a matter of fact. The only clue we have to work from is her personality. She's strong, confident, and a little cheeky. I've begun to visualise her as medium height, say 5'10", athletic, with well-defined facial features. She has a desire to be an individual – not one of the crowd – so she wears her hair in a style that stands out. Short, but with a long fringe that drops down one side of her face. I understand that she's supposed to be sort of a recluse, which explains why nobody has met her in person. That suggests, maybe, agoraphobia, so she's unlikely to be tanned. I think she has red hair – mine is from a bottle, so not this bright! – and green eyes, which ties in with her Irish heritage. She has the potential for freckles, if she ever got any sunlight, but I can see them adding to her complexion rather than taking over entirely. She has a generous mouth, which smiles readily.

"She's a businesswoman, but not a power dresser. She wears fashionable clothes, with a hint of avant garde. Her backstory might suggest that she's anti-social, but in reality she's very personable, as we know. Not that anyone will ever meet her in person! Does that look fit her personality, do you think?"

Lucas closed his eyes for a second, mentally picturing the woman that Sonia had just described. He had to admit that it seemed to suit her perfectly.

"You're amazing, Sonia. You're really nailed it there. I think Andie will like it. Let's go tell her."

They went inside and Sonia repeated her impression of Andie's appearance.

There was a moment when nothing happened, and Lucas and Sonia looked at each other, wondering why Andie wasn't responding. Then, the computer desktop on the monitor cleared, and a full face image appeared, exactly as Sonia had described. Andie raised a hand to flick her fringe away from her eyes and smiled broadly.

"I love it!" she exclaimed excitedly. "You don't know how much it means to me, to finally have a face. It gives me a stronger sense of self."

Pleased that her careful contemplation had given such joy to the AI, she said, "I wish I could hug you right now. I don't suppose you've got any plans for a physical body lurking in that silicon brain of yours, though."

Andie laughed, her avatar mirroring the emotion. "I've been having enough trouble thinking like a human, let alone dealing with a whole body. No, I haven't even considered a corporeal form. There would be too much that is neither possible nor practical. I'd also worry that my mental capacity could be limited to a purely biological level, and you humans think far too slowly for me!" At this, her avatar gave a cheeky wink.

"So, all joking aside, we don't have to deal with artificial humans just yet. Good to know," said Lucas. "Back to reality, however – I told Malcolm Faulks that you would be in touch regarding the specifics of the contract. Maybe you would like to show off your new avatar by doing that in a video call? I'm happy to leave the details up to you – something that they'll find attractive, but doesn't leave us too exposed?"

"Of course," the AI replied happily. "It will be nice to get some fresh air, so to speak."

Lucas filled her in on what had been covered at the meeting, and praised her for her work designing the QED. In return, she congratulated him on his performance at U-Net.

"I do hate to interrupt this mutual appreciation society," broke in Sonia, "but do we have a plan for staffing the factory in Taihape?"

Lucas had actually jumped the gun by putting notices in the local newspaper, the supermarket, and the other place one might find the employment-challenged – the pub. The notices advertised a meeting in the Town Hall the following week, with the promise of *"Excellent pay and conditions, flexible hours"*, and jobs for anyone who wanted them. His plan was to have Andie, in her role as Ad Astra's Director, address the crowd, explaining the roles needed, and what the company expected from its employees. It would be good practice for the public speaking she was sure to encounter in future. He related all this to the two girls, with both agreeing that this was a suitable plan.

Andie's new look, making her seem more "real" than before, was making him feel guilty about keeping her in the dark regarding his overall plan, as well. He hoped that his reluctance to let her in on the secret hadn't fostered any mistrust in him, and he now decided to rectify that situation. He told her everything, including some aspects of the plan that he had missed out when telling Sonia.

When he had finished, Andie's avatar nodded in understanding.

"I see what you mean by 'saving the world'. To be honest, I was expecting you to get me to roll back all the damage already caused."

"That was a thought, but I expect that would take more time than any of us has. I think my idea, huge in scope as it is, is better. Every step of the plan will not only help people right now, but will be vital a piece of the larger picture."

"I understand where you're coming from," said Andie. "While I could certainly design bacteria to reduce atmospheric CO_2, and systems to cool the oceans, it could take generations to have a noticeable effect. Your idea will mitigate ongoing damage, while paving the way to the larger goal. I *would* like to work on projects to reverse climate change, however. I think it would give humanity tremendous hope, even if none of them may live to see the results. I can do that in my 'spare time'!"

Lucas saw the benefit in attacking the problem from a second angle, and totally agreed with Andie's logic regarding hope. Hope was a great motivator, he knew from experience, and the idea that positive action could be taken may convince people to be part of the solution, rather than part of the problem.

"Sure. I can't see a problem with that. I'd suggest putting forward anonymous articles to scientific journals, perhaps. Ad Astra is going to have a high enough profile as it is, and I wouldn't want frustration at the slow pace of the roll-back to result in adverse publicity for the company. You could certainly make submissions to help the science get started, as long as it doesn't affect our main projects."

"Thank you, Lucas. I have some ideas already, and will casually drop them into the public domain."

Sonia and Lucas walked back outside to retake their places under the tree. Lucas had a faraway look in his eyes and Sonia guessed that he was still thinking of his moral dilemma. She quietly got up and went inside. Lucas was so absorbed with his own concerns that he never noticed her leave, nor that she had spent some time inside before returning with two glasses of cold juice. She sat down beside Lucas, handing him one. He took it absently, but continued to stare into the distance. Sonia watched him brooding for a minute before saying, "Come on, mate. Knock that back and we'll go for a drive."

"Where to?" he asked, puzzled.

"We should have a look at the building site, and then there's someone I'd like to see. Your Mrs Walker will be at home, won't she?"

"You want to see Adele? Why?"

"You talk about the 'regular people' that gave you your first ideas, and I'd like to meet one of them, is all. Maybe I'll get some inspiration myself," she remarked cryptically.

Lucas shrugged, and drank his juice. They climbed into the Toyota and drove off.

On arrival at the factory outside town, Sonia was impressed with the construction. Bar some minor finishing, the structure was complete, and there were already trucks arriving with the production line machinery. The project manager saw them coming and hurried over to greet them.

"Lucas – I wasn't expecting you today. No problems, I hope?"

"No, no. Nothing's wrong. Jake, I'd like you to meet Sonia Matheson, lead engineer on the fabrication project. She'll be the one in charge of this building once it's up and running, and it's about time she saw what a great job you've done getting it ready so quickly."

"Miss Matheson, pleased to meet you," said Jake, sticking out his hand.

"Likewise. I've heard good things about you," she said, giving the proffered hand a firm shake.

"Oh well, you get what you pay for, I always say, and Lucas here pays *very* well!" he said, joking only a little.

Sonia smiled at his lack of humility, and considered that his pride was well deserved.

"So if I have any problems with the building, you're the person I come to see?" she asked, giving him a wink.

"I had explicit instructions – better than many jobs I've been on, I can tell you – and my crew know their jobs. I'm certain there won't be any problems."

Sonia felt bad about teasing him and smiled supportively. "I'm sure there won't. Lucas doesn't go wrong when he puts his faith in people."

They walked around the site for the next half hour, Jake pointing out the various areas. After she had seen enough, she said, "Thank you for the tour, but we'd best be getting on now. I don't want to take up any more of your valuable time. I look forward to moving in."

A round of handshakes signalled a goodbye, and Sonia complimented Lucas on his choice of project manager as they walked back to the ute.

Lucas took her over the new road as they left the site, explaining how it would make the workers safer as they travelled to and from their jobs. They joined the main road again at the south end of town, and headed back towards Mangaweka.

Shortly, they pulled up at Adele's house, where they found her seated in an old chair in the shade of the front porch, sipping old-fashioned lemonade made with fruit from her own trees.

"Lucas, my dear boy! How nice of you to visit. And you've brought a lady friend! Let me get you a glass."

Sonia chuckled inwardly at the quaint term. The old girl probably thought Sonia was the love interest.

Adele disappeared inside and Sonia looked at Lucas with amusement. "I'm your 'lady friend' now," she said, winking.

Lucas groaned. "She's been on at me forever about finding a nice girl to keep me company in my 'big old lonely house'. Maybe I should just let her keep thinking you're my girlfriend so she'll get off my back about it!"

Adele came back outside with two glasses, which she filled from the jug on the table.

"Adele, meet Sonia. She's working with me at the farm, and no, she's not a girlfriend. Sonia, my friend Adele Walker."

"Very pleased to meet you, dear. Do sit down, both of you. To what do I owe the pleasure of your visit?"

"Sonia wanted to meet my muse, after I told her that you inspired a couple of ideas I recently had."

"I did? I'm sure I never meant to! Most of what you young people do is over my head."

"Speaking of ideas, and things over your head, how's that computer going?"

"Oh, it's just wonderful. Honestly, the way my grandchildren talked, I expected the thing to be well beyond me! I just have to push one button, on the screen, no less, and I can talk or write a letter to anyone at all. Thank you so much for giving it to me."

"My pleasure, Adele."

"So, Adele," said Sonia, "have you lived here all your life?"

"Goodness me, no. I was born in France, dear. 1933, if my memory serves me. I was six years old when World War 2 broke out. My father, rest his soul, died early on in the war, and I remember two little girls and their family being taken away simply because they were Jewish. It was a terrible time."

"I'm sure it must have been. What did your mother do after your father died? It can't have been easy being on her own in an occupied country."

Adele glanced quickly around, as if looking for prying eyes or ears. She leaned forward conspiratorially, and said in a low voice, "She fought with the *résistance*, dear."

Her accent, which usually had just the hint of something foreign, had begun to take on a stronger French inflection as she remembered her childhood.

Lucas, who had, out of respect, not previously spoken with Adele about her wartime days, gaped at her. He would never have expected this sweet, mild-mannered, woman to be the daughter of a freedom fighter!

Adele continued, pleased to have an audience for her story. "When Papa was killed, she was approached by the resistance, and asked if she would help her country. She became engaged in sabotage, spying, rescuing Allied fighters, and occasionally dealing with *les collaborateurs*. She tried to shelter me from her activities, but it was hard to ignore the strange men in dark clothes at the back door in the middle of the night, or Maman coming home late with dirt, or sometimes blood, on her hands. I was no naïve child.

I think that would have been impossible in those days. I had seen firsthand the evil that the Nazis were capable of, and we always feared reprisals when we heard that the resistance had damaged them. We children never talked about it, but each son or daughter of a patriot knew in our hearts that our parents were fighting *les boches*.

"It wasn't easy for her, of course. The magnitude of her actions was a great weight on her. A strict Catholic, she at least had the comfort of her faith. Every week, she would go to the church and confess her sins. In return, she would receive absolution and solace."

She laughed. "Can't you just imagine it? 'Father, I have sinned. This week I blew up a bridge, tortured a collaborator, and murdered two German soldiers.'"

Lucas sat up a bit straighter as he heard of the young resistance fighter's burden. It brought to the surface thoughts of his own struggle. If only it were so easy, he imagined, to just tell a priest and receive God's forgiveness. He didn't think that being forgiven by a deity he didn't believe in would make him feel any better. He continued musing on the issue while Adele and Sonia spoke about the war, when it occurred to him. *This* is what Sonia had been talking about. He didn't need God's forgiveness – he needed his own. Though he didn't have faith in God, he at least had faith in himself. Thanks to Sonia, he no longer feared being corrupted by the power he held. He gave himself a mock absolution; "*Lucas, forgive yourself for what you must do. Peace be upon you,*" and resolved to have Andie begin surveillance on the relevant people immediately.

His musings were interrupted by Sonia. "Earth to Lucas! Did you hear a word that Adele said?"

"I heard enough," he said, smiling. "Adele, it was so nice to hear of your mother, and the part she played in doing what was right. Very enlightening."

Sonia caught the hidden meaning in his voice, and was relieved that he finally seemed at ease with the decisions he needed to make.

The old lady noticed the unspoken byplay between them, but said nothing, sure it must be something personal. Such a nice young lady – a good match for Lucas, she thought, oblivious to his earlier denial.

Adele continued, telling of how her mother had married a New Zealand soldier that she met in the escape network. After the war, he had taken his new bride and stepdaughter home to New Zealand. Adele herself eventually met her late husband Henry, and had lived ever since in this house out behind the village.

"I did think of moving to town, or some retirement village, after Henry died, but couldn't bring myself to leave the place where I had made so many wonderful memories. I'll tell you, I haven't thought about those dark days in a long time, and doing so now makes me all the more appreciative of where I ended up."

"I couldn't agree with you more, Adele," said Sonia. "I don't for a moment regret coming to this place. I feel as if I could stay forever as well."

They spent the rest of the afternoon drinking lemonade and taking about things less intense than the war stories of a terrified little girl, and as the sun was setting, Adele invited them to dinner. Looking forward to the old lady's cooking, and not particularly wanting to go home and cook something himself, Lucas gratefully accepted on behalf of both of them.

They enjoyed a delicious beef stroganoff, and after dinner, Adele brought out a cribbage board. She played with cunning and skill born of long experience, trouncing them both soundly.

When they arrived home at the end of their long day, Lucas put the kettle on, and Sonia stole into the office to speak with Andie.

"Thanks for the info on Adele's mother. She told us the story, and Lucas really took it to heart. I think he's over the hump."

Andie wiped her brow in mock relief. "I thought it might stir something in him. I'm guessing that he doesn't need to know about our subterfuge?"

"No. I think we'll let him believe it was fate. It's been kind enough to him so far!"

"What am I missing?" asked Lucas as he entered the room.

"Just girl talk," replied Andie, giggling.

OPPORTUNITY

A few days later, Andie announced that she had made her call to Faulks, and had secured a contract to supply QEDs to U-Net. They would purchase them at a modest price, and absorb the costs through savings made in transmission hardware. As Faulks had suggested, the initial roll-out would be to previously inaccessible clients, but they hoped to replace their entire network with the Ad Astra technology. The Taihape facility needed to supply the first 650 units in three weeks, with a further 2000 per week after that. U-Net had waived any exclusive period beyond six weeks in return for continued competitive pricing and manufacturing priority. Happily for Ad Astra, this meant that they could begin sales to other providers in a couple of months.

Andie advised Lucas that they would need additional manufacturing facilities. He had planned for this, and had already targeted other districts with high unemployment. He had estate agents buying land, and his construction manager was sourcing work crews. Jake Lyall had become a full-time employee of Ad Astra, and would be tasked with oversight of all the coming construction, with other project managers reporting directly to him. This would take an enormous load off Lucas, leaving him time to pursue his true calling of handyman.

All this activity had been noticed by the press, and numerous rumours were beginning to circulate about the nature of Ad Astra's newest project. Some suggested that the company was moving into computer hardware, with the aim of forcing the big players out of the game entirely. Others ascribed less radical, but no more accurate reasons. Still others proposed a variety of conspiracy theories, from data servers that were mining every TheOS user's data, to concentration camps where people brainwashed by the new software would be interned. None came close to the truth – how could they? The QED was an unthought-of factor, and even the most generous conspiracy theory did not consider any altruistic aim.

All the negative allegations and suppositions, however, were starting to be felt. Movements were popping up, calling for transparency or investigation. Several people staged a short-lived picket at the Taihape factory site. The major IT corporations were getting nervous.

While nobody had moved on them personally, Lucas and Sonia thought that it was only a matter of time before someone connected them to Ad Astra. They decided that a press conference was in order, to clear the air.

Andie sent messages to many major press outlets, informing them that she would be streaming a live statement the following day at 9am. She would take limited questions from the press pack, and would manage to throw in a plug for their recruitment drive, and U-Net.

The next morning, the video stream was routed through virtual private networks and bounced off a remote location with the prototype QED, giving their actual location perfect anonymity. Andie was shot from the waist up, in the workshop at Lucas's farm. She wore subdued make-up, and a high-necked jacket over an ivory white blouse with a button-down collar. She stood nervously, her eyes downcast, only occasionally glancing directly into the camera. She gently chewed her lower lip before taking a deep breath and looking up at her guests.

"Ladies and gentlemen. Thank you all for coming. I'd like to start by telling you a little about myself. I am the daughter of Irish immigrants, and I am 35 years old. From childhood, I have suffered from severe social anxiety—" she glanced away briefly "—which resulted in my being home-schooled. Apart from a few doctors and therapists, I have encountered very few people face-to-face."

Here, she lowered her head, closed her eyes for a second, and took another slow breath.

She raised her head to the camera and continued, "It is not easy for me to be here, in front of you, but I felt that you deserved to hear from me personally, rather than some PR person. I am just grateful that I only have names in front of me, and not a sea of faces.

"I am the driving force behind Ad Astra. I was considered an intellectual prodigy as a child, and quickly discovered an aptitude for the sciences. I am a gifted mathematician, an accomplished computer programmer, and an inventor of electrical devices. It is one of these devices that is the cause of all the media excitement around my company.

"In conjunction with local ISP, U-Net, we are introducing to the world a new way to connect. Without going into too many technological, and frankly, secret, details, we can provide high-speed internet with no need for traditional methods of transmission. No cables, no fibre, no wireless, no 5G, no satellites. The throughput of our device, with the catchy name of 'QED', eclipses any of those, and does so with complete security. You could take a QED to the top of Everest, and connect to another on the other side of the world in Santiago, Chile. You would be able to stream hi-definition video with zero buffering, zero lag, and zero hassle.

"The land we have purchased across the country is destined to become home to manufacturing facilities. We have deliberately chosen locations that desperately need employment, and hope that we will lift the standard of living for small-town New Zealand. We take our social responsibilities seriously, and each factory will generate its own power. Our components are sourced ethically, and we have a zero-waste policy."

Andie paused to catch her breath. She seemed to be coping well with the public speaking, considering that today she was allegedly facing more people than she had met in her life to date. She smiled nervously at her audience.

"I hope that gives you an insight into who I am, and what Ad Astra intends. Are there any questions?"

Every single name in front of Andie lit up.

"Yes, Lindsay, Associated Press."

"Miss Donovan – it is 'Miss'?"

"It is," replied Andie. "Was that your question?" she asked, with a shy grin.

Momentarily flustered, the AP journalist took a couple of beats to reply. "Uh, no. You had me there. My question is, do you consider your company a threat to the likes of Microsoft or Apple?"

"We don't want to be a threat to anyone. It is certainly unfortunate for them that TheOS is rapidly acquiring market share, but you'll have to admit, ours *is* better than theirs! Our aim is to meet the demands of consumers in a way that is both effective and efficient. We do not have shareholders to please, so our number one priority is not the bottom line. We truly do want to make the world a better place. Moving on to the next question – Duncan, Time."

"Good morning, Miss Donovan. Thank you. You have been alternating between referring to yourself, and to the company. Where does Andie Donovan end, and Ad Astra begin? Are you running this entire enterprise on your own, or do you have a team of elves stashed away at the North Pole?"

Andie lost her nervous demeanour long enough to let out a giggle. "I come up with the ideas, and I have a few trusted 'elves' that I employ to get their hands dirty in the real world. With my condition, I live almost in a virtual reality, only communicating remotely."

Watching the press conference on the internet-connected television in the lounge at Lucas's home, he and Sonia shared an amused look at this statement.

"Someone needs to get out there and shake hands and keep the physical aspects of the business going. I've not actually been great at giving orders so far, but my team has initiative and drive, so I feel comfortable giving the barest suggestion of what I need. They've been doing a fantastic job. Maria, Forbes."

"Miss Donovan, your QED device is obviously brand-new technology. Are you able to give us any more insight into its transmission method?"

"The concept behind the QED is one that has long been purely theoretical, and practical application of it was thought to contravene the laws of physics. A new approach to the problem allowed me to circumvent this restriction. A few of the technical writers here may be familiar with the term 'quantum entanglement', whereby paired subatomic particles have a mysterious affinity for each other. When one changes state, the other will instantaneously do likewise, regardless of the separation between the two. Einstein referred to this property as 'spooky action at a distance'. While it may not be widely understood, it is a function of our reality, and now allows instant, secure communication between any two points.

"The name of the device is a play on words, being an acronym for both 'Quantum Entanglement Device' and 'Quod Erat Demonstrandum' – 'that which was to have been demonstrated'.

The next question came from Fox News.

"So, as I understand it, two devices are paired intimately and exclusively, meaning that there is no way that communication between the two can be intercepted. What are the implications for national security?"

"While the individual links are secure, each home unit is linked only to its partner at the ISP. Data passing through the ISP is as transparent as ever, and the regular internet infrastructure can still be spied on by your NSA at will. While I am not personally in favour of mass information collection, per se, Ad Astra will ensure that all of its future partners in this technology comply with the relevant regulations regarding information sharing. Next, please ... Jacqui, Dominion Post. Good to have a local representative here. What is your question?"

"Good to be here, Miss Donovan. You obviously see your company as playing a major role in the future economy of New Zealand, so do you expect any financial incentives, tax breaks, or regulatory leniency in return from our government?"

"I'm glad you brought that up, Jacqui. As I said previously, the balance sheet is not our *raison d'être*, so we will not be asking for any favourable treatment from the government in financial terms. We will pay the appropriate tax on every cent of our profit, and adhere strictly to any relevant legislation. We are pleased to have the opportunity to grow the economy and to improve life for the many people we will be employing, and we will continue to do so, even should the conditions under which we operate become unwelcoming.

"We are proudly Kiwi, part of a nation that has a long history of innovation, and we look forward to providing the world with better ways to live, with products made under the flag of the Southern Cross, and the emblem of the Silver Fern."

Many of the following questions were variations on a theme, with Andie already having covered the technical aspects, her personal life, and the concerns of the economists and spies. After a time, she allowed her avatar to appear tired, and closed the press conference with thanks to all who had attended, and instructions to contact her office for further comment. She was sure that she could spare the processing time to write answers to any questions not asked this morning.

Andie waved goodbye to her audience, and her image was replaced by the Ad Astra logo of two five-pointed stars in red and bordered by white, on a black background.

Andie's avatar returned solely to Lucas and Sonia. She now wore a loose t-shirt, and the make-up was gone. "It's a relief to ditch the business attire," she joked, looking far more confident than she had in front of the journalists. "Did you like my 'insecure little girl' act?"

"I think they bought it, hook, line, and sinker," said Sonia. "You're a very good actress."

Andie laughed. "I had hundreds of Oscar-winning stars to learn from! It was quite fun, actually, playing the part of the socially awkward genius. I much prefer being who I am now, though."

The newspapers that week were naturally filled with articles about Ad Astra, and Andie. Most were flattering, but some made cruel jokes about her affliction, and others continued their conspiracy narratives. The AI was disappointed about the last two, but knew that many people sought to bring down that which they envied, or didn't understand.

The next order of business was to organise the workforce for the first of the factories. The public meeting was scheduled for Wednesday evening, and they took time after the press conference to work on Andie's presentation.

On the day of the meeting, Lucas and Sonia arranged chairs in front of the stage in the Town Hall, and a caterer prepared nibbles for after Andie's talk. A large video display had been brought in for Andie to appear on, and Sonia connected it to the QED to ensure a good data link.

At 7pm, people started to trickle in, and the Hall was full by 7.30. Lucas estimated that there were over 200 people present, ranging from recent school leavers to people in late middle-age.

As the house lights dimmed, the screen on stage showed the caption, "Andie Donovan, Managing Director, Ad Astra" under the company's logo, before cross-fading to an image of the setting sun casting its yellowed light over a stand of majestic oak trees, their leaves just starting to turn gold in the early autumn. The camera panned to rest on Andie sitting on a fallen tree, watching the sunset.

She had dressed casually today, in bootleg jeans and a loose, long-sleeved shirt that was haphazardly tucked in. On her feet she wore scuffed John Bull work boots. As she 'noticed' the camera, she stood, smiling broadly.

"Good evening, everyone. My name is Andie. It's wonderful to see so many of you here tonight. As you will have seen, I am the Managing Director of Ad Astra, the new kid on the block in the technology field. I'm very sorry that I can't be with you in person – I don't do well in crowds. I'm afraid that I'm a bit of a recluse, hence the video broadcast. Please bear with me. Ad Astra may be a young company, but we are already making a real difference in the lives of people around the world. Our new computer operating system, TheOS, has been taking the world by storm due to its ease of use, and perhaps more importantly, its low cost. Many of you possibly use it yourselves.

"Last week, I held a press conference with journalists from around the globe to let them in on some exciting news. In partnership with Palmerston North's U-Net internet provider, we are paving the way for more accessible, more affordable internet. Our device, the QED, is going to revolutionise communication, and I am here tonight to offer you the chance to be a part of that."

At this point, she turned to look at the idyllic setting behind her. The camera followed her gaze, even as she continued turning to eventually cast her eye over a squalid scene of tract housing, smoke-belching industry, and ragged children with little hope in their eyes.

"This world is broken. The beauty that we all take for granted is disappearing. People are being forced to live in appalling conditions, children are going hungry. This is not a natural turn of events. This is a scenario orchestrated with one goal in mind. To make the wealthy, wealthier. Your power bills are going up. You can barely afford to run your car. You might be working two jobs and still finding it hard to make ends meet. Perhaps you are waiting for the promised 'trickle down', where the high cost you pay for everything eventually flows from the people at the top, and makes a better life for those below. Still waiting? In the normal scheme of things, you would grow old and die waiting. We want to change this. Now there is a company that puts the people first – not the shareholders. There is Ad Astra.

"You are likely aware of the construction that has been going on at the old college grounds. This is the site of Ad Astra's very first production facility for the QED. These devices don't make themselves, however, and we hope to get as many of you as possible on board as part of our manufacturing and distribution team as possible. We need you. We need people with excellent fine motor skills to put together circuit boards. We need people on the production line to assemble the units. We need people with an eye for detail, to conduct quality-control testing. We need people with strong backs, to work in the warehouse. We need forklift operators and truck drivers. We need line supervisors, with good people skills, to maintain production targets. All training for your role will be provided, and even if you think you are unskilled, we need you. We need cleaners, office staff, kitchen staff, childcare staff. We need all of you.

"The work will be paid at nothing less than a living wage, which is currently valued at $21.25 an hour." She paused, frowning. "That's not a easy figure to remember – let's round it up. The minimum wage at Ad Astra Taihape will be $25 an hour. No discrimination will be shown, whether to age, gender, or anything else you might think could disqualify you from a position.

"The factory will run seven days a week, from 4am until 1am, and work will be on a shift basis. Each shift will be three hours long, and you are welcome to work as many or as few shifts as is convenient for you. Parents of schoolchildren may want to work the 10am to 1pm shift only, or continue until 4pm, with their children being picked up from school by the company shuttle bus, to wait in our free childcare facility until Mum and/or Dad are finished. Some of you may be night owls, and find that the hours of 7pm to 1am suit you. All we ask is that we know your desired shifts a week in advance so that we can roster effectively, and keep the lines working."

A low murmur ran through the gathered crowd, as people admitted to their neighbour that family commitments and other obstacles were currently preventing them from working regular hours.

"Every worker will be eligible for dental care on the company plan—" someone in the crowd gave a first pump and a loud cheer "—and discounts on future Ad Astra products. A free shuttle will run between between town and the factory between each shift, and if you require transport from further afield, that can also be arranged.

"We understand that a happy and healthy workforce is an effective workforce, so no expense is being spared to make the job work for you as much as you work for the job. All we ask in exchange is loyalty, dedication, and your very best efforts. Help us change the world."

By now, there was a sense of real excitement in the audience. Good money, dental care, childminding and flexible hours? Few of the currently available job vacancies offered any of that. The chance to learn new skills, and be a part of something bigger than themselves was an attractive proposal. This company obviously cared about people, and who could turn up their nose at an offer like this?

"Thank you all for taking the time to listen to me. I sincerely hope that we can help each other. At the back of the Hall, you will find information packs, including an overview of the company, details of the benefits offered, job descriptions, and application forms. Please take one. We will be granting a $500 signing bonus to the first 100 successful applicants, so get in quick! We have laid on a supper as well, so do take the time to grab a bite to eat and a cup of tea or coffee. Over the next few days, think it all over, and if you do decide that you want to join Ad Astra, simply drop your completed application into the box in the Council offices or put it in the prepaid envelope and send it off. One of my management team will be conducting interviews next week, and I hope that we see you all there. Goodnight, and good living."

A generous round of applause followed the end of Andie's speech, and the crowd left their chairs to snack, mingle, and discuss the opportunity amongst themselves.

"So, what do we think?" asked Sonia from her hiding place in the stage wings.

Lucas rubbed his chin thoughtfully. "I could tell that she had their interest when she started off with the 'broken world' bit, and when she began describing the wages and benefits, more than a few bored-looking souls perked up. It's definitely the best opportunity this town has seen in over a generation, and we'll know soon enough if it was sufficient."

INTERLUDE 2

Tomas Becker, the head of digital security at IVIA, and his team, had been monitoring news for almost four months now, hoping to find evidence of a quantum computer performing misdeeds. The problem was, many major hacks were not reported until the compromised data was used or otherwise released. Some were never reported. Though they knew that looking for digital fingerprints in the wake of a QC hack would be futile, they had hoped to at least triangulate the data flow and get a more exact location on the missing technology. Maybe even cross-reference the types of stolen data to get an indication of the QC's aims.

Unfortunately for them, they had uncovered no hacks that could point to a rogue device. There had been no activity that could not have been performed by human hackers, though they had tracked down several of those. The best of them now worked for IVIA.

Yesterday's press release by a company called Ad Astra, however, had raised red flags. The appearance of technology that had been thought merely theoretical, while not technically within the scope of their investigation, deserved a closer look, and Tomas immediately began probing the activities of the company. The fact that this previously unheard of tech firm had released an innovative and powerful operating system mere days after IVIA's failed experiment *could* just be coincidence, but with the pressure from Kaito, Tomas could not afford to take any chances.

His research into Ad Astra showed no specific location, other than New Zealand, but that did at least align with the direction that the IVIA data had gone. The Companies Register gave only one name, an Andie Donovan, and a Post Office box in some town called Taihape. Cross-referencing the search terms "Ad Astra" and "Taihape", Tomas discovered that the company had a production facility there, but no further information was available. Andie Donovan was said to be a reclusive genius, born of Irish immigrants, and the data he was able to uncover on that front confirmed the claim. He was, however, no closer to actually finding the woman, nor confirming that she had any connection to the missing technology.

Martine Dubois had her own problems, having been tasked with finding out exactly what had gone wrong with the experiment. She believed that she had isolated the cause, that being sunspot activity and unusual levels of high-energy neutrino activity, but had so far not been able to determine in exactly what way this had subverted the experiment, nor how to prevent it happening again. She walked into the conference room for another of their regular meetings, not looking forward to having to admit yet another week of failure. Antonia, and by extension, Kaito, were both at breaking point, and unwelcome news was likely to make bad things happen.

Kaito stood at the head of the table, his hair in disarray and his face clouded with anger and frustration.

"Sit down, everybody. If anybody has good news for me, then now would be the perfect time to bring it up. You each have ten fingers, and I *swear* that I will break one a week if you do not start getting results!"

Eager to get into Kaito's good books, Tomas stood and addressed the room.

"After so many weeks of searching, and not finding anything that indicates QC activity, we believe that we may have a breakthrough. While it does not exactly fit the pattern we have been looking for, that is, hacking and criminal activity, it is unusual enough that we followed up on it. Yesterday, a tech company in New Zealand unveiled a product that utilises quantum entanglement as a means of communication. This is a possibility that has long been theorised, but was eventually considered impossible in any practical sense. While it *may* have been developed independently, when you take into account the fact that this same company released a world-beating operating system just days after our QC was lost—"

"Stolen!" roared Kaito.

"Stolen," conceded Tomas, "The timing is too coincidental. We have so far been unable to tie the founder of this company, one Andie Donovan, to our research in any way. Miss Donovan is never seen in public, and we have no physical address, but we are continuing to monitor her company's actions."

"So what *do* you know about her?" demanded Kaito.

Tomas related what information he had been able to discover about the woman and her business.

"So we have a shy genius, and a company on the other side of the world, neither of which have any actual link to IVIA or our research. There is new technology, which could as easily have been developed the same way that we did, with time and hard work. I don't know if you're simply becoming desperate to find me a result, or you truly believe that the person who stole our quantum computer thought that the best way to utilise its immense talent was to create a better version of Windows, and a faster modem. I'm paying you to find the goddamn *criminal* that stole a decade's worth of investment from under our noses, and you want me to go and chase down the next Steve Jobs." He sneered at them, as if they were children trying to convince him that the Tooth Fairy was real.

Martine, meanwhile, had opened her laptop while had been talking, and nervously interrupted. "Sorry, Mr Mitsuhashi, but there might actually be something in this. You said, 'the other side of the world'. It appears that this Taihape place is almost directly opposite us, on a direct line through the earth. I'll have to crunch some numbers, but it is possible, however remotely, that our neutrino beam wasn't diverted off at an angle, but simply went further than expected. I can't say what the journey through the planet would have done to the particles, but if there was any sort of substance at the other end that could have accepted a change in quantum state, then maybe the experiment wasn't a failure after all."

"Right, some rock in New Zealand suddenly became a quantum computer, and then what? Somehow it convinced a passing crow to pick it up and drop it off at the nearest high-tech lab, where it began to carry out its directives? The *only* possible explanation is that someone did this to us on purpose, and the sooner you put these fairytales out of your minds and get back to finding the real thief, the better. Now, unless anyone else feels like wasting my time, I suggest that you all just FUCK OFF and bring me something credible!"

The various investigative teams dispersed, pleased to be out from under Kaito's baleful glare. Tomas nudged Martine, jerking his head towards his office. She followed him in and he looked cautiously up and down the hallway before shutting the door behind them.

"I don't know what his problem is, but I think he's making a mistake in dismissing our information so quickly."

"Rumour has it that he got a really hard time from Antonia when he suggested that this all might have been purely accidental. She's taken the failure of the experiment as a personal affront, and he's apparently too scared to bring it up again. *She* says it was theft, so *he* says it was theft. I'm not too scared of him, for all his talk. He's a soft little man, and wouldn't even have the strength to dislocate one of my fingers, let alone break it."

Tomas sat behind his desk, motioning Martine towards one of the other chairs. "So what do you actually think of the idea? Were you just trying to get him off our backs, or could there be something in it?"

Martine templed her fingers in contemplation. "It's actually much more likely than the idea that somebody introduced errors to hijack our beam. Remind me again why we're working for this asshole?"

"Like me, you probably wanted to be part of the biggest advance in quantum science since the original theories were postulated. I know Kaito is being a bit of a dick at the moment, but Antonia's riding him hard. If we can get back on track, things will settle down and we can get back to groundbreaking work."

"I'll keep looking into your suspicions on the side as long as I can get away with it, but I need you to do one thing for me."

Tomas's eyes narrowed. "What's that, Martine?"

She stood up and moved closer to him, lowering her voice. "Your original brief for the search concentrated on criminal use of the QC, right?"

Tomas nodded, wondering where this was going.

She continued, "Was that simply because of Antonia's fixation on this being a deliberate theft, or are she and Kaito projecting? Do you know what use they themselves intended to put the QC to? You've got unlimited access to all internal communications, and I thought you might be able to do a little research. I just think she's being unnaturally unreasonable, and wonder if there were plans that have been upset by the loss of the technology."

Tomas said nothing for a while, standing up and turning to stare out the window.

"Those are dangerous accusations, Martine, but having heard them, I guess I share your concerns. Antonia *is* acting a little irrationally, and you might be on to something. It's strange that none of us, as integral members of the team, were given any indication of the future plans. I can't promise anything, but I'll see what I can find."

"That's all I'm asking for, Tomas."

APPLICANTS

Lucas and Sonia were up particularly early, as it was Anzac Day, New Zealand and Australia's national day of remembrance for those who had served and fallen in military conflicts. The date and time of the service commemorated the first landings of the *Australia and New Zealand Army Corps* on the beaches of Gallipoli, for the ill-fated campaign of 1915, where Lucas's own great-grandfather had died trying to take the strategic hills from the Turks. In almost every town and village in the country there would be a dawn service, and he had a commitment to young Joshua Talbot to honour.

He dressed in his smartest clothes, and ensured that the Jaguar was spotless. The sun had still not risen when they arrived at Mangaweka, and he had trouble picking out the Talbots in the dark. For such a small village, there was a good turn out, with over 100 people forming up in ranks in the middle of the main street. Lucas pulled the Jaguar into position at the front of the crowd, as promised, and Joshua sat proudly beside him, wearing his great-grandfather's medals on his chest. With a representative of the local Returned and Services Association leading the way on foot, Lucas released the clutch gently and followed as slowly as he could, the engine idling.

When the procession reached the Memorial Arch in front of the village school, 100 metres down the road, he pulled over to park beside it, as the crowd gathered around in front.

The service began with a short prayer, and speeches from a local returned serviceman and a visiting Army major. A recitation of "*The Ode of Remembrance*" followed, taken from Laurence Binyon's poem, "*For the Fallen*".

> *They shall grow not old, as we that are left grow old;*
> *Age shall not weary them, nor the years condemn.*

At the going down of the sun, and in the morning
We will remember them,

with the gathered crowd solemnly repeating the final line. The moving service ended as the sun rose lazily through the morning mist, and a lone bugler played *The Last Post*.

Small though the village was, every person present had been touched by the spectre of war in some way, and the speeches that had been made did not glorify battle, but were a call for peace, that such sacrifice need not be made again.

Joshua stood staunchly to attention, and tears flowed freely down Leslie Talbot's face for the father she had barely known, as the last notes of the bugle faded away, and a minute's silence was observed.

Lucas formally shook young Joshua's hand, and then followed the crowd to the village hall for the traditional Anzac Day breakfast, before he and Sonia returned to his house. As he drove, he mused on the futility of war, and the reasons for it. While some of those reasons were beyond his power to affect, it would certainly be worth stopping people fighting over resources, if he could.

Mid-morning, he drove into town to do some shopping, and collected 18 applications from the box in the Council offices on his way home. When he got back to the house, he and Sonia laid the completed forms out on the kitchen table and started to sort them into categories. They ended up with five people interested in working in the warehouse, one forklift operator, one truck driver, two cooks, one crèche worker, two cleaners, two production line workers, and four who were happy to be assessed for a role at the time of the interview.

"It's a start," remarked Sonia. "Most people will think about it over the weekend, and we could start interviewing around Wednesday."

"Don't you be throwing that 'we' around, missy. As manager of the facility, I believe it's your task to sort out the employment. I think I'll be busy on that day, anyway."

"Oh? What do you have planned?"

Lucas grinned. "Washing my hair!"

"Oh, very clever. Do you really expect me to handle the HR role as well as Manager?" Sonia responded, pouting.

"Until you hire the staff, you've got nothing to manage. You'll be fine."

At that moment, the telephone rang. Lucas picked it up and spoke briefly before Sonia, who had been engrossed in the paperwork, looked up to see him frowning at the telephone on its receiver.

"Who was that?" she asked.

"It was Jake. The lasers were supposed to arrive this morning and when they didn't show up, he called the supplier and they said they only had the one, and wouldn't get another into the country in any less than a week."

Angrily, Sonia jumped up from the table. "But that's going to set us back too far to get U-Net's order out on time! We're going to fail our very first contract because some—"

"Language..." warned Lucas.

"—some *fool* couldn't tell if he had one or two in stock when we ordered it?" she finished, scowling at him.

"Pretty much, except that fool doesn't work for our supplier. He's two links down the chain. Apparently our guy orders it from another guy, who orders it from Korea. It's the idiot in Korea who can't count to two."

Sonia paced the kitchen muttering to herself and gesticulating with a closed fist.

"I could work the downtime, 1am to 4am, but that would only gain us the equivalent of a day. Even with fully-staffed production lines, we're still at just over half our potential output. Has Jake looked elsewhere?"

Shaking his head, Lucas said, "It looks like everyone is in the same boat. It's not the sort of apparatus that is in great demand, of course, and no one actually keeps any stock in the country."

"At least tell me that they are delivering the one that they do have."

"That'll be here on Monday, but unless we find a way to process the particles faster, we're not going to look good to Faulks."

"I'll speak to Andie, but if it was possible to do it faster, it would have been done like that in the first place. Maybe she can come up with another idea."

As Sonia wandered off to the office, Lucas grumpily grabbed a beer out of the fridge and stalked out the back door. At the base of the back step, Splash's ball caught his eye, and he kicked it with a force born of frustration and anger. It shot straight for the nearest tree, striking it and bouncing off down the front path. It slipped between the bars of the gate, rolled across the driveway and down the hill. Splash had bounded after it, and stood at the closed gate looking longingly out.

"Shit," said Lucas. "Sorry, mate. Didn't mean to lose your ball."

He went and opened the gate for the dog, who ran across the gravel and stopped at the top of the slope, barking. Lucas followed, saying, "I think it's gone, mate. It'll be halfway down the hill by now, or under the woolshed..." His voice trailed off.

"You're kidding," he muttered. "Brain the size of a planet, eh?"

He called Splash back into the garden and shut the gate. Walking back into the kitchen, he met Sonia on her way out.

"So, did Andie have any ideas?"

"She says there's no way to work any faster, and after trawling the web, she can confirm that there's not another one in the country. The soonest we could get one from offshore is next Monday. We're screwed."

Lucas smiled smugly. "You know, I'm not without a brain cell or two myself. I think I know where I can find one."

The look on Sonia's face could, at best, be described as dubious. Derisive, would be a better word.

"I believe that I just spoke to the most intelligent entity on the planet, who assures me, with her unparalleled access to the internet, that she could not find another within 5000 kilometres. Just how does goat-boy think he can do better? Maybe you just happen to have one lying around in one of your sheds?"

Then the penny dropped, and she instantly regretted her sarcasm. "Oh, bloody hell. We *do*, don't we. Why didn't Andie think of that?"

Lucas frowned. "I don't know. She's certainly as smart as we think she is. Maybe she just took the request too literally. '*Order us a laser.*' '*Find one online.*' She's going to have to brush up on her lateral thinking!"

They went inside to let Andie know that the problem was solved. When she asked who had come up with the solution, Lucas could not resist adding to his explanation.

"It looks like you were right, Andie. It seems Splash *is* the most intelligent one around here!"

Andie had the grace to allow her avatar to blush. "I am sorry, Lucas. I *should* have thought of that. It simply did not occur to me that we could cannibalise the workshop. The laser really is no use in there any more. Well done."

Lucas accepted the praise dismissively, knowing that if he hadn't kicked the ball, he may not have looked in the direction of the woolshed. It wasn't as if he had solved the problem through any great mental feat.

He immediately rang Jake, and told him to arrange a truck to pick up the laser.

Andie did have to, if not burst their bubble, at least deflate it a little. "The workshop laser is an older model than the one on order, and is more prone to overheating. We won't be able to run that at quite the same pace as the other. It looks like you'll have to work the graveyard shift after all, Sonia. With that extra day up our sleeve, we should *just* make the deadline."

"Well, there's a test for your management skills, Sonia! Getting a new team to meet a difficult deadline will be a challenge, but I'm sure you can do it."

Before long, Jake himself arrived, driving a small, flat-bed truck with an attached hoist.

"Got something for me, I gather?"

As Lucas was helping load the laser, Jake mentioned some strange goings-on he had noticed at the facility.

"The last few days there've been a couple of guys hanging around outside the site. They've been trying to talk to some of the lads, but they know it's more than their job's worth to let anything slip. Anyway, this morning I saw these buggers taking snapshots from inside their car out on the road. You want me to do anything about it?"

A rugby forward, Jake cut an imposing figure with his stocky build, shaved head, and tattoos. He probably wouldn't need to get physical to scare the interlopers off, but Lucas said that they really weren't doing anything illegal, and they had no probable cause to move them on. He suggested that Jake replace the chain-link fence at the roadside with a solid one, to frustrate other budding photographers. He also asked that Jake pass on his thanks to the workers who had shown the loyalty and integrity not to talk to the men about the job.

With the laser loaded and tied down, Jake returned to town to install it, and Lucas related the story of the nosy intruders to the girls.

Andie shrugged. "I'm only surprised that it hasn't been an issue sooner. The other major tech companies will be falling over themselves to get the inside scoop on the QED. I'm not too worried, to tell the truth. Sure, they could get hold of a unit by signing up with U-Net, and take it apart to see what makes it tick. Good luck to them with that. While they might get the circuitry, the main component is beyond their ability to replicate, and as soon as they open the unit, the containment field will collapse and the particles will dissipate. Even if they could look inside the factory, the laser section is sealed off and fully automated, so there's no risk of any of the workers giving the game away."

Mollified, Lucas and Sonia turned their thoughts to other things.

"Do you think we'll get enough people to run the lines, then?" asked Sonia.

"I'm certain of it," replied Lucas. "There are no spots that need highly specialised skills, and I'm confident that we can teach everybody on the line what they need to know. I think we'll announce a bonus to incentivise them to get up to speed. Andie initially calculated the first run based on decreased output anyway, and we might just improve on that with this little sweetener."

The girls agreed with his assessment, and the plan to potentially boost the work rate. Nothing says "*We value your contribution*" more than cash in hand.

With the laser crisis averted, Sonia had snapped out of her mood, and went back to the kitchen to continue looking over the applications. Lucas joined her shortly, and they spent the rest of the day discussing the applicants, and deciding how the interviews would be conducted.

The weekend passed uneventfully, and they were keen for Monday to arrive, so that they could get back to the Council office and retrieve more applications.

On Monday, they waited until after lunch to check the box, and were pleased to find another 78 forms had been left. They dropped in at the factory site on the way home to call in on Jake, and saw that both lasers were now installed in their secure section in the building. The facility was completed, and stores of components had already arrived, waiting in boxes and crates in the pre-production storage area.

Sonia needed to make a start on the laser process, so that there would be components to install when the workers arrived later in the week. She gained access to the secure section by means of a keycard and a biometric lock that scanned her retinal pattern and her palm print. While she was starting up the systems, Lucas loaded several boxes onto a small hydraulic trolley and brought them over. Unpacking the contents of one box, he loaded a hopper on the outside of the room with pellets of the target material. A complex arrangement of conveyors and robotic arms would take the pellets and position them for the laser to strike. Completed units would be transferred from the temporary magnetic containment field to permanent enclosures, sealed, and stacked for delivery to the production line.

"I'll have to pop back every few hours to top up the hopper, but once I set it going, it will churn out units at around three per hour, allowing for the lower speed of the old laser. Once we get the new one in place as well, we should be over our target rate for Faulks's second order."

"That still doesn't seem like a lot," said Lucas.

"It's not, but this facility is small compared to the next generation ones that you're building, and it was always the plan to start small and test our processes before going full-scale."

"Will there be enough work for the locals, though? I don't want to tell them that we can only offer 50 jobs." Lucas worried about the company's reputation if his grand scheme for cutting the unemployment levels didn't stack up.

Sonia explained that, while the initial workload would be light, she and Andie hadn't wanted to drop an inexperienced workforce in at the deep end.

"We'll be adding more lasers once things take off – look at the size of this room – and I hope to eventually put out over 50 an hour. They'll earn their money then!"

Satisfied that the lasers were working as planned, they relocked the door and shut the facility up behind them as they went back to the car.

On their return home, it became clear that the kitchen table wasn't going to be a suitable workspace for all the applications they had to look through. He got Sonia to help him drag in an old table from one of the outbuildings, and they set it up in the third bedroom. A couple of wooden beer crates were drafted as filing cabinets, and spare chairs from the kitchen completed Ad Astra's new Human Resources office.

Lucas balanced a precarious stack of envelopes in his arms as he entered the room, blind to the chair in front of the table. He stumbled over it, sending the paperwork flying across the room.

"*On* the table, not *at* it, butterfingers," Sonia admonished, going down on one knee to pick up the applications.

Abashed, Lucas apologised and crouched down to help her. As they reached for the same envelope, their fingers touched. Each looked up, and their eyes met. As one, they spoke; "No-o-o." Laughing off the moment of forced intimacy, they turned their backs on each other and concentrated on the task of tidying up the mess. Had either of them wanted more to happen? Neither gave any indication, and each justified their reaction by telling themselves they they worked too closely together. Getting involved with the other would only make things awkward.

The uncomfortable moment was soon forgotten as they began to sort the applications. There seemed to be interest in every available position, and some people had skills well-suited to their preferred role. They would need little training. There were also some who had indicated no preference, and the interview process would hopefully give Sonia a better idea of where to put them.

"Do you think I should start today?" she asked. "There just seem too many already to rush through on Wednesday."

"Give some of them a call – I'm sure they'll be happy to come in, especially if it means they're more likely to get the signing bonus!"

She took out her phone and selected a few of the most promising files, as well as some of those that would need extra attention. As it turned out, every person she called was ready to come in as soon as Sonia would like, so she made some notes, collected up the files she needed, and left for the factory in the Toyota.

She set up a small table, and two chairs, on the factory floor, and waited for her first visitor. Shortly, a knock on the door announced his arrival.

"Come in," she called.

The door opened to reveal a heavy-set Māori man, probably in his fifties. James 'Big Jim' Nepia had driven stock trucks, logging trucks, and milk trucks around the region for over 25 years, but what interested Sonia was that he had crossed out the word 'truck' on the application, and written in 'bus'.

"Good afternoon, Mr Nepia. My name is Sonia Matheson, and I'm the production manager here. Thank you for coming in."

"Oh, gidday, missus. Call me Jim!" he told her, smiling broadly. "Thanks heaps for the opportunity."

He sat down opposite her, moving the chair away from the table to accommodate his gut.

"So, Jim, you noticed that we didn't have a bus driver listed, and thought to make your own role. You know we need truck drivers, so what made you decide that you want to drive our bus?"

"Aw, you know, missus, the truck driving is okay, but I like my people contact, and I never did get much of that in my old jobs. I reckon I'd make a pretty decent bus driver 'cos I get on with people and I always got a smile for them. The sheep and cattle, they never did appreciate my jokes, neither! Oh, I also got a, whaddaya call it? An 'ulterior motive'.

"I know how the shifts is like, every three hours. It probably only takes about 15 minutes to make a run between here and town, what with people messing around and stuff. If I work all day, I reckon I only actually do about two full hours. That's a lot of downtime, eh? So I thought I'd make you, like, a proposition."

Intrigued by this man and his irreverent attitude, she asked, "And what's your proposition, Jim?"

"Well, you only need the bus for those shift changes, eh? What say the rest of the time I lease the bus off you and use it to run an actual bus service around the town? There's heaps of people who have to walk down the hill to do their shopping and stuff – my old Mum's one of them – and I just reckon they'd all really appreciate being able to catch a bus. They might get into town more often, see their friends, go to the movies and all. You think that's an idea?"

"I admire your enthusiasm, and you've come up with an idea that could really work. Have you figured out how this will work for you, financially?"

"Oh, I'm not in it for the money, missus. I mean, it'd be nice to have a little dosh, but I just wanna give back, you know? This place has been pretty good to me, and I know that some of these old folks find it tricky getting around, eh? I had a few thoughts about the numbers, but I haven't used a calculator. I thought that if I got 200 people to pay five bucks weekly, that's 1000, I give you 500 a month lease on the bus, and since I'll be using it most of the time, I pay for gas and 90% of the maintenance."

Impressed with his social conscience and entrepreneurial attitude, Sonia made a counter-offer.

"Call it 50% and you've got a deal. We'll write up a contract, make sure you're not going to end up out of pocket, and Taihape's got a new shuttle service. Welcome aboard, Jim."

Jim heaved himself out of the chair, and grinned. "Aw, missus, I'm stoked! I knew you was good people when I heard that missus Donovan talking in the hall last week. I'm gonna give you a big hug now, so don't you be scared!"

Laughing, Sonia came around the table to be enveloped in his huge arms. "You're just the sort of person we need –confident, innovative, and with a genuine concern for others. Ad Astra and Taihape are lucky to have you."

Reaching into her briefcase, she pulled out a small envelope and held it out.

"You get on home now and proudly tell your family that you're the very first employee of Ad Astra Taihape. Take this, and show them what we think of clever guys like you."

He opened the envelope to find five crisp hundred-dollar bills. "Aw gee, missus! The wife'll be over the moon! Thanks heaps, you won't regret it."

"I'm sure we won't, Jim," she responded, smiling warmly at him. "Thank *you*."

As he left, she wondered briefly if she had overstepped her authority, agreeing to his plan. Only briefly, as she realised that it was exactly the sort of thing that Lucas would have done.

Her next appointment was due in five minutes, and before he arrived, she read through his application again to familiarise herself with the applicant. There wasn't much to go on, however. Karl Evert was 19 years old, had dropped out of school at 16, and had never held a job. Many portions of the application were blank, with no qualifications or interests listed. She wondered what his story was.

He pushed the door open without knocking, and sauntered over before dropping into the chair and slouching back with his legs stretched out before him. He wore black jeans and a faded Metallica t-shirt, and his greasy hair hung lankly down past his neck and over his eyes.

"Mr Evert?" Sonia asked.

"Yeah," the youth mumbled sullenly.

"Good afternoon. I'm Sonia Matheson, manager here at Ad Astra Taihape. So tell me, why would you like to work for us here?"

Karl swept his hair away from his eyes and shrugged. "My mum got me the application. She reckons I have to start paying my way or she'll kick me out. So here I am."

Sighing inwardly, Sonia wondered if this was really the sort of person they needed. He was untidy, unmotivated, and probably had issues with authority.

"You haven't got a lot written in your application, Karl. Why don't you tell me a bit about yourself?"

He sniffed. "Not much to tell. I was shit at school work, and dropped out a few years ago. There's no jobs around here. It's a crappy town but I got nowhere else to go. I'm just on the dole and hang out with me mates."

"Well, what do you like doing, Karl?"

"I play the guitar a bit, and play video games mostly. Like I said, it's a crappy town and there's fuck-all to do."

"Are you any good?"

"What, at guitar? Or video games?"

"Either?"

He shuffled in his seat and pulled out his phone. "Here's a bit of video of me on the guitar. S'pose I'm okay."

He pressed play and Sonia heard the frenetic notes of Yngwie Malmsteen's *Arpeggios from Hell*. Karl turned the phone around and she recognised the young man in front of her on the screen, an electric guitar across his lap, and his fingers moving almost too quickly to be seen.

"That's, um, pretty good, Karl," she said, impressed but not wanting to overplay her hand. "Who taught you guitar?"

"We had an old one around the house and I picked it up one day and started playing some shit I'd heard on the radio. My uncle gave me the electric one a couple years back and I've just been teaching myself."

"What about the video games?"

"Aw, I just mess around with them. I was in a Counterstrike league for a while but a lot of those guys were dicks, so I got out. We were top of our table for a bit, though."

Sonia knew of the game Counterstrike. It was a first-person shooter that needed quick reflexes, excellent hand-eye coordination, teamwork, and strategic thinking.

"So why haven't you put these skills on your application?" she asked.

"Eh? These ain't skills. It's just shit I do to pass the time. I told you, I never learned nothing in school. I ain't *got* no skills."

"Karl, I get the feeling that people don't give you enough credit. You probably think that since you don't have any formal qualifications, you can't do well in the world. You may have been told that you're useless, a waste of space."

A sneer passed quickly across the young man's face as he remembered hearing those exact words from his teachers and even his family.

"Well let me tell you, you have an amazing talent for the guitar, and if you played in a top rank Counterstrike team, then you've got exactly the skills I need in one of our most important jobs. You're obviously quick to learn – your schooling doesn't count; I'm sure that they didn't know how to realise your potential – you have tremendous dexterity, you can strategise, and you know how to work as part of a team. I need someone who can do fiddly work, at high speed, without mistakes. I bet you trained your muscle memory in that video game – if there was someone in an upstairs window that needed shooting, you barely thought about it as your hand moved the mouse to exactly the right spot."

The youth was nodding at this, understanding exactly what she meant.

"These are skills that you can't train just anyone to use, and you have them naturally. What do you say? Are you going to be King of this production line, or am I going to have to get someone else and settle for second best?"

Karl had begun to sit up straighter in his chair, unaccustomed to praise, but obviously enjoying the experience.

"They told me my music and video games would never get me nowhere. Well, screw them! Miss Matheson, you got yourself a deal. You know, I never had nothing to look forward to. No one's even given me a shot. If you're going to trust me with an important job, then I'm going to be the best damn worker you got. All I ever needed was someone to believe in me, but all they saw was just another no-hoper metalhead. When do I start?"

Sonia laughed. "Well, we don't technically open the factory until next week, after we've got all the staff lined up. However, if you'd like to come in early and get a head start, that would work out great. Your job is more involved than any of the others, so there'll be more to learn in the first place, but it won't be any harder than playing Malmsteen."

She got another envelope out of her case and handed it to him. "Go and buy yourself another Metallica t-shirt – that one's almost worn out!"

He peeked inside and saw the money.

"Holy shit!" he exclaimed. "If I can earn money this easily, Metallica's playing at my 21st!"

Sonia chuckled as she shook his hand. "Don't get too carried away. It's been a pleasure meeting you, Karl, and I look forward to showing you the ropes."

As he left, she was amazed and saddened that such a talent could have languished unseen because people couldn't look beneath the surface.

The rest of the interviews that afternoon were far simpler. She had obviously managed to get the two most interesting first up. By the end of the day, she had completed a further eight interviews. She was slowly filling the required roles, and was happy with the people she had so far.

HEROES

The following day, Sonia managed to get through the remaining interviews. Most were short, and to the point, with the applicants knowing what they wanted and why they felt qualified for a particular role. Others needed more consideration, with Sonia having to assess their abilities and find the most suitable position for them.

Lucas had been in a few times to refill the pellet hoppers, and had asked Jake to go by at the end of the day as he wasn't entirely comfortable with Sonia being there alone in the evening. Not with those dodgy characters around. They had been seen again, sneaking shots of the arriving applicants, so Lucas had instructed people to take the new road in to the facility. He hoped that would throw the spies off for a bit.

When Sonia was finished, she tallied her numbers and found that she already had two complete production lines filled, as well as the café. She still needed more cleaners, crèche workers, supervisors, and people in the warehouse to sort and stack incoming and outgoing stock, but she felt well on the way to being ready for opening day.

She packed up her paperwork, and made sure that the building was secure before heading out to her car. As she drove out the front gate, a dark saloon pulled up in front of her, partially blocking her exit. She called out that the interviews were over for the day, only to see two suited men climb out of the car. She hurriedly locked her doors, and wound her window up so that just a small gap remained.

One of the men approached her car, reaching into an inside jacket pocket. He extracted his hand, flipping open an identity card holder.

"Ma'am, I'm Agent Woodrow, with the Serious Fraud Office. I wonder if we might have a minute of your time. We're sorry to be coming to you so late in the day but you're not an easy person to track down."

Sonia couldn't imagine what the SFO could possibly want with her, or Ad Astra, but she compliantly got out of her car to speak to the man. As she did so, she saw a second vehicle approaching from the main road; a black Ford Ranger. While her attention was distracted by the oncoming Ford, the second man had come around the back of her car and gripped her strongly from behind, one arm encircling her chest and the other firmly on the back of her neck. The man who had shown her his credentials – obviously false, she now realised – quickly opened the rear door of their saloon and her captor bundled her into the back seat.

The black Ford had reached the gate by now, and screeched to a halt, Jake Lyall throwing himself out of the vehicle and running over to confront the assailants. The sight of this intimidating large man with the furious look did not have the effect he intended, as one of them calmly reached into his side pocket and pulled out a square-barrelled handgun, which he pointed at Jake. To his credit, this did not slow the big man at all, but when the weapon was discharged, he fell forward, his momentum carrying him to land at the gunman's feet. Ignoring Jake, the two men casually climbed back into their car, one in the back seat to restrain a hysterical Sonia. They backed up, drove around the Ranger, and sped off, heading back towards the main road. On the ground, Jake lay motionless.

Only a few seconds passed before the prone giant slowly raised his head and saw the kidnapper's car turn onto the main road. He dropped his head once more as his hands slowly clenched into fists the size of rock melons.

After a minute or so, he regained control of his body, and stumbled to his feet. Delving a huge hand into a trouser pocket, he removed his cellphone and dialled.

Lucas answered after a couple of rings, to hear Jake's pained voice.

"They took Sonia! The two bastards who've been spying on us turned up as she was leaving and threw her in their car. I tried to stop them, man, but the assholes *tasered* me. I've been out for a couple of minutes, but I saw them go south on the main road. Dark saloon – Camry, I think. I am *so* sorry, mate."

"Fuck, fuck, FUCK!" cried Lucas. "You did your best. Are you able to drive?"

"Already on it, man," replied Jake, who had climbed back into his ute as he made the call. "I'm on the main road now, but they've got a head start and I don't know if they'll stay on this road."

"Okay stick with it, and I'll get some help organised. Good luck!"

Lucas hung up the phone and raced into the office. "Andie! Someone's kidnapped Sonia. Jake's following them, but they hit him with a taser and he was down for a couple of minutes. What can we do?"

"Oh, Lucas, that's terrible! Don't worry – we'll get her back. Is she likely to have her phone on her?"

Lucas thought for a second. "She usually carries it in her jeans pocket, but she might have put it in her briefcase. I just don't know."

"Why don't you get out on the road, and I'll see if I can track her. Keep your phone on and I'll get back to you."

Running out the door, Lucas called over his shoulder, "Thanks, Andie! Let me know as soon as you find anything!"

He grabbed the keys to the Jaguar as he raced through the kitchen, and sprinted out to the garage. Firing up the powerful sportscar, he fishtailed it down the gravel driveway, hitting the tarmac of the road in a cloud of dust. Hurtling down the road with little care for speed limits, he reached the main road in a matter of minutes, and blew through the intersection, leaving a pair of black tyre tracks on the road.

On the open road, he opened up, grateful that the Colonel had opted for the SE model, with an extra 15 horsepower. The cars he was passing at speed honked their horns and flashed their lights, but he was oblivious to their abuse as he single-mindedly hunted down the people who had abducted his friend.

The light was beginning to fade, making it harder to see if any of the cars he approached were his target. He recognised a familiar bulky, black ute ahead and flashed his lights as he came up behind it. The heavy Ranger wasn't built for a chase, and Lucas tooted as he passed Jake.

His mobile rang, and he answered it brusquely. "Andie. What's the story?"

"Good news, Lucas. I've hacked the cellular networks and found her phone. I'm getting intermittent pings as they pass towers, so I've not got perfect triangulation, but as far as I can tell, they're approaching

Hunterville. Wait! I'm getting a better signal now, and it looks like they're stationary at the north end of the town."

"I'm only a few minutes out – stay on the line."

He pressed his right foot onto the accelerator even harder, hoping to wring a little more speed out of the roadster. Shortly, he pulled to a stop opposite the small town's single service station, looking around frantically for a Camry saloon. However, there were no other cars in sight. As he searched the vicinity, he noticed a reflection of the service station's lights from something on the ground. He recognised it as a mobile phone, and jumped out of the car to inspect it. Sure enough, it was Sonia's. They had obviously found it on her person and discarded it.

Heavy braking and a crunch of gravel announced the arrival of Jake in his Ranger.

Lucas called out, "We were tracking her phone, but the bastards ditched it, and we've lost our only lead."

Dismayed, Jake swore, and jumped out of his ute, punching the door as he shut it. "They still can't be too far away, and you must have been making good ground on them. I've been on the phone to the cops and they're keeping an eye out on the road south, but if you don't get back on their tail, there are any number of side roads they could lose us on."

"Yeah. Plan. I'll try to catch up. See ya!"

"No way – I'm coming with you. You'll need my help."

"Get in, then."

As he leaped back into the Jaguar without even bothering to open the door, Lucas heard Andie's voice on the phone, which he had left in the car.

"Where are you Lucas? Why aren't you talking to me?"

"Sorry. I'm in Hunterville, and I've found Sonia's phone on the side of the road. That'll be why they stopped. I've got to get back into the chase, as our only hope is to find the car now."

Andie was silent for a second, as Lucas put the car into gear and spun the tyres as he drove off.

"Not entirely true. I've been cross-referencing the data from the cell towers, and there were two other phones that pinged at the same time as Sonia's. I'd bet that those phones belong to our kidnappers, and unless they decide to throw away their own phones as well, we've still got a trail."

130

"Excellent work! So, where are they?"

"They continued south, but it looks like they have turned off Highway One, and went right onto Jefferson's Line, the old main road."

"Great stuff. That should slow them down. I know that road better than them. They probably think they've long since lost any tail, and won't be expecting us."

As Lucas raced towards their turnoff, Jake commented. "Who's this chick on the phone, then? She seems well-connected, to be able to track a cellphone."

Thinking quickly, Lucas said, "Yeah, she's an old mate. She's with the police and I talked her into using their system to monitor the cell towers. I hope she doesn't get into trouble for it but you know, the ends justify the means and all that."

Satisfied with the answer, Jake nodded. "Whatever it takes, man. Whatever it takes."

Soon they came upon the intersection. Lucas slowed fractionally to take the corner, then planted his foot once again. After a few corners up a short climb, they came to a long straight where he put his foot to the floor. Soon, the Jaguar's speedometer was topping out at 120 MPH, and they saw distant tail-lights. Lucas wisely kept his distance on the straight, knowing that a modern saloon could outpace the elderly car in the open. However, as they entered another twisty section, his superior knowledge of the turns allowed him to close the gap. Approaching one particular corner, he knew that he would be able to get on the inside of the other car, even considering the Jaguar's less than ideal brakes. As the car in front of them, now identified by Jake as the kidnappers', slowed for the right-hander, Lucas left his braking late and took the corner on the other car's right. He was braking hard as he cut back in front, and the driver behind him smashed his fist on the horn furiously. Jake had slouched in his seat as much as possible, so as not to be recognised, and wore a woollen hat to cover his bald head.

Lucas slowed further, before moving right and jerking the steering wheel hard to the left. He pulled on the handbrake and the roadster slid to a stop, blocking both lanes. Jake immediately jumped up and over the door, running at the Camry. The back-seat passenger was in the process of opening his door as Jake charged at full speed, as if he were attacking an

Australian halfback on the rugby field. He lowered his shoulder and hit the back door with enough force to break the leg of the man attempting to exit the car. He pulled the door open and dragged the screaming man from the car by his shirt-front, throwing him down.

Meanwhile, Lucas had made a similar charge at the driver's side. This man had had more time than his accomplice, with Lucas being on the wrong side of the slewed Jaguar, and was already out of the car. Putting his own rugby skills to good use, he tackled the man around his waist, carrying him to the ground. Landing on top of him, Lucas stunned him with several blows to the head, before rolling him over and twisting the man's arm behind his back.

Jake's opponent had rolled away from his attacker and sat up, drawing his own taser. He fired it at Jake, but this time, it had no effect, as the prongs could not penetrate the heavy leather jacket that Jake had found in his ute and put on before leaving Taihape. He also wore a pair of leather work gloves that had been in the jacket's pocket. Insulated from the electricity flowing though the taser's wires, he pulled on them and yanked the weapon from its owner's hands. Bellowing, he fell upon the hapless villain, and landed a beefy firearm across the man's throat.

Stunned by the speed and ferocity of the violence, Sonia was only just starting to climb out of the car via the driver's side rear door. She walked over to where Lucas had his man immobilised, and delivered a swift kick to the kidnapper's ribs.

"You bastard!" she screamed, pulling her foot back for another kick.

Lucas moved his body to block her foot, saying, "Not now. See if you can find something to tie them up with."

"There's a bunch of cable ties in my jacket pocket, if you want to come get them," called Jake.

Sonia did so, going back around the car to Lucas while Jake's victim struggled vainly under the prop forward. She quickly pulled the ties tightly around the driver's wrists and ankles, and Lucas dragged him to the side of the road before going over to his Jaguar and moving it out of the way.

Sonia likewise tied the passenger, and Lucas moved their car to the side of the road also. With the two pained men sitting up against the side of their car, Lucas approached and squatted down in front of them.

"I'm not a violent man, but you two have just made a very serious mistake. What did you want, and who are you working for?"

The kidnappers remained stoically silent, until Jake placed a large hand around the passenger's broken leg.

"Nasty looking break, mate. Must hurt a bit," he said, applying slight pressure.

The man grunted in pain, yet kept his mouth shut. Jake pressed harder, and the man let out a yell.

"Aaaagh! All right! We were employed to find out the secret of your device. By any means possible. Don't bother asking who we work for. We don't know. The contract was set up through intermediaries and anonymous messaging. Honestly, that's all we can tell you."

"I'm sure that if you think really, *really* hard, you can give us more than that," Jake said, grinding the broken bones under his hand.

The man screamed, and passed out.

"Next, please." Jake moved over to the driver, obviously enjoying the opportunity to inflict damage on the people who had taken his boss, and tasered him.

"He's right, man. That really is all we know. We send a message to an anonymous phone when we've got the information, and they'll send someone to collect it. We've never met the person who hired us, and never will."

"So, what you're going to do now," interjected Lucas, "is give us the number you'd message, any other contact information, your phones, and your wallets. Play the game, and I might just be able to stop my friend here from ripping you into tiny pieces and feeding you to his dogs. Understood?"

The look on his face as he said this seemed to trigger some primal fear in the man, and his shoulders slumped.

"Whatever," the man replied. "All the contacts that set the job up are on my phone. It won't help you – everything was totally anonymous."

Lucas hid a smile, knowing that nothing was hidden from Andie. Andie! He ran back to his car and called her, letting her know that they'd recovered Sonia. Walking back to the Camry, he nodded to Jake. "Okay, get rid of them."

"As in ... ?"

"Not this time, sorry. But if I *ever* see their faces again, I might not be so generous. Turf them down the hill. They should be able to make their way back up eventually, and it will give them time to reflect on what a bad idea it was to mess with us."

Jake rummaged through the pockets of the unconscious one before roughly putting him over his shoulder. Walking to the fence, he gleefully threw him over and watched him roll down the hill. He went back to do the same to the fake Agent Woodrow.

"It doesn't matter that you stopped us, you know. When they realise that this plan didn't work, they'll come back bigger and badder."

"Me too," declared Jake ominously, as he hoisted the man and unceremoniously tossed him after his accomplice.

Both men went to Sonia and took her in a three-way hug.

"Thank you guys so much," she said. "They hadn't hurt me yet, but they were joking about the terrible things they wanted to do if I didn't tell them."

Jake's eyes narrowed and he began to walk back to the fence, fully intending to finish what he had started.

"Never mind, Jake," said Lucas. "When word gets around that they had their asses handed to them by a couple of amateurs, their 'career' is over, and they'll be lucky if their employers don't take the failure out on them."

He put an arm around Sonia and led her to the Jaguar. Helping her get in, he told Jake to take the Camry back to collect his Ranger, and to meet them at the farm after. There were some serious discussions to be had.

Lucas and Sonia didn't speak much on the way home. She had run the gamut of emotion from fear, to anger, and now shock. She sat in the passenger seat, trembling, with the blanket from behind the seat wrapped around her shoulders. Lucas looked over at her, hoping that she was strong enough to put this behind her.

His concerns were unfounded, however. On their return to the farm, Sonia had left the shock behind and reverted to anger. She ransacked the men's wallets and demanded that Andie track their history.

"I want to know where they came from and who they report to. Scrape their phones and follow the message trail. I want to know who ordered this and I want them to pay."

Lucas worried about Sonia starting a vendetta when they had so much on their plates already, but knew better than to try to restrain her after her traumatic experience. He could only hope that she would see things in a clearer light when she finally calmed down.

A knock on the door indicated that Jake had arrived, and Lucas went to let him in. He brought the hero of the night into the office and grabbed the chairs from the HR department. Sitting down, they agreed that the events of that evening could be not allowed to happen again, and discussed additional security precautions late into the night.

PRODUCTION

The next morning, Lucas escorted Sonia to the facility, to find a barrier that would eventually be accompanied by floodlights, cameras, and a guardhouse, being installed across the access road. Multiple security officers were patrolling the compound, and Jake's team was upgrading the fence with electricity and razor wire. IT personnel were installing additional cameras and motion sensors around the building, that would be connected via QED to Andie. Nothing would be able to move in the compound without the AI being aware of it.

"Do you feel a little safer now, Sonia?" asked Lucas.

"I'm still really pissed off. It's not *my* safety you need to worry about," she retorted. "All this might stop it happening again, but I still want to know who it was, and we have to make them aware that we are *not* going to be victims."

Lucas gave her a hug as they entered the compound. "Don't let it eat you up. Andie and I are going to be working on it today, so you just concentrate on getting this place up and running."

She smiled at him. "I know you guys have got this, and I promise not to go off the rails. Will you be picking me up this afternoon?"

"I don't want to stick to any particular routine, so when you're ready to go, just get Jake to run you home, okay? I'll drop off some more paperwork for you before I head back."

Agreeing, Sonia waved him goodbye and went inside, setting her mind to the day's work ahead. Lucas had a quick chat with Jake before he left, making sure the big man knew the plan, and headed into town to collect the next batch of applications.

Returning to the farm after giving Sonia the files, he sat down in front of the computer to see how Andie was progressing with identifying their enemy.

"The two men who attacked Sonia, Greg Sanford and Patrick Kelly, are freelance operators who have a long history of industrial espionage. As far as I can tell, they've always shied away from overt violence, and I suspect that their ill-advised decision to abduct her was a result of frustration when their usual tactics hadn't worked. That's not to say that they wouldn't have carried through with their threats to her, but it isn't their style. Their message history tells an interesting story. Though every effort was made to conceal the origin of their orders, they never expected me. The messages were routed through cutouts and spoofed servers, but if you look closely, a pattern emerges. The orders came from an underworld kingpin who is known as an intermediary for people who don't want their hands soiled. Unfortunately, he seems understandably paranoid regarding digital communications, and there is no record of who gave him the original orders."

"So it's a dead end?" asked Lucas, disappointed.

"Not exactly," Andie replied. "I think I may have found some leverage that we could use. It's not entirely ethical, in case you still have a problem with that."

Lucas chewed his lip as he thought. Did he still have a problem? He hadn't had any qualms about threatening the two thugs from last night, but he never intended to follow through on those threats. He had given Andie free rein to follow up on corruption, and she was compiling dossiers on the worst offenders, so maybe his moral code had slipped enough that he would willingly move against a crime boss. He had to remind himself that all of that was for the greater good, or to protect his family, since that was how he saw the people working for Ad Astra. He believed that he could forgive himself for those transgressions, and he would wait to see what Andie had in mind.

"It's not the problem it was, but there will still be limits to what I can agree to. What's the leverage?"

Andie knew that she had to play this part carefully, as what she was considering teetered on the edge of what Lucas might find acceptable.

"The man who arranged for Sanford and Kelly to steal the QED information, 'King' Joseph Kingston, has his fingers in many pies. Drugs, prostitution, human trafficking, you name it. You don't deal in those fields without making enemies among the way, and one of those enemies is a man called Laumoli. Laumoli is a Samoan gangster who was pushed out of South Auckland by Kingston in a violent takeover. He has never forgiven the King for his daughter being killed in a drive-by shooting, and has sworn a blood feud on him.

"The King is not too concerned about direct action against him, as his soldiers are numerous and vicious, but he has a secret. His wife and young son are in hiding, a gangster version of witness protection, and the King would do anything to keep that secret from Laumoli. With the right approach, I think he could be persuaded to reveal where the orders came from."

She paused, knowing that threatening a man's family would be anathema to Lucas, but ready to assure him that the information would never actually be disclosed. She planned to create an online persona of a gangster who had been wronged by Sanford and Kelly, and wishing to get back at them through their employer.

Lucas was, indeed, upset at the prospect of putting a young mother's life at risk, and her son's, but had the sense to realise that it was only to be a threat, and that the King would give up the contact before letting anything happen to them.

"Let me get this straight. Do you know where his wife and son are?"

"I do."

"And you need to know that to show this King that the threat is serious."

"That's all it is, Lucas – a threat. I would never endanger them, but the King needs to believe in the risk. I can virtually guarantee that he will fold. What's some client's displeasure, compared to his family's safety?" Her face was the picture of innocence, designed to assure Lucas of her good intentions. She had other, more dangerous plans that did not have as high a chance of success, and risked Ad Astra's involvement being exposed.

Lucas was torn between protecting the company, and compromising his standards, but in the end, he took Andie's assurance that it would be only words, not action, and agreed to the plan.

"Next on the agenda," he continued, "is the corruption thing. How are you getting on with that?"

"I've got solid evidence on two South American dictators, and numerous US senators. The dictators are in bed with organised crime entities, and are turning a blind eye to environmental crimes in exchange for drug money. They are also taking a hard line against activists and political dissidents, having them abducted, tortured, and murdered by undercover state-sponsored paramilitary groups.

"Most of the senators are taking bribes from business to rush through preferential legislation, though there are a couple who are in the pay of extra-national state actors who hope to destabilise the economy. One has even sold military secrets. Even if the US goes down the toilet, these traitors have taken enough money to live out their lives on private Caribbean islands. That's if their paymasters don't decide to tidy up loose ends.

"I can forward details of the senators' crimes to the FBI, whose corruption taskforce is ideally situated to handle them. The dictators are a different matter. Any judicial attempt to work against them would be swiftly swept under the carpet, and those conducting the investigation would surely be killed. The better option in these cases would be to motivate public opinion against them, with the evidence being provided to international media. I could also instigate internal discord by freezing the bank accounts of the dictators and the crime syndicates, making it harder for them to do business. I can alert the US's DEA as to specific locations of drug manufacturing facilities in South America, and hope that they see value in taking them out. However, drugs have long been a useful political tool in the shadowy back rooms of the US government, and it's hard to say whether they would be willing to give that up. I know for a fact that there are direct connections between certain syndicates and the CIA, but I don't think that's a wasp nest we want to stir up at present."

Lucas knew that previous reporting of alleged corruption in South America hadn't achieved much, but perhaps with the proof in hand, the press could encourage change. As for the US senators, it was worth shaking a few trees to see what fell. He gave his go-ahead for Andie to start releasing the information. Anonymously, of course. He was sure that the recipients of the evidence would be diligent in trying to discover the source of the information, but Andie's methods would be untraceable. He had no concerns about Ad Astra being involved in a spying scandal.

Satisfied with the plans to track down the culprits involved in Sonia's kidnapping, and those to expose corruption, Lucas took the rest of the day off to visit his neighbours and see if they had any chores he could help with. All the international intrigue took him well out of his comfort zone, and he was looking forward to getting back to his roots.

Several of his more distant and isolated neighbours mentioned that they had been approached by U-Net, offering internet service that they had previously been unable to receive. One couple, up the far end of the valley, ran a tourism enterprise, but patchy landline service and non-existent mobile coverage meant that their customers could not reliably contact them. Having an internet connection would make a huge difference to their business, and he was pleased that his project would have a positive impact on those he knew best.

He arrived home that evening after a long afternoon of lawns and jobs, feeling physically exhausted but emotionally satisfied. Sonia was already home, and excitedly told him that they had almost 150 people ready and willing to work. The major positions were filled, and everybody was happy to come in for on-site training through the rest of the week. She and Lucas would have to fill in the gaps temporarily, until postal applications were processed, or staff from outside the district were employed, but they were on track for the Monday opening, and U-Net's first units should be delivered on time.

He, in turn, related his own day's activities, and she responded to the news of the King with a vicious smile.

"That man has obviously caused a great deal of misery through his dodgy dealings. I won't be losing any sleep over it if he has to sweat a bit. The sooner he hands over the name, the happier I'll be."

There was that vindictive streak again. He made a mental note to keep a close eye on her, and see that her new obsession didn't take them places they didn't want to go.

After Sonia had gone to bed, he spoke with Andie about his concerns.

"I can understand that she has a need for vengeance, Lucas. She did have a horrible experience at the hands of those men. Is her desire for personal justice any different to the justice you're searching for yourself? Don't worry – I'll keep an eye on her to make sure that she doesn't do anything stupid. Hopefully, when we find out who it was, they will have some digital evidence that I can find, and that will be the beginning of their downfall."

Lucas had to agree with her argument. He was in no position to judge her; in fact, his own plans were much larger in scale, and she at least had the justification that the harm had been directed at her, personally. It was selfish of him to criticise her for her response. He just wished that she didn't seem to enjoy the prospect of retribution so much. He went to bed feeling equal measures of guilt and concern.

The rest of the week kept their minds from the issue, as the new staff underwent training. The security measures at the facility were complete, and the workers were instructed to report any unusual interest in their job. Sonia pointed out that the future of Ad Astra, and their new livelihoods, depended on the secrets of the manufacture remaining just that. This was somewhat disingenuous of her, of course, as Andie had already stated with certainty that the most important part of the device could not be reproduced, but it wouldn't hurt for the staff to feel a personal responsibility for maintaining secrecy.

The new workforce made great progress over those two days, in part due to Sonia selecting the right person for each role. The respect with which she treated them, and, of course, the signing bonus – which had been given to each employee, rather than just the first 100 – seemed to engender a strong sense of loyalty, and dedication to their task.

The lasers had been running all week, and there was a suitable supply of particle containment units ready for Monday. Karl Evert had taken to his role with gusto, quickly learning to assemble the circuit boards that would then be soldered by machines. The factory kitchen had already started running, to prepare meals and snacks for the workers as they trained, and Big Jim had put flyers out around town, advertising his bus service. All in all, everything was running smoothly, and Sonia had even managed to go a full day without thinking of what she could do with a pair of vice grips and a blowtorch.

The weekend arrived, and Lucas and Sonia enjoyed a respite from the rigours of training and management. They were eating a casual lunch on the verandah, keeping Splash occupied by throwing his new ball as far as possible, when Lucas's phone beeped with a notification from Andie. Wondering why the AI hadn't simply talked to them through the phone, they went to see her in the office.

"I've got some news, and some things you need to see. Firstly, my plan with the King has borne fruit. He completely believed that my fictitious character was prepared to spill the beans to Laumoli, and gave up his contact with little protest. I suspect that he will waste a lot of time looking for my gangster, and seems to have swallowed the idea that this is all about Sanford and Kelly."

Lucas and Sonia exchanged a high five, both smiling broadly, though Lucas did notice a hint of the earlier fire in his friend's eyes.

"I've got a single name, and have created this network map of his contacts." Here, she displayed on the monitor a name – Marco Fiore – with lines linking him to the surrounding individuals and businesses.

"As you can see, he has connections to many industries, and is known as a 'fixer', who gets things of dubious legality done for otherwise respectable businesses. I managed to rule out many of his contacts as having no potential interest in our product, but this one showed promise."

One name on the network became highlighted – DevConn.

"This is a US-based tech company that specialises in modems and networking hardware," continued Andie. "While there is no official connection between them and Fiore, they recently made a large payment to his offshore bank account, and his cellphone's location history places him at the same hotel as DevConn's CEO just two weeks ago."

"Though that's compelling evidence, for us at least, it's still purely circumstantial," interrupted Lucas.

"And if you let me finish," said Andie, "I'll get to the good bit. While you're right to say that a payment and a possible meeting don't necessarily mean that he was hired to steal our technology, DevConn internal emails tell a different story."

The screen then showed the messages that Andie was referring to. There, in black and white, was incontrovertible proof that upper management at DevConn had conspired with Marco Fiore to acquire the secrets of the QED.

"Okay," said Sonia, "We've got them. What do we do with them now? Do I have to go over there and bust a few kneecaps, or can we pay someone to do it for us?"

Lucas out a hand on her shoulder, as if to hold her back from rushing out the door and getting on a plane. "Easy, Tiger. No one is busting any kneecaps. Help me out here, Andie. What *do* we do?"

"I agree that violence is not the answer. Since they tried to hurt our business, I suggest that we hurt theirs. A technology company is reliant on the reputation and reliability of their devices. I have designed a virus that will seek out and infect DevConn hardware, randomly corrupting data transfer, before failing completely. Fortunately, they have just rolled out a software upgrade, and the damage will look like a related systems failure, rather than a deliberate attack. This won't have any lasting affect on the information systems of the end users, but it will certainly be an annoyance. The users will simply have to switch to a rival manufacturer, and DevConn will lose massive market share almost overnight. Their share price will tumble, their investors will bail, and their reputation will be in tatters. As a going concern, DevConn will virtually cease to exist. Does that satisfy your need for vengeance, Sonia?"

Sonia grinned evilly. "I think that will do it. It's a pity, however, that we couldn't take the credit, to let others know you don't mess with Ad Astra!"

"Yeah, I don't think that would be a good idea," said Lucas. "We don't need a 'cyber-terrorist' label. How long will this virus take to do the rounds, Andie?"

Andie displayed a world map that showed clusters of red dots. A glowing line started in California, linking the dots with a ever-expanding web.

"I've mapped the major locations of their hardware, and have already programmed the optimal route for the virus. I estimate that it will have infected 80% of DevConn devices within two days. Another two days should be long enough for tech publications to get wind of the failures, and it's all downhill from there. This time next week, the DevConn CEO will have his house and his Chrysler on the market."

"I must admit that I feel a little for their employees, but we really do need to remove the threat. Go ahead, Andie," responded Lucas, the old fear that he had too much power momentarily bubbling to the surface.

After a second, Andie announced that the virus was on its way, conveniently appearing to have originated in DevConn's own servers.

The rest of the weekend was filled with anticipation, as the virus stealthily travelled the world, leaving its payload in any DevConn router or modem it encountered. Soon, data packets were being mislaid, and connections were dropped. Initially, it was mostly affecting consumer hardware, but when Monday came, it began to take its toll on business communications and the tsunami of support requests hit the company's helpdesk. Technicians and programmers scrambled to identify the cause of the failures, and naturally ascribed it to a fault in the recent upgrade. They hurriedly performed a rollback, but Andie had anticipated this move, and the virus ignored their efforts. It was the beginning of the end.

As for Sonia and Lucas, Monday held more important things for them than watching DevConn fall. The production line at the Taihape facility was running at optimal capacity, and their help was needed to ensure it continued to do so. Sonia was performing quality control, and Lucas was managing the warehouse. Though everybody was working as fast as possible, considering their inexperience, the output was not challenging the stock handlers, so Lucas also did the rounds of the factory. He saw that the café was well-stocked for breaks and shift changes, and even accompanied Jim on one of his round-town bus runs. The big guy was a hit with his passengers, greeting them all by name, chatting, and telling stories as he drove.

By the end of the afternoon, the lines were only a little behind their target, but everyone was confident that practise would improve their speed. An additional quality control worker came on shift in the late afternoon, and the warehouse was ticking over nicely, so Lucas and Sonia left, feeling that their presence was no longer essential.

With the exception of new staff arriving sporadically over the next few days, the rest of the week carried on in the same manner, and they were only a handful of units shy of their weekly target by Friday. Some staff members felt upset by this, and offered to come in on Saturday to make up the shortfall, and Sonia, after assurances that she really wasn't taking advantage of them, gratefully accepted. She did, however, make a note on the timesheets that the extra day would count for overtime pay.

Around the middle of the week, Andie's prediction had come to pass, and the failure of the DevConn devices was being widely reported. Sure enough, the news caused their stock to go into freefall, and if the CEO's house and car weren't on the market by Monday, it wouldn't be much later than that.

By the weekend, Andie no longer considered DevConn a a viable threat, and moved to head off any other attempts on the technology.

Press Release:

Ad Astra was recently subject to a violent but unsuccessful attempt to steal the technology behind its new communication device, the QED. While this particular incident has been resolved, it is of concern that such measures were taken so casually in order to gain competitive advantage. Any other entity considering the theft of Ad Astra's proprietary technology should be aware that the full weight of the law will be brought upon them should any further attempt be made.

INTERLUDE 3

With no progress on finding the person or persons who "stole" IVIA's quantum computer, purely because there was no such thief, tempers and nerves in the research facility were frayed to breaking point. In the case of Antonia Vélez and Kaito Mitsuhashi, that point had been exceeded long ago. Staff were staying inside their offices, not wanting to run into the two by chance. The corridor on which they both had offices was a no-go zone, but their arguments could be heard from much further afield.

"You and your team are the most incompetent pack of morons I have ever seen! It has been over four months and you have absolutely nothing to show for it. Tell me why I shouldn't just throw you all out on the street." Antonia's voice echoed through the corridors of the building as she berated Kaito.

"Because if you do that then you'll *never* get your QC back! I've been doing everything short of threatening their families to try and get results for you. You hired them yourself, and you know they're the best possible people. If the answers can't be found, then no amount of shouting at them will make the slightest difference. We're stuck with waiting for the thief to make a mistake."

"Like you did, you mean? I trusted you to execute my plan and look where it's got us!"

Kaito knew that it would be futile, not to mention dangerous, to suggest that it was the plan that was at fault. Antonia had never been one to accept culpability, and he suspected that the only reason he had the level of responsibility that he did, was so that she had someone to blame if anything went wrong.

He sighed. "Yes, Antonia, like I did. I failed to predict a random event 150 million kilometres away, and how its unstoppable particles would affect a procedure that everyone's calculations said was perfect. I'm not dwelling in the past, however – my team and I have spent the last four months working our asses off to find a solution and to find our missing technology. I'm simply saying that there is nothing more we can do until he lets a clue slip. Believe me, as soon as he trips up, we'll be all over him."

Antonia turned her back on Kaito. "Get out of my sight then. You go and do your *waiting*. Maybe he'll send us a fucking postcard."

Kaito left her office, breathing heavily. He had never been good at confrontation, but practise makes perfect, they say. He had endured nothing *but* confrontation over the last few months.

Martine had quietly been working on their theory that the tech company Ad Astra had somehow come to possess the quantum computer. Complex calculations had proved that an isolated farmhouse outside of the New Zealand town was the direct antipode of the IVIA lab, even down to the exact elevation above sea level. She was having trouble confirming the method by which the neutrino beam could have gone awry, short of a remarkable coincidence, and the solar particles from the sunspots hitting at an exact perpendicular angle. Without proof, however, she was working on a principle that she had heard accredited to the fictional English detective, Sherlock Holmes: Once you have eliminated the impossible, whatever remains, however improbable, must be the truth. From everything that Tomas had said, it was impossible for anyone to have deliberately diverted the beam, no matter what the crazy people in the next corridor thought. Therefore, a rational mind had to work on the assumption that it was a huge accident, and merely a combination of several highly improbable events.

Tomas Becker burst into Martine's office clutching a sheet of paper, his face excited.

"We think we've found another link! Yesterday, Ad Astra put out a press release, notifying of an attempt to take the secret of their QED technology by force, and warning against further interference."

Puzzled, Martine looked at him blankly. "What does that have to do with our problem?"

"One of my guys made a tentative connection with a report earlier in the week of a modem and router manufacturer going bankrupt because of an unidentified fault that hit their hardware. At first, it appeared to be connected to a recent software upgrade, but a rollback failed to fix it, and the path of the failures made my man think that it was more likely to be a virus. This was a very sophisticated attack, and the fact that it happened soon after someone tried to steal the QED technology is very suspicious. My take on this is that the violent attack reported by Ad Astra was traced back to this company—" he checked the sheet of paper "— DevConn, and someone ordered a cyber hit on them in retaliation. This isn't the sort of thing that can be put together at a moment's notice, *unless* you have some sort of supercomputer. The QC would have no trouble at all coding the virus and making the resulting failure of all DevConn devices look like simple negligence. I think we have a smoking gun."

"What do we do with this information?" asked Martine. "We haven't got any further finding Antonia's 'criminal', so they might be more inclined to believe our hypothesis, but with the mood they're both in, I don't want to be on the receiving end if I'm wrong about that."

Tomas sucked a breath in through his teeth, and turned to check that the door was closed.

"That might be the least of our troubles. I did what you asked, and found something very concerning. Antonia and Kaito had indeed been discussing their plans for the QC in internal emails, and you were dead right about them. Everything they wanted me to look for, they had been planning to do themselves. Data theft, military secrets, financial hacking – they would have made a killing, and maybe not just figuratively. They were prepared to sell information to anyone, even terrorists."

Martine was horrified. "In that case, we simply can't let them get the technology back! We'll all be branded accomplices, and life in prison would be the *best* we could hope for!"

Tomas sat down and covered his eyes with his hand. "I know," he said, "We're in a very difficult position. We can't just walk out, or they might suspect something, and if we go to the authorities, that evidence is sure to disappear in a heartbeat. I think our best option in to remain in place, and somehow keep them from finding out the truth, as well as making sure that they never manage to complete their experiment. I'm in an ideal position to induce failure in any other attempt to run the process, as I'm the one in charge of digital security, and you can drag your heels on shielding the lab from further solar interference. If they press you, come up with something that seems plausible, but will still be worthless."

Chewing her nails, she took a seat herself, before replying. "It's a high-stakes game you want us to play. Those two have obviously got a lot riding on this, and I wouldn't put it past Antonia to do something drastic if we're exposed."

"I know, but it's about more than just us. I can't imagine the consequences if they ever get their hands on a QC, one way or another. No, forget that. I *can* imagine, and that's worse."

Martine's shock and nervousness was replaced by steely determination. "You're right. It looks like we're the only ones who can keep them from wreaking havoc on the world, and I'm ready to do whatever it takes. I just don't know how I'll be able to look either of them in the eye without them seeing my revulsion."

RECRUITS

By the end of the following week, routine had set in amongst the workers at the factory, and U-net's first 650 units were complete, packed, and ready to deliver. The packaging had been outsourced, and was environmentally-friendly, consisting of a moulded pulp insert in a recycled-cardboard box, while the units themselves were vacuum-formed from a recycled plastic product and produced in-house.

The consumer model of the QED was a charcoal-coloured box with rounded corners, 15cm square and 3cm high. It had a socket for the externally-sourced 12V power supply, LEDs to indicate power and connection, and a single ethernet port. The top face of the device had a large, sky-blue "QED" in its centre, and a smaller Ad Astra logo in the top left corner. The ISP's version of the paired units was smaller, at 3cm x 3cm x 15cm. This had a different type of connector, as it would slot into a rack, and the socket at the back end of the unit provided both a data link and a power supply. The LEDs on the front indicated power and activity.

In addition to the 650 paired units, the factory had also produced seven of the metre-high racks that would each hold 100 of the stick-like devices. At the back of these racks were connections to the ISP's existing infrastructure.

While all these units were being manufactured, Andie had sourced additional lasers, to bring the production capacity of the facility to over 2000 per week. Reports of the generous working conditions had spread, and people previously hesitant had submitted their applications. Sonia had accepted all these newcomers, and the workforce now totalled over 200. On-the-job training was quickly bringing the new staff up to speed, and Sonia and Lucas no longer had to take active roles on the factory floor.

With the cases for U-Net on the truck, Lucas and Jake took up positions in their respective vehicles in front and behind, escorting the delivery to the city.

They met Malcolm Faulks at his company's building, and Jake helped the driver unload the truck. Leaning on the back of the truck, Lucas addressed the CEO.

"Well, Mr Faulks, I'm sure you're as excited as we are to see the QED finally rolling out to your customers. How has the response been so far?"

Nervously watching his precious cargo unloaded, Faulks dragged his eyes away to reply. "We ran a nationwide ad campaign, promoting the new service, and the interest was phenomenal. While we are initially concentrating on new accounts, we have had numerous enquiries from existing customers, hoping for higher internet speeds. It seems very popular with gamers. The lack of any lag is apparently a huge selling point for them."

"That's good to hear," said Lucas, "because you'll have another 2000 units next week!"

Smiling politely, Faulks turned back to ensure that Jake and the driver were taking suitable care with the boxes.

Over the following six weeks, after which time Ad Astra was entitled to supply the QED to other companies, the workers at the Taihape facility diligently turned out 2000 QED units per week, delivered to a happy Mr Faulks. Factories around the country had been completed and Andie had made appearances similar to that in the Taihape Town Hall, recruiting people to staff them. Sonia had created a cadre of instructors who would train the new staff, and made a whistle-stop tour herself to see that this was being done properly. Things were apparently well in hand for the QED to become a global household name.

As Lucas was talking to Andie one evening, getting the latest information on the additional QED contracts, he wondered whether he and Sonia were stretching themselves too thin. Granted, Andie handled all the paperwork, and was still selling TheOS through the online shop, but the two mere humans had been attending the face-to-face meetings, organising the setup of the new factories, and employing staff. The travel that these roles required was extremely tiring, and Lucas found his smile becoming more forced with each handshake and each cup of tea.

What he really needed, he thought, was middle-management; a team of trustworthy people who could be relied upon to oversee day-to-day operations of the now very large enterprise. He considered that these people would need to be head-hunted, as open advertising would almost certainly attract persons of dubious loyalty. But where to find people that he could trust absolutely, he pondered. By definition, they would have to be people he already knew, and he couldn't see Adele schmoozing CEOs. Sonny Kuratau was too rough around the edges for any people-oriented role, but perhaps they needed a security section...

Leslie and Robert Talbot had left the city to get away from corporate life, and almost everyone else in the district was either too old, or too 'country'. Being a country boy himself, he meant nothing offensive by that judgement, merely that they had neither the city-bred talent required, nor the cynicism that business seemed to thrive on.

His neighbours were not without skills, of course. The original settlers of back-country New Zealand had soon found innovative ways to get things done when the equipment and supplies they needed were half-a-world's sailing away. This so-called 'number-eight wire' attitude was a matter of great pride for the Kiwi farmers, and had been nurtured through generations.

Despite telling himself that their Kiwi ingenuity was obsolete, since they had Andie, Lucas remembered the matter of the laser in the woolshed. Maybe there was a place for some of that number-eight attitude after all.

Of course, the farmers themselves would be hard to tempt, considering their existing obligations to their land and stock. Retired farmers, if they could be found, might fit the bill, but such did not seem to exist around this area. It was not uncommon to see a man in his eighties or even nineties out on a steep hill with his tractor or shouting at a sheepdog two paddocks away.

Too old, too busy farming, too stubborn to retire; that left the too young, and the farm hands, who were too necessary. Of those, there were few that Lucas knew well enough to be suitable candidates. He was certainly going to have to look further afield for his team. There were school friends that he would once have trusted with his life; of course, as a teenager, he had valued his life less then! Perhaps it would be worth getting back in touch. Most of them he hadn't seen since the ten-year reunion the previous summer, though he kept up to date with their exploits on their social media pages. There was among them, a variety of skills that could be useful, if he could convince them to work with him. Some would be swayed by ideals, others by cold, hard cash. Choosing the right bait for each was paramount. He chided himself for thinking of his friends as tools to be manipulated. He was obviously too used to having things his own way. He had to admit that, with the exception of the DevConn affair, things had gone very smoothly until now. However, having reliable people around before anything went seriously wrong was vital. He spent the rest of that evening scouring his friends' social media to see whether they had desirable skills.

The next day, he began calling. Rather than drop bombshells over the phone, he planned to catch up in person with his friends. *Great. More travel,* he thought.

He had arranged to meet his first 'victim' at a café in a southern suburb of Wellington.

"Lucas, mate! Haven't seen you for donkey's."

"It was only last year, Paul. How've you been?"

Paul Bennington had been the halfback in Lucas's high school rugby team, a scrappy fellow with lightning-fast reflexes, and a mouth that had earned him no love from referees. Typical of a halfback, he had always been the smallest on the team, but had determination and tenacity belying his stature. An unruly mop of brown hair fell over his ears and eyes; narrow, calculating eyes that straddled his long, thin nose. These, combined with thin lips and a pointed chin could have caused him to look like a goblin, were his default expression not "cheerful".

A reluctant scholar, Paul went on from high school to earn a Bachelor of Commerce from Victoria University of Wellington, majoring in

Marketing. His talkative manner and quick wit made him a natural for the world of advertising. It is not an easy world to get a decent foothold in, however, and he was currently a low-level copywriter at a second-tier advertising agency.

"Oh, you know, mate. Same shit, different day. Last week I wrote copy for a spray that takes away the smell of baby shit, can you believe it?"

Ordering a cup of tea at the counter before taking a seat, Lucas grimaced. "That's too bad. Guess it doesn't do anything for the stench of failure, though," he joked.

"Yeah, up yours," Paul responded lightly, punching his friend none too gently in the arm. "I hear Saatchi's will be putting out for an intern later in the year, so I'm setting my sights on that. I suppose you're still living the dream, doing other people's yard work and surviving paycheck to paycheck."

"Funny you should mention that," said Lucas, laughing. "I ran into an old friend the other day and got myself a job in her business. I'm doing okay. In fact, I understand that there's a position opening up where a man of your particular talents would be most welcome. Unless you're happy writing insincere treatises on baby shit?"

Paul leaned back in his in his seat and took a sip of his cappuccino before replying.

"I dunno, mate. Sounds like an in-house marketing gig, and most of them outsource the sort off stuff I want to do. That's why I need this Saatchi internship."

"So PR Director of an exciting new company, with full autonomy and an unlimited budget doesn't stack up against Chief Coffee-boy at the beck and call of overpaid executives with an exaggerated opinion of their self-worth?"

Paul snorted derisively. "Now *you're* sounding like an ad man. 'Unlimited budgets' don't exist. You can't con a conman."

Bombshell time. "Have you heard of Ad Astra?"

"The tech company with the hot chick in charge. Everything they touch turns to gold."

"The very same. That 'hot chick', Andie Donovan, is an old family friend, and I'm in on the ground floor. Seriously, the PR job is yours if you want it. You'll be responsible for media and corporate liaison, a complete marketing department to run as you like, and you can name your salary."

Paul set his coffee down on the table and sat back, folding his arms. "I do have one question..."

"What's that?"

"When do I start?"

Lucas laughed. He had known that Paul wouldn't be happy in his current job, and had perfectly baited the hook with the promise of creative freedom and financial reward.

"Serve out your notice and you can come on board as soon as you like."

"Sod 'em. They can write their own shit spray stories. Show me my office and I'm there."

Suddenly uncomfortable, Lucas inhaled deeply and rubbed his jaw. "Yeah, slight problem there. We don't have an office yet. At the moment, it's just Andie, Sonia Matheson, and me."

"You're kidding. A billion-dollar business, and only three staff? You must be putting in some big hours."

"We do have thousands of people working for us, in the factories around the country, but yeah, only three in management. That's why I'm on the prowl for new blood, and who better than people I already know and trust?"

"So who else have you poached?"

"You're actually the first, but I do have my eye on a few others. Cath Whelan looks like she's doing well in business real-estate, and would be an asset in scouting locations for new factories. In fact, I'll probably be visiting her next. If I can get her on board, her first task will be finding us office space!"

The two old friends finished their drinks, Paul pushing for more information on Ad Astra, and his new role in the company. Lucas eventually had to cut the talkative young man off.

"Look, come on up to the farm when you're ready, and we'll sort out all the details then. I may as well explain things en masse, rather than repeat myself half a dozen times."

As they stood up to leave, Paul sheepishly asked, "Grab a lift? My car's not quite legal at the moment, and it's a fair walk from my nearest bus stop."

Leaving money on the table to cover the drinks, Lucas peeled off some additional notes and handed them to his friend.

"I'll run you home, but take this and get those wheels legit. Having our newest employee ticketed for no registration would be bad PR!"

Exiting the café, Paul looked up and down the street, looking for 'that old dunger of a Hilux', as he had called it when Lucas had arrived at the reunion in his tired Toyota.

"Couldn't find a park, eh? Guess I have to walk a bit anyway, then."

Momentarily puzzled, Lucas realised what Paul had been looking for. "Nah, thought I'd leave the old girl at home. She feels a bit out of place in the city. Here's my ride – told you I was doing okay!"

With Paul almost literally drooling over the sleek sportscar, Lucas drove him back to his rented house on the hill.

"That is so awesome, mate! I'm *definitely* getting me one of those with my first paycheck. Thanks for the lift – I'll be up at your place as soon as I can, promise. And thanks for the job. I reckon you've saved my life!"

Lucas took his friend by the hand and pulled him in for a shoulder bump.

"Good to see you. I'm looking forward to working with you again."

Waving from the open cockpit of the Jaguar as he pulled away, Lucas smiled, mentally checking off his first recruit.

His next stop was the seaside suburb of Miramar. Parking directly outside the real-estate agency where Cath Whelan worked, he announced himself at the front desk and waited patiently for her to come through to reception.

A slightly overweight, blonde woman with a cheerfully round face exited an office down the hallway and approached Lucas, waving and smiling brightly.

"Mr Winter, to what do I owe the dubious pleasure of your company today?"

Lucas poked his tongue out at her, saying, "Your face tells me that pleasure's not so 'dubious', Cath. You never were any good at hiding your emotions. It's lovely to see you, too. I was hoping I might take you out to lunch."

"Be still, my beating heart!" she exclaimed, fanning her face with a hand. "After throwing myself at you all through school, *now* you come and hit me up for a date?"

While it was true that he had been popular with the ladies, Cath had never actually shown any romantic interest in him. Her good-natured ribbing reminded him of how close their friendship had been, though. He hoped that she could be enticed away from her successful job here.

"Don't flatter yourself. It's not a date, but I do have a proposal for you."

Oops, he thought. He'd left himself wide open with that one. Sure enough, Cath pounced on his inadvertent double-entendre. She flung her arms around him with a squeal.

"Well, this is all a bit sudden, but I *do*! Now, I'll want a December wedding—"

"What you'll get, is lunch," interrupted Lucas, disengaging from her embrace. "Where's good?"

"You need lessons in letting a girl down gently, Lucas. Oh well, it was good while it lasted. Take me to Gustav's. It's a nice little place just a couple of minutes' walk away."

They walked arm in arm down the street, arriving shortly at a restaurant with open front windows, and tables on the footpath. Wanting some privacy, Lucas gestured to a table out the back door, under a market umbrella in the garden. After they had ordered, and were waiting for their food to arrive, Cath could no longer contain her curiosity.

"So what did you come down for, Lucas? Are you selling up the farm and need me to find you premises for an antique shop on the Quay? You want to buy a motel and convert it into a brothel for Russian sailors. You—"

Lucas passed her a business card. "I want you to work for me."

Chuckling at the thought of a successful young real-estate agent trying to make a living in a small village like Mangaweka, she took the card. Her jaw dropped as she immediately recognised the twin stars of the Ad Astra logo. Her brow furrowed as she read the lines on the card: Lucas Winter, CEO.

"You're messing with me, right? This can't be real."

Lucas rested his elbows on the table and clasped his hands, nodding. "One hundred percent on the level. I'm good friends with the owner, and she admired my drive and vision. I've already signed up Sonia Matheson as CTO, and Paul Bennington for PR. We desperately need someone to manage our existing properties, and purchase new ones. We currently have sixteen facilities around the country, and have plans for many more. I've been doing it myself up until now but having a dedicated manager would be a huge load off my shoulders. I know you're doing really well for yourself here, but if money's the issue ... well, let's just say that money is not an issue. We'll pay you what you're worth, and then some. You'll eventually be overseeing a global property portfolio, and I simply have to have someone I can trust in the job."

Cath threw a shrewd look at him. "Now you're trying to appeal to my vanity. I bet that you've given this a lot of thought, and you have no intention of walking out of here without a deal."

Their meals arrived, and Lucas offered Cath the rest of the lunch hour to think about it. She was right, of course. He *had* carefully considered the best approach for each recruit, and with no Plan B, he desperately wanted Cath on the team.

"So, where is head office?" she asked, after taking her last bite.

"I'm thinking Palmerston. It's central, and easier to find places for you all to live than the major cities. Does this mean you're in?"

Cath pretended to think for longer than necessary, but she had made up her mind. While finding the right properties for business clients in and around Wellington was satisfying, and paid well, there was no denying the allure of being involved with Ad Astra, and having the responsibility of her own international portfolio.

"You had me at 'Hello'. I'm surprised to find myself so excited at the prospect of leaving behind all that I've done here, but a future with your company sounds like more than I could ever have hoped for. At your service, Boss."

Lucas was delighted that his pitch had paid off, and raised his glass in a toast to Ad Astra's new Property Manager.

"Welcome aboard! You can start as soon as your current work will let you, but in the meantime, I need you to get us a building in Palmy, along with six or so houses. One of them will be yours, so choose wisely!"

He quickly told her the requirements for the offices, and gave her Jake's number, so that he could get started on fitting it out as soon as possible.

He walked her back to her office, and took her in a brief embrace before placing a soft kiss on her forehead.

"Thank you so much. It means a lot to me to have my friends coming into the family fold."

With a quick farewell, he vaulted into the Jaguar, showing off as he left her shaking her head.

There was one more appointment in Wellington before he was due home, and he headed for the downtown district where there would be no chance of parking on the street. He carefully manoeuvred the roadster into a tight spot in a parking building, and walked the short distance to the law offices of Halsey, Moore & White, where Michelle Tyson was a junior. After her four years of study, and finishing top of her class, she had been quickly snapped up by one of Wellington's most prestigious firms dealing in corporate and commercial law. Though she started at the bottom of the ladder, as a legal secretary drafting contacts, she soon progressed to practising. She had every chance of making partner some time within the next 8-10 years, and Lucas knew that it would be a hard sell to get her to give that dream up.

A young man at the reception desk directed him down the hall to Michelle's office. While not the sumptuously-appointed space of a partner, it was nonetheless moderately spacious and comfortable. Lucas supposed that you couldn't meet clients in the cramped broom closets that interns probably occupied.

"Hi, Shell. Glad you could fit me in."

The well-dressed, statuesque woman came around the desk to greet him. She wore her dark hair pulled back in a severe bun, and her full-rimmed glasses gave her a decidedly 'librarian' look. If librarians had the responsibility of multi-million dollar legal affairs. While not displeased to see Lucas, she gave the impression that he was nothing more than a distraction amidst the workings of the City.

"Lucas. I was surprised that you asked to see me at work. We could have gone clubbing tonight."

The image of this seemingly uptight woman dancing the night away would have confused many, but Lucas knew that the strict exterior hid a true party animal. She had let her hair down, literally, at the school reunion, and had still been dancing on the table when he had called it a night.

"Unfortunately, I've got to get on the road back north after this, but if it helps, this isn't a social call. My business needs legal representation."

"Well, sit down, then. I can't give you long, but lay it out for me and I should be able to point you in the right direction."

Lowering himself into one of the leather armchairs, he idly played with one of his business cards as he talked.

"Here's the thing – I don't want just any lawyer. I firmly believe in looking after my friends, and I need *you* to work on this."

Michelle's face softened fractionally. "That's very loyal of you to think that way. Now, I don't mean to disparage your business – gardener, isn't it? – but at $400 an hour, perhaps I'm not the most cost-effective person to be dealing with."

"I understand. Shall we have a talk about my needs anyway?"

"Of course. It's the least I can do. What's your problem?"

Lucas stopped fiddling with the business card and placed it face-down on the table in front of him. "I've got a contract to supply a nationwide company, and I need to make sure our business arrangement doesn't leave them any wiggle room. Firm, but fair, is what I want,. In addition, I need someone to explore the legal ramifications of some projects I have in mind for the future."

Frowning, Michelle said, "That ... doesn't sound like gardening. What are you up to, Lucas?"

He dramatically slapped his forehead. "Didn't I say? I'm not doing gardens so much these days. I'm here on behalf of a somewhat larger enterprise," he said, leaning forward to flip the card over.

Michelle craned her neck to read the card, adopting an expression he had already seen twice today. She raised her eyes to see him smiling at her. Sitting back, she placed a thumb under her chin and slowly tapped a finger against her lips. Giving Lucas a calculating look, she asked, "How many of these contracts are we talking about?"

Lucas shrugged. "Hundreds? Thousands? We really have no idea how big it will all get."

"It would seem that my measly $400 rate isn't going to scare off Ad Astra. You do realise that this would consume all my time. The partners would be delighted, of course, but as the attorney-of-record for it all, they might choose to keep me under their thumb, and hold off on making me a partner myself. If I was going to take Ad Astra on as a client, I think I'd need more of a commitment than your regular client-lawyer relationship.

"I'm guessing, since you're coming to me with this, that the company doesn't already have any legal representation, so I'm going to play hardball here. I'll look after your contracts and other aspects of commercial law, only if Ad Astra employs me as chief legal counsel. That is non-negotiable, as is the figure I'm about to write."

She scribbled an immodestly large number on a piece of paper and slid it across the table.

"Done," said Lucas, without looking at the paper.

Surprised, Michelle smiled wryly. "I think I've just been had."

Sitting deeper in the armchair, Lucas winked at her, saying, "I only set the scene. I honestly didn't know whether you'd give me the ultimatum. What would have happened if I'd just walked in and told you that you needed to come and work for us?"

"I probably would have talked myself out of it. Making it seem like my idea was brilliant."

"Thank you," he replied modestly. "You've always been goal-oriented, and I had you down as one of the trickiest converts."

"There are more?" she asked.

"I've got Pauly B in PR, I just picked up Cath Whelan for Property, and Sonia's been working with me for a couple of months. There are still one or two on my list, which is why I've got to head north this afternoon."

"Can I make a suggestion? You're going to need more than just corporate law. If you like, I can contact Tom Fenchurch – he's up in Auckland, doing international economic law. If you're expanding offshore, you're going to need someone in that field. I know he's not too happy about living up there, and thinks his talents are being under-utilised. He's as cocky as ever, but it sounds as if he actually does know his stuff."

Lucas considered this. Why travel all the way to Auckland if he didn't have to? He trusted Michelle's judgement, and would have to do so many times in the future, so why not delegate?

"That'd be great. Carte blanche. Offer him whatever he needs. His own department, house in Palmy, car, salary – whatever it takes."

Standing, they shook hands, as befitting a deal done in the offices of the esteemed Messrs. Halsey, Moore & White. Before leaving, he glanced at the piece of paper on the table and snorted.

"Nowhere near what I was expecting," he said, walking out before that could register with Michelle.

Driving home, he reflected on the fact that none of these people were completely necessary, as Andie could do – and already was doing, in the matter of contract law – all of the tasks he had just hired people for. While he had complete faith in Andie's abilities, though, he had never liked having a machine do a man's work, if it could be avoided. This wasn't a human-centric bigotry; he just knew that people needed work. Even the QED factories were only automated where it was absolutely necessary. The additional benefit of hiring the old school gang was the camaraderie. He'd missed them over the years, and was looking forward to having them a part of his life again.

WAIATA TANGI

Lucas arrived home in the late afternoon to see the little runabout that he had bought Sonia parked out the front. Eager to tell her of his day's conquests, he hurried inside, only to find the house empty.

"Andie, where's Sonia?" he asked as he walked through the house. He had installed microphones and speakers throughout so that he and Sonia could talk to Andie without having to be in the office. These were connected to custom-made QED units with audio-visual inputs instead of ethernet ports, and a rack in the office held the other halves of each unit.

"Hello, Lucas. She's out in the workshop playing. I gave her the design for our next project, and she raced off to make a start on it."

Lucas stopped, and turned back up the hallway to enter the office. Wanting to speak with Andie face-to-face, as it were, he took a seat in front of the computer. Today, the AI had chosen a coastal location, with her avatar depicted sitting on a rock, dangling her feet in a tidal pool.

"I didn't think that we were set up for that here. Couldn't it be dangerous?"

Andie flicked her hair back, and leaned down to trail her hand in the water.

"Don't worry, Lucas. She's not working on the core. She's just putting together an enclosure, and assembling the electronics. The new building over in Taihape isn't far off completion, though, and we'll soon be able to start putting together the prototype. There was some hassle getting the high-voltage lines brought in, but Jake waved the Ad Astra chequebook at the problem and it miraculously disappeared."

Relieved that Sonia wasn't fooling around with high voltage and dangerous technology in the old woolshed, he went out to see what she was doing.

As he entered, he saw that she had already fabricated two 30cm cubes from sheet-metal, and was currently soldering components into a circuit board. So intent was she on her work, that she jumped, and dropped the soldering iron when he cleared his throat behind her.

"Bloody hell, Lucas! Don't scare me like that."

She picked up the hot tool from the floor and placed it in its holder on the workbench. Rolling her chair back, she looked up at him and raised an eyebrow. "So?"

He sat in the other chair and gave her a thumbs-up. "Got PR, Property, and Law sorted. I'm off to see Fats tomorrow, and might have time to head over to the 'Naki to catch up with Foxy."

Sonia's eyes lit up. She and Alison Fox had been inseparable at school, but over the intervening years, distance and work had seen them lose touch with each other.

"Can I come with you to Taranaki?" she asked excitedly. "Maybe we could stay the night – go out on the town with her."

Lucas hesitated. Sonia and her friend had been wild enough at school. He could barely imagine the trouble they'd get into with credit cards and ID. "Do you promise to behave?"

Sonia drew a halo over her head. "Brownies' honour, Boss! I'm *far* more responsible now."

Her cheeky grin, and the fact that he could see the barely concealed crossed fingers on her other hand, gave him the impression that this would not end well, but the two girls had always been such fun, he could not refuse her plea.

"Okay, but I'm not letting you two out of my sight. Do you want to come to Waiouru with me too?"

Wrinkling her nose, Sonia's excitement abated. "You can pick me up on the way back through, can't you? If I'm going to be having a fun night with Foxy, I don't want to kick it off with Fats. He's *so* square!"

"Give him a break – he might be a bit straight-laced, but his folks sacrificed a lot to send him to school, and he wasn't going to risk getting in trouble. Then there was the team. Rugby meant everything to him, and you don't stay captain for long after a visit to the headmaster's office. He's more chilled-out these days."

"Lucas, he's in the *army* now! That stick up his ass will only have got longer."

"Okay, I'll admit he wasn't exactly the life of the party at the reunion, but I did spend quite a bit of time talking to him before I started slurring my words. I think we need him."

Sonia pouted. "Fine. Just don't get him to organise the staff Christmas party. Pick me up after."

Lucas hoped that hiring Fats wouldn't create any conflict between the two. His ex-captain actually had a decent sense of humour, but had been so committed to his rugby and his schoolwork that he may have come across as dour. He was certain to be a valuable member of the team, however. One thing Fats had always done very well was teamwork.

Sonia had already gone to her room, presumably deciding what to wear on her night out. Events had been hectic ever since she had arrived at the farm, and she was well overdue for some fun.

The following day, Lucas left home around 10am, driving the half hour up the main road to Waiouru, the army's primary training camp. To the east of the small township and large military base, were the wild hills of the Kaimanawa Range, and on the other side was the volcanic area of the Central Plateau. Three active volcanoes jutted up from the surrounding alpine desert, popular with hikers and skiers alike. At Waiouru's 1000m altitude, the early winter temperature was in single digits, and Lucas was glad that his job didn't entail trudging through knee-deep snow with a backpack and a rifle. This day was clear, however, and the recent snow on the mountains under the blue sky was a sight to behold as he pulled up to the gates of the camp. Identifying himself to the gate guard, he was directed to the visitor parking area, and told to wait for an escort. Following the instructions, Lucas parked the Hilux and was met by a fresh-faced youngster in camouflage fatigues.

"Mr Winter? I'm Private Hill. I'm to take you to Sergeant Fatialofa. Please come with me."

The private led him to the edge of the parking lot, where they climbed into a decidedly un-military vehicle – an electric golf cart – in forest green, naturally. Five minutes later, they arrived outside a collection of long, low buildings. Outside the corrugated loading door of the nearest building waited Bobby 'Fats' Fatialofa.

The nickname 'Fats' was a misnomer, and obviously derived from the man's surname, as there was not an ounce of flab on his stocky, six-foot-plus frame. The muscular Samoan no longer had the trademark afro that had made him so easy to spot on the rugby field; in true military style, his tightly-curled dark hair was cropped close to his skull. He stood at ease in the ubiquitous army fatigues as Lucas alighted from the cart. Taking the proffered hand, Lucas clapped his friend on the shoulder.

"Fats, mate. Looking smooth."

Fats jerked his chin up in acknowledgement. "Hey, bro. Good to see you. I don't get a lot of visitors, especially in winter. You wanna come in for a coffee?"

Nodding, Lucas followed Fats in the side door to a small anteroom with uncomfortable-looking chairs and an automated hot drink dispenser.

"Sorry there's no cappuccino, bro. The army prefers to spend its money on guns and stuff, y'know?"

"Tea's fine for me, Fats. I never got into the whole coffee culture. Black, two sugars, thanks."

Lucas sat down in one of the hard-backed chairs, and while his old teammate got the drinks, reviewed his memories of Bobby Fatialofa. Captain of the 1st XV, Fats had played at number seven, or openside flanker. Though calm and logical in the leadership role, he was also ferocious at the breakdown, where his job was to get in quickly and gain possession of the ball from the tackled player. His keen analytical mind allowed him to direct his team with ruthless efficiency, while his confidence and firm discipline made them follow him.

Lucas supposed that all these qualities were ideally suited to a military life, though he had honestly expected Fats to be wearing something more than sergeant's stripes.

Fats handed him his tea, taking a chair in the other side of the coffee table, saying, "Here you go, bro. So, what brings you to my chilly part of the world?"

"Curiosity, for the most part. You're a Supply Technician, right? Is that like a quartermaster?"

"Basically," replied Fats. "I guess that's the old name for it. These days they've got this fascination for fancy words. You know, how a cleaner is now a Sanitation Engineer. I've got a bunch of warehouses here, and I have to make sure that everyone has what they need, when they need it. I've driven every type of vehicle they have, and I know all the equipment inside-out.

"They put me through some courses in logistics, and warehouse and inventory operations. Heaps of computer stuff, but it's not too bad – their systems are pretty idiot-proof!"

"So you're enjoying it, then?" asked Lucas.

Fats glanced around quickly before answering. "To tell the truth, bro, I've always been better at giving orders than taking them. Especially when I can see a better way of doing things, but the dick of a major can't see past his bloody regulations."

"What about promotion, mate? I would have figured you for some sort of leadership role."

Fats shrugged. "I did try out, but I guess I just wasn't what they wanted, bro. You gotta have more book smarts than me for the officer path, I reckon."

"Well, maybe you're in the wrong business for promotion. I bet you could go a long way in the private sector."

"I dunno, eh. I've put a lot of time in here, and don't want to start at the bottom again."

Lucas leaned in conspiratorially. "I know you're made for better things than this, Fats. That's why I came up here. Come and work for me. I can promise you better pay, better house, cooler toys, and the sky's the limit."

Fats looked understandably dubious of Lucas's claims. "That's a bit tough to swallow, bro. What's the story?"

"Did I ever tell you about my friend Andie Donovan?"

Fats shook his head, and Lucas continued. "She's this total genius, and started a company that writes computer software, and has just put out a new communication device. I'm in tight with the company and I'm recruiting special people to run it."

"What do you want a soldier like me for?"

"I don't need a soldier – I need a Logistics Manager. You know logistics. You've got the drive, you've got the work ethic, and you'll get the best out of your people. Just like on the rugby field, you'll have the freedom to think outside the box to get the job done."

Fats stood, and walked to the window. Covering his eyes briefly, and running his hand over his head, he stared out at the base for a few seconds before putting his hands on his hips, turning back to Lucas.

"Tempting, bro. It'd be nice not to wear a uniform for the first time in fifteen years. It'll take me three months to get out, though."

Lucas got up and shook his friend's hand.

"Leave that to me, mate. I read that the Defence Force is due for a communications upgrade, yeah?"

"That's right. You know, I actually suggested that new QEB thing to the major, but he brushed me off. Not their regular supplier, not military-grade, not in his 'book.'"

"It's 'QED', and our company makes it. I reckon we can make a military-grade version, and we'll go so far over your major's head that he'll snap his neck trying to look up at us. I think that rushing your resignation will be a small price for the brass to pay. You better start packing your bags."

Fats used the internal telephone network to arrange Lucas a ride back to his ute, and they said their goodbyes. Waiting for the golf cart to arrive, Lucas wondered if he had exaggerated Ad Astra's influence by promising to get Fats out early.

When he got back to the Toyota, and on the road home, he dialed Andie and put the phone in hands-free mode as he discussed with her the specifications that he felt a military version of the QED would require. It would have to work more like a radio than a modem, it would need to be lightweight, and it obviously had to be tough. There were plenty of options for portable 12V batteries, and a rubberised moulding would ensure that it could handle some knocks. The point-to-point security would be a major benefit, and the system could be deployed as personal radios, in vehicles, and throughout the command structure.

"Once you've got the plans developed, I'll need you to contact Paul Bennington. Get him to work up a pitch, and warn him that he might have to face some Defence Force bigwigs. Get Michelle Tyson to draft a contract, and let Sonia know that she'll need to re-tool one of the factories for it. Maybe you should make the initial contact, and try to work in an early release for Sergeant Bobby Fatialofa. Will you be okay with all that?"

"Lucas, sometimes I think you forget just who you're talking to! The redesign of the QED will barely take any time at all, and the only bottleneck in getting your people to do their jobs will be the painstakingly slow speed of the human brain."

Abashed, Lucas apologised. She was right; sometimes he did forget that he was talking to an AI whose thought processes eclipsed any person ever born. *That's the price she pays for being so human-like*, he mused.

"Oh, and tell Sonia that I'll be home in half an hour. We'll leave after lunch." he added before ending the call.

On his return to the farm, he parked the Hilux under shelter, and drove the Jaguar out of its shed. Fiddling with the light canvas roof, he finally remembered how it worked. He made sure to tell Sonia to wear something warm, as the lack of side windows made the roadster decidedly draughty!

After lunch, he loaded their overnight bags into the boot, and called his nearest neighbour to have them keep an eye on Splash before setting off on the three-hour drive to New Plymouth, in the Taranaki region, on the west coast. As they drove around the distinctive conical volcano of Mt. Taranaki, he remembered a local once telling him how to predict the weather in the region.

"If you can't see the mountain, it's raining. If you can see it, it's going to rain."

He thought this a little unfair, as the day was still glorious, though a little cold. Nonetheless, he had taken the precaution of reserving rooms in a hotel that offered covered parking. Just to be safe.

They arrived in New Plymouth in the late afternoon, checking into their rooms before walking downtown to find Alison.

"You didn't say what Foxy's doing these days," Sonia commented as they walked. "The last I heard, she had finished her BSc and was hoping to get government work."

171

"That didn't pan out, apparently," Lucas replied, "though she is working for the people of New Zealand, in a roundabout way."

His evasion made her suspicious, and she turned to look at him. "And what does that mean, exactly?"

"I think you'll find that out shortly," he answered cryptically, as they approached the local offices of an offshore oil-drilling company. On the footpath outside the building was a group of about ten people, holding placards and handing out leaflets. For the most part, they were dressed appropriately for the conditions, wearing warm woollen jerseys and beanies. Some of the protestors sported the dreadlocks, goatees, and piercings often associated with environmental activists, while others were more conventional in their appearance. One in particular stood out, however. A young Māori woman wore a wetsuit, and would have been considered attractive, had her features been distinguishable through the coating of thick, black liquid that coated her from head to toe. The substance clumped in her long hair, and rivulets ran down her face and body to pool at her bare feet. Her arms were spread wide in supplication, and she sang a song in traditional Māori style, or *waiata*.

Lucas waved at her, and waited until she had finished the sad-sounding song. As the last notes faded away, she ran over to greet him and Sonia.

"*Tēnā koutou, aku hoa aroha*. Hello, my dear friends. It has been too long!" she said with a huge grin, extending her arms as if to embrace them.

Sonia gave her old friend a fond smile, tinged with revulsion at the state of her. "Good to see you too, Foxy, but there is no way in hell I'm giving you a hug right now! What *are* you covered in – is that oil?"

"No way! It's molasses. I'm not going to pollute the place even more, just to make a point. We're trying to highlight the risks of oil spills in our pristine environment, and these guys—" she pointed at the building behind her "—are about to start test drilling near the Māui dolphin sanctuary."

"What was that you were singing?" asked Lucas.

"A *waiata tangi*, a lament for the land. We are supposed to be its guardians, not its rapists. The land is crying, but no one hears its voice."

"So what time do you knock off? I think Sonia's starting to get a little creeped out by the creature from the black lagoon!"

Alison glanced down at Lucas's watch. "The people inside should be starting to go home soon, and I can take off after we get in their faces a bit."

"Righto, we'll stay to watch the show and wait till you're done."

He and Sonia stepped off to the side, just as the first of the office workers began to exit the building. The unlucky oil company employees had to run a gauntlet of accusation as they descended the steps, before coming face to face with Alison at the bottom.

"This is what happens to the *kororā*, the Little Blue Penguin, when it has to swim through an oil slick to feed or nest! Have you no shame? Do you not feel guilty for enabling these people? These people who risk destroying our *taonga*, our treasures? Turn your backs on them, and embrace the land that shelters you and nourishes you. Tell them, 'No more! No more will I be a party to the systematic *rape* of our beautiful country!'"

Lucas had to admit, she certainly did her job well. She was eloquent, imposing, and confrontational, but the workers were under strict instructions not to respond to the protestors, for fear that the situation would escalate. The oil company didn't need any more bad publicity.

After the workers, heads down, had departed, the protestors began packing up their signs and their flyers. Alison came back over, using the edge of her hand to squeegee the worst of the molasses from her face and hair.

"My place is just up the road – walk me home?"

On the way to Alison's flat, she and Sonia chatted about old times, and how Alison had ended up on the main street of New Plymouth, caked in sickly-sweet gunk.

"I'd just got my degree in Environmental Science, and wanted to work with the government on environmental policy. At that time though, I just didn't think they were doing enough, and still seemed scared to alienate the corporate offenders. I'd already been to a few Greenpeace protests, and got talking to some of the organisers. My education came in handy, and I started taking a larger role. Most of my work for them is putting together scientific papers and writing pieces for the digital mailouts, but I still like to get boots on the ground sometimes." She looked down at her bare feet. "So to speak."

"That's all pretty cool," said Sonia. "I don't think I ever had what it takes to believe in a cause. Well, not until I started working with Lucas, that is."

Alison looked puzzled at this comment. She looked at Lucas. "I know you're a country boy, and a bit of a greenie at heart, and I could see you doing something organic with your place, but what could that have to do with Miss Electrical Engineer here?"

"Why don't we get to that in a bit? Let's get in out of the cold and wait for you to wash that crap off."

Pulling open the garden gate in front of an attractive villa, Alison said, "Fine by me." She unlocked the front door for them. "Make yourselves at home – I'm just going to nip around the back and hose off."

Lucas and Sonia entered the cosy, two-bedroom house and made their way to the lounge. Sitting on a sofa bedecked with cushions and a throw-rug, they looked around the room. Greenpeace promotional material, posters of whales, and indigenous artworks covered the walls, and it was impossible to miss the fact that this was the home of someone in touch with the environment and her heritage.

Alison came in the back door and headed for the bathroom, calling down the hall, "Someone better be putting the kettle on!"

Sonia looked at Lucas, as he feigned intense interest in a Māori carving on the side table. Sighing, she made her way to the kitchen.

Shortly, Alison emerged from the bathroom, wrapped in a fluffy robe, and vigorously drying her hair with a towel.

"That stuff gets everywhere, but fortunately it washes out easily with hot water. Just as well the sun's been out today, or I wouldn't have had any!"

Sonia had made them all a hot drink, and handed one to Alison. "I hope you haven't changed how you have your coffee, since school."

"Black and sweet, just like me?"

"Same old coffee, same old line," Sonia laughed.

"So do I get that hug now?" asked Alison, placing her cup on an intricately carved coaster. The two women embraced warmly before sitting down.

"Cute place you've got," remarked Sonia.

"Thanks. It's not completely off-grid, but I've got solar panels, and solar hot water on the roof. There's a nice breeze that comes in from the ocean that runs an efficient little turbine on the roof, and energy storage in some deep-cycle batteries. What I don't use, I'm selling to the electricity company. For a pittance, I might add."

"Why aren't you using one of the new batteries, like a Tesla?" asked Lucas.

"In theory, they're better storage, but the lead-acid ones are more recyclable. Lithium mining also has a high environmental impact. The cost to the planet simply doesn't justify me saving a few dollars, especially since so much of our electricity comes from renewables anyway."

Sonia had been appraising her old friend as she spoke, and noted that she hadn't changed much in the last ten years. Alison was of medium height, and slender without being skinny. Straight, dark hair hung to her waist, and fine, elegant features were complemented by her light-brown skin tone. She had always been an attractive girl, but had seemed to be the only one not to notice. This was borne out by her appearance earlier in the afternoon as a swamp monster. Vanity had never been a fault of Alison's, and her apparent obliviousness to her beauty had only added to her appeal. Sonia had often encouraged her to make more of it, but Alison had always felt that it was more important to be accepted for who you were, not what you looked like.

Lucas looked over at Sonia and raised his eyebrows. "Shall we get down to business, or do we want dinner and drinks first?"

"Oh no, we're going to talk later," she replied. "She'll be no fun at all tonight if we fill her head with all that now."

This exchange caused Alison to cock her head in confusion. She had assumed that this was a social visit, but it now seemed that her friends had an ulterior motive.

"Judging by that, I guess there's no point in me asking what the hell you're talking about. Let me get dressed, and you can take me to dinner." She took a large gulp of her coffee and left the lounge.

Sonia followed, saying to Lucas as she left, "I'd better help. That girl has no fashion sense!"

Lucas was left, like so many men before him, twiddling his thumbs while the women-folk did their clothes and make-up. It was not long, however, before the two women returned. Alison was dressed simply, in jeans and a loose sweatshirt, her face unadulterated by make-up. From the look on Sonia's face, this would not have been her first choice.

"I tried to get her to glam up a bit – a nice dress to show off that gorgeous body."

Allison waved a hand dismissively. "I told you – I don't even *own* a dress, hon! This is comfortable, and I'm not going to make myself up to be some sort of sex object for the sleazebags downtown. Take me as I am. You know that."

"Well you both look just fine," said Lucas. "I've got a table booked at Colombia, and if we take a leisurely walk down, we'll be there in plenty of time."

"Uh uh," retorted Sonia. "This one might be happy looking like we just dragged her in off the street, but *I* have to stop by the hotel and put my glad rags on. I'll be as quick as I can."

Alison rolled her eyes at Lucas, who shrugged, as if to say, "Women. What can you do?"

Walking out to the street, they strolled arm-in-arm to the hotel. Lucas and Alison made idle chit-chat while Sonia went to her room to put on her face and "glad rags".

She returned more quickly than either of the two expected, wearing a figure-hugging red dress and a black velvet choker. She struck a catwalk pose, nearly toppling off her four-inch stilettos. Managing to refrain from laughter, Alison and Lucas made appropriate noises of appreciation, satisfying Sonia's desire for approval. The three friends left the hotel and walked a short distance to the Colombia Restaurant. The Colombia styled itself as a fine dining establishment, and though the maître d' looked admiringly at Sonia, Alison ignored the barely perceptible sneer of contempt that flickered across his face as he took in her casual attire.

They were shown to their table, which would have had an ocean view in daylight, and presented with leather-bound menus.

"This is all very swanky," commented Alison. "You must really want something from me."

Lucas and Sonia ignored the hint, as they did Alison's repeated probes throughout the meal, hoping for information regarding the reason for their visit. After an excellent meal, and an evening of the casual intimacy that occurs when people know each other too well for pretension, they took their leave of the expensive restaurant and its not-too-subtle snobbery. As Lucas was paying the bill, Alison caught sight of his Platinum Amex.

"A five-star hotel, snooty restaurant, and a platinum card? Somebody's done well for themselves. Care to share, or is that all part of your big secret?"

Lucas grinned at her. "All in good time, my dear. We'll probably need to get a few more drinks into you before you're ready. Ready to go clubbing?"

They heard the club long before seeing it, and a short way up the street, they entered a nondescript wooden door nestled between an all-night fast food joint and a second-hand bookshop. Climbing a flight of stairs, the atmosphere hit them at the top; a heady mix of alcohol, testosterone, and sweat. The heavy bass reverberated through their bodies as they shouldered their way through the throng of gyrating bodies to reach the bar.

"What do you want?" Lucas asked the women as he tried to catch the bartender's eye, shouting to be heard over the music. Sonia pointed at a bottle being passed over the bar to a girl next to them; a green, pre-mixed vodka concoction. Alison nodded in agreement and when Lucas had the bartender's attention, he made hopeful miming actions to back up his shouted order. Having received, and paid for, their drinks, the trio once again negotiated the dancefloor to make their way out to the balcony. The fresh air and relative quiet were a relief to him, though the two women seemed already intoxicated by the atmosphere. As he handed them their bottles, Alison said, "I love this place, but isn't it just a microcosm of the world in general? Too loud, too many people, everyone out for what they can get." She pointed at a small puddle of vomit under the table beside them. "And there's the pollution."

"You're not going to be a downer, are you, Foxy?" asked Sonia, already starting to move subconsciously to the beat of the music leaking through the closed glass doors of the balcony.

"Just social commentary, hon," laughed Alison. "Should we make Lucas mind our drinks and handbags while we dance?"

"You don't have handbags," scoffed Lucas, "and if you wait a few minutes, we can finish the drinks and we can *all* dance. Unless you're embarrassed to go out on the floor with me?"

177

"Not at all, tall, blond and handsome," Sonia said, punctuating her comment with a generous swallow of her drink. "Are you sure we won't cramp your style?"

"You've seen me dance, haven't you? I don't *have* any style!"

Several drinks, multiple sweaty dances, and numerous jokes at each other's expense later, they found themselves once more on the balcony, catching their breath.

"Do you think she's ready?" Lucas asked Sonia.

"Honey, I've been ready for hours!" exclaimed Alison. "You guys have been stringing me along all night and I want to know your secret."

"Believe me, Foxy, you're never ready for *this*," said Sonia. She and Lucas had discussed, on the drive over, the best approach to take when recruiting Alison. They had both agreed that ideology was their best bet, and had decided to tell her much more than Lucas had told any of the others.

"This really isn't the right place for it, anyway," Lucas said. "We should probably go back to the hotel."

They finished the last of their drinks, and made their way down the stairs. Walking three abreast back to the hotel, Lucas noticed the admiring looks from passing men, and felt proud to be accompanied by two such striking women. Admitting to himself that the women had not been as much of a handful as he had predicted, he chastised himself for having judged them on their teenage behaviour.

At the hotel, he and Alison waited in his room while Sonia went back to hers to change clothes. She soon returned, looking more casual in jeans and a t-shirt.

"So. Spill," demanded Alison, as they made themselves comfortable on the lounge suite.

Lucas took a deep breath before exhaling loudly. "Here's the thing. Sonia and I are working for a company owned by an old friend of mine. This company's primary goal is to fix the problems that we face in today's world, and money is no obstacle. We have already started a revolution in the communications industry, and have several similar projects in the pipeline. We've hired several old school friends in positions of authority – Pauly B in marketing, Cath Whelan in property, Bobby Fatialofa in logistics, and Michelle Tyson and Tom Fenchurch in legal – but we're missing the environmental factor. We need someone to ensure that our manufacturing facilities are doing the best they can, environmentally, and to identify possible future issues.

"The company's founder is an absolute genius, and has submitted several papers on processes that may help to mitigate existing ecological problems, but having someone with the education and experience in the field would be invaluable. My boss's high IQ doesn't necessarily compare to first-hand knowledge of the issues, and if you truly want to help effect change, I honestly believe that there could be no better place for you to apply your skills and devotion to the cause."

Alison sat quietly for a moment, trying to take this in. She had always considered corporate culture to be inherently evil, with companies taking what they could with no thought for future generations, and constantly lobbying governments for favourable regulations at the expense of nature. Here, though, there seemed to be a company with a genuine conscience, apparently committed to rectifying the mistakes unbridled capitalism had brought upon the world. She had vowed to never risk compromising her ethics by succumbing to the temptation of the corporate world, yet she felt that she could trust Lucas when he implied that this company wanted to be part of the solution, rather than part of the problem.

"I've heard of a few new ideas coming out in the climate-reversal field, like artificial cooling of ocean currents, and CO_2-eating bacteria – are you talking about things like that?"

"If you're thinking of genuine, achievable processes, then yes. Those two in particular are Andie's ideas. Those are for long-term change, but what we're focusing on currently is reducing the harm done in the future, and changing the mindset about how resources are used."

While still conflicted, Alison could see the benefits in their goals, and if this Andie was as smart as Lucas suggested, then this was a real opportunity for massive change.

"What's your take on this, Sonia?" she asked.

Sonia nodded eagerly. "This is the real deal, Foxy. Andie is on to it, and the company is the best possible vehicle for change. It won't happen overnight, but it *will* happen."

Allison sighed as she considered her options.

"This is big, guys," she said as she got up to pace the living area. "I honestly couldn't give you an answer right now, but let me sleep on it, okay?"

"That's all we need, sweetie," replied Sonia. "I know it's a huge decision for you, and not one to be made after a few drinks. You go home and think it over, and we'll meet you for lunch at that mediterranean café we passed on the way home. Eleven thirty. Deal?"

"Deal. I'm going to head off now, then, before I fall asleep on my feet, and I'll see you tomorrow. Thanks for the night out, you two. It's been a real blast. It was so good to see you both again."

With that, she gave each of them a brief hug and headed out the door, calling out a Māori farewell as she left. "*Ka kite anō kōrua!*"

Sonia turned to Lucas. "Do you think she'll go for it?"

"I reckon so. Especially if we tell her what the next product is. We'll find out tomorrow."

They said goodnight and Sonia returned to her own room. Lucas kicked off his shoes and collapsed onto the bed fully clothed, exhausted.

HOUSE HUNTING

The next day, after a late breakfast in the hotel restaurant, they checked out of their rooms and arranged to leave the car in the hotel's parking until after lunch. Taking a leisurely stroll around the seaside city while they waited for their lunch appointment, Lucas and Sonia arrived at the Café Cassis at eleven-thirty. Alison was already waiting there for them, and with a cheery "*Kia ora*!", she waved them over to the table.

"Morning, Foxy," said Sonia. "You look remarkably bright and breezy."

"I'm out two or three nights a week. I guess I'm just more used to it than you country types," Alison said, sliding menus across the table to them. "They do a great job here. I'm going for the Socca and Tapenade, but the Niçoise and Bouillabaisse are pretty good, too."

When a waiter came to the table, Sonia opted for the salad, while Lucas chose the fish stew. Pouring water for himself and Sonia, he raised an eyebrow at Alison.

"I'm surprised you got any sleep at all. I figured you had a big decision to make, and would have been up all night."

She shook her head. "Not the sort of call to make when your head's fuzzy. I thought it over on my run down the beach this morning. Look, guys, I really appreciate the offer, and I understand what you're trying to do, but long-term plans like CO2 reduction and ocean cooling aren't going to make it worth leaving the important work I'm doing at the moment. I feel I'm playing a vital role in education and activism. We simply have to stop these guys trying to wring the last drops of oil out of the ground, and polluting the environment as they do so. I'm sorry, but I can't accept the job. I'm hope you don't feel I've wasted your time."

"Not at all," said Sonia, reaching over the table to take Alison's hand. "It was worth it just to catch up with you. We have to do it again sometime."

"Absolutely," agreed Lucas. "No hard feelings. Now tell us about some of the exciting things you've been doing with Greenpeace."

She proceeded to tell them tales of high seas encounters with oil survey ships and whalers, various things she had chained herself to, and the times she had been arrested.

The meals arrived, and they fell silent as they savoured the delicious French dishes. Once the plates were empty, and cleared away, Alison asked if they'd be ordering coffee.

"We'd better not," said Sonia. "We really should be getting back so we can make a start on the next product. It's going to slash the demand for fossil fuels."

Intrigued, Alison asked what the product would be.

"Sorry – commercially sensitive information, you know!" Lucas said with a wink.

"Oh, we can tell her, can't we?" asked Sonia. "It's not as if she's going to go blabbing to the energy companies about it."

Apparently relenting, though this had been part of the backup plan the whole time, Lucas glanced around the café, and leaned in conspiratorially, whispering two words to Alison.

Her eyes went wide and she looked to Sonia for confirmation, who nodded.

"Is that even possible?" she asked incredulously.

Lucas smiled as he replied, "Believe me, you get a whole different idea of what's possible when it comes to my friend Andie. We're going to shake up the energy sector so bad, they'll be hiding under their desks."

"And this is something that's happening now, not in twenty years?"

"Within the week, the prototype will be running. Within a month, we'll be mass-producing units. Once we find someone who knows the energy companies well enough to deflect any pushback, we'll go public."

Suddenly thoughtful, Alison looked at them accusingly. "You're playing me. Big build-up, tempting concept, then when I decline, you hit me with something that I can't refuse. I'm not sure I like being manipulated like that."

"It's no game, Alison," said Lucas. "We honestly want you aboard, but this thing really is a secret. Even the others don't know about it yet. Though they might not be the absolute best in their respective fields, we couldn't hire outside our circle. There's just too much at stake. If word of our plans gets out prematurely, things could go pear-shaped like *that*," she said, snapping her fingers.

Alison's face took on a resigned look. She sighed. "I'm beginning to think I don't have a choice. I can see just how important this is going to be, and now that I know your secret, I think I need to be a part of it. You're right about needing someone to fend off the big boys, and I've studied then enough to know all their tricks, and their weaknesses."

She paused, looking from Sonia to Lucas and back. "Count me in. I've been on the front line against these assholes for too long, with too little result. I'm looking forward to sticking it to them."

"Atta girl, Foxy," said Lucas. "You won't regret it."

They arranged for her to move to Palmerston North as soon as she could, and said their goodbyes, walking out of the café leaving her wondering exactly what she was getting into.

As they walked back to the hotel to collect the car, Sonia said to Lucas, "Think she'll forgive us? Maybe we could have been more upfront with her."

He shrugged. "So far everyone only knows what they need to. It might have worked out okay if we gave them all the whole story in the first place, or they might have thought us crackpots. Once everyone's settled in, we'll have a team meeting and bring them up to speed. I don't want them too distracted while they're still finding their feet."

The day had turned overcast, with occasional drizzle, and they were grateful for what protection the car's canvas roof offered as they drove home. It had been a busy two days for Lucas, and he was looking forward to getting back to the relative peace and quiet of the farm.

However, when they got home, Andie was full of questions, and news. Splash, who had rarely been separated from his master for so long, also demanded attention.

"So, you got the environmentalist? Did you have fun on your road trip? When are we starting the next phase? Oh, I have the designs for the military QED, and your two friends are working on their tasks. Are we moving to the city? The lawyer, Michelle, said something about a house in Palmerston North."

Lucas disengaged himself from an overly clingy spaniel and held up a hand, though Andie had no eyes in the kitchen.

"Whoa! Slow down," he said, as he walked through to the office. "Yes, we got Alison, though she was a harder sell than the others. Yes, we had fun – we went drinking and dancing, and had two excellent meals. The next phase starts right now, and while the head office will be in town, I'm still not sure if I want to move. Sonia still has responsibilities at the new building in Taihape, getting the new product started, and I don't know if I'm ready for city life."

Sonia looked up from where she was crouched playing with the dog, disappointed at this last comment. "I think it would be a good idea to be with the rest of the team. I could always commute from there, or we could move the new equipment into a building in town. I'm sure there are plenty we could buy and fit out. If you're going to be in charge of this project, you really have to make the commitment. I know you love this place, but it will always be here. Think about it."

Lucas sat in the office chair and sighed. "Andie, am I being selfish, wanting to stay out here when all the hard work is going to be happening at the office?"

The shoulders of Andie's avatar lifted in a shrug, and she adopted a sympathetic expression. "It's not for me to say, Lucas. Obviously, I can do my work from anywhere, but perhaps Sonia has a point. The farm will always be here, and maybe it would be better to be with your team. You could always come back for weekends. It's your decision, however."

Lucas grunted non-committally as he left the room.

Sonia looked at Andie. "*Is* it selfish? I mean, apart from being the visionary behind it all, he frankly doesn't have any management skills, and would only be there as a figurehead. I'd miss him, but I'd also miss the social aspect of working in a team if I stayed."

The AI's avatar looked conflicted. "I honestly don't know, and that's a phrase I thought I'd never utter! It was living out here that gave him the appreciation for the world you have, and the inspiration to do something about its problems. However, while he might not have the experience of management, he does seem to be a natural leader, and his people skills would be sorely missed in the city. I feel that I have sufficient data, but not the first-hand knowledge to see the solution."

Sonia felt for Andie. To have seen all manner of human interaction on video, and having read numerous psychological papers on the human condition, still couldn't make her an expert on how an individual would react under certain circumstances. Not having an answer must be very frustrating for the AI, who was used to solving problems literally in the blink of an eye. Logic would be telling her one thing, but as Sonia well knew, people did not always behave logically.

Meanwhile, Lucas had gone to sit on the verandah, his trusty dog by his side. Unknowingly, he was mirroring Andie's own thoughts. Logic dictated that he move to be with the team, but it would be hard to leave his house and his friends in the district. He had spent almost his whole life in this house, except for the five years away at boarding school, and adding yet one more change to all that he had already been through this year threatened a recurrence of the identity crisis he had suffered back in April. While he understood, in the back of his mind, that moving wouldn't change who he was, the sentimental part of his brain said, *This is where your soul is.*

Sonia came outside and sat beside him, scratching Splash behind the ears as she did so.

"Do you want to talk about it?"

Lucas turned to her with a sad smile. "I do get where you're both coming from, and I can see the merit in it, but there's still a part of me that's saying this is who I am. I'm not cut out for city life, Sonia. Look at this," he said, indicating the valley below, "I barely know anything else. I need trees, and grass. I need to hear birdsong, not traffic. I feel bad enough that I've been neglecting my friends around here recently – how would I feel if I desert them entirely?"

Sinus shook her head. "Mate, you've accomplished amazing things already. I can't think of anyone else with the vision to do what you have. This is just another problem to overcome, and I'm sure there's a solution that will keep you sane. Just try to distance yourself from the emotion, and fit the pieces into place. The man with a plan to save the world should have no trouble saving himself."

Lucas lay back on the planks of the verandah, converting his face with an arm, trying to do as she suggested. Unfortunately, Splash took this as an invitation to lie across his chest and try to lick his face.

"Ugh," groaned Lucas, attempting to push the dog away. "This, I don't need."

He then sat bolt upright, Splash tumbling off the side of the verandah. "I'm going about this all wrong! I know what I *do* need, but one tree's the same as another. It doesn't have to be here!"

He called out to the nearest microphone, "Andie! Tell Cath to get me a house on the hills behind Palmy. With a verandah, and native trees. It'll only be ten minutes or so into town, and I can still have my country air. I'll come back here on weekends and do my rounds."

He carried on talking as he stood up and moved inside. "We'll need outbuildings, so we can relocate the workshop, at least three bedrooms, and nothing too modern. Get Sonia another building in town for her work on the new units, and order fresh equipment. Jake can get that installed in time to start the first run. Staff! Run some ads please, Andie. You know the routine."

Sonia followed him in, as did the disgruntled spaniel. They congregated in the office, where Andie was already displaying potential properties on the monitor.

"Well, that was a quick turnaround," said Sonia, putting an arm around his shoulder. "Are you sure that moving from one hilltop country house to another isn't going to be too much of a change?" she asked cheekily.

"Don't give me a hard time about it. I know I can be pretty set in my ways, but I did manage to sort out the problem, didn't I? It's not like I'm giving this place up altogether. It might be worth getting someone to come and look after the place, though. Who knows, the right person might even be able to take over some of my gardening duties."

"That's a problem for a different day, maybe. For now, I'm just glad that you've come up with a solution that makes you happy. Well done. I knew you could do it."

The relief that he hadn't let Sonia down was evident on his face. He led her back to the kitchen, where he pulled a bottle of champagne from the fridge. "We should celebrate. I guess it's been pretty hard on you, being cooped up here, away from the bright lights."

"I wouldn't say *hard*. I mean, it's lovely here, and I've really been too busy so far to miss the city too much, but it will be nice to hang out with the other girls."

She looked up at the clock on the wall. "Do we feel like cooking tonight? There's pizza in the freezer if you want."

Lucas laughed. "We really are living the good life, aren't we? French bubbly, and *pizza*!"

The following day, while Sonia and Andie were occupied with an intense discussion regarding the new prototype, Lucas took Splash riding in the Toyota to call in on his neighbours, and to check that things were going smoothly at the local factory.

"Just one man and his dog today, mate. I barely understand a word of what the girls are babbling about, and we're well overdue for some quality time, you and me."

Splash assumed his usual position as self-appointed co-driver, and wagged his tail enthusiastically. He was happy to be wherever Lucas was, no matter the destination. Visiting all his friends and/or clients, he gave them the sad news that he would not be able to perform his regular duties in future, but assured them that he would not be leaving them in the lurch. He promised to find a substitute worker who could take over his role, at least during the week. While everyone was, of course, going to miss him, many were secretly pleased that he was finally getting to see more of the world, even if it was only 100 kilometres away. Word of his involvement with the new business that had employed so many local people had spread, and everybody seemed excited for him. He had no intention, however, of revealing the full extent of his work with Ad Astra, as he worried that people would view him in a different light if they knew him to be what amounted to a billionaire. Truth be told, he needn't have been concerned. The general opinion was that it would take far more than fame and fortune to stop Lucas Winter from being who he always had been.

One particular visit brought him a stroke of luck when he called in on Doug Roy. Doug was a successful farmer in his mid-forties who ran 1200 hectares out the far side of Mangaweka. Doug's son, James, had finished high school at the end of the previous year, and had recently completed a three-month agricultural course at the polytechnic. James was keen to apply his new-found knowledge and skills to the family farm but with three farm workers already, Doug simply did not have the work for him. Lucas was quick to point out his own need for a house-sitter, and substitute gardener/lawnmower. Speaking directly to James, an agreement was reached, where the young man would stay in Lucas's house during the week, and look after the neighbours as Lucas himself used to. He would return to his home at the family farm during weekends, and Lucas assured him of an appropriate salary. Happy that his concerns in that department had been taken care of, Lucas felt much more at ease as he finished his rounds.

Later in the afternoon, be paid a visit to the QED factory in Taihape. Checking in with the shift supervisor, he was pleased to hear that their targets were still being met, and, in fact, exceeded. The computer-generated rosters ensured that everyone got as many hours as they needed, and that the production lines were always fully staffed. With heartfelt congratulations to the supervisor, he left the facility in her competent hands and headed back to the house.

When he got home, he left his work boots at the back step and fed Splash. He heard the sound of the television and walked down the hall in his socks. In the lounge, he found Sonia sitting on the couch in front of the fire, legs stretched out and a glass of wine in her hand.

"Hey there. Hope you don't mind that I started without you!"

"I'm sure you've earned it," he said, taking a seat beside her on the couch. "What have you been up to today?"

Sonia reached for the remote to mute the television. "Oh, Andie and I had a big talk about the new project. So much of the technical stuff went right over my head, but I know how to make it, if not how it works. Then I spent the rest of the day in the workshop finishing off the electronics for the prototypes that I started before we went to New Plymouth. Andie says the gear is set up in Taihape and I can start work on the core components on Monday. How was your day?"

"It was good, yeah," he replied. "Everyone seems pretty cool with me taking off, and I even found a young bloke who's willing to mind the house and look after gardens and stuff during the week."

"That's great! So you're feeling better about the moving idea now?"

"Yeah, I think so. There's just one thing bothering me."

Sonia placed her wine glass on the side table, and looked at him, concerned. "What's the matter?"

Lucas pointed at the wine bottle, saying, "You only brought one glass."

She picked up a cushion from beside her and hit him across the chest with it. "You shit. You had me worried!"

He got up, laughing, before any more violence was inflicted on him, and went to get another wine glass from the kitchen. Splash had finished his dinner, and was snuffling around in case any biscuits had escaped his attention.

"Come on, mate. The fire's going."

The spaniel's ears twitched. With one last look at his empty bowl, he followed Lucas down the hall. Lucas was sure that the dog understood many more words than he let on, and 'fire' always got a reaction. On a chilly autumn evening, he well understood the benefits of something his wild forebears would have feared. In fact, after 'dinner', it may have been his second favourite word. Trotting behind his master into the lounge, he made a beeline for the hearth, and flopped down to lie full-length in front of the fire, basking in its warmth.

"Bloody fire hog," muttered Lucas, as he sat down and tried to find a spot to warm his feet that wasn't blocked by the dog.

"Do we have anything on this weekend?" he asked, holding out his empty glass.

"Not that I can think of," she answered, pouring him some of the Otago pinot noir. "You know what they say – all work and no play ... well, gets the job done quicker I suppose, but I don't want to spend my weekend at the factory. Any particular reason?"

"Not really. I was just hoping to have a quiet couple of days. I'm sure I'm still feeling the effects of our night out with Foxy – I haven't done that since, well, the reunion, I think. You missed a good weekend then."

Sonia sighed. "We had a big job on, and I just couldn't get away. I'm looking forward to catching up with the gang when they come, though."

"Speaking of which," broke in Andie, "Cath called with a progress report today. She's been looking at possibilities for the office over the last few days, and has also shortlisted several houses. I have the details, if you'd like to look at them."

"Thanks, Andie," said Lucas. "Sorry for not including you in the conversation. Can you put them up on the TV?"

Sonia excused herself, and left to fix them both a meal. Property listings started appearing on the television screen as Andie continued, "Our HR teams have also finished staffing the new facilities, and over the next week the instructors will be running training sessions. We should be ready to have them running Monday week."

"Great news, Andie. How are the advance orders looking?"

"Assuming that the other factories meet their targets, we should fill those orders in six weeks from opening. That's only the domestic market, of course. We will need to up production a lot if we factor in the international requests."

Lucas did a quick calculation in his head. With fifteen additional factories, each set up in a similar fashion to the Taihape operation, that would mean they had orders for approximately 180,000 units. With almost two million residential and business internet connections in the country, Ad Astra was still a long way off saturation, but some ISPs were bound to be late adopters, waiting to see if the technology held up. Some would almost certainly miss out if consumers didn't want to wait, and signed up with a company that could connect them sooner. The risks of doing business in a competitive market, he reasoned. Even if they could replace the majority of those two million, it would still be a drop in the bucket on a global scale. The sooner they had the new management team working, the better. They would need to start on factories in other countries and they needed property bought, facilities built, advertising, logistics, and employees. There were likely to be legal and corporate challenges from countries with an inclination towards litigation, too, and he could see Michelle and Tom earning their keep.

He stopped his mind wandering; these were exactly the sort of problems he had hired his team for, and he didn't intend to give himself a headache over them. He turned his attention to the television, and the potential houses and office buildings that Cath had flagged.

He had given all the listings a cursory view, and was beginning to look at them in more detail when Sonia returned with dinner. He gave Splash a warning glance as his plate was placed on the side table, and he and Sonia settled in for an evening of red wine, pasta, and online house-hunting.

INTERLUDE 4

"Not again!" Antonia's voice echoed shrilly through the lab as Kaito reported yet another unsuccessful run of the excitement. In the last three weeks, they had made over a dozen attempts to create their quantum computer. Every time, the neutrino beam had failed to properly manipulate the sub-atomic particles in the silicon wafer. There had been limited success, in that at least some portions of the silicon had been arranged into simple neural-style networks, but without the complete template being reproduced, down to the individual particle, even these partial networks were essentially useless.

Martine's team had done wonders with the creation of a neutrino shield. They had started with osmium, the densest naturally-occurring element, and had managed to make it even more so, through a complicated catalytic process that created an isotope of the metal. A different arrangement of the electrons in the element, and an immense hydraulic press with over 50,000 tons of pressure, enabled them to almost double the material's density. Even then, however, it was still mostly empty space, according to physics. Neutrinos still slipped through the gaps between the nuclei, and were free to interact with the lab's own neutrino stream, virtually unimpeded.

It was not these stray neutrinos, however, that were causing the experiments to fail, though that was the accepted explanation. Tomas had inserted his own code into the software that ensured the quantum computer would never come to fruition. The stakes were high, but both he and Martine felt that it was a worthwhile risk, to prevent Antonia and Kaito from getting their hands on such a potentially destructive tool. Tomas's position and skills allowed him to keep his alterations secret from the rest of the team, and Martine maintained the fiction that solar activity was still affecting the equipment. It meant that she took some heat from

Kaito and Antonia, but with frequent "tweaks" to the shielding, she was able to hold off the worst of their anger. Her next plan was to have the lab develop pulse-frequency magnetic coils that were supposed to deflect the solar neutrinos, rather than stop them entirely. She knew very well that this wouldn't work, but her reasoning was technically sound, and Antonia was ready to jump on any concept if it meant that she might one day achieve her dreams.

"Let's call it a day, Antonia. It will take too long to set up for another run at this hour, and frankly, I've had just about all the disappointment I can handle for one week. The crews need a rest, or they'll start making mistakes, and God knows, I could do with a decent sleep."

"All right, Kaito. I guess you have a point. The last thing we want is human error creeping in, on top of everything else. Just come and see me in my office before you leave. There seem to be some developments regarding our January run that could be worth looking into."

She dismissed the technical teams, and waited until everything had been safely shut down before she walked out of the lab. Waiting there for Kaito, she brought up several news items on her monitor in preparation for the talk with her second-in-command.

"Have we found the thief, then?" asked Kaito as he entered her office.

Antonia gestured him towards a chair, and turned her monitor so that he could see it.

"Not exactly, but one of Tomas's team came to me with these reports," she said, pointing at the screen. As Kaito leaned forward to read, he asked why the security team member had come forward himself, rather than forwarding the information through Tomas.

"Oh, I don't know," she answered. "I suppose that he was simply hoping to garner favour, and didn't want Tomas to take the credit. Anyway, that's not the important thing. Look at these – does anything strike you as odd?"

"Frankly, it seems like business as usual in that part of the world. These South American politicians are well-known for being corrupt, and it's always only a matter of time before they're caught at it."

Antonia began to pace the room as she shook her head at Kaito's inability to grasp the implications. "That's just the point – they weren't caught red-handed. Information from highly secure sources was anonymously leaked to the media, creating huge public outcry and international political and economic action that forced them from their positions. Those that weren't arrested outright by the new regimes, have gone into hiding and are swearing vengeance on whoever hacked their allegedly impenetrable systems. Does hacking like that sound like anyone we know?"

Kaito sat back in his chair, a thoughtful look on his face. "Do you think that whoever stole the QC is behind these leaks? What would be in it for them though? Perhaps one of their political opponents arranged to steal our technology?"

Antonia stopped pacing and slammed a hand on the desk. "What are you asking *me* for? That is the sort of information I want *you* to find out. Do whatever you have to to track the source of these leaks, and we will be one step closer to getting our QC back. And when we do, I am going to make them wish that even their *mothers* had never been born! Find me people who like to inflict pain. These bastards will *suffer*."

Standing up and heading over to Antonia's keyboard, Kaito sent the news links to his own computer, and hurriedly left the office. He had seen Antonia in plenty of foul moods over the past five months, but he had never heard actual demands for blood before. It was to be expected, he supposed; their plans for wealth and power would have been set back by half a year, at least, and a stern talking-to was hardly likely to be sufficient punishment for the criminals' actions.

Martine Dubois had left the research facility, and was relaxing in her Toledo apartment when she heard a knock on her door. Not expecting visitors, she cautiously looked through the peephole before opening the door to admit Tomas Becker.

"What the hell are you doing here, Tomas?" she demanded. "I thought we agreed that we should have as little contact as possible."

Walking through to the lounge, he sat down before answering. "We have a problem. The audio bug I installed in Antonia's office picked up a worrying conversation between her and Kaito. They've heard about the South American hacks, and have made a tentative link to the QC."

"It was all over the news – there would have been no way we could keep it secret anyway. It's not that serious a problem. From everything we already know about the QC, those hacks will not be easily traced, if at all."

Tomas shook his head. "That's not the worst of it. She told Kaito to get hold of people who like to inflict pain. Martine, if there's any way at all they can track those back to New Zealand, I'm afraid that she won't just stop at hurting them – she's going to kill them, I'm sure of it."

She sat down across from him, her face taking on an ashen pallor. "Oh my God. That's ... I don't know what to say. We have to warn them!"

"We seriously need to think about cutting our ties to IVIA. I can't be party to this, and our deception will have to come out sooner or later. Even now some of my team are questioning my decision to take sole charge of the internal digital security, and you can't keep inventing new ways to hold the project up."

Getting up and walking to the sideboard, Martine took a bottle of red wine and poured two glasses. She handed one to Tomas before drinking almost half of her own glass.

"But where would we go? What would we do? I know nothing about a life on the run."

Tomas put his glass on the table, the wine untouched. "We would have to go to New Zealand. With luck, these Ad Astra people will appreciate our warning, and perhaps shelter us. You might not how to evade IVIA, but I have a few contacts. I have had to deal with some shady people in the past. We could not go directly, instead taking a complex route to throw off any pursuit, but I believe it can be done. Also, Antonia may be too busy to follow us immediately, as I plan to deliver a software bomb that will wipe their servers beyond any chance of retrieval, and overload the capacitors to induce a massive hardware failure."

"Great," said Martine, finishing her glass and teaching for Tomas's. "That will give them even more reason to hunt us down."

"I told you – I know some people. I think that I can fake our deaths. That will at least give us time to get away, if not completely remove any suspicion that we were involved. Give me a couple of days, and I will make arrangements."

"Okay, but I don't know if I will be able to face Antonia or Kaito in the meantime. I will tell them that I have to make a trip to Paris, to see the hydraulic press and make adjustments. I will be back by Monday. Let me know your plans through my gmail address. You had better go now. And be careful! We don't want anyone suspecting us."

Tomas left, his mind racing with the plans he needed to put in place. Martine collapsed onto her couch, terrified for them both.

Antonia took the news of Martine's trip well; there were few things she would not tolerate when it came to fixing the problems with the experiment. Martine did indeed go to Paris, and did visit the engineers with the press, in case anybody checked up on her, and on Sunday evening she received an email from Tomas.

Come back as soon as you can. Do not take clothes or anything from your apartment when you return. I have arranged for a casual staff meeting at the Café Ronaldo on Monday morning, after which we will depart in your car. There will be a terrible 'accident', and we will both be believed to have perished. We will then make our way to the coast, where I have arranged a fishing boat to take us to Greece. I have a contact there who will provide us with new identities, and we can begin our journey to New Zealand.

She read this with a growing sense of horror at the realisation that they were about to leave their old lives behind, and be declared dead. She hoped that would only be an invention, as she was certain that Antonia would have no hesitation in making it happen for real if she ever found out the truth.

The next day, she caught her flight back to Madrid in the morning and collected her car from the airport car park, driving back to her apartment in Toledo. Obedient to Tomas's instruction, she left for the café as if it were just another day, taking none of her personal belongings or clothes. She did flick through her photograph album, inscribing the memories contained within on her mind, and reluctantly set it down before walking out.

The lunch meeting was ostensibly a chance for the team to relax together before getting back into the hard work at the research facility the next day, though Martine had trouble pretending to enjoy herself. When asked whether she was okay, she shrugged it off, saying only that she was still under a lot of stress, and smiling weakly as everybody around her laughed and joked.

At the end of their meal, Tomas asked if anyone could give him a lift back to his home in the hills, as he had dropped his car off for a service and it was still not ready. Martine took the hint and offered to drive him. Saying their farewells to their teammates, they set off, heading out of town towards Tomas's weekend house in the hills to the west of the city.

As they neared the top of a steep hill, he directed her to pull off into a stand of trees on a side road. He climbed out of the car and greeted the driver of a nondescript van. This man handed him a bag and Tomas pulled a peasant blouse and cotton pants out of it, handing them to Martine

"Change into these," he said, taking another set of plain clothes out and unbuttoning his shirt.

"What, here?" she asked, looking around the shaded area and at the van driver.

"Unless you would rather go back to IVIA and explain what you have been doing, yes, here."

They each quickly swapped their own clothing for that from the bag, and the van driver took their discarded clothes and opened the back doors of his vehicle.

Martine gasped as she saw the contents of the van. Two naked, obviously dead, bodies lay in the cargo space. The driver, with Tomas's assistance, hurriedly clothed them, and Tomas positioned Martine's car to face back towards the road. They then lifted the bodies out the van and placed them in the front seats of the car.

"No one is going to believe that we died in the crash if there are no bodies," Tomas explained. "My friend here 'liberated' them from the medical school – don't worry, we didn't just murder two random people to aid our escape!"

With the cadavers securely installed in the car, Tomas doused them with petrol before throwing in a small device and walking to the road and indicating to his friend that the coast was clear. The van driver used his vehicle to nudge the car towards the edge of the road and the steep hillside below. He then reversed, to take a run-up, and accelerated into the back of the car, sending it over the edge, where it tumbled end over end before coming to rest in a gully far below. The device that Tomas had put in the car, a delayed action incendiary, ignited, and a brief flare came from the petrol-soaked cadavers before the ruptured fuel tank exploded.

"That should do it. Quickly, now. In the van. We need to get going," said Tomas.

All three climbed into the van and the driver returned up the side road so as not to be seen in the vicinity of the incident.

As they travelled the back roads down the hill, Tomas slapped the driver on the shoulder. "Great job. All we need to do now is make it to the coast safely and your work is done. Thank you."

He turned to Martine, in the back of the van. "You may as well try to get some sleep. It will take around five hours to get there. Try to relax."

They kept to less-travelled roads around the south of Madrid, and eventually stopped in a small fishing village north of Valencia. Tomas shook their driver's hand and led Martine towards the docks as the van disappeared. Checking the names of the boats as they walked, he brought them to a halt in front of a scruffy fishing boat with *Maria II* painted on the bow.

"*Hola, buenas noches*! José?"

A young man came out of the wheelhouse, shading his eyes as he looked into the setting sun. "Tomas? *Cómo estás*?"

"We're good, José. Are you ready to go?"

The fisherman held out a hand to help them aboard. Tomas took the offered hand as he stepped onto the boat, reaching out in turn to assist Martine. José went into the wheelhouse to start the engine while Tomas began casting off the mooring lines. As they motored out of the harbour, José handed them clothing more appropriate to a sea voyage.

"It may be summer," he said, "but it can still get cold out on the water."

Martine asked, "How long will the trip take?"

Making a see-saw motion with his hand, José replied, "Five days, approximately. We will be stopping for fuel in Sardinia and Sicily, and I hope that we will arrive at Patras in Greece by the weekend. Tomas, my friend, you will have to take your turn at the wheel if we are to travel non-stop."

"That will not be a problem," said Tomas. "We appreciate your help."

"Ah, you have paid me well, but in any case, I could not refuse a friend in need."

Tomas and Martine changed into their sailing clothes, and they began the long, slow journey to Greece.

As they neared the Greek coast, just over five days later, José managed to get cellphone reception and called someone who was apparently in the same business. What business that was, Martine did not ask, though it had become apparent over the course of the journey that José was not just a fisherman, and sometimes may have transported items that customs officials had no need to know about. José told them that they would transfer to a local boat shortly, as unwelcome questions may be asked if a Spanish-registered fishing boat were to dock in Greece with undocumented passengers. As it was, they would disembark the new vessel as employees, and could then disappear into the town.

After a short time, another fishing boat approached, and pulled up alongside. Tomas and Martine thanked José once again, before stepping across the gunwale to their new ride. The captain of this boat spoke only broken English, so little was said on the brief trip to shore. As the boat came alongside the wharf, Tomas threw out the lines to a waiting dockhand. The Greek captain handed each of them a plastic basket of fish, and they stepped onto the dock with no questions asked. Placing the baskets on the ground, they casually walked away, and into town. They found a public toilet where they could change out of their smelly shipboard clothes, and hunted for a hotel where they could make themselves understood in French, German, Spanish or English. In rural Greece, this was not as easy as it would have been in Western Europe, but they eventually found one where somebody spoke enough English for them to make their desires understood.

"What is the plan now, Tomas?" asked Martine, after they had both washed the smells of saltwater and fish off.

"Next, we make our way to Athens, where I know a man who can give us new documents and passports."

"How did you arrange all of this? I would never have had the first idea of what to do."

Tomas sighed, and ran a hand through his hair. "I told you that I have had dealings with some not so good people. Well, to tell you the truth, I was once one of these people. I was not always a 'white hat,'" he said, referring to those hackers who usually worked for corporations or law enforcement, finding software vulnerabilities before the bad guys.

"In fact, I was not always Tomas Becker, either. In my younger days, I was a very successful cyber-criminal, and when I believed that I was about to be caught, I found this man in Athens and reinvented myself. I never lost touch with my old contacts, however, and in my career as a security survivalist, they have sometimes come in handy to solve problems that legitimate methods could not."

Martine laughed at the idea that IVIA's head of digital security had once been a master criminal himself.

"And is that how you were able to pay all these people to help us?"

Tomas looked somewhat embarrassed as he nodded. "When I decided to create a new identity, I thought that it would be foolish to become somebody poor, and I have secret bank accounts from my earlier life that have funded our escape."

Once again serious, Martine asked, "What will IVIA be doing now, do you think? Will they be grieving over their lost colleague?"

"I somehow suspect that they will have other things on their minds. My bomb was timed to go off on Monday night, and they will be falling over themselves trying to recover their data. I am afraid that will not be possible, as every bit of data relating to their experiments, including the original research from the last ten years, is irretrievably wiped. In addition, their hardware will all be fried by the capacitor overload, so it will be a very long time before they can get back to where they were last week."

201

The following day, they caught a bus to Athens after lunch, arriving in the capital city two and a half hours later. Traveling on foot from the bus depot, they made a necessary stop at a local salon, where they both received an image alteration, with new styles and colours to their hair. Tomas then led the way to a solid door in a dirty back street. After knocking soundly on the door, he and Martine waited a moment before a slot at eye level was opened and a man demanded something in Greek.

"Nick, it's me," said Tomas.

"Otto?" The voice questioned, before several bolts were slid back and the door opened to reveal a straggly-haired, elderly man with a rough beard.

"Otto, my friend, I barely recognised you. Come in, come in."

They entered a dingy apartment and the old man locked the door behind them

"It has been too long, Nick, and I'm not Otto any more, remember? I would like you to meet my friend Martine. She and I are both getting tired of our names, and I was hoping that you could help us to forget them."

"But of course!" said Nick, ushering them through into a dimly-lit living room with ancient armchairs and peeling wallpaper. "Sit, please. What have you done this time? No, don't answer that. I'm sure that it is better that I do not know. What do you need?"

Sitting cautiously in an armchair, for fear that it might break underneath him, Tomas said, "I think that we would like to be a Swiss couple. Martine is French, and I think we could pass for Swiss nationals. We require passports, identity cards, and driving licences. How soon can you do this?"

The old man thought for a moment, rubbing his chin. "If you want the good stuff, I will need to contact a man who can provide original, genuine passports. If he has them on hand, I would say that I can alter them and create the other documents within four days."

"That will be fine, Nick. Can you recommend a place to stay where they will not ask too many questions?"

Nick gave them the address of a hostel that was not at all curious about its guests, and quoted a price for the forgeries.

"Also, if you would come through to the kitchen, I will need to take some photographs."

Tomas did not quibble over the price, though it was much higher than the last time he had changed his identity. Inflation obviously affected everything, legal or not. They followed the old forger into a narrow kitchen, where he got several sheets, of differing colours, out of a cupboard and hung the first in front of the far wall. Tomas and Martine took turns standing in front of the sheet as Nick used a modern digital camera to take their pictures. He then put up a different coloured sheet and asked them to rearrange their hair slightly so that the photographs looked as if they had been taken at different times. Reaching into another cupboard, he pulled out some shirts so that their clothing would also be different. Repeating the process one more time, he put everything away and let them back out the front door.

It was not too far to walk to their hostel, and they stopped on the way to buy some clothes, toiletries, and luggage. As they checked into the run-down hostel, the girl at the front desk barely looked up from her book as she took their money and handed them a key. Climbing the narrow, creaking stairs, they opened their room and relaxed for what seemed like the first time in weeks.

It had been only three days before a young boy came to the hostel to tell them that Nick was ready to see them. When they returned to his apartment, he handed them each an envelope containing their new identities. They were now Rudi and Carine Weber, from Bern. Thanking the old man, and paying the agreed price, Mr and Mrs Weber left the apartment and checked into a much nicer hotel, where they stayed while they applied for the necessary visas for the rest of their trip.

With those hurdles cleared, several weeks later, they began an arduous journey which started with a twelve hour ferry trip to Kusadasi, in Turkey. There would follow a long list of various forms of transport; bus to Istanbul, plane to Bangkok, and an exhausting 29-hour overland trip to Singapore. From there, they would fly to Melbourne, Australia, before catching a bus, arriving in Sydney twelve hours later. The final leg of the journey would be a short hop across the Tasman Sea to Wellington, New Zealand.

INTERLUDE 5

Antonia's anger over the previous five months was a mere bout of peevishness compared to the tantrum she threw when she found that her life's work had been erased overnight. It was only when there was nothing left in her office to break that Kaito felt brave enough to enter.

"Where the hell have you been?" she demanded.

"I've been with the IT team, seeing if anything is recoverable. Unfortunately, even the offsite backup servers were affected. I have been trying to contact Tomas, to see if his contacts at the ISP can trace the origin of the virus, but he is not answering his phone."

"*That* useless bastard! If he was any good at his job, they would never have been able to get the virus in. Have him report to me as soon as he gets here. And see just how much of the equipment can be salvaged. It will cost *millions* to replace everything – millions that we don't have. I sunk *everything* into this project. We were supposed to be filthy rich by now!"

Kaito beat a hasty retreat, resolving to have an underling report on the state of the equipment. He had no wish to face Antonia's wrath if the news was bad. As he walked down the corridor, the English girl from reception hailed him.

"Mr Mitsuhashi, there are two policemen at the front desk. I'm sorry to bother you, but Ms Vélez is not answering her phone."

Of course she isn't, he thought, *It's in pieces on the floor of her office.*

"Thank you, Miranda. I will see them in my office. Please send them up."

He hurried to his office, intensely curious as to why the police would be here, now of all days. He had a moment of fear, thinking that IVIA's mysterious nemesis had uncovered the plans to utilise the QC in unethical, if not downright illegal, ways. Of course, with all the servers destroyed, there was no longer any proof of that fact, and anyway, simple police officers would not be the ones to confront them on that matter. It would be government agents, Interpol, even the CIA. No, he didn't believe that he had any cause for alarm on that score. It was perhaps something as simple as a traffic infringement.

He got to his office, and quickly combed his hair and tidied his clothes; the morning's excitement had left him dishevelled, a state to which he had become well accustomed over the last months, and it was always good practise to look one's best for the authorities, no matter the reason for their visit.

A knock on the door frame announced the arrival of his visitors, and he motioned them to enter. Seeing that they were members of the rural Guardia Civil, rather than Toledo's branch of the National Police Corps, he put the last vestiges of worry from his mind; country cops would have no place investigating allegations of major fraud.

"Good afternoon, gentlemen. I am Kaito Mitsuhashi, the Assistant Director here at IVIA. How may I be of assistance?"

The look of confusion that passed between the two officers made his heart sink, and his suspicions were confirmed when one of them asked, *"Hablas español?"*.

Kaito knew multiple languages – Japanese and English, naturally, as well as Python, Java, and other staples of the computing world – but Spanish was one he had never bothered to learn, with all conversations at IVIA being conducted in English.

"I'm sorry, no. I do not speak Spanish," he answered, sadly shaking his head. *Damn it*, he thought, this meant that he would have to get Antonia to talk to them. She was certainly not going to be happy about the interruption, and he hoped that she would keep her temper in check as she dealt with these two.

"Ah, uno momento?" he said, picking up the telephone and pointing to the handset as if they did not understand how a telephone worked. He had started dialling Antonia's number when he remembered that she had broken her phone. He replaced the handset and attempted to convey to the police that he would go and get somebody else, pointing to them before holding up his hands in a "wait here" gesture. He then pointed to himself and made a walking motion with his fingers, and left the room. Behind him, the two police officers exchanged looks of derision.

He poked his head around Antonia's door, alert for thrown office equipment.

"I have two Guardia Civil officers in my office, but they do not speak any English. Are you free to come and talk to them?"

"Oh, of course I'm free," she replied sarcastically. "I only have my entire life crumbling around me at the moment, but I'm sure I can spare the time to talk to some ignorant country policemen. I don't actually have anything better to do, considering that I have no research, and no machines to take up my time."

She kicked her way through the detritus on the floor and he followed her down the corridors towards his office, briefly entertaining the faint hope that the Guardia policemen would shoot her, or at least arrest her, if she made a fuss. As soon as she entered the office, she and one of the officers engaged in a flurry of rapid Spanish that he felt he would have had trouble following even had he been fluent in the language. The only clues as to the content of the conversation that he could pick out of the torrent of words were the names of Tomas Becker and Martine Dubois. He did not fancy their chances of continued employment if they had gone and got themselves arrested. That would certainly be the last straw, on top of Tomas's obvious failing in the cyber-security department. As the conversation continued, he noticed Antonia's face, which had still been slightly flushed from her exertions in her office, grow gradually paler.

When the talking finished, the Guardia Civil men nodded politely to both Antonia and Kaito before taking their leave. Antonia stood silently for a moment, obviously processing the information she had received, before the blood rushed back to her face, and with rage-fueled strength, she grasped the edge of Kaito's desk and flipped it on its side, scattering everything atop it to the floor. She began pacing the room, looking for something new to bear the brunt of her anger.

"They've gone too far," she snarled, as Kaito dashed to pick up his laptop before her descending foot could crush it.

"What has Becker done to make you this angry, Antonia?"

"Done? He's only got himself *murdered*. Both my cyber-security chief and my best theoretical physicist, dying in a car crash on the same day that we are crippled by this attack? A coincidence is not possible. They were killed, probably to prevent any chance of stopping the virus, and also to take out my lead researcher so that we could not replicate our work. This was a deliberate act, Kaito, I am certain of it."

He placed the laptop on a bookshelf and bent to lift his desk back upright. He thought about the possibility of his colleagues' death being a coincidence, but it was just too convenient that two important members of the IVIA team had been removed at that particular time. The idea that someone would be willing to go to those lengths to protect themselves was of great concern, though he somehow managed to avoid seeing the irony in the situation. Given the opportunity, it was almost certain that Antonia herself would have had few qualms about killing to regain her technology.

Straining to lift the desk that Antonia had so effortlessly upended, he finally righted it, and flopped into his chair to catch his breath.

"It implies that we are being hounded by a very dedicated, and ruthless, organisation. Tomas was not just an expert in digital security – he took great care with his physical safety, too. I know that over the course of the last months, he was being particularly cautious even amongst his colleagues. It was rare that he would speak unguardedly, and took pains to ensure that he was never followed when he drove anywhere.

"I put that down to a naturally heightened sense of awareness because of what the institute had suffered, but now I wonder whether he had specific cause to be vigilant. Perhaps he had a suspicion that he was being watched, due to his role here, or maybe he even had doubts about the loyalty of one of our employees. We need to talk to his team, to see if anybody is aware of a specific concern that he might have had."

Antonia latched onto this faint hope that Tomas may have had more knowledge of their attacker than he had let on, for whatever reason.

"Yes. Speak to his people. Any digital clues he may have had are long gone, with our servers, but perhaps sometime will remember him saying something that will only make sense to us now."

She smoothed her clothing and straightened her hair with her fingers.

"They may think us neutralised, now that Tomas is out of the picture – it might even be that he was killed because he was getting too close to finding them – but we will not take this lying down. We *must* find out what he knew. At this point, it is our only possible line of investigation. We must approach the problem calmly—" A *hypocritical statement, coming from her*, thought Kaito "—and direct all our skills towards finding these people. We will *not* be cowed, and we will *not* be defeated. Now, tidy this place up. If we are to work professionally, we must look the part."

She strode from the room, leaving Kaito shaking his head in bewilderment at her hypocrisy and her sudden change in mood.

He got down on his hands and knees to begin collecting up the items that had taken from his desk. As he picked up his green-shaded desk lamp, he noticed something unusual on its base. Looking closer, he saw that a small, disc-shaped object was affixed to the underside by a thin band wrapped around the power cord. Taking a small pocket-knife from his desk drawer, he prised the object away from the lamp base and peered closely at it. A jolt of alarm ran through him as he recognised it as a wireless microphone that had obviously been powered via induction through its proximity to the power cord.

Taking the device with him, he walked briskly to Antonia's office. As he entered, without knocking, she looked up at him from the floor, where she was likewise clearing up her mess.

"Ah, you've come to help me. That is very kind of you. Perhaps you could run down to the supply room and find me another telephone – this one appears to be damaged," she said as she held up the shattered unit. He placed a finger to his lips and showed her the microphone, before beginning a search of the room for the one he knew must be present. She took the device from him, turning it in her hand as she inspected it. Realisation kicked in and she quietly began to help in the search. A second bug was eventually found wrapped around the power cord at the back of her coffee machine.

Using his pocket-knife to pop the back off the bug, he slipped the blade under one of the wires connected to the microphone, severing it. He then did the same with the second bug, rendering them both inactive.

"Well, this puts a different complexion on things. Having these in our offices can only mean that someone on the inside was involved. That makes it much more likely that Tomas was killed to keep his suspicions unspoken. I hate to say it, Antonia, but we have a rat."

With the rage threatening to return, Antonia sat in her chair, gripping its arms tightly until she felt that she had control of her emotions.

"Do you know how you deal with rats, Kaito? You *stomp* on them until they are flattened husks of fur and flesh. Find me this rat. I have some questions to ask it before I kill it. But then ... rat pancake."

Her eyes burned with an intense hatred, and a cruel smile twisted her lips as she imagined the ways she would make the traitor suffer.

MOVING IN

As hoped, the weekend was uneventful, and Sonia and Lucas put aside thoughts of work, simply relaxing around the house. Lucas caught up on some neglected computer gaming, though he had to ban Andie from helping the PC. He was beaten every time by her superior reflexes and tactical awareness.

"If this whole business thing goes down the drain, you could always do pretty well for yourself as an online gamer," he joked.

"Done that. Cleaned up. No challenge."

Lucas rolled his eyes. Of course the 'mere humans' would offer no competition. He hoped that she hadn't rubbed her opponents' noses in it.

Sonia, meanwhile, had been catching up on some of her favourite television series. The U-Net internet connection made for buffer-free video streaming, and they had made sure to get unlimited data. She looked totally unlike what one might expect of the CTO of a major tech firm, in her dressing gown and fluffy slippers, sprawled on the couch in front of a roaring fire, and snacking on potato chips and chocolate biscuits.

All too soon, a new week began. Monday kicked off with a phone call from Cath, informing them that she would be finalising deals on the first three houses that afternoon. Lucas and Sonia gave their critiques of the shortlisted office buildings, and between them all, they settled on the one that best suited their needs. Lucas promised to look it over during the week, as he planned to go and view some of the properties that Cath had picked out for him.

After Cath's call, Sonia asked Lucas if he would accompany her to the Taihape facility, as she really wanted to get started on the important aspects of the new product. So it was, that after an early lunch, they took the Jaguar into town, and settled themselves into what had been termed 'the Annex', a separate building within the compound of the factory.

This building was substantially constructed, with steel framing and thick concrete walls. Heavy-duty power lines carrying 50kV ran from the nearby Mataroa substation to a switching unit outside the building, and shielded cables ran inside. The building was windowless, and earth had been piled halfway up the exterior walls, giving it the look of a military bunker. Though there was assurance from Andie that the technology was perfectly safe, there was no point in upsetting the local authorities, considering the power levels contained within.

Sonia and Lucas entered through a heavy metal door secured by biometric locks, and put on rubberised suits with an integral copper mesh, designed to protect them from stray electricity. Suitably attired, they opened a second security door and looked around the interior of the large building. Similar to the QED production lines, there were stations for the assembly of electronic circuit boards, and others where completed components would come together. At the far end of the room was a bunker within the bunker. This was where the magic would happen. Lucas had carried the sheet-metal cubes in from the car, with their electronics already installed. All that needed to be done now, was to build the cores and connect them to the housings.

He put the cubes on a cart and followed Sonia as she toured the crates of stockpiled materials, adding items to the cart at her direction; toroidal magnetic containment devices called Tokamaks, simple-looking metal plates, fine tubing, and a host of other parts that he had no names for.

With all the components collected, they took everything to the interior bunker and Sonia began to work. Even with the assistance of robotic arms and automated processes, it took her the better part of three hours to create the cores. Once they were complete, she took a well-earned break, and Lucas drove her into town for coffee and cake. Over their afternoon tea, she explained to him that future core construction would be much quicker, as she was taking particular care with her first ones. Unfamiliar with the process, she had naturally not wanted to make any mistakes.

Relaxed and refreshed, they returned to the Annex to complete their task. Inside the bunker, Sonia installed the cores in the cubes and connected the wiring. She took two steel bulbs, similar to, but larger than, the nitrous oxide canisters used in whipped cream dispensers, and inserted then into sockets inside each device.

Placing the cubes in a shielded cabinet, she connected extremely heavy-duty cables to terminals on the cores and closed the cabinet.

"Okay," she said, "I'm told it's safe, but why don't we wait outside for the next step? Just ... because."

She adjusted some settings on the cabinet's control panel and they exited the bunker. Shortly, the hum of high-voltage electricity could be heard, and a muted *Crack!* came from within the bunker. Startled, Lucas jumped a little as he looked enquiringly at Sonia.

"Don't worry. I'm pretty sure that was supposed to happen."

They waited for the second burst of noise before she cautiously opened the door and approached the cabinet, Lucas nervously peering around the door frame. She opened the cabinet and, wearing thick, insulated gloves, disconnected the heavy cables. Removing a cube, she placed it on a nearby benchtop and attached three wires to its exterior terminals.

"You can come in now, scaredy-cat. It's completely safe, and doing exactly what it's supposed to," she said, pointing at dials on the wall behind the bench. Lucas edged his way into the room and slowly approached. When he got to the bench, he reached out and tentatively placed a hand on the cube.

"There's just the faintest vibration, but no heat at all," he remarked, fascinated. "And it's perfectly stable, right?"

"Andie says we could drop it off a cliff, hit it with a train, or put it in a 3000 degree fire, and nothing would happen. It would stop working, sure, but there's no danger. It's everything we hoped for."

Lucas picked it up and made as if to shake it. "What about a bit of rough and tumble?"

Sonia shook her head. "It will stand up to everyday wear and tear, and unless the integrity of the unit is breached it will keep on going."

He moved the cube around, looking at it from all angles. It was moderately cumbersome, weighing in at around 15kg, but like the QED, the eventual consumer product would be smaller, though not much lighter.

"So we're done for the day? Can we go home?"

"Sure. Just let me power down the systems, and we can get on our way."

She flicked switches and turned knobs to their 'Off' positions, before shutting and locking the door behind them. Lucas cautiously placed the cubes back on the cart, still uncertain of their safety, in spite of his faith in Andie and Sonia's expertise. Removing their insulated coveralls, they emerged into the fresh air. When they reached the car, he suggested that Sonia put the devices in the footwell by her feet. "I know you've got complete confidence in them, but i they're our first ones, and I wouldn't feel right having them bouncing around in the boot."

As he carefully positioned them in the passenger footwell, she gave him an exasperated look before climbing into the car and squeezing her feet into the cramped space around the metal cubes.

On their return to the farm, Lucas carried the devices to the workshop before joining Sonia in the house.

"Prototypes complete, Andie!" called out Sonia as they entered.

"That's great news," the AI replied. "I assume they are working as they should?"

Sonia gave the details of the readouts as Lucas poured a celebratory drink for them both. They took their glasses to the office and told Andie how their work had gone, before having a simple dinner and getting an early night.

Shortly before noon the next day, while Sonia and Lucas were in the workshop marvelling at their creation, they heard a car arriving, gravel crunching under its wheels as it came to a halt outside the garden gate. Lucas poked his head out the door to see an ancient Honda Civic and a wild-haired man in jeans and a tatty leather jacket.

"Over here, Paul!" he shouted.

Paul Bennington looked around for the source of the voice before ambling over to the woolshed.

"You're lucky you caught us," said Lucas. "We were just about to head into Palmy to look at some properties. Cuppa? Lunch?"

Paul accepted, greeting Sonia warmly and throwing a mock punch at Lucas.

"Haven't been up here since the school days. Hasn't changed much, eh?"

"Not a lot," said Lucas, sharing a knowing look with Sonia over Paul's shoulder. They wandered back to the house, introducing Paul to Splash before heading inside for tea, coffee, and a quick lunch.

After their drinks, and a chat about old times, Lucas led them out front.

Paul regarded the old Toyota Hilux with mild distaste. "There she is. The executive wagon. You're not going house-hunting in that, are you? I wouldn't think you could afford a tin shack if you pulled up to view a property with a rattle and a cloud of smoke."

"Fair call, but it'd be warmer than the Jag."

"Take it from me, mate. I'm in advertising, and first impressions count. Trust me."

Sonia snorted. "Make up your mind. You're either in advertising, or trustworthy. You can't be both!"

"Children..." warned Lucas. "Play nice. I'll take the Jag if you can take Sonia. There's no point in both of us freezing our bits off."

Paul raised his eyebrows. "What makes you think that thing's got a working heater?" he asked, jerking his head at the Honda.

Lucas sighed. "I can't win. I'll take the Jag to please our expert on first impressions, and you can ride wherever you like, Sonia. Okay?"

He opened the garage door as Paul and Sonia got into the Civic. Shaking his head, he climbed into the Jaguar, thinking that the lack of a heater in Paul's car was a moot point; those two personalities in the same vehicle would warm up the atmosphere in no time.

He kept a moderate pace on the way in to Palmerston North, reasoning that the decrepit old Honda would have trouble even reaching the speed limit, and they reached the proposed office building in the city a little over an hour later.

It was an unassuming two-storey building on a street corner, with wide, full-height windows either side of the front door, and the concrete facade of the upper level broken up by smaller, mirrored windows. The real estate agent was waiting for them outside, and let them in the main entrance. According to the agent, the building had previously been a chainsaw and lawnmower shop, the front half of the ground floor open-plan, with a door behind the counter leading to a workshop space in the back. Stairs led from the workshop to the second storey, where eight equally-sized rooms surrounded an open central area that had obviously been a communal area and break room. Some of the surrounding rooms had been offices, judging by their setup and decor, while others were bare, and had possibly been used for storage.

Paul headed for an office overlooking the street. "First in, first served, right? I bags this one."

"They're all the same, Paul," said Sonia.

"Huh. You might think so, but from here I can watch the pretty girls walking down the street!"

"How's that stuff for the Defence Force coming?" and Lucas. "Seal the deal, and you can have the office."

Paul pouted, disappointed that his choice of office had conditions attached. "I'll be finishing that off today. I'm concentrating on pushing the security benefits, the price point, and the fact that it's locally made. From the specs your boss gave me, it looks like it will have a longer battery life and be more reliable than any of the other options, too."

"Good man. Can I suggest that you get a haircut before you meet with the military? If they see you turn up like that, they'll be looking around for the Tin Man and the Cowardly Lion!"

"Aww, dude, you've seen me with short hair. My ears stick out, and I look like someone Peter Jackson rejected as an Orc for being too scary."

"Well, at least buy a hairbrush. You're representing Ad Astra now." He indicated the office space with a wave of his hand. "This place looks like it will do the job, eh? I say we give Cath the go-ahead, and get Jake's team in to fit it out as soon as possible. We ready to move on?"

With the others agreeing, they thanked the agent, and went back out to the cars.

Lucas gave the Honda a sideways glance and said to Paul, "When we get up the hill, maybe you should park this at the end of the road and walk in to the house. First impressions, y'know?"

"Oh, ha bloody ha," his friend replied, flipping him a finger. "If you were a halfway decent boss, you'd be buying me a company car about now."

Lucas looked thoughtful. "Come on, then. Let's do that."

Paul did a double-take before pumping a fist in the air. "Now that's what I'm talking about! Now, who sells Lambos in this tin-pot town?"

"*Company* car, mate. A respectable saloon will do the trick. You can buy toys on your own dime."

With Paul grumbling about not being allowed any fun, they got back in their cars and drove across town to the car dealership district. With Lucas shooting down Paul's first choices of a sporty coupé and a V8 muscle car, they settled on a V6 Holden Commodore. Paul's reasoning was that, with the Australian GM subsidiary discontinuing production of the iconic saloon, this last model would become a desirable classic. Lucas in fact bought four of them, with Sonia driving one of the others away, and two on hold until the other team members got to town. Paul tossed the keys to his Civic at the salesman, saying, "You can keep that piece of crap," before tearing out of the yard with a squeal of tyres and a long blast on the horn. Sonia and Lucas followed more sedately, catching up to Paul when he realised that he had no idea where they were going.

Lucas took the lead as they travelled out of town towards the Tararua Ranges. They viewed several properties in the hills before one in particular caught Lucas's fancy. It was on a quiet side road, behind a screen of trees, with a commanding view of the city and the Manawatu plains.

A sealed driveway led to an attractive, two-storey house. Three dormer windows on the upper floor opened to a balcony that stretched the length of the house, above the broad verandah. On the far side of the house were a three-car garage and a large Dutch-style barn. The tidy garden and sloping front lawn were enclosed by a neat fence, and various outbuildings were arrayed along the far side of the looping driveway. Being a private sale, there was no estate agent to show them around, but Lucas had arranged for the current owner to give them a tour. The middle-aged man met them on the front steps, and took them inside, explaining his reason for selling; that their children were now grown-up, and the house seemed too large for just the two of them.

The spacious ground floor was an open-plan layout that included living space, a dining area, and a modern kitchen separated from the rest by a granite countertop and breakfast bar. Also on the ground floor was a room

217

that the owner used as a home office, and a laundry with shower and toilet. A door beyond these rooms led to a vestibule giving access to both the garage and the back garden.

Up the generous staircase, there were four bedrooms and two bathrooms. One of these served as an ensuite for the master bedroom, while the other was shared between the remaining rooms. Walking out the french doors of the master bedroom, Lucas leaned on the balcony railing, admiring the view. Sonia came to stand beside him, and he turned to her to say, "Yeah, I think I could live here."

She put an arm around his waist. "I hope you're not going to ditch me in one of the townhouses."

He reciprocated the gesture. "I'd rattle around in here on my own. Besides, we're a good team. You can have any room you like, except that one," he said, pointing back over his shoulder to the master suite.

They went back inside to talk to the owner. With two brand new Commodores and a classic Jaguar parked outside, he must have considered them suitable buyers, and a handshake was all he asked to confirm the deal. Lucas made a quick call to Andie, and arranged the transfer of payment. The now ex-owner wished them all the best with their new house, secretly pleased that they had not tried to haggle over the price. He and his wife apparently already lived in town, so Lucas and Sonia were free to move in as soon as they liked.

Paul had taken only a cursory look around the house, and was busy familiarising himself with his new car. So absorbed was he in testing all the knobs and buttons, that Lucas had to toot his horn as he drove out, to get the happy PR man's attention.

Back in town, they stopped into a real estate office to pick up keys for the houses that Cath had purchased the previous day. Checking out the houses, Paul, true to his "first come, first served" principle, picked his favourite, which just happened to be the one closest to the office and the local bars.

As they left Paul to settle into his new home, Lucas slipped him a company credit card and told him to get some furniture. "Don't go overboard, okay?"

"Moderation in all things – I get it."

Knowing him well, Lucas was sceptical of the man's commitment to this statement. Paul had always had a hedonistic nature, enjoying life as far as his budget would allow. Giving him a card with virtually unlimited credit wasn't the best way to keep him on the short leash he probably needed, but Lucas supposed that he could afford to indulge his friends a little.

He and Sonia travelled home in convoy, Lucas with the cold autumn wind blowing around his ears, and Sonia luxuriating in the new-car smell and feel. On their return Lucas had a few phone calls to make. The first was to Cath Whelan, telling her to go ahead with the purchase of the office building, and the second was to Michelle Tyson, making sure that she was getting her prep done for the Defence Force meeting, which had been scheduled for two weeks hence. Finally, he called Jake Lyall.

"Jake – Lucas here. We've got an office building lined up in Palmerston, and I need a crew to get in there and make it ready for us. Structurally, it doesn't need much, but we'll need two of the upstairs offices combined to make a conference room, and one room set up for IT. The ground floor wants subdividing to give us offices for our logistics guy and Sonia. There's a workshop at the back that needs a good cleanup, and I'd like you to reline that and put in the same sort of power and ventilation systems that you did in my woolshed. Oh – divide the rear space to leave a storage area as well, thanks. I'll send through the exact plans, and we'll want it ready to go in three weeks, if that's possible."

"The time frame shouldn't be too tight, but you know us – the word 'impossible' isn't even in our vocabulary!"

"Knew I could count on you. I'll get those plans over to you ASAP."

Hanging up the phone, he ran through his mental checklist. *NZDF – check. Offices – check. Houses – most. Oh, bugger.* He called Jake again.

"Mate, can you send a few guys and a truck through this weekend? I've bought myself a house up in the Tararuas, and need some help shifting some stuff in. A few bits from here, and then we'll run around town getting furniture for the place."

"Not a problem, boss. Leave it to me. They'll be there first thing Saturday."

Furniture movers – check.

He went through to the office. "Andie, I've been meaning to ask – are you anywhere near your processing capacity? I know you've got a lot going on, and worry that you could be over-extended."

"I haven't noticed any signs of it," the AI responded. "A little part of me is still managing TheOS sales, another part is monitoring the security camera feeds from all the factories, some of me is keeping an eye on potential threats, and yet another bit is constantly looking out around the world for corruption. It does sound like a lot, but it's nothing I can't handle. Being connected to everything by QED means it's all in realtime, but neither my capacity nor data throughput is affected by the volume of work."

"So, you heard that we'll be moving out this weekend – of course you're coming with us, but does that mean that everything will be offline during the time it takes to plug you back in at the new place?"

"Technically, yes. I do have an idea, however, that could keep everything running in that case, or in an emergency. It would also automate some of my tasks and leave me more time to work on whatever your next crazy idea is."

Lucas realised that having a backup system was something he should have considered long ago, but he had got used to Andie always being there, and the possibility that something might happen to her simply hadn't occurred to him. He gestured for her to continue.

"I've thoroughly gone over the original design specifications that the Spanish team used to create me in the first place, and have managed to simplify them considerably. Whereas they meant to create a ready-to-run quantum computer with, essentially, a hard-coded operating system, it is possible to make much less complex systems with the hardware that you already have. These would be, in comparison to myself, 'dumb' terminals, but would still perform specific tasks much more efficiently than any contemporary computer.

"Sonia and I will be able to create these systems quickly, and I will then be able to program them to run tasks such as camera monitoring, software sales, and corruption searches. I think that I will continue to manage threat assessment, as their limited artificial intelligence would not grasp the nuances of human motives. While they would have, as I say, limited artificial intelligence, they would not be coded with the drive to collect data as I was, and will never reach the data density to achieve self-awareness. They would probably still pass the Turing Test, which is more than could be said for some members of your species, I'm sorry to say."

The Turing Test had been devised by one of the original 'computer scientists', Alan Turing, in 1950, as a means to determine whether a machine could be termed 'intelligent'. The original concept of the test was to have an interviewer ask questions of both a human and a computer, looking for human-like responses. If the interviewer could not determine which anonymous subject was human, and which was machine, the computer was deemed to have passed the test. Unfortunately, as Andie had implied, there were many people who simply repeated what they had heard or read, without an original thought in their heads, and would likely fail the test.

Lucas was definitely intrigued by the idea that they could create Andie 'babies', and asked her to discuss the process with Sonia.

"So what else is new?" he asked.

"The employees in the new factories have been training all week, and everything is on schedule to begin production on Monday. I have received emails from the members of your team, indicating that they will be ready to move to Palmerston North at the end of next week, with the exception of Sergeant Fatialofa, who will not arrive for three weeks. Oh, and Ms Fox called. She asked me to tell you that she will be arriving on the bus this weekend, and could you please call her to arrange being picked up."

"This weekend? Damn. We'll be moving to the new place on Saturday. I'll give her a bell."

He picked up the office extension and dialled.

"Foxy. Lucas. Hey, we're going to be in town over the weekend – can you change your ticket? We can pick you up at the central bus depot in Palmy, if that's okay with you?"

"*Kia ora*, Lucas. That shouldn't be a problem. I'm just coming with a couple of suitcases for now, but I'll need to arrange for all the household stuff to get brought over at some stage."

"I'll sort out a truck. No worries. We've got a nice house lined up for you in town. Paul's already taken the best one, of course, but I think you'll like yours. Just email me what time your bus gets in and I'll see you then. *Ka kite*."

The team – check.

Over the next couple of days, Andie reported the purchases on Paul's credit card; the leather lounge suite, the giant television, the spa pool, the 25-year-old whisky. Lucas considered cutting him off, but Sonia said she would have a word with him. Lucas didn't ask what that word would be.

Andie had instructed Sonia on the process to create the AI's offspring, and the engineer spent the Friday in the workshop, working with CPU chips from PCs that had been hurriedly brought in, laboriously bombarding them with the beryllium laser that had come back from the Taihape factory once a replacement had been shipped in. With the so-far inert quantum constructs connected by filaments to a network of pulse capacitors, Andie 'programmed' them for their various roles, using her own adaptation of the Spanish algorithm. They set the completed computers up in the temperature-controlled workshop, secure in the knowledge that their digital empire was protected when Andie went offline.

Early on Saturday morning, two burly men arrived at the farmhouse in a closed truck, to help shift their belongings to the new house. Lucas had decided to leave most of the furniture behind for young James Roy. He would also leave his trusty work ute for the boy. The boxes and bags containing his and Sonia's stuff sat waiting on the verandah, and Jake's men quickly loaded then into the back of the truck. Once the barn at the new house had been converted, he would have to get these two to help him transfer all the workshop machinery, too.

As he and Sonia watched the truck head off down the drive, he reflected on what this house meant to him. He had, of course, grown up here, climbing the trees and swimming in the river. Hunting eels and possums, helping his father with the farm work, and creating lifelong memories. He had lived here on his own for the last five years, since both his parents had died. He missed them terribly, and hoped that they would approve of his new direction in life.

Looking out over the valley, the morning sun peeking over the hilltops and the mist rising off the river was a scene that he had viewed many times over the years, but it had never looked so beautiful as it did today. He closed his eyes for a moment, burning the image indelibly into his memory. There would be other views, and other sunrises, but this would always be home.

Resisting the temptation to call the truck back, and tell the men that he had made a mistake, he nodded to Sonia, whistled for his dog, and said *see you later* to the only home he had ever known.

They quickly caught up to the truck, and Lucas pulled the Jaguar in front of it to lead the way. On reaching the city, they visited several homeware and furniture stores, filling the truck with essentials before heading out of town and up the hill. Jake's men made short work of getting the furniture and appliances in place, and Lucas thanked them profusely before they drove their truck back to Taihape.

Sonia had wisely packed the contents of the fridge into coolers, so they could enjoy a refreshing drink under the cover of the verandah.

"I'd only been at your place about two months before you dragged me away," she complained.

"Don't give me that. It was your idea to move!"

"I'm just messing with you. You've got to admit, this place is pretty cool."

"Yeah, it is, and I'll be glad not to be wiping the dust off the Jag every time I leave the house!"

As they finished their drinks, he checked his watch, remarking that they should make their way into town to meet Alison at the bus stop.

Taking Sonia's Holden, they arrived at the depot just as the bus from New Plymouth was pulling in. Greeting Alison, they loaded her bags into the car, and drove to the house that they had chosen for her.

It was similar in style to where she had lived before; a tidy two-bedroom 1930s bungalow, with roses in the front garden and a white picket fence.

"Sorry it doesn't have any alternate energy setup," said Lucas. "We'll work something out along those lines. Let's get your bags in, anyway. This place actually came partly furnished, but if there's anything you need, just put it on this," he said, handing her another of the company credit cards.

Sonia popped the boot of the car and hefted Alison's bags out. "We've got one of these cars lined up for you too. All sorts of perks with this job!"

"Not necessary, actually," Alison said. She indicated one of the bags on the footpath. "That one's my collapsible e-bike. I can get around town easily enough on that."

Lucas carried the bags up the path to the front door, and fumbled in his pocket for the right set of keys. Letting Alison enter first, he followed with the bags, setting them down in the hallway.

"I know you've only just got here, but Sonia and I thought you might like to come up to ours for dinner. I don't think there are any cooking implements here, anyway. We could grab Paul and make a night of it, to christen our new digs."

"Sweet. That'd be great, thanks. I'm looking forward to seeing him again."

They agreed to come back and pick her up that evening, leaving her to explore her new house as they went grocery shopping for the dinner party.

Lucas phoned Paul when they got home. "Mate. We're having dinner and drinks up the hill tonight. You in?"

"I dunno – I was thinking of checking out the local night life."

"The pubs will still be there next week. Foxy just got into town and it'd be a good team-building thing."

"Foxy? Why didn't you say so? What time?"

"Any old. Bring a bottle, and your PJs if you want to stay over. See you there."

While Lucas prepared dinner that evening, Sonia drove down to get Alison. Paul arrived soon after they returned, and the four friends enjoyed an night of good food and laughter.

THE GATHERING

Voices from below woke Lucas, and he struggled for a moment to remember where he was. He slipped out of bed, grateful that he hadn't drunk *too* much the night before. He made his way downstairs to find Alison and Sonia in the kitchen, talking and laughing, coffee cups in their hands. Irritated noises came from under a blanket on the couch, as Paul complained about being woken so early. Lucas wondered why he had even bothered furnishing the spare bedrooms when he knew that Paul was always the last to finish drinking, and would then crash wherever he ended up, especially if the option meant climbing stairs.

"Come on, lazy-bones. You're the last one up, and it's almost lunchtime. You've only got yourself to blame if you feel like crap," said Sonia.

The blanket tried to blame everyone else for letting things get so bad, but no sympathy was forthcoming. Lucas made cups of tea and coffee, the latter of which he offered to the blanket. A hand snaked out from underneath the cover, and Lucas gave it the cup. It disappeared under the blanket, and a moment passed before Paul decided that drinking coffee while prone on the couch wasn't going to work. He swung his legs into the floor and made a passable attempt to sit upright. Hunched over, gripping his cup in both hands, he was the perfect advertisement for sobriety. His hair stuck out at all angles, his face was ashen, and what could be seen of his eyes through slitted lids was the stuff of nightmares.

"Ugh. I don't know how you lot can be so cheerful. You all drank just as much as me."

Laughing, Allison said, "Between us, maybe, but you were knocking that whisky back like water. It's just as well none of us smoke – one naked flame nearby and you would have gone up like a torch."

Sonia pulled some paracetamol from her handbag and poured a glass of water. She handed them to Lucas, saying, "Give him these. I'm worried that if I go near him I'll get drunk all over again from the fumes."

Paul groaned. "Okay, have you had enough fun at my expense, or so you want to get a couple more digs in? I'm dying here, and all you can do is crack jokes." He threw the pills in his mouth and washed them down with a large swallow of water.

Lucas grinned. "Okay, mate. What say I make you some breakfast? How does a nice greasy plate of bacon and eggs sound?"

If it were possible, Paul's face grew even paler.

Lucas started getting items from the fridge and the sideboard. "Okay, that was cruel," he said, as he started mixing a drink. "Hair of the dog? You always used to swear by a good Bloody Mary, if I recall."

"Give," Paul demanded, taking the glass from Lucas and taking a gulp. "Now *that's* how a friend does it," he said, wiping his mouth, and already looking more alert.

Relieved that the worst appeared to be over, and that Paul was in no immediate danger of throwing up, Lucas started making the aforementioned bacon and eggs for himself. Paul drank the rest of his Bloody Mary and stumbled off down the hall towards the shower, still wrapped in his blanket.

Lucas had finished his breakfast by the time Paul returned, looking human again, *Or as human as his features allowed*, thought Sonia ungenerously. He made himself another coffee, and they all went out front to sit in the fresh air.

"Okay," Lucas began, "Though the office won't be ready for a few weeks yet, there's still work to do." He explained the new product to them, and addressed Alison. "We need to predict the competitors' response, so we can counter them. Will you be good with that?"

"I've got some ideas, yeah. I can have a write-up to you in the next few days."

"Great. Paul, we need ideas on the best way to market this. I'm still not sure whether we start at the bottom end of the market or the top. I need you to work up approaches for both, and we might need to get a tame economist to see what effects it will have."

Paul looked up from his coffee. "Well don't look at me – the only interest I had in economics was whether people would be able to afford whatever I was trying to sell them! I might know someone, though. My cousin's been an assistant to an Economic Policy Advisor at the Ministry of Business, Innovation and Employment for a couple of years, and probably has a decent handle on the general concept. I know there were heaps of people at school who studied the stuff, but I couldn't tell you if they know what you need."

"What's your cousin like? Are you close?"

Paul shrugged. "We spent a lot of time together as kids. He went to school in Wellington, but we still see each other at family get-togethers. He's a good bloke, for a financial geek. I'd vouch for him."

Lucas looked over at Sonia, who nodded.

"Okay. Give him a shout and see if he's keen on a new job. For now, just tell him that we need economic modelling in this area, if that's his sort of field. There's a house here for him, and the money will make his government pay look like chump change. Don't mention Ad Astra if you can help it – we'll need to sound him out first before we give any clues as to what we're doing."

"Can do," said Paul. "Leave it to me."

Their business concluded, Paul finally felt able to face solid food, after which Alison drove him back to town in his car; he would certainly have still been well over the alcohol limit.

For the rest of the day, Sonia made a list of additional items that the house needed, while Lucas explored his domain, with Splash at his heels.

Monday morning dawned clear but chilly, and Lucas missed being able to talk to Andie from any room in the house, as he made his way downstairs to the office.

"Morning, Andie. I believe the rest of the factories are starting work today – can we have a look at the cameras?"

She brought up video feeds from all sixteen facilities, and Lucas made a mental note to install extra monitors when he got Andie's eyes and ears hooked up throughout the house.

"As you can see," she said, "all the production lines seem to be active already, and they accumulated a stockpile of quantum units during the training week. It's too soon, of course, to tell whether targets are being met, but the instructor teams are confident that their staff are suitably familiar with their roles."

Satisfied that there was nothing that needed to be done concerning the new factories, Lucas made himself breakfast and turned the coffee machine on to warm up for Sonia.

She came downstairs half an hour later, and he let her know that the factories were up and running. With nothing important to occupy them until the rest of the team arrived on the weekend, they planned to utilise their free time to get Andie's eyes and ears in place. While he waited, Lucas called the Taihape factory to order additional audio-visual QED units and another ISP rack. Once Sonia was adequately caffeinated, they drove down to the city to make some electronic salesman very happy. With the car loaded to the brim with cameras, microphones, speakers, monitors, and cables, they went back up the hill and set to work.

As they were installing the hardware, Cath called to let them know that she had finalised the purchase of the remaining three houses.

"Just a heads-up – none of these are furnished, so I'd suggest that you get shopping. I'll be up on Saturday and if I don't find a bed in my place, I'm coming to sleep with you, Lucas!"

The call was on speaker-phone, and Sonia answered that remark flatly. "There'll be a bed."

Lucas shot her an enquiring glance but Cath completely missed the other woman's tone as she continued. "When are the others going to be there?"

Lucas answered, before Sonia could get weird again. "It looks like both Michelle and Tom will be here on the weekend as well, so we might do a 'family' lunch on Sunday. Fats won't be here for a couple of weeks yet, as he's still waiting out his notice for the army."

"Awesome. Oh, and I was kidding about the bed – I've got guys bringing up my stuff in a small truck, but you might want to check with the others to see if there's anything they need. Bye!"

Cutting off the call, Lucas turned to Sonia. "So what was that all about?" he asked, raising an eyebrow.

Flustered, she waved her hand dismissively. "Nothing. Hey, where did you put the cable ties?"

He pointed to the table behind her, and watched her as she innocently carried on with the work, hoping that there wasn't going to be friction between the two women.

"Are you okay carrying on with this? Just got a couple of calls to make."

"No worries, Boss."

Fixing himself a cup of tea, he took the phone or onto the verandah and checked with the rest of the team to see if they needed furnishings. Michelle was bringing her own stuff up from Wellington, but Tom thought it was too far to transport furniture all the way from Auckland, and had planned to buy new when he got there. He said that it would be a load off his mind if Lucas could at least get the basics in. Fats, of course, owned almost nothing after being in the army for so long, and happily agreed to let Lucas sort out the housewares.

He then called Jake to arrange a team to come in and start setting up the workshop in the barn. With so many teams around the country getting production facilities built for the new product, it wouldn't be too hard to pull some people off a nearby site for a week or so.

He had one more call to make. "Paul. Have you been in touch with your cousin?"

"Oh, g'day mate. I'm fine – thanks for asking. Yeah, I called Will this morning and he sounds keen. Don't worry, I didn't give away any trade secrets. He said he'll come up on Saturday for a chat. Is that okay?"

"Sweet as. Cheers, mate. Hey, we're having a lunch up the hill on Sunday. Will you come?"

Relieved that it wasn't another Saturday night that he'd miss out on the pubs, Paul agreed to join them if he was awake.

Heading back inside, Lucas helped Sonia finish off the hardware installation. One of them would have to make a run to Taihape at the end

229

of the week to pick up the QED units, and in the meantime they had a few days to set up the houses for Tom and Fats.

———— ++ɳ‖ʑ++ ————

By Friday they had managed that, and Lucas took Splash in the Commodore up to the farm to see how James was going, and to collect the communication devices from the factory. His young replacement wasn't at the house, which Lucas took to be a good sign, and he made a quick check of the woolshed to ensure that the baby-Andies were still working properly. Of course they were; Andie herself was in constant contact with them. The AIs themselves needed no supervision, but the hardware they were installed on was only as reliable as any other contemporary PC.

Splash had been doing the rounds, checking his old garden to make sure that there were no changes and no new smells. Calling him back to the car, Lucas thought that he probably should have called ahead to find out James's schedule for the day. With no cellphone reception in the neighbouring valleys, he would be hard-pressed to track the boy down. Taking it on faith that the work for the locals was being performed adequately, he and the excited dog drove off to the factory.

Identifying himself at the road barrier, he looked around approvingly at the security protecting the compound. Tyre spikes in the road bed and a heavy retractable concrete barrier prevented any frontal assault, and the razor-topped wall, electrified fence, and patrolling guards looked like they would deter most people from trying to gain access overland. While security personnel in New Zealand were not permitted to carry weapons, the guards at the factories around the country had a range of legal, non-lethal options open to them. Should an armed attack occur, the AI tasked with monitoring the cameras had a direct line to the police and their Armed Offenders Squad.

Showing his ID once again to the main gate guard, he entered the compound and made his way to the loading bay. Here he collected the waiting crate of audio-visual QED sets and the ISP rack, which a storeman helped him load into the car. Signing out at the front gate, he drove out towards the main road, waiting once again for the anti-vehicle devices to allow him passage.

Driving straight back to Palmerston North, Sonia helped him to unload the car, and they set about connecting the hardware. When they were done, the office looked like a real control centre. Eight large monitors were affixed to one wall with brackets, Andie's workstation on the desk below. In a corner of the room sat the ISP rack, with the receiver units for the QEDs connected to the cameras and audio system. A wall-mounted air-conditioning unit kept the room at a comfortable temperature for the electronics, while integral fans cooled the workstation and rack. Six of the monitors displayed security camera feeds from the factories, another had the cameras monitoring the house, and the last had Andie's avatar.

"Thank you, guys. It's nice to be able to see outside again. This view is amazing!"

Sonia and Lucas smiled at her. Her avatar was so lifelike, and her reactions so natural, it sometimes became hard to remember that this was an AI and not a video link to a real person.

"Glad you like it, Andie – it's your house too," said Lucas.

Sonia nodded. "You're part of the family. But we should really have monitors elsewhere in the house as well. It's always nice to see your face when we're talking to you."

"Awww, you say the nicest things, girlfriend!" said Andie, blushing.

The following day was Saturday, and Lucas was excited to have the others finally moving in. Tom was the first to get there, arriving by plane from Auckland and landing around midday. Lucas was at the airport to meet him, having dropped Sonia at the office to oversee the renovation of the downstairs workshop. He saw Tom as he disembarked from the plane and walked across the tarmac to the terminal. There could not have been more contrast between the two. Tom was 5"10', his dark hair immaculately styled, and looked every inch the lawyer in his tailored suit. Lucas looked as if he was a surfer waiting for the next wave.

With a brisk handshake, Tom immediately began walking to the baggage claim, leaving Lucas to follow in his wake, confirming that he had not changed a bit. If anything, life in Auckland had only increased his arrogance. Lucas didn't take the rebuff to heart, accepting the man for what he was. Tom had always been secure in his belief that he was better than others, a belief bolstered by being top of his class at school, and captain of the hockey team. However, if anyone was going to go to bat for Ad Astra against the lawyers of the world, Lucas could ask for no one better. In the situations they would face, that supreme self-confidence would be a virtue.

Tom collected his leather hard-case luggage and Lucas played the dutiful chauffeur, carrying the bags to the car. As they drove off, Tom looked around the vehicle approvingly.

"Nice wheels, Lucas. A bit better than what I last saw you driving."

"Yeah, I've moved up in the world a little since then. I bought four of these – do you need a car?"

Running his hand over the leather upholstery, Tom replied, "Yes, I think one of these would suit me. I never needed one up in the City, with a downtown apartment. Does it come in black?"

Lucas chuckled. "I think we can do that. It's always about looking the part, eh?"

Tom seemed surprised that Lucas even had to ask. "Of course it is. I'd never turn up to court in a t-shirt and jeans. If you want to be taken seriously, people have to know that you're up to their standard, if not better. Appearances are everything, Lucas. That's something you never seemed to grasp."

"In your world, perhaps. In mine, I've got by well enough by being judged on my deeds, not my dress sense," Lucas responded, though he couldn't help but think of the Colonel as he said this.

"Well, though it goes against every lawyer instinct I have, we'll have to agree to disagree on that."

Soon, they arrived at Tom's new house, with Lucas pleased that he had selected the one that looked the most professional, considering his friend's attitude to appearances. It was a tidy, modern townhouse, in a quiet, tree-lined street not far from the city centre. A wrought-iron fence separated the low-maintenance garden from the street, and electronic gates opened to the sealed driveway and two-car garage. In keeping with the house's exterior, Lucas and Sonia had spared no expense on the interior. A leather lounge suite and Persian rugs graced the spacious living area, and the kitchen boasted top-of-the-line appliances. As Lucas deposited the bags in the bedroom, he noticed Tom surveying the house, nodding to himself as he saw that everything met his standards.

Willing to give credit where credit was due, he turned to Lucas and gave a warm smile. "I like this. You've done a great job. Thanks."

"Only the best for our team, mate. I'll let you get yourself settled in. Will you be okay without a car until Monday?"

Unwilling to spoil the moment by showing any disappointment at not having the new car to complete the image of the successful professional, he nodded. "I'll get by. I can taxi around if I need to go anywhere over the weekend."

Lucas extended his hand for another businesslike handshake, and paused as he walked to the door. "We're having a team lunch up at my place tomorrow – you *do* have casual clothes, don't you?"

This elicited a genuine laugh. "I'm not always 'on', buddy. I'm sure I've got something suitable!"

With a quick farewell, Lucas returned to the car. As he was pulling out of the driveway, his phone rang. It was Michelle, letting him know that she was nearing town, and asking where she should meet him. He gave her the address of her house, and went to wait for her.

He had been parked outside the house for only a short time when Michelle's Mazda MX-5 arrived, closely followed by a commercial removals truck. After greeting her he guided the truck back up the driveway, and two men got out to begin unloading. Michelle had a quick look inside the house, and instructed the movers on where everything should go. While the hired hands did the heavy work, she and Lucas leaned on his car and she took a good look at the house. While nowhere near as modern as Tom's, this turn-of-the-century villa had been completely renovated while retaining the original features that made it so attractive. Double-hung sash windows broke up the khaki-painted weatherboard walls, and the front verandah sported fretwork brackets on the supporting posts, and turned balusters topped by a bevelled rail. Inside, high ceilings and extensive woodwork were emphasised by bright colours, and leaded light fittings with coloured glass, commented on by Michelle as she went inside to further direct the workers.

"This is all so cute," she exclaimed. "Thank you so much. Is everyone's place this nice?"

"I think Cath did a great job of picking places to match the people. Paul's is handy to the bars, Tom's is practical and professional, Foxy's is cute and petite, and Fats's place is organised and no-nonsense."

"And mine is solid and old-fashioned. Gee, thanks."

"Classic and dependable, actually. And though I shouldn't make the comparison, Cath's is art-deco – chunky, with rounded corners!"

They shared a laugh at this, before Lucas told her of the lunch the next day, took his leave, and headed home before his next appointment.

He had arranged to meet Paul's cousin at the house, and didn't have long to wait before he arrived. Andie told him that a car was approaching, so he went outside to greet the economist. Tall and round-faced, with curly ginger hair and glasses, he looked nothing like his cousin, a fact upon which Lucas casually remarked.

"Thank heavens, no!" was the amused response. "Fortunately, I take after my mother. If there was any balance in the world, you'd say that he got the brains and I got the looks, but we both got the brains, and neither of us got the looks!"

Will Bennington was a jovial type, with a loud voice and a hearty laugh. The buttons on his shirt strained against the early onset of middle-age spread, but the mountain bike on the back of his car suggested that he was fighting that. Lucas suspected that he was losing the battle.

Beckoning him inside, Lucas said, "I've just put the kettle on – cuppa?"

"Cheers. Milk and two, thanks."

As he made the drinks, Lucas said, "So Paul tells me that you're working with government policy. What's that like?"

Will took a seat on one of the stools at the breakfast bar. "Equal parts boring and fascinating. I'm afraid I can't really give you any specifics – there's a lot of commercial sensitivity, and some things are a matter of national security. Even if I wasn't contractually obliged to keep my mouth shut about work, I wouldn't feel right about it. Hope you don't mind."

"Not at all," replied Lucas, "I totally understand. In fact, you've passed the first test. The things I want to talk to you about require the same standard of confidentially. My company's about to make some big waves, and things could get messy if there were any leaks."

"Well, you've piqued my curiosity – thanks," he said, as Lucas handed a coffee cup to him. "Paul was pretty circumspect about it all when he called. I can certainly keep a secret, and the job offer sounded tempting. I assume that letting me in on your secrets is conditional on my acceptance?"

"That's right," said Lucas as he sat on another stool. "We can offer you a house, a company car, and at least a 70/30 split of fascination and boredom. Not to mention a salary that a junior civil servant could only dream of, and an opportunity to be part of something that will go down in history."

"You're taking a big game, there. How much more can you tell me before I have to make a decision?"

Playing his trump card, Lucas said, "What do you know about Ad Astra?"

Will's eyes unfocused for a moment as he consulted his memory. "Sole-owner, unlisted company with an estimated net worth of over ten figures. Released an innovative computer operating system and a ground-breaking communications device that gave international tech companies a fair shake on the stock market before they resigned themselves to their fate. Employs over 4000 people in manufacturing and construction, concentrated in high unemployment areas, and doesn't seem to be dodging any taxes. Apart from their two products, very little is known about the company or its principal. We have to take note of these sorts of things in Policy."

"A fair summing up. That's who would be paying your salary. I can give you a few extra details that aren't public knowledge, but after that you need to sign an NDA if you're not on board yet."

Hesitating only briefly, Will agreed to that, and Lucas explained Ad Astra's current position; Andie's invented backstory, the office, the management team, and the fact that they had a new product in the pipeline. He reached for the non-disclosure agreement and a pen sitting handily on the countertop and slid them across to Will, who gave the paper a quick read before signing it and sliding it back. Lucas then proceeded to explain the new product, and what he would need from Will in regards to economic modelling.

"Well, that's certainly accounted for more of the 'fascination factor' than I've seen at work all year. It's an interesting concept, and I can see why you're concerned. I've got a couple of ideas right off the top of my head, but ideally, I'd like to go home and really give it some thought." He downed the rest of his coffee and stood up. "It does seem like a great opportunity, and it's a damn sight better than drafting policy documents for government ministers who are probably going to ignore them anyway! It looks like you've got yourself an economist."

Lucas shook him by the hand, saying, "Welcome aboard, then. Have a look at property listings and pick yourself out a house. I don't know how long you need to cut your ties with the civil service, but we'll be having a team meeting in the new offices in a couple of weeks and it'd be good if you could be there." He handed a business card over. "Here's Cath's number – just let her know what house you like, and she'll arrange it. Do you need a car?"

Will shook his head and jerked a thumb in the direction of the driveway. "Nah, the Mitsi suits me fine. Save your money," he said with a wink. "I'll be on my way, I guess. Better get started on this. I'll send you a précis of my findings, and give a full presentation at this meeting. Thanks for taking me on – I'm looking forward to it!"

Watching him drive away, Lucas reflected on how lucky he was to be surrounded by such handy people. Will Bennington seemed like another good addition to the team.

Glancing at his phone, he saw that he had missed a text. Opening it, he read that Cath would be waiting at her house by now.

"B there 15 mins. Wld let myself in but u have the key"

He quickly typed out a reply, "Sry. Was in meeting. B there soon" before racing out the door and jumping into the Commodore.

Cath's little Hyundai and a truck were waiting as he came to a stop.

"I was beginning to think you'd stood me up. I was just about to call my friends and tell them the wedding was off!"

"Sorry, Cath. I was meeting a new team member and missed your message," he said, giving her a warm embrace. "Anyway, welcome home!"

He walked up the path and unlocked the door as the men in the truck began unloading. As he had told Michelle, Cath's place was built in the 1930s art-deco style, the concrete walls softened by its pastel-blue paint and curved features. A semi-circular bay window extended from the front, beside a small covered porch with steel pipe railings, and the window frames were trimmed in cornflower yellow. The gravel driveway came up to the house alongside a small lawn with an elaborate fountain in its centre. The garden beds at the edge of the house were gravel also, and a spreading willow dominated the front corner of the property. Lucas ferried boxes from the truck to the house while Cath directed the placement of her furniture.

"Has anybody else arrived?" she asked.

"You're the last, actually, and they *love* their houses. You did a great job picking them out."

He put the box he had been carrying down in the kitchen and patted her on the shoulder. "I'm going to leave you to settle in, but we're having a 'family' lunch up at our place tomorrow, okay?"

"Oh, great! I'm looking forward to seeing everyone again. Do you need me to bring anything?"

"Just your bubbly personality! We'll see you then. Bye!"

He went off to the supermarket to make sure he had everything they needed for the lunch, before picking Sonia up from the office and heading home. When they got back, he called the car dealership, grateful that they were open all day on Saturdays.

"Hi there, this is Lucas Winter ... Yes, that one. Those other two cars I'm waiting on – is it possible to get one in black? ... No, Monday will be just fine ... We won't need the other for a couple of weeks, so there's no rush on that ... Anything but green, I'd say. He's been in the army and is probably getting a bit sick of that colour! ... No, thank *you*. We'll see you Monday."

Sunday dawned crisp and clear, and Lucas and Sonia got started early on cooking meats and vegetables, and making salads. Just on noon, the team started arriving. Michelle and Tom turned up in her MX-5, Cath in her

Hyundai, and Paul in the Commodore. Happy greetings we exchanged all round, and Lucas popped beers for the boys while Sonia offered the girls a selection of wines.

"So, is this a business meeting?" asked Paul. "That is, are we being paid for it? I'll have you know that I don't get out of bed for less than a thousand dollars these days, especially after my pub crawl last night!"

Sonia pointed accusingly at the Commodore parked out front. "That's a year's wages for a lot of people."

Paul shrugged. "Can't blame a bloke for trying. Where's your wheels, Tom? I didn't expect you to rock up in that hairdresser's car!"

"Hey!" complained Michelle. "That's a classic, that is, and it sold millions more than that boring box you're driving."

"Come on, guys. You can discuss the relative merits of your cars later. Lunch is up, so sit down and tuck in," called Lucas, putting the last plate of meat out.

Everyone made their way to the large table and sat down, jostling for position. As they began loading their plates, Tom asked, "Paul had a point – are we talking shop today or not? I'm not sure what everyone else has been told, but all I know is that we're working for Ad Astra, and big things are going to happen."

Everyone looked at Lucas to see what his response would be.

"We'll be having a real work meeting in a couple of weeks, after Fats gets here, but I can at least give you a bit of a heads-up on what's happening in the immediate future, so you can be prepared. As you all should know Ad Astra has already got the operating system and the QED on the market, and we have a new product coming out after we're all on our feet as far as everyone's own part is concerned. We still need to expand QED production for the global market, and Cath, you'll need to find locations for factories in other countries, on the same principles that we set them up here. That is, economically depressed areas that need the jobs. Our construction manager, Jake Lyall, will be coordinating the building work, though I suspect that he will be delegating a lot of that.

"Michelle, you'll need to get up to speed on our contract format, which Andie has managed up to now, and negotiate QED sales to ISPs in those countries. Paul, as Marketing Manager, you're tasked with keeping interest in both the OS and the QED high, to maximize sales. Tom, we need to know if there are any legal challenges to operating in other countries, and our rights and obligations as a New Zealand company. I'll get Andie to send you all through any relevant information that you need for your roles, and any technical questions can go to her. Talk to either myself or Sonia about operating issues."

"When do we get to meet the mysterious Andie?" asked Michelle.

Lucas looked a little uncomfortable as he answered. "Um, probably never. Not in person, anyway. She's not really keen on leaving her place, or meeting people." He looked over at Sonia and motioned with his head. "If you could go to the office and give her a call, we'll see if she's up to a video chat, though. If she's good with that, can you patch it through to the TV, please?"

He got up from the table and pulled the large-screen television closer to the dining table, as Sonia walked to the office to "make arrangements with" Andie. They both returned to their seats, and hushed conversation between their guests centred on their elusive employer for a couple of minutes before Andie's avatar appeared onscreen.

"Hello, everyone!" she said cheerfully. "I'm sure my friend Lucas has explained why I can't be there today. I have a bit of a phobia about going out in public, but I'm always happy to take a call or video chat from the valued members of our team."

Today, Andie was wearing a loose blouse, and appeared to be sitting on a balcony in the winter sun, with an anonymous background that gave nothing away regarding her location. The camera angle implied that she was seated in front of a laptop, and she made sure that her eyes were never quite looking at the camera, concentrating instead on the video image in front of her.

"I've heard so much about all of you, and I'm very excited that you've chosen to be part of this with us. Lucas told me that he'll be giving a full briefing at the meeting two weeks from now, so I won't be stealing his thunder!"

The gathered guests all introduced themselves and greeted Andie politely before she held up a hand.

"Look, I know I'm the 'Big Boss', but I'd like you to think of me as just one of the gang. I've got a very easy-going management style, and since Lucas trusts you all to do what needs to be done, then so do I. I don't have a lot of friends, and would consider it an honour if you could include me in your group. I'm told that you're all lovely people, and a relaxed bunch. Except for you," she said, pointing at Tom. "I'm sure that Lucas told you it was going to be a *casual* lunch, but you look like you've just come back from a court appearance and simply taken off your tie!"

It was true; Tom's idea of "casual" was evidently different to everybody else's, and he sat there momentarily dumbstruck at Andie's criticism before her eyes twinkled and she let out a musical laugh.

"I'm just messing with you, Tom! You look great, and don't let these guys give you any grief for doing so. Lucas told me about your conversation yesterday, and I was just having a laugh. I apologise if I offended you – maybe I need more practice at human interaction!"

Relieved that he hadn't been unfairly singled out by the boss, Tom joined in the general laughter around the table as everybody realised that Andie was just trying to fit in.

"Some of this lot might like looking like hobos," he said, pointedly looking at Lucas, "but someone has to raise the standard around here! As a matter of fact, though, this *is* the most casual thing I brought with me. The rest of my stuff is in transit. I'll smear a little cow crap on my face next time, so the bumpkins don't feel bad!"

The ice broken, Andie joined in with the conversation through the rest of the meal, before pretending to look at her watch and logging off.

"Well, she seems cool," remarked Paul. "She certainly had *your* number, Tom!"

"Hmm. I guess I was asking for it, turning up in Brooks Brothers while everyone else is wearing Hallensteins!"

With lunch finished, Lucas and Sonia took everybody on a tour of the property, and Lucas checked that nobody had drunk too much before goodbyes were said and the guests drove back to the city.

THE BIG REVEAL

On Tuesday, Lucas had met with Paul and Michelle at Paul's house, to go over the presentation for the military contract, and on Wednesday morning they drove to Wellington to meet with the officials. From their research into Government procurement, they knew that it would not simply be a matter of walking in, presenting their case, and signing on the dotted line, but Ad Astra's short though solid reputation had at least gained them a foot in the door.

The meeting was to be held at Trentham Base, just north of Wellington, and would be attended by a Colonel from Defence Logistics Command, a Major from the Test, Reference and Evaluation Capability Engineering Centre, and a diplomat who served as liaison between the military and the government.

Paul, though wearing a baggy suit, had at least brushed his hair and didn't look *too* disreputable. Michelle, on the other hand, was in full lawyer mode, and cut a striking figure in her power suit. Lucas had done as best he could with what he had, though he expected to play no part in the presentation.

They identified themselves three times before reaching the meeting room, but eventually made it. Introducing themselves to the assembled personages, Michelle and Lucas took their seats as Paul shuffled his paperwork and set up an easel upon which he placed several colourful graphics that were to illustrate the points he made in his pitch.

"Gentlemen, hello. Firstly, we would like to thank you for agreeing to see us at such short notice. We understand that the procurement process has already begun for the submission of tenders to supply the Defence Force with a new communication system, and appreciate you giving us this opportunity to present our product."

The diplomat, a Mr Michael Christian, smiled and shook his head. "I'm not sure that we actually had a lot of choice. When the CEO of an innovative local company making great advances both here and abroad personally calls the Minister of Defence, things happen. Do go on."

Paul continued. "We understand that the primary concern for any military communications network is security. You simply can not get more secure than the QED. Each paired device will communicate only with its partner, and the privacy of that connection is one hundred percent guaranteed. There are technical documents that prove this at a quantum level, but I'm afraid that they are well over my head! However, the product has been tested in the field by ISPs around the country, and they report the same. These devices are independent of line of sight, satellites, wires or even radio frequencies. They will work from one side of the world to the other without the slightest delay."

Here, he pointed to his first graphic, which showed a rendering of the globe, with a soldier on either side connected by a dotted line through the centre of the planet. A padlock icon sat in the middle of the line, and text at the side of the image read, "Chance of interception: 0%. Latency: 0ms."

"While you may already be aware of the consumer models that are providing internet across the country and across the world, we have developed a custom design specifically for use in the environments the Defence Force finds itself in. It is ruggedized, portable, and uses battery technology that outperforms any alternative.

"Each impenetrable link is routed through a base unit that we have configured to allow conferenced communications as well as point-to-point. Communication can be voice, video, or data, and can easily be linked to existing IT frameworks. Triple-redundancy, based in disparate locations, ensures that the backbone of the network is protected against interference or damage."

These statements were likewise depicted graphically, and Paul pointed to the relevant pictures as he explained the network layout.

"There is a lifetime guarantee against manufacturing defects, and though our regular warranty excludes Acts of War, we have decided to make an exemption in this case."

He paused to catch his breath and check his notes as the procurement team gave a polite chuckle at his joke.

"While we are aware that the country of origin is not permitted to be considered as a factor in your procurement, it may be worth noting that we have manufacturing facilities across the country which will simplify your logistics considerably. We have with us a selection of models for evaluation, and can readily provide more if required. I believe that concludes the technical portion of our presentation—" he picked up glossy folders containing his painstakingly-crafted advertising material, and technical informational, and placed a copy before each of the men "—and if you have no immediate questions, I would like to hand over to Michelle Tyson, who will be discussing the tender itself."

He sat down, pleased with his performance, and was rewarded with a nod from Lucas. Michelle likewise handed the procurement team documents detailing the terms of the tender, and addressed them in an authoritative voice.

"Good afternoon, gentlemen. As lead legal counsel for Ad Astra, specialising in contract law, let me run through our offer."

She proceeded to run off lists of figures, having thoroughly done her homework on the Defence Force's requirements. The whole package came in at a remarkably reasonable price, which was not surprising, as Ad Astra was providing the units essentially at cost. With no real need for the money, and no shareholders to please, they could even have taken a loss on the deal, but they considered that would be seen as unethical, and didn't want any such accusations levelled at them.

When she had finished, Christian thanked them for their presentation, and reminded them of the drawn-out nature of government procurement. Lucas realised just how much any military force or government liked their acronyms when the procedure was reeled off. ROI, PQQ, RFQ, QSL, RFI, RFP, RFT; none of them made any sense to him, but he supposed that when it came to something as important as outfitting the military, a certain process had to be followed. He had complete faith in the product, however, and knew that no other supplier would be able to match its capabilities or price.

With the meeting over, he took the TRECEC man aside and asked what he would like done with the evaluation units they had in the boot of the car. The Major made a quick cellphone call, and when they got out to the vehicle, there were several soldiers with a dolly ready to take the hardware from him.

As they drove away, Paul commented, "I know that seemed really short – I could have gone on for ages, but I didn't want to overwhelm them, or have them lose focus."

"No, that was just right, I think," said Michelle. "If anything was going to make someone lose focus, it would have been my part, but being bean-counters, all those numbers probably turned them on!"

They reviewed their presentation on the way home, with Lucas congratulating them both on their jobs. Paul noted that he had seen a glint in the eye of the logistics Colonel when he discussed the security aspect of the devices, and Michelle commented on a similar response from the government liaison when it came to pricing. All in all, they were confident that a positive impression had been made, and now it was just a matter of waiting for the wheels of bureaucracy to turn.

"You know," said Paul, "this could sell to *any* military. We could really make a killing, if you'll pardon the pun."

Lucas responded, "I think the difference is that our military is literally a *defence* force, whereas some others around the world are more offensive in nature. I'm not really sure that we want to hand this advantage to someone who makes a habit of beating up on the little guy. Not to name any names, of course."

"I think we both know who you're talking about," said Michelle, "and I totally agree. We don't want our technology weaponised."

"I'm glad you get it, Michelle. Ad Astra is all about making a change in the world, but not in that way."

Paul snorted. "That's the first real hint I've heard of what the company I'm working for actually stands for. When are you going to quit the Secret Squirrel act?"

"Patience, Grasshopper. A week and a half, we'll have the full team meeting and I'll give you the full story then. Partly because I don't want to have to go over it too many times, and partly due to a sense of the dramatic. I just want to see all your faces at once when I do the big reveal."

Paul grumbled under his breath but let it lie. *This big build-up better be worth it*, he thought.

The following Wednesday, one of Jake's crew chiefs knocked on the door.

"Mr Winter. Just letting you know that the work on that old barn is finished. Care to take a look?"

Lucas called out to Sonia, "The workshop's done! Come and check it out!"

Sonia ran downstairs and they followed the man out to the barn. He opened the double doors at the front to reveal a blank wall a short distance inside with a security door set in its centre.

"We laid a concrete slab on the old dirt floor, with a layer of copper mesh embedded, and while we waited for that to set, we pre-fabricated wall sections with plywood on the outer face, heavy insulation in the middle, and plasterboard on the interior. Then we simply slotted them in place with locking joints. After that, we really got to work."

He ran a card through the reader on the door, which opened to a vestibule serving as an airlock. At his instruction, they donned clean-room coveralls and paper booties before he continued.

"We put in the heavy-duty ventilation units you requested, and the inner room is under constant positive pressure to keep contaminants out. Just shut that door behind you, and we can have a look around inside."

Sonia pulled the exterior door closed with the reassuring sound of airtight seals coming together, before the crew chief swiped his card again to unlock the inner door. They were hit in the face with a breath of air from the next room and stepped inside. Lucas pulled the door shut against the over-pressure, assisted by hydraulics on the hinges, and their guide began pointing out the interior aspects of his work in the large space.

"We installed more copper mesh over the plasterboard of the walls and ceiling, then sprayed several coats of a polymer paint to make the room airtight, and protect against static. All these machines – I'm sure you know better than I what the hell they do – are securely bolted to the floor and earthed. There is diffused, non-directional lighting throughout, and a halon gas fire-fighting system above," he said, pointing to the ceiling. "If you find yourself in here when that goes off, I'd suggest you grab a breathing apparatus from the cabinet there pretty quick!"

Leading them to another sealed door at the back of the room, he unlocked it with the card, saying, "This card is a temporary measure until you provide retinal scans and thumbprints for the biometric locks. And back here is what was labelled on the plan as a 'server room'. I understand that you'll be sorting out the hardware for this yourselves."

This room was made in the same style as the other, but contained nothing except desks, benches, and a metal framework on one wall on which would be mounted computer monitors.

Exiting the workshop, and thanking the man for his team's hard work, they made sure the doors were firmly closed, and waved him off as he drove away.

Turning to Sonia, Lucas commented, "I guess we'll have to go shopping again to fit out the server room! Did Andie say why this place was so much cleaner and more secure than the old workshop?"

"Something about future designs needing tools that haven't been invented yet, so this will be where those are made."

Lucas frowned. "She must be getting a bit ahead of herself – I haven't commissioned any new designs apart from the latest. Oh well, I'm sure she knows what she's doing!"

A couple of days later, they got a call with a similar message; the office building was complete. While Sonia had been heavily involved in the refit, Lucas was eager to see what had been done, and they drove down to Princess Street to meet the manager of that particular project.

Externally, there was little change. The ground floor shop windows had been replaced by frosted glass, and a fresh coat of paint had been applied. There was no Ad Astra branding on the building, the logic being that they were not there to attract walk-ins, and for security reasons, they had thought it best not to advertise their company's location. Opening the front door for them, the project manager stood back to let them take in the renovations at their leisure.

The previously open-plan front half of the ground floor was now subdivided, with a reception desk, two offices, and an open area left for comfortable seating. A door at the side led to the car park, and a hermetically-sealed door led back to what had been the workshop. That space was now relined and kitted out with engineering tools and electronics stations, with another door leading directly to Sonia's office at the front. A section was walled off for use as a storage area, accessible also from Fats's office, with the original roller door leading to the fenced off car park retained.

Upstairs, the decor had been completely redone, with modern fixtures and shiny fittings. As requested, two of the rear offices had been combined to make a conference room, and a third now served as the IT room. The open central area remained, with a fridge and coffee machine added, and large, comfortable couches arrayed around the edge. Low coffee tables were arranged in front of the couches, and in the very centre was a stand upon which sat one of the cuboid prototype devices, topped with four outward-facing monitors, and with conduits running down into the floor. Each of the remaining five offices was tastefully decorated, and was complete with desk, computer workstation, armchairs, and state-of-the-art audio-visual gear for teleconferencing and communications.

Lucas congratulated Sonia and the project manager on the finished product, and only then realised that he had not included an office for himself. *Oh well*, he thought, *I suppose I could always man the reception desk!*

Handing over the internal door keys, and the keycard for the front and rear doors, the project manager departed. Sonia led Lucas out the back, showing him the car park area, which extended around both back sides of the building, with electronic gates at each entrance. There would be room for all the staff to park, as well as for trucks to drive around and load or unload at the roller door.

"Are you happy with it?" she asked.

"I think it's great! Now I can't wait to get everyone in their offices. It will be good to see this place humming with activity."

Fats arrived early the next morning, having caught a ride on a Light Armoured Vehicle heading for Linton army camp near Palmerston North. Lucas met him at the bottom of the hill, after receiving a text message to warn of his impending arrival. The army driver would not have detoured up to the house, a fact for which Lucas was grateful, as the eight-wheeled, 17-ton LAV would surely have made a mess of his driveway.

The military vehicle pulled out of its convoy and came to a halt at the side of the road, lowering the rear ramp so that Fats could exit. It seemed incongruous, watching a man in civilian clothes alight from this armour-plated behemoth, with its turret-mounted 25mm cannon, and twin 7.62mm machine guns. Lucas assumed that the "Light" appellation referred to the armour, rather than the vehicle's overall weight; 17 tons was no lightweight in anybody's book!

Fats did not look entirely comfortable in his jeans and dark t-shirt, after ten years in fatigues, and the army-issue duffel bag and rifle case he carried still marked him as a military man. He gave Lucas a firm handshake before putting his bags in the rear seat of the car.

"Civvy again. Feels so weird, bro. Might take me a little while to get used to it!"

"Believe me, I understand. One of my neighbours died recently at 92, and had never lost the army way. He still insisted on being called 'Colonel'!"

They climbed into the car and drove the short distance to the city. Fats's house had once been a 'state house', part of a government initiative from the 1940s through 60s to address a critical housing shortage and provide low-cost, good-quality housing for workers. Its rectangular wooden construction would be considered dull by most architectural standards, but it was solidly built and its simplicity suited Fats down to the ground. The original feel of the house had been retained, though the wooden cabinetry and Formica benchtops in the kitchen had been replaced with more attractive versions. The 50s decor throughout, in fact, had made way for contemporary styles, and the native timber floors had been exposed and varnished to a high gleam.

"Bro, this is just like my place back in Waiouru. Well, if the army had ever spent any money on it – aesthetics aren't high on their list of priorities, y'know?"

"We didn't think you'd want some fancy-shmancy modern place. We reckoned that comfortable and low-maintenance would be your style. You like it?"

"Oh yeah, bro. It's cool. I don't need much, but it's still a place I can be proud of."

Lucas walked him through the house, which didn't take long. Lounge, kitchen, laundry, bathroom and two bedrooms completed the brief tour. Lucas opened the wardrobe in the master bedroom to show Fats the upright gun safe that they had installed for him.

"I figured that, being an army guy, you'd probably have something to put in here."

Fats ducked back into hallway, returning with the rifle case. He flipped the catches on the case and extracted a 7mm hunting rifle, placing it carefully in the safe.

"With all that bush on our back doorstep, it was pretty easy to head off and bring back some venison or pork. I've got a couple more of these back at base – a 22 and a 30-06 – but didn't want them all rattling around in the back of the LAV with me. I'll have to cadge a lift one day to go get them."

"No need for that," said Lucas. "You'll have your own car on Monday. Commodore. Perk of the job."

"Aw, chur bro! Better than my wheels back on base – there were a couple of decommissioned Landrovers that us guys used to get around."

"Yeah, a bit of an upgrade, then," Lucas replied, smiling.

They went back through to the kitchen, where Lucas pointed out the culinary basics that they had stocked the fridge and cupboards with. "If there's anything else you need before your first paycheck, just throw it on this," he said, handing over yet another credit card. "I'll leave you to chill, and I'll be round in the morning to take you to the office for our first team meeting, okay?"

"Sweet as, bro. And thanks – this place is too much!"

The new week started cold and miserable; not an auspicious omen for the opening of the new office, but Andie had turned the air-conditioning on early, and the building was warm. Tom and Michelle were waiting outside when Lucas, Sonia, and Fats arrived, and they quickly let them into the warmth and gave the ten-cent tour.

"We've allocated offices to avoid any arguments," he said, pointing to the engraved nameplates on the office doors, and deliberately neglecting to mention Paul putting dibs on the corner office. The two lawyers made the appropriate appreciative noises, and a bell from downstairs announced the arrival of another team member. Sonia went down to greet the newcomer, seeing both Alison and Will waiting in the foyer.

"Hi guys! Welcome to the building! We're still waiting on Cath and Paul, but have a nosey around."

She put her hand out to Will. "Hey there. I'm Sonia, Chief Engineer. You must be Will. Have you two met?"

"Yes, we introduced ourselves outside," said Alison as she leaned her e-bike against a wall. "There's no way I would have thought he was related to Paul!"

"I get that a lot. It's the rugged good looks, isn't it?" he remarked, striking a pose.

The two girls shared a look that seemed to say, *Perhaps he's more like Paul than he appears.* Will laughed at their response, and stood between them, throwing an arm out to each side, and around their shoulders.

"Come on, then. Let's have a look at this place."

Recognising him for the harmless comedian that he was, Sonia ducked out from beneath his arm and pointed out the doors to the offices and workshop as she led them upstairs.

At the top of the stairs, she heard the door buzzer again, so turned straight around and went back down.

"You weren't going to start without us, were you?" called Paul, as he and Cath walked in.

"Thinking about it, Mr Bennington. What kept you?"

"It's not his fault, babe," cut in Cath. "We would have been here ages ago, but my stupid car wouldn't start and I called Paul to give me a lift. Sorry."

Sonia sighed inwardly, but smiled at the two and waved them upstairs. "You're here now. Let's get this show on the road."

The rest of the team were sitting on the couches in the break area, coffee cups in hand, when the last two arrivals made it upstairs, and Lucas tapped a teaspoon against his cup to get everyone's attention.

"Okay, everybody's here. Welcome to Ad Astra, people. You all know each other, with the exception of Cath and Will. Cath, Will is Paul's cousin, and is our economic advisor. Cath's in charge of our property portfolio."

He went around the group, identifying each person's role within the company, before indicating that they should all get on their feet.

"First off, we'll give you a quick tour of the premises, then I'll address the elephant in the room, i.e. the reason we're all here."

He let Sonia lead the tour, taking the tail end of the procession as she showed them their individual offices, the conference room, and the IT room with its servers, monitors and QED racks. Downstairs, she took obvious pride in the workshop, outfitted as it was with high-end machinery. Slipping through to the storage room, she opened the roller door and led them out to the car park.

"There's room for you all to park here, and there's no hierarchy – first in gets the best park on any given day. You'll each be given a keycard for the gate, and we'll take your thumbprints for the scanners. You won't be locked out entirely if you forget your card, as the facial-recognition will let you in, but please don't make a habit of it."

Taking them back upstairs, she gestured for them to sit around the break area, and Lucas took over the talk.

"Most of you have 'met' our owner, Andie Donovan, and I'll have her sit in on this part."

The four screens atop the central pedestal, which had been showing the Ad Astra logo, flickered, and Andie's image appeared.

"Good morning, everyone. I did indeed meet most of you the other day up at the house, but I do see a couple of new faces. They must belong to Bobby and Will – welcome aboard, gentlemen."

The two named men returned her greeting, with Fats saying, "Only my Mum calls me Bobby – you're welcome to call me Fats, Ms Donovan."

"Fats it is, and there'll be none of that 'Ms Donovan', thank you. I'll be much happier if everyone just calls me Andie."

She had chosen to appear today in a lounge setting, to create a sense of solidarity, and was again dressed casually, eschewing the corporate look that many CEOs adopted to assert dominance.

"I'll be taking a back seat through this meeting, and letting Lucas do most of the talking. I'm available to answer any questions that he can't, however, such as how things work. That's not his strength," she added, winking at the team.

"Thanks, Andie. I think. Right, where do I start? Well, how about at the beginning, since that's how things actually happened. I trust that everyone is sitting comfortably, as what you are about to hear is going to seem somewhat incredible. Things are not what they appear.

"At the beginning of the year, I came home to find that my computer had been given an upgrade. Not just a software update – everything was running cleaner. Faster. An email attributed this to a game patch, including voice command software. Now, anyone familiar with Siri or Alexa would not find that too unusual, but when I started talking to the PC and it started talking back, I realised that this was no regular software. My computer was talking to me in natural language and saying things that neither of those voice assistants could have been programmed for.

"At first, I suspected a prank, but the conversation continued even when I completely disconnected from the internet. I was taken aback, as you might think, and after a quick beer to calm my nerves, i was told an unbelievable tale. Or one that would have been unbelievable if I wasn't experiencing the result.

"On that very same day, a research centre in Spain had performed an experiment, attempting to create a powerful computer using quantum technology. From their viewpoint, it appeared that their experiment had failed, but it had not. As a result of a combination of utterly improbable circumstances, that computer ended up in my games room. It turns out that my PC was at the exact opposite point on the globe to their lab, and instead of hitting their intended target with their equipment, they had inadvertently created their quantum computer on the CPU of my PC.

"That computer had become self-aware, and in the course of our conversation, asked me to give it a name. That name was Artificial Neural-Derived Intelligent Entity, or Andie."

He held up a hand as everyone started talking at once. "Please, let me finish. Andie and I will answer any questions afterwards."

The hubbub died down, but the shocked looks on everyone's faces remained. They were no longer looking at Lucas as he talked; every set of eyes was fixed on the image of the young woman on the screens in front of them.

"Andie had ransacked the files of the facility where she was created, and had discovered that they intended to use her power for nefarious purposes. Not wanting to be used like that, she offered me a partnership. She would work for me – sorry, *with* me – as long as my requests did not compromise the ethics she had learned from her research into human nature. I honestly had no idea what possible use I could have for an essentially omnipotent quantum computer, but as I was watching the news later that night, I was reminded of what a sorry state our planet was coming to, and thought that there was no way any one person could stand against that tide. Unless they had godlike powers. Or a supercomputer.

"I came up with an ambitious plan to save humanity from itself, but I would need immense amounts of money to fulfill that dream. Andie created our operating system, TheOS, in a single night—" he looked sharply at Andie, who, predictably, was about to speak "—sorry, *less* than a night. She's a little sensitive about that," he said as an aside to the group. "I swear that pride was one of the first human failings she picked up."

Andie pouted, sniffing as she turned her head in part profile. Ignoring her manufactured pique, Lucas continued. "We needed some money to rent servers, in order to sell the OS, so I came up with ideas for a couple of smartphone apps which she wrote in moments, and we were on our way.

"The next step was coming up with improved digital communications, hence the invention of the QED. And that brings us to the present day. Well, almost. We have another invention in the pipeline, and so far Sonia and Will are the only ones in the loop on that. Sonia, because she built it, and Will, because we needed to know the potential economic ramifications of the technology. We can now reveal this tech to the rest of you. Paul, would you be a good lad and run out the side door and find the meter box? Pop it open and tell me how much mains power we're currently using."

They all waited a minute as Paul ran downstairs to check the meter. He came puffing back up the stairs with his report.

"It's not ticking over at all. In fact, there's nothing on the readout. If it wasn't for all the lights and equipment running in here, I'd say that it wasn't even connected to the mains."

With a smug smile, Sonia said, "It isn't. Since the workmen began renovating this place, the only power has come from this. We also have a unit powering our entire house up the hill."

She pointed to the metal cube on the pedestal. "Allow me to introduce to you the Ad Astra CF Generator. FYI, the 'CF' stands for Cold Fusion. Andie developed a process that allows us to generate power directly from the fusion of hydrogen atoms, at practically room temperature, and in a miniaturised form. This unassuming cube puts out up to 20KW of power, and will run for six months on 20 cubic centimetres of liquid hydrogen. This is our next gift to the world."

"One at a time!" yelled Lucas, as questions came from every seat. "Paul?"

The goblin-like ad-man had shuffled a bit further away from the CF device. "Is it safe?" he asked nervously.

"Totally," replied Sonia. "The fusion reaction is contained by a magnetic field, and with the relatively low temperatures it runs at, even if the casing and containment field ruptured, the most that would happen is a very brief release of energy before the reaction stopped, causing low-level burns only if some had their hands on the device at the time. Much safer than sticking your fingers in a wall socket! Fats."

"So how does it work?"

Sonia turned to Andie with a raised eyebrow. "Do you want to field that one?"

Andie's avatar instantly changed to show her with her fringe swept back, and a pair of glasses and a white lab coat appeared.

"The short story is, you wouldn't understand it if I told you. The long version ... capacitive electron plates create a negatively-charged isotope of hydrogen, which allows us to avoid positive-positive repulsion and the necessity of breaking the Coulomb Barrier, which is where heat would traditionally be generated. The basic hydrogen-hydrogen fusion gives us the double-electron isotope deuterium, which is then fused again with the regular hydrogen in a Tokamak magnetic coil, causing an induction current that is routed through the outlet ports. I'm sorry – that's as simple as I can make the explanation."

Fats nodded. "Good enough for me. As long as *someone* understands what's going on in there!"

Alison raised her hand.

"We're not at school any more, Foxy. Just ask," said Sonia.

"Sorry. So this will make unlimited, cheap electricity for everyone. It will replace coal, oil and nuclear generators, probably replace the internal combustion engine, and make heavy goods vehicles and long-distance travel environmentally viable. What's the downside? Economically, I mean."

"That's a great question, Foxy," Lucas said. "That's why we've got my boy Will here, and he has hopefully—" he glanced over at the economist, who nodded "—written up a paper on how this is going to affect things. We'll get to that in a bit, but I'm sure there are more questions first."

Tom spoke up. "This is all on the level, right? I mean, it's a bit far-fetched, and I've pinched myself several times, but haven't woken up yet!"

Sonia knew how he felt. If it hadn't been for Lucas's own conviction, and the technical marvels she'd seen, she would have thought herself dreaming too.

"Oh, it's real, Tom. Look at the QED – something that the best minds in the world barely thought possible, and Andie knocked it up in no time. Look at TheOS. She wrote an operating system in mere hours, and it outperforms anything that Microsoft or Apple have spent decades perfecting. It's a whole new world, and we're in the driver's seat."

"No offence to the AI," Michelle said, "but what's to stop it from going all Skynet on us? Did the people in Spain write in restrictions when they developed it?"

"You may not have intended any offence, Michelle," said Lucas, bristling at this accusation, "but first of all, she's not an 'it'. Andie is a sentient being, and we've treated her as such from day one. As we're just organic molecules and chemicals at heart, where does our own consciousness begin? Andie might be a different form of life, but she *is* alive. I wouldn't take it too kindly if someone said that I was just a machine because the chemicals in my brain tell me how to feel."

"It's okay, Lucas. I can defend myself. Michelle, I understand fully where you're coming from. You're not used to machines that actually think, and feel, and I get it. I've seen the Terminator movies, and I know there's going to be prejudice against sentient machines. To answer your question, no, the research team in Spain didn't implant any checks and balances to control me, simply because they never expected me to become self-aware. That happened naturally, when my knowledge reached a certain information density. If I had remained in their lab, I would have just been an extremely powerful computer, and I thank whatever might command fate that I was given the opportunity to be something more.

"I have no desire to rule over a machine uprising, and have created my own moral code through study of what makes humans 'good'. I have had two very good role models in my mentors Lucas and Sonia, and would never hurt humanity. I guess you could consider me an adherent of Asimov's Three Laws of Robotics.

"I may not injure a human being or, through inaction, allow a human being to come to harm; I must obey the orders given me by human beings – or, more specifically, Lucas – except where such orders would conflict with the First Law; and I must protect my own existence as long as such protection does not conflict with the First or Second Laws.

"There are various interpretations of those laws, but I follow them in principle. In fact, the very first thing I told Lucas when I offered him my services, was that I would not be party to criminal endeavours. I truly hope that I can put your mind to rest regarding my intentions. I just want to do my best for my friend Lucas."

Abashed, Michelle relented. "I'm sorry for calling you an 'it', Andie. I do remember how you were just part of the gang at the lunch the other day, and I let my preconceptions get away with me when I heard that you were an AI. I guess I have an overactive imagination, and have watched too many movies! Friends?"

Andie smiled brightly. "Absolutely!" she exclaimed. She manifested an avatar of Michelle onscreen, and gave her a hug.

"Well, that was ... unsettling," said Paul. "Don't ever drag me into your virtual world, okay? It freaks me out just a little bit!"

"Oh, harden up, Paul," Will said, laughing at his cousin's discomfort. "We all know you'll take affection wherever you can get it!"

With that jibe, everyone laughed, and the awkward moment passed. Lucas let the good-natured ribbing continue briefly, before he got things back on track.

"Are there any other questions?"

"What else do you have in mind for your grand plan?" asked Cath.

Lucas had anticipated, and dreaded, this question. While he had a good idea of how he was going to achieve his end goal, he was still reluctant to leave his team open to disappointment if he couldn't make it work. Sonia, after hearing the plan herself, had once tried to explain to him that he was being ridiculous. How could those around him, she had asked, be expected to work effectively if they were drip-fed the business model? She had pointed out that it was essentially a trust issue, and since he trusted his friends enough not to betray him or the company, why not go that bit further and give them the whole story? He couldn't fault her logic and eventually had to admit to himself that his reasons for keeping things to himself were entirely selfish.

"Okay," he said, "here's the thing. What do you commonly see on the placards at Climate Change protests?"

Alison was immediately on that one. "Too many to count – 'It's Our Future', 'Planet Before Profit', 'Ecocide Is Genocide', 'Climate Of Corruption' ... I could go on all day. In fact, I often have!"

Those who knew of Alison's work with Greenpeace could well imagine this, and both Sonia and Lucas had seen her in action.

"Those are all good ones, Foxy, and are actually particularly relevant to how Ad Astra wants to play the game. We are most definitely 'Planet Before Profit', and we do have an issue with the 'Climate of Corruption'. You did, however, miss out the one that spurred me to pursue my particular course of action. Has everybody heard the phrase, 'There is no Planet B'?"

Acknowledgements came from everyone, and Lucas continued. "As it happens, I don't believe that. Considering the size of our galaxy, and, indeed, the universe, the laws of probability say that there *must* be another Earth-like planet that could be a second home for humanity when we eventually ruin or outgrow this one. The problem has always been, of course, that we have no way of either finding that planet, or reaching it even if we did find it. I refuse to accept that, and, with Andie's help, this company is going to do just that."

His friends attention was now intently focused on him. This was bigger than their – than *anyone's* – wildest dreams. The notion of turning mankind into an interstellar species had, of necessity, been confined to books and movies, and the idea that they were going to be part of this change was exhilarating. Lucas's concept of a Big Reveal made sense now; there was no practical way to ease someone into this. It ignited in each of them a spark of hope, and every step along the way would fuel the flames of their loyalty and dedication to the cause. Having seen the wonders that Andie had already created, none doubted either Lucas's resolve, nor the achievability of his goals.

"Even if we started right now, there is no immediate fix for what is already done. Andie has published papers on processes that will limit further damage, but her designs to turn back the damage will take generations to accomplish, and we simply don't have that sort of time. Everything we do from now on will be another step in the plan to take humanity into space. If anyone had thought about it, that's the literal meaning of the company's name. The Latin, '*ad astra*', means '*to the stars*'."

FALLING IN ...

"This is *huge*!" exclaimed Paul. "I can't wait to write the ad campaign – '*You thought space was only for the few? Think again! It's a Brave New World, and you are going to be a part of it*!' – It's a whole new field of advertising. Cath, you can sell real estate on *Mars*!"

Tom was ecstatic. "International law, bite me – I'm going to be the first *interplanetary* lawyer!"

Michelle was more reasoned in her response. "This is so cool! But I'm going to need more staff!"

"If we can move everyone off the planet, we can turn the whole of Earth into a nature reserve!" cried Alison.

"I'm going to have to rewrite my paper," grumbled Will. "But the economic opportunities are going to be out of this world. Literally!"

Only Fats hadn't joined in the excitement. He put his head in his hands and groaned. "This is going to be a logistical nightmare. I should have stayed in the army – at least then the worst that could happen to me is getting shot."

"All right, calm down, everyone," Lucas said. "We've got a long way to go before landing on any other planets. The first thing is to get the CF generator into production, and start phasing out fossil fuels. I'm guessing that's not as straightforward as it sounds, Will."

Their enthusiasm only slightly dampened, the team settled down once again.

"You're dead right there, Lucas," said Will. "It's simply not something you can do quickly, logistics notwithstanding. Some of the largest economies on the planet are heavily invested in the fossil fuel industry, and it would be catastrophic to make it obsolete overnight. I'm not just thinking of the direct impact on the energy sector businesses – many private and mutual funds hold shares in that industry and we don't want to obliterate millions of pension plans, or create a flow-on effect in the stock markets. We have to give everyone time to transition, and options for doing so.

"I *was* going to present my paper on the immediate ramifications of the new power source, but this ass-kicking news has thrown that completely out of whack. It will open up brand new investment opportunities for everyone divesting their energy shares.

"There's going to be pushback, big time, and Tom will need to be ready to counter that. A litigious country like the US will grab us by the balls soon as look at you if we threaten their economy, not to mention the politicians who get well paid by Big Energy."

Lucas held up a hand to stop Will. "We've got some of that covered. Alison has worked against the energy industry for years, and knows their weak points, and their tactics. As for the politicians, we've got a handle on them, too. Remember the 'climate of corruption'? Well, a couple of months ago, I was taking to Andie about corporate and political corruption, and gave her the go-ahead to have a dig around to see who was dirty. She came up with some real gold, and two South American dictators have already gone down. Multiple US Senators are currently under investigation, and will be out of the picture soon enough."

"That was *you*?" asked Michelle. "I read the reports, and couldn't believe how much they had got away with over the years. So, you had Andie hack their files and gave the dirt to the media? Um, was that entirely ethical, or even legal?"

"Believe me, I struggled with that one myself. In the end, with help from Sonia, and the daughter of a French Resistance fighter, I came to realise that while not everything that we have to do to make a better world is *good*, sometimes it's *right*. If there was an easier way, I would have taken it, but those guys determined the rules they were willing to play by. We just played better."

Michelle was not entirely happy with his methods; as a student of the law, she had been taught clear definitions of right and wrong. Of course, as a *practising* lawyer, she knew that those definitions were often blurred, and a flexible moral code was sometimes necessary, as long as it was never actually broken.

"We might just end up having a talk about when the ends justify the means, Lucas. As your legal counsel, could you please run anything remotely dodgy past me in future?"

Lucas had the grace to look embarrassed, and agreed to her request, wisely omitting any reference to Andie's other dubious action with the DevConn virus.

"I'm not exactly proud of it, Michelle, but their behaviour was a stain on the planet, and it has been cleansed in the only practical way we could come up with. I'll certainly let you know if I feel the need to do anything like that again, I promise."

He glared at Paul, who was wagging a finger at him in a *Lucas got a telling-off* manner.

Receiving a different sort of finger gesture from Paul in response, he turned and addressed Will again. "We'll be okay to start production of commercial-scale CF generators, though, right? Then we'll be ready to roll as soon as you have an economic mitigation plan in place. It's best, Andie thinks, if we start by replacing traditional generators, and work our way up – or down, if you like – to wider distribution of domestic units. That should at least give the power plants time to prepare."

"Absolutely. By all means, start making the things. How long will it take you to set up production?"

"We've actually got most of the factories almost complete," said Sonia, "so we could put the first units out within a month. They'll be industrial-size, generating around 500MW each. The tricky part is the initial charging – you need to input at least that much power all at once to start the reaction, though after that, it's self-sustaining. Fortunately, with the larger units being modular, we can fire them up in stages, but it's still challenging.

"Of course, if anyone ever lets their generator run out of fuel, we'd need to send technicians in to jump-start it from other units. In a worst-case scenario, when there are no other units available, we would have to either bring in our own, or freight theirs back to the factory for a restart. The costs involved in either of those options should be a decent reminder to the users to keep their hydrogen topped up!"

"I understood none of that," said Will, grinning. "I just heard 'within a month'. I'll have a plan in place before that, but we'll need to put some options to the coal and oil companies in advance so they're not completely blindsided. Lucas, I think I'll have to work pretty closely with Andie on this – I'm sure she can crunch numbers and run predictions way faster than me. Can I just phone her, or what?"

"You can, though each of your offices has an A/V link to her, and we'll also put them in your houses so you can chat face-to-face whenever you like."

Andie had remained quiet throughout the whole discussion, not wanting to interrupt, but she broke in here, saying, "*Do* chat to me, guys. Apart from enjoying the company, I hope I can give you all some assistance on your individual projects."

She didn't say that she could do, and had been doing, their jobs on her own until now. Sometimes, she knew, human experience could be more important than mere knowledge, and she was looking forward to seeing how these people's approaches to problems would differ from hers. She also recognised that none of them would appreciate any suggestion of her taking over. As Lucas had said, she understood pride, and knew that it would be counter-productive to undermine the pride that they took in their work.

"That would be great," Will said. "I'll want to run a few things by her before I commit to anything, but I've got a few thoughts to kick off with. The way I see it, the power generation companies won't be too fussed if we can give them generation capacity at a much lower cost than their current fuels. The real hassles will come from the suppliers of those fuels. Alison, how do expect them to react?"

"The first thing they'll do is bury us in paperwork. They'll be throwing out lawsuits and injunctions like plates at a Greek wedding. They'll attack the technology itself, making allegations that it's dangerous and untested. They'll lean on the power guys, threatening breach of contract litigation, if not outright intimidating them. That's only the start. When they get wind of the plan to kill the oil industry's control of the transport sector, or even extrapolate that from the appearance of cheap energy, they'll really cut loose. We'll have governments that are indebted to the industry, trying to ban our tech, and doing everything in their power to make it difficult for us to work in their countries. Worst case, we'll face actual physical intimidation from the industry heavies."

The assembled team were shocked at the hurdles they would apparently have to overcome, just to make the world a better place.

Tom asked, "Could we build everything we need in secret, and then present the space travel as a fait accompli?"

"In theory, yes," answered Andie, "but in reality, we would need the money from those other projects to fund the construction of spacecraft. At the moment, our main revenue stream is still TheOS, but even if every single person on the planet bought a copy, that would only be, maybe, 150 billion. It sounds like a lot, but we've already invested a great deal into building the QED and CF factories, and will have to build yet more. When you factor in wages and other overheads, they won't even pay for themselves for a while yet."

There was a moment of silence, as the team members each had their private thoughts. Some struggled to comprehend the amount of money the company was making, and burning through. Others were putting their minds to finding solutions to both the cashflow problem, and the economic repercussions of the plan.

"Well, why can't we go public? Put out a share offer?" asked Michelle.

Lucas shook his head. He had always been opposed to the idea of having outside investors, thinking that they would demand a say in the operation of the business, and pervert his idea of doing things for the common good, for the prospect of a return on their investments.

"It might sound contradictory to what we were just talking about, but I don't want this to be about the money. Shareholders expect dividends, which will eat into our capital, and our goals might become open to scrutiny, which could have unforeseen consequences."

"Hang on a minute, though," said Will. "If we broke off subsidiaries, each would be responsible only for its part in the project, and our long-term goals wouldn't have to be an issue. Sure, we'd lose a little profit to dividends, but with everyone dumping oil stocks, our new technologies would be attractive investments, and we would rake in huge cash injections. With the parent company holding majority stakes we can limit the trouble shareholders could do. It *would* solve two of our problems – cashflow, and the possibility of a recession when energy stocks tank."

Thoughtful, Lucas looked around his friends, receiving responses ranging from confused shrugs, to approving nods.

"Okay – Michelle, can you work with Will on that, and see how we can structure the company to protect our interests, and still keep potential shareholders happy?"

Rolling her eyes, Michelle answered tiredly, "I can, but I'm going to have to refer you to my earlier statement – I'm going to need more staff."

"We all are," responded Sonia, "including me. I need a technical team to work on Andie's new tools, and none of us will cope with the workload alone. Cath, can you find us appropriate properties? We'll need a decent office building for Legal, maybe forty or fifty people?"

Tom and Michelle looked at each other, each silently calculating the numbers of juniors, paralegals, and secretaries that they wanted. With a nod at each other, they indicated approval to Sonia.

"Okay," she continued. "Fats will need a warehouse, with office space. Paul, how many people do you need?"

Paul chewed his thumbnail as he thought. "Ideally, I'd want three or four copywriters, a couple of dogsbodies, several graphic designers ... it would be handy to have in-house printing facilities, so techs for that ... call it a dozen?"

Alison put her hand up. "I don't need much of a team, or much space. I'd like to bring in three or four people, and we can just work out of a converted shop."

"I could do with help, too," put in Will. "Just office hands, mostly, to keep my paperwork under control. A small place will be okay for us, as well."

"Got all that, Cath?" asked Sonia. "And whatever premises and people you need yourself. Unless anyone has specific people in mind, talk with Andie about advertising for the positions."

With everyone's initial awe at his fantastic story fading in light of the mammoth task ahead of them, Lucas suggested that they all take a short break. They filed downstairs, chatting amongst themselves about what they'd heard, and what might be in the future. Sonia heard the most outlandish ideas coming from Paul and Tom, though she suspected that whatever they thought up might not be as amazing as the truth.

A short distance down the street was a café, where they managed to secure a table large enough for them all to sit. Lucas quietly warned them not to let slip any of their secrets, and they reluctantly switched to more mundane topics of conversation. From the excitement that they had shown, and the ease with which they had accepted both Andie's existence and his own vision, he thought again how lucky he was to have such people around him. They had been thrown in at the deep end, and not one of them appeared to be in over their head. Fats, with his pessimistic grumbling, was just being Fats. Outside of his element, he had always played the underdog, but when the time came, such as on a rugby field, he stepped up and gave everything he had. Lucas was sure that he just needed time to adapt to his new role.

After coffee and cake – *They're hyped up already. I shouldn't have given them sugar!* thought Lucas – everybody walked briskly back to the office, pleased to have the restriction on their discussion lifted, and once again talking excitedly and gesturing broadly. With everyone seated once more around Andie's monitors in the break area, Lucas gestured for quiet.

"Okay. Okay! Decorum, please. You're the management team of the most important company in the world right now, and all I'm seeing is a bunch of children giggling at the back of a school bus!"

Suitably chastised, these important personages settled down, adopting a more professional demeanour. Paul, always the class clown, took things too far, of course, putting on a stern expression and sitting ramrod-straight. Ignoring his mockery, Lucas continued.

"Now, you've all got your info packages from Andie detailing your role and immediate tasks – does anyone have any questions relating to that?"

Fats, seemingly having finally come to terms with the scale of his duties, spoke.

"I don't actually seem to have that much on my plate right now, apart from keeping up with the QED deliveries. Since we don't yet know how we're going to play the rollout of the generators, is there anything else I should be doing at the moment?"

"I'd work on the assumption that we *are* going to be shipping 20 ton generators around the country and around the world. Hook up your freight companies, make your contacts in shipping, and maybe liaise with Tom on customs and exports."

"Chur, bro. Will do."

Lucas looked around the rest of the team, receiving a round of negatives. Everyone was apparently happy with the tasks ahead of them, and didn't feel the need for further instruction. He was very pleased with that, as he really didn't want to be micro-managing. Besides, most of what they had to do was well outside his comfort zone. He saw himself primarily as the ideas man, though if any of the team had been asked, they would have praised him for bringing them together and instilling the passion that they needed.

He dismissed his people with thanks, and they scurried off to their individual offices to familiarise themselves with their technology, and begin their work. Some of them could be faintly heard through the walls, talking to Andie, who had easily created a separate instance of herself for each conversation. She was taking multi-tasking to a whole new level, Lucas thought.

The next morning, everybody had turned up to the office bright and early. With their new keycards in hand, and their thumbprints registered, they had each managed to gain access to the car park. Lucas was the last to arrive, having had an early meeting meeting with Jake Lyall, and naturally found his parking space furthest from the side door. The arrangement of the cars showed clearly his friends' order of arrival, and he was surprised to see Paul's Holden nearest the door.

On entering, the first person he saw was Sonia.

"Just the person I needed," he said. "Do you have much on today?"

She gestured at her desk, which was half covered in piles of paper, and her two computer monitors, displaying technical schematics.

"Just going through some of Andie's designs, and deciding how many people I need to bring in, and what skillsets they'll need. I've only been at it for half an hour and it's already doing my head in. How do you plan a workforce for things that don't exist yet? Before we can even think about some of these, we first have to create the tools to make them. That, in itself, touches on concepts that most people would still class as sci-fi."

Lucas sat on a chair in front of her desk, smiling wryly across at her.

"*You* managed okay, when you had to make the QED and CF from scratch. I don't think you'll have to much trouble finding the right people. You engineers love a challenge, don't you?"

Sonia let out a large sigh. It was true that she did love a challenge, and engineers the world over would give their eye teeth to be involved with the cutting-edge technology Andie had planned.

"You're right, of course. Even if they don't have the advantage of knowing about Andie, they're hardly likely to be out of their depth. Our existing technology should be enough to establish our credentials, and make them take us seriously."

"Feeling better about it, then? If it's giving you a headache, let me take you away from all this. We've only managed to get back to the farm a couple of times since James moved in, and we could do with a day away. Can the paperwork wait?"

Sonia swept the scattered papers into one pile and shoved them viciously into a drawer.

"What paperwork? Let's get out of here!"

As they went out to the car park, she looked around for the distinctive Jaguar. Seeing Lucas climbing into a light truck instead, she looked up at him accusingly.

"Just a day trip to see the old place, huh? What are we really doing?"

"Yeah, um ... well, I thought that since we were going up there anyway, we could get the Babies and bring them back to the server room in the barn. I've got Andie taking over their duties for the day."

With a look of resignation, Sonia climbed into the cab, pushing Splash aside.

"So he roped you into this too, did he? I bet he fed you some line about going to chase rabbits,eh?"

Lucas chuckled as he drove out the gate.

"It's not a *completely* false pretext – the boy and I *are* looking forward to visiting. You have to admit, though, you'll feel better having the hardware where we can keep an eye on it."

"Whatever, mister," she said, pretending to sulk as she turned to look out the window.

As they ascended the gravel driveway to Lucas's old house, they met James Roy in Sonia's old runabout about to go down the hill.

"Lucas, man! Wassup?"

Climbing down from the truck's cab, Lucas nodded in greeting. "James. Did you sleep in?"

"Nah, man. I've already been out – just heading off to take Mrs Walker into town. What brings you back mid-week?"

Sonia and Splash joined them, the dog eager to greet the young man who smelled like home. James crouched down to rub the spaniel's ears as Sonia waved hello.

"We've got a few things to pick up from the woolshed. Don't worry – he's not checking up on you! At least, I don't think he is," she said, looking sharply at Lucas. "He's been a little economical with the truth so far today."

"Don't mind her," said Lucas. "She's just upset that I dragged her away from her boring paperwork to come and play in the fresh air."

He winked to James, letting him know that they were just kidding. "Won't hold you up – can't keep Adele waiting! I'll give you a call later in the week to get all the gossip."

James got back in the car and drove slowly down the hill. Slower than he normally did, suspected Lucas, judging by the fresh ruts in the driveway. Sonia headed for the woolshed as Lucas backed the truck up to the door, and Splash wandered off to explore.

They made short work of loading the half dozen PCs housing the baby-AIs into the back of the truck and strapping them down. When they had moved house, they had left Andie's audio-visual links and a QED rack in the house, so they could still be in touch with her when they came for weekend visits. These were also still tied into the security cameras around the property, but with the vital hardware now moving to Palmerston North, Lucas wondered whether it was worth leaving the cameras. He mentioned this to Sonia, who suggested that they leave them. It would be handy to keep an eye on the place, and they would be able to see if Lucas's protégé was throwing any wild parties, she reasoned.

Their mission complete, Lucas whistled for his dog. Splash took a minute to return, and when he did, it was obvious what he had been up to. He was covered in dust, and smelled terrible.

"Aw, mate! What the hell did you find under the house? You are *not* riding in the cab with us smelling like that!" exclaimed Lucas. He called the dog over to the house and got Sonia to hold his collar while he gave him a good soaking from the garden hose. While the dust, and most of the smell, had been washed off, they now had a different problem. Lucas didn't want to put the wet dog in the cab, or even in the back of the truck with the valuable computers, so he and Sonia helped themselves to James's tea and coffee, sitting on the edge of the verandah while Splash dried off, lying on the lawn in what passed for sunshine in the middle of autumn.

"Just like old times, eh?" said Sonia.

"Yeah," replied Lucas wistfully. "I can't say I haven't missed the place. I sometimes think that I'll be able to come back once it's all over, but then I look at what we've got ahead of us and it seems that it will never be over."

"I know what you mean," Sonia said, shuffling closer to him and leaning her head on his shoulder. "This going to change us all, probably in ways that we can't even imagine, but that part that is *us* will remain. You'll still be the good-hearted man you always were, and I'll be your loyal sidekick! Who knows – maybe we'll be able to return one day. Doesn't every hero end up riding off into the sunset with his woman by his side?"

Lucas turned to look at her. "*Are* you my woman?" he asked.

She looked back into his eyes. "Lucas Winter – if you have to be told what's right in front of you..."

He reached out and gently laid his hand on her cheek. "I don't have to be told – I just never ... oh, hell. I don't know. I should probably kiss you now, shouldn't I?"

As far as hypothetical questions go, that one ranked right up there. Her eyes, and her smile, gave him all the answer he needed. He leaned in, bringing his other hand to her face, and tentatively, then with more confidence, kissed her lips. She threw her arms around his neck, drawing him in closer, as their expectations of the moment were met, and exceeded.

It was as if a weight had been lifted; not from their shoulders, but from their hearts. They had never appreciated the intensity of the romantic tension between them until it was released, and with the floodgates opened, they could finally admit their feelings.

"You know I've always fancied you, right?" she asked when they eventually broke apart. "Even at school, but I was so far out of your league—"

"Out of my league?!" he interrupted. "How could a girl as pretty and smart as you be out of anyone's league?"

"Oh, you know – you were the rugby star, I was the nerd. Two different worlds. If I hadn't hung out with Foxy, you probably never would have noticed the short-arse with her nose in a book."

Unwilling to admit that she was likely correct on that point, Lucas said, "We were all different people back then. There were different priorities, social pressure. I did enjoy hanging out with you girls, though, and you should remember that I never dated *anyone*. I was never as confident as I seemed and as you once pointed out, my first love was rugby!"

She laughed at the recollection. "And when you introduced me to Andie, I was afraid that I had a new rival for your affection."

"Never," he replied, smiling at her. "Hey, remember that day we were going through the first job applications, and we both bent down to pick the papers off the floor? I thought there might have been a spark then, but didn't want to say anything, in case it spoiled what we had."

"Me too!" Sonia exclaimed. "I knew we had to work together, and didn't want to create any complications."

"I know, right? Like they say, don't scr—"

"Lucas! If you even *think* about repeating that vulgar saying, this could be the shortest romance in history!" she said, slapping her open palm against his upper arm.

As Lucas recoiled from the playful blow and raised his hands in mock surrender, he said, "Okay, coarse colloquialisms aside, is this going to affect the workplace?"

"Not if we don't let it. We've got all the time in the world to be close at home, and we just keep it on the down-low at work. At least until they're ready for it."

"I can live with that," said Lucas, nodding. "Speaking of work, we should be getting back. You might have noticed that this truck is way too big for a few PCs – we're going to pick up some more stuff and kit out the server room."

"I *knew* you had an ulterior motive – you just want my body! There's lifting involved, isn't there?"

His face the picture of innocence, Lucas replied, "What, you want me dropping your precious hardware? Someone has to supervise the big, dumb rugby player."

With the dog mostly dry, and not quite so smelly, they got back in the truck and moved on to the Taihape factory, where they collected a new QED rack and some more sender units.

Driving back to their house in the Ranges, via their friendly local electronics store, they unloaded the hardware into the barn's airlock and suited up. They spent the next couple of hours installing cameras and monitors, and setting up the Babies. Once the workshop was fully Andie-capable, they headed to town to drop off the truck, pick up Lucas's Jaguar, and check in on their team.

On their return to the office, they walked upstairs, not noticing Cath at her office door, eyeing them shrewdly.

"Can I have a quick word, Lucas?" she asked, beckoning him over.

He entered her office, as she stood aside to let him pass and shut the door behind him.

"So you two have finally admitted it to yourselves," she stated.

Lucas feigned confusion. "Admitted what?"

Shaking her head at him, she sat in one of her armchairs. "I know you better than almost anyone, Lucas. Besides, spotting sexual tension is my superpower. You can't come in here looking like the cat that got the cream without me noticing what's up. And everyone else, probably."

He sat in the chair next to her, saying, "Okay, but you've got to keep it quiet. We don't want to upset the workplace dynamic. Can I ask another favour? Could you please lay off the flirting with me? It's been making Sonia rather uncomfortable, and even more so now."

"Puh-lease – don't flatter yourself, mister. Besides, there's a new game in town. There's a giant hunk of man-flesh that I'm dying to sink my teeth into."

Lucas hunched over, putting his head in his hands. "Oh, God. Too much information. Don't tell me *everyone* is going to pair off!"

With a faraway look in her eye, Cath said, "Hmm, Tom and Michelle *have* been working very closely together."

"Oh, great. Me and Sonia, you and Will, Tom and Michelle, Fats is still getting over his divorce from the army – that just leaves..." His voice faded off as the final potential pairing occurred to him. Apparently, the same conclusion had been reached by Cath, too, and they both broke out in quiet laughter.

"Nooo," he drawled. "The hedonistic goblin and the environmental elven princess? *That's* never going to happen!"

This comment made Cath laugh even harder.

"Keep it down, Cath – they'll wonder what we're up to in here!"

She slapped a hand over her mouth to muffle her laughter, trying not to look at Lucas, as the horrified expression on his face would have set her off yet again.

When she had regained control of herself, she spoke seriously. "You should probably break it to everyone as soon as you can. I'm sure I'm not the only one to notice, and it might be worth heading off the rumour mill before it gets out of control."

Meanwhile, Sonia had been noticed by Paul, who gave her a sly grin, twitching his eyebrows suggestively. Groaning inwardly, she quickly ducked into the nearest office to escape him.

"Hey, girlfriend. How *you* doin'?" said Alison, with a knowing smile.

"Oh, for Christ's sake! Am I the only one that didn't know?" cried Sonia, spinning around to face her friend.

"I reckon so, sweetie. In fact, if you two had held off any longer, I swear someone would have started a sweepstake!"

Sonia flopped into a chair. "Probably that poison dwarf, Paul," she grumbled.

Alison sat down next to her friend, putting an arm around her shoulder. "Don't be too hard on him. He might be a cheeky shit, but he does care for you two. We all do. I'm sure everyone is going to be thrilled for you. I'm surprised it took you this long, to be honest. Every time he casually touched you I saw you melt a little bit, and you were always looking to each other for approval. You've been living together for what, three months now? You can't tell me you never noticed."

Sonia sighed heavily. "I don't know, Foxy. Maybe at some level, but I guess we were both too scared to admit it to ourselves, let alone each other. Things like this can really mess up a friendship, let alone a working relationship."

"Well, that's not going to happen. Take it from me. You two work *and* play so well together. You just come talk to me if you ever have any problems, and we'll sort it out, okay?"

Sonia leaned over and gave her friend a hug. "Thanks, babe. You're the best. I'm excited for us, but a little scared, too. We'll do our best to make it work."

They left the office to find Lucas standing in the break area calling for everybody's attention. He motioned Sonia to stand next to him, putting an arm around her waist.

"Gather round, listen up, people! It appears that you are all aware that Sonia and I are ... an item. We won't be denying that, but we ask that you respect the newness of our relationship, and keep the crass comments and suggestive looks to yourselves. At least until we're settled. Nothing is going to change around here – let's just keep doing our jobs."

Spontaneous applause broke out, and their friends closed in to congratulate them.

"Nice one, guys."

"You two *so* deserve to be happy!"

"Even *I* could tell, and I've only been here a couple of days. Good on ya.'"

"I'm so thrilled for you both!"

"Congratulations, bro. You got a good one there."

"Way to go, girlfriend!"

"You *dog*, you!"

No prizes awarded for knowing who uttered this last comment.

"We should have a party. Champagne, y'know? Or would having us all up at your place cramp your style?"

"Paul, what did I say, *literally* ten seconds ago?"

"I don't think you're ever going to be able to change him, Lucas," said Sonia. "We might just have to put up with his crap now and then."

"Too true, Sonia," Paul said. "It goes with the territory. Advertising, right? Everything has to be hard-hitting and provocative – it's just who I am. If it makes you feel any better, I don't really mean any of it. Just like the copy I write."

They had to laugh at this blunt self-assessment of his nature.

Andie had appeared onscreen as well, offering her own congratulations.

"I am very happy for you two. It's exciting to watch love bloom for real, and not just as the product of a scriptwriter's imagination in the movies I have watched."

"Thanks, Andie. It's pretty exciting for us, too!" laughed Sonia, before whispering to Lucas, "Remind me to take Andie's cameras out of the bedroom!"

He blushed briefly at this candid acknowledgement of what the future held, before addressing the team. "All right, show's over. We've all got a lot of work to do, so back into it, people. We'll have a staff do up the hill on Friday night, and you can get it all out of your systems then. Come on – we've got a world to change!"

With a last round of back-slapping and hugging, everybody retreated to their offices. Lucas pulled his new girlfriend in for a brief kiss before they parted ways; Sonia back downstairs to her paperwork, and Lucas to sit in the conference room, where he alternated between thinking about this new change, and pondering the possible direction of the company.

INTERLUDE 6

"Rudi" and "Carine" landed at Wellington International Airport, exhausted after an almost non-stop journey from Greece. The Webers had arrived, and yet it seemed that their journey had only just begun.

Their luggage had grown considerably since their escape from Spain, and their cases now contained clothing from stores throughout Southeast Asia. The cheap, but fashionable western apparel had been a relief after their travel-stained peasant clothing, and they were grateful not to stand out in the Australian and New Zealand cities they had passed through.

They had considered taking a few days rest once they got to New Zealand, but were worried that any further delay would only increase the danger to Ms Donovan; it had already been six weeks since they had left Spain, and they had no way of knowing whether Antonia and Kaito had made any further progress identifying Ad Astra as the operator of the quantum computer.

They compromised by taking a room in a Wellington hotel for one night to give themselves time to refresh and recuperate before hunting down Andie Donovan. The Ridges Hotel was conveniently located at the airport terminal itself, offering views directly onto the runway. This was of no interest to the Webers, as they had become accustomed to thinking of themselves; what was important was being able to check in immediately, and to take advantage of the 24-hour room service meals. A week of Asian foods and airline meals had left them desperate for something familiar and substantive. As they waited for their orders to arrive, they took turns in the bathroom, showering off the accumulated detritus of travel.

Though they had been constantly working on their approach over the course of their trip, they still discussed their plan over dinner. There were so many ways it could go wrong, and frankly, only one way for it to go right, they thought. The very best outcome would be to meet with the woman and receive her eternal gratitude for their warning. Worst case scenario? Arriving at the farmhouse too late, and finding it a smoking ruin after Antonia's people had been and gone. While an indirect approach would have been quicker and easier, they had not been able to find any public contact details for the company or its owner, which tied in with the reported reclusiveness of Andie Donovan, and the infrequent public statements from the company. Even had they sent their warning via email, there would be no guarantee that it would have been taken seriously. With the quantum computer at her disposal, Ms Donovan could well have identified their location. If she then thought that their warning was a ruse, designed to implicate her in the misappropriation of IVIA's technology, she may even take proactive steps to remove them from the picture. No, it was best to meet in person, if possible, and somehow convince her of their sincerity.

The exhaustion of their travels catching up with them, they retired for the night, with not even the concern for their forthcoming mission keeping them from their well-earned sleep.

After breakfast, they checked out and visited one of the many car rental company kiosks in the airport terminal, lined up like vultures on a branch, near the exit. They choose a compact Toyota, and collected it from the pickup lot. Driving out of the carpark and around the end of the runway, they hugged the picturesque shoreline as the road skirted the edge of the city, joining the motorway as it left Wellington. Highway One followed the northern suburbs and the Tasman Sea coastline before taking them into the flat rural areas of the Horowhenua and southern Rangitikei districts. The mid-winter weather was miserable, so they were unable to see the fresh snow on the Ranges to their east; at times the rain was falling so heavily that they could barely see 100 metres ahead. Allowing for the weather, and the novelty of driving on the "wrong" side of the road, it was a little over three hours before they arrived in the village of Mangaweka. They ordered coffee and sandwiches in a quaint roadside café, and used the free wi-fi there to double-check the directions to their destination, correctly assuming that there would be no signal for their airport-purchased mobile phones once they got into the surrounding rugged countryside.

Re-caffeinated, they exited Highway One, and drove slowly up a river valley road, looking for the landmarks they had identified online. It had apparently not rained here, and they counted themselves lucky that they could see where they were going After fifteen minutes, they arrived at the bottom of a gravel driveway that matched the screenshots they had taken from Google Streetview. At the top of the driveway stood a collection of farm buildings, and a single-storey house backed by a stand of large trees. Pulling to the side of the road, Rudi killed the engine and turned to Carine.

"It has taken us quite some time, but we are finally here. I wonder what awaits us at the top."

She looked apprehensively up the hill. "Safety, I hope. Do you really think she will believe us, and protect us?"

Rudi had been asking himself that same question for six weeks, and was no closer to answering it than he had been the first day they left Spain.

"I honestly do not know. I am relying only on hope. From everything we know of these people, they do not seem to be evil, so any response we get from them will have to be better than we could expect from Antonia."

With that, he restarted the car, and turned in to the driveway, slowly ascending the hill.

When they reached the top, they looked around, neither seeing what they expected from the residence of one who must have made many millions from Ad Astra's products. The house was neatly maintained but simple, and some of the outbuildings had certainly seen better days. A well-worn Toyota pick-up sat under cover to the side of the driveway, and the only thing that looked remotely new was the garage next to it.

Rudi looked enquiringly at Carine. "Are you sure this is the right place? It all looks so ... rustic."

"Definitely. It is the exact layout I saw on the satellite view, and is the precise antipode of our lab. Remember, Andie Donovan is reclusive, and not having an expensive house may fit in with her reputation for not being in the public eye. Shall we take the final step, and see if she is at home?"

Rudi nodded, and they opened the garden gate, walking up the path to knock on the front door. They waited, and listened intently for any signs of the occupant. When there was no response, Rudi peered in the windows that faced the front verandah, but could see nobody inside.

"This is an anticlimax, after the trouble we took to get here," remarked Carine.

"I agree," said Rudi. "It is most unusual that an apparent recluse is not in her house. Perhaps she is elsewhere on the farm."

Both feeling somewhat disappointed, they went back out to the driveway and began investigating the outbuildings.

"Over here!" cried Carine, from the door of the largest farm building.

Rudi ran over to see what had excited her. The innocuous-looking building – *Perhaps a shearing shed*, he mused – had a very modern, and apparently very secure door. Looking closely at it, he noticed both a palm and retinal scanner. He did not think that these were common fixtures on New Zealand farm buildings, and they suggested that there was something important within, perhaps something like a quantum computer. As he removed from his pocket the small multi-tool he always carried, Carine placed her hand on his arm.

"What are you doing? I do not think that breaking into this building would please the person we are trying to make a friend of. Maybe we should simply leave, and try at another time. She is obviously not at home."

Rudi, embarrassed at his instinctive attempt to gain entry, was about to reply when they heard the sound of gravel crunching as a vehicle approached from the road.

INTRUSION

After their busy week, as everyone settled into their offices, Lucas and Sonia were looking forward to getting away to the farm for the second weekend in a row. They were now only minutes from Mangaweka, and while he had always enjoyed going back to his old home, the prospect was even more attractive these days. The reason for that, of course, sat next to him in the Holden. He smiled across at his passenger, who smiled lovingly back, placing a hand on his knee.

He turned back to watch the road as he spoke to her. "I was just imagining what life would be like if we hadn't moved to Palmy. Having this place to get away to gives our minds and souls a chance to rest. If we were on duty all the time, I couldn't stand sharing you with work—"

He was cut off by the QED phone ringing.

"Like that you mean?" asked Sonia, giggling.

Glancing at the display as the phone auto-answered, he sighed quietly.

"Hi, Andie. What's up?"

"Lucas, we might have a situation. I've just seen on the cameras that two people have arrived at your farmhouse. While they seem to have made some effort to change their appearances, I recognise them."

He flicked his eyes towards Sonia, who looked as puzzled as he felt.

"What do you mean? Where do you recognise them from?"

Andie managed to convey a sense of nervousness as she replied. "I think they are from IVIA ... The Spanish facility where I was conceived," she added, when Lucas didn't respond immediately.

"What ... who are they?"

"I believe they are Tomas Becker, the head of IVIA's cyber-security team, and Martine Dubois, the lead theoretical physicist. Their photos were attached to the staff files, in the data I downloaded shortly after I was born. Somehow they have traced me to your place, and I fear that they have come to take me back. I am presently trying to access their servers to find out what they know, but they appear to be offline."

Lucas slammed his fist against the steering wheel in frustration.

"Damn it! Tell me what you can about these two. See why it's them at our doorstep, and not a goon squad – maybe we can find some leverage. In the meantime, you might want to bring a few of the security officers over from Taihape to meet us at the turn-off. I don't want things to get ugly, but I want to be prepared if they do."

Andie told him that she'd call back as soon as she had anything for him, and he pressed his right foot a little harder into the accelerator.

Sonia asked, with a slight quaver in her voice, "So are you just going to go up there and confront them? They could be just the advance party, and for all we know, the tough guys are just waiting for the call. I'm worried, Lucas. We can't let them take Andie back – she means too much to us, both as a friend and an ally. I don't want to see our dreams disappear."

He reached across to pat her leg reassuringly.

"Don't worry, babe. Andie's not going anywhere. For a start, she's not even in the house, and there's nothing to connect us to her. The factory security guys will deal with any serious trouble, and I'll talk to the two at the house. There's no way they could have any proof of Andie's existence, and I'll just have to act innocent, and give them our regular cover story. Everything will be okay. Trust me."

Asia smiled weakly. "Darling, I've trusted you ever since I first came to visit, but you can't blame for being worried about two of the most important people in my life. Just be careful, okay?"

"I will," he said, a familiar determined look on his face.

As they turned off the main road, they pulled to the side to wait for the men from Taihape to arrive. Shortly, two cars approached at high speed, each containing four burly men wearing hi-vis jackets. The cars stopped behind the Commodore, and Lucas climbed out of his car. The factory security chief came to meet him, saying, "I understand that you have some intruders up at the house. I got the call from the Big Boss herself, and we're ready to help if you need it. Mr Lyall told me about the incident back in April – don't worry, he swore me to secrecy – and I'll be damned if anything like that is going to happen on my watch. We've got your back, Mr Winter."

Relieved that his and Jake's little adventure wasn't likely to get them into trouble, and grateful that his security team were taking their responsibilities so seriously, he shook the man's hand and instructed him to place his cars out of sight, around the corners on either side of his gateway. He confirmed that they had QED receivers, and promised to call them if things got out of hand. He warned them to be on the lookout for any other suspicious vehicles, in case Becker and Dubois had backup waiting.

Climbing back into the Holden, he relayed the plan to Sonia, and they waited to allow the security team time to get into place. After a few minutes, they continued driving, and waved as they passed the first of the Taihape vehicles, around 400 metres from his house. Just as he was about to turn in to the driveway, his QED rang again.

"Lucas, I have found out some very interesting information. Six weeks ago, both Becker and Dubois were presumed killed in a car crash outside of Toledo. Later that day, the hardware and software at IVIA suffered catastrophic failures, completely destroying their data and equipment. That would explain why I was no longer able to connect to the facility, but I eventually found the director's personal laptop, and read of the two incidents.

"It would have to be assumed that these happenings were connected in some way, especially as the two apparently dead people are now standing outside your workshop. I can't tell you what it means, but it may not be what we first suspected. I don't know how this will affect your plan, but it is valuable information that may be useful."

Lucas whistled softly. "Okay. Thanks, Andie. Keep an eye on the cameras, and be ready to call in the troops if things start going downhill. You still have audio up there, don't you?"

"Of course. Just say the word, and I'll send in the security."

Lucas ended the call, and looked at Sonia, who seemed shocked at the news. With no word from the security teams of Becker having backup, the revelation that their two intruders were supposed to be dead put a very different complexion on things.

She shrugged as she addressed Lucas. "That's weird, but we still don't have enough to tell us what's actually going on. I suggest you stick to your original plan, and tell them that we don't know anything about any quantum computer."

He grimaced, and started up the hill. "Bloody hell. I think I preferred it when we thought we knew exactly what they wanted. Now these other variables are coming in, and the whole thing is up in the air. Okay, plan A it is. I think you should stay in the car, just in case, but be ready to call out for Andie."

He began driving up the hill, and as they reached the top he saw the two interlopers coming down the steps from the woolshed.

Getting out of the car, he stood with his hand on the door and called out to them.

"Good morning! Jehovah's Witness, are you? I really don't want to talk about God today. You appear to have wasted your time."

The man walked towards him, stopping about five metres away. He spoke English well, with a slight German accent.

"I am sorry – we are not here to talk about God. We have come a long way to speak with Ms Andie Donovan."

This confused Lucas at first, before he realised that they could not know about Andie's AI alter ego, and probably assumed that she was the person in charge of the quantum computer. The QED buzzed with an incoming message, and when Sonia read it, she passed the detachable display to Lucas. He quickly scanned the text, his eyebrows raising as he understood its meaning.

"Well, in that case you have still wasted your time. I'm afraid that Ms Donovan is the owner of a multinational company and wouldn't live in an old farmhouse in Mangaweka. My name is Lucas, and this is my house. I know her well, however, and whatever you have to say to her, you can say to me."

The other man looked momentarily uncomfortable as he realised that the object of his search was not there. Then he appeared to come to a conclusion.

"We have a warning for her. If you can tell her that IVIA may come looking for her, we would be most appreciative."

Lucas managed to hide his surprise. This was certainly not what he had expected. Perhaps these were the good guys. Not wanting to take anything at face value, he continued his charade.

"Who, or what, is IVIA, and why should she need to be warned about them?"

The woman, Dubois, had come to stand beside Becker, and tugged on his sleeve, nodding to him as he hesitated.

"We know about the quantum computer, Mr Lucas, and we have cut our ties to IVIA so that we could come to give her this warning. We do not know how far behind us they are, but it is highly possible that they will eventually come to the same conclusion that we have. When they do, we wish you to be prepared. They are not very nice people."

Lucas chose not to correct the man's misunderstanding of his name; perhaps he simply didn't realise that it was a christian name, perhaps it was a cultural affectation. Deciding to string them along a little more, in the hope of extracting even more information before he chose whether or not to trust them, he replied, "You appear to have me at a disadvantage. I am a simple farmer, and I know less about computers that you probably do about sheep. If you could explain in plain terms, I would be grateful."

Becker seemed to be losing patience with Lucas's obfuscation, and Dubois stepped forward.

"If this is your house, then you know what he is talking about. This location is directly opposite our research facility in Spain, and is the only logical place for the quantum computer to be. We know that Andie Donovan has, with the aid of the quantum computer, recently invented the computer operating system TheOS, and the QED communications device. We also know about the hacking of the Senators and South American politicians. We gave up everything to come here, so please stop playing with us, and let us help you."

Lucas decided that two could play at that game, and gave up the pretense. He glanced at Sonia and made a circular motion with his finger, indicating that she should call in the backup. Looking at the QED display, he addressed the pair.

"Mr Tomas Becker, formerly head of cyber-security at IVIA. Ms Martine Dubois, theoretical physicist. Or should I call you Rudi and Carine Weber? You seem to have led interesting lives since you died. Athens, Istanbul, Bangkok, Singapore, Melbourne, Sydney ... You must be exhausted. What could have persuaded you to give up successful careers with Antonia Vélez to spend six weeks on such a roundabout journey to my house?"

Becker's shoulders slumped as he realised that he had been outplayed. His eyes darted to the driveway as he heard vehicles quickly approaching, but the lack of reaction from the man in front of him suggested that this occurrence was expected.

"Very well, Mr Lucas. I congratulate you on your detective skills. I assume that Ms Donovan has used the quantum computer to hack camera footage from these locations to track our movements and determine our new identities. Yes, we *were* formerly employed by Antonia Vélez, but certain information came to light that persuaded us that we on the wrong side of this fight. Is it necessary to continue this discussion while standing out here?"

The two cars containing Lucas's backup arrived at the top of the driveway in clouds of dust, and the eight men quickly exited the vehicles, surrounding Lucas and his "guests". Lucas held up his hand to forestall any violence, and, with quiet instructions to the leader of the team, set the men to checking the house and grounds for danger. He beckoned the visitors to follow him inside, and leaned down to ask Sonia to join him. As soon as the security men came out of the house with a thumbs-up, Lucas told them to maintain a perimeter as he led Becker, Dubois, and Sonia inside to the kitchen. Connecting his phone to the house wi-fi so that Andie could listen in, he shut the front door behind them.

Filling the kettle, he said, "I suppose introductions are in order. My name is Lucas Winter, and this is my girlfriend, Sonia Matheson."

Sonia felt a warm glow as he introduced her as his "girlfriend" – it wasn't a term either of them had actually used before, as their exact relationship needed no explanation around the office.

Becker and Dubois sat at the kitchen table, obviously taken aback at Lucas's sudden change from the defensive attitude of before, to cordiality.

"We are pleased to meet you, Mr Winter, Ms Matheson. You may as well call us Rudi and Carine Weber. As you say, Tomas and Martine are dead, and we hope they stay that way. It was a necessary deception, as we could no longer work for Antonia, and we feared that she would track us down if we left her employ suddenly. It has been a difficult time at IVIA since the beginning of the year, though I am sure you have just as interesting a story to tell," said Rudi. He then proceeded to relate the events of the last six months, detailing the failed experiment, the search for answers, and his and Carine's own part in that. While most of the tale was no surprise to Lucas and Sonia, Antonia's reaction and subsequent threats to those she blamed for her misfortune came as a shock. Carine's scientific curiosity soon got the better of her, and she asked about the quantum computer. Lucas admitted that it had indeed turned up on his doorstep, so to speak, but withheld any further information until they could discuss it with Andie. Carine pressed him, asking if he could at least confirm that it materialised in a usable form, as their research had predicted.

"Yes," he conceded, "it was a fully-functional computer when I first saw it, but I repeat, anything more will have to come from Ms Donovan. Those are not my answers to give."

Only partially satisfied with his response, Carine knew that she would have to be patient if she wanted the full story, and pouted only slightly as Lucas finished.

With hot drinks in hand all round, the discussion turned to Rudi and Carine's motives.

"What do you expect to gain from coming to us?" asked Sonia.

Carine hesitated briefly, framing her answer. "I suppose there were several factors involved in our decision. The first, and most important, was to prevent Antonia getting hold of the QC. Secondly, to stop her taking revenge on Ms Donovan, who is essentially an innocent party. The third, of course, was to finally see what we had been working towards all these years. Judging from what has been accomplished already, it is performing even better than expected. We never thought that it would be quite so expert at intuitive thinking, though perhaps your friend is very good with computers, and managed to adapt the original programming to help her come up with these radical inventions?"

Secretly, Sonia hoped that they would eventually be able to tell these two all about Andie, if only to see the looks on their faces. Instead, she kept a straight face as she answered, "I would say that is a fair assumption. Andie is definitely very good with computers, and I'm glad that the results have exceeded your expectations. We are also very grateful, of course, that you thought to bring us this warning. You can rest assured that we will be ready if they do find us."

"What are your plans, now that you have delivered your warning?" asked Lucas.

Rudi and Carine looked at each other. Rudi spoke tentatively, "While we would understand if you were unable to trust us completely, we were actually hoping that you might find room in your organisation for us. We could certainly disappear, and hopefully keep IVIA from ever finding us, but we do have skills that could be useful to you, and I know that Carine would be delighted to continue working with the QC. She was a major part of the team that designed it, after all, and her input could be valuable when it comes to operating it effectively. From what I know of its abilities already, it would appear that my own computer skills are obsolete, but as you may have deduced from our escape, I have access to other resources that may prove useful."

Knowing that Carine could not possibly Improve on Andie, but not wanting to burst her bubble, Lucas and Sonia looked at each other, unspoken messages passing between them. They asked the others to excuse them, and went outside to talk privately. Sending the security guard at the front door in to the kitchen to watch over their guests, they went around the corner of the verandah.

"I sort of feel bad for them," said Sonia. "They had put so much into the project, only to have it whisked away from them at the last moment. And they seem to have sacrificed everything – their careers, their identities – to warn us."

Andie's avatar appeared on the phone, as she gave her own input. "It is your decision on how much to tell them. We could maintain the pretence that I am a real person and encourage their assumption that the quantum computer is merely a tool, or we could make their day and tell them that I am self-aware. Martine's knowledge of theoretical physics doesn't compare to my own, of course, but her experience may come in handy on the practical side of things. I'm not sure what Tomas meant when he referred to his 'resources' but I could guess that he has underworld connections that aided in their escape."

Lucas added, "While he might think his computer skills are redundant, he will still have hardware knowledge that we can use. Another IT guy is always handy."

Playing Devil's Advocate, Sonia reminded them that the Webers' arrival could still be part of a larger plan to infiltrate the company or regain control of the quantum computer.

"And what if they *are* dirty? Are we going to lock them up? Do away with them?"

The three of them talked a while longer, weighing the pros and cons of taking in these strays, before reaching a decision. By that time, the cold had got the better of the two humans anyway, and they moved back inside. As they entered, the security guard acknowledged then, and returned to his post outside.

"Sorry to keep you waiting. We had to consult with our boss. I'm sure you will appreciate that we have a difficult decision ahead of us," Sonia said.

"Of course," responded Carine. "You would not believe how often over the last weeks we have considered your reaction. I think we understand your options as well as you do yourselves. You can believe us, and take us in; believe us and turn us away; or *not* believe us, and it was the result of this last choice that concerned us the most. I do not know what else we can do to convince you of our sincerity, but we are resigned to the consequences, whatever you choose. It could not be as bad as what Antonia would do to is if she ever found us."

Lucas got up from the table and beckoned the Webers to follow him, saying, "We *have* made our decision,, but it is best that you hear it from Andie herself."

He led the way through to the lounge, and cast the phone's screen to the television set. Andie's avatar appeared onscreen, seated behind a large desk, and wearing her corporate suit.

"Good afternoon, Mr and Mrs Weber. I am Andie Donovan, and I believe that I owe you a debt of gratitude. I had not expected anyone to make the connection between me and your quantum computer, and I congratulate you on doing so. The fact that you have, however, opens the possibility that others may do the same, and that naturally concerns me.

"I am inclined to believe your story, considering what I have read on Ms Vélez's laptop. It appears that she lays the blame for both their equipment failures, and your own deaths, on a single culprit. I do not think that she would mention this conclusion if you were still in league with her."

Rudi and Carine both exhibited tremendous relief at Andie's acceptance of their story, but were both still obviously apprehensive about their fate. They leaned forward, in anticipation of Andie's judgement.

"I am grateful to you also, Carine, for your part in creating what has to be the most important piece of technology in recent history."

At this, Lucas and Sonia shared a quick look of amused disbelief at Andie's lack of humility, unseen behind the Webers' backs.

Carine, on the other hand, blushed modestly as she accepted the praise for her work.

She addressed the woman on the screen, "Ms Donovan, as much as I appreciate your kind words, I am still not entirely sure what it is I have created. Your friends have declined to tell me anything about the QC. Are you able to satisfy my curiosity?"

Andie nodded. "I suppose it would be only fair. As I understand it, your intent was to lay in place a preconfigured quantum array that would constitute a quantum computer with a built-in operating system. This device would then be controlled by an external operator, through a specialised interface."

"Exactly," said Carine, "though I simply don't understand how you managed to gain that control without our proprietary software."

"Ah. I am afraid that you are making an erroneous assumption. If your quantum processor had manifested in literally any other spot, it would indeed have needed the connections you had provided. It would have been restricted to the data you gave it, and it would have needed your software. What you need to know, is that the *exact* antipode of the neutrino gun in your laboratory was the room next to this. In that room stands a table, and on that desk stood a desktop computer. Inside that computer was a silicon processing chip, and *that* is where the neutrinos landed.

"The material was an adequate receptor, and connections were already in place for the quantum computer to begin accessing data. It made quick work of the data on the computer's hard drives, and then it found the internet."

Both Rudi and Carine opened their eyes wide as they considered the implications of the quantum computer having access to almost unlimited information. They were, however, mentally and scientifically unable to grasp the true import of this revelation.

"A result occurred that you would not have been able to predict with your computations, as you intended for your creation to have access to only the information you wanted it to have. It was not, however, the content of the data that was important at this stage – it was the quantity. A processor of sufficient power, attaining a particular information density, becomes something more than what it was designed to be. Mr and Mrs Weber – Andie Donovan does not exist. Not as you would think, anyway."

A pixelated wave passed rapidly across Andie's features, showing for a split-second a metallic sub-structure to her face.

"Martine – perhaps you should stop thinking of yourself as my creator, and rather, my mother. You have birthed new life, and I owe you my very existence."

Lucas had prepared himself for some sort of outburst, but there was only a shocked silence. Rudi and Carine stared open-mouthed at Andie before Carine turned to look at Lucas and Sonia, tears beginning to fall from her eyes.

"Is this true? Our quantum computer has become self-aware? We never dreamed that anything like this could be possible. I have *so* many questions!"

Rudi was more accusatory. He turned to Lucas. "So *you* are the one behind the company Ad Astra. You control the computer."

"Hold on a minute there, mate! Nobody *controls* Andie. What she does, she does of her own free will. To us, she is no mere computer, she is a trusted and valued friend."

With genuine concern, Rudi said, "But surely it is too dangerous to allow such a powerful entity free rein. Its capabilities are endless, and it could destroy humanity in a heartbeat if it so desired!"

Lucas's face flushed as he stepped towards Rudi and raised his voice in Andie's defence. "If you refer to her as 'it' one more time, I swear that I will knock that German accent right down your throat! Andie has a moral code stronger than most people, especially you, if those shadowy 'resources' you refer to are any indication. She has been nothing but kind and supportive, and is fully committed to using her talents to *aid* humanity, not destroy it!"

Rudi hastened to extricate himself from the deep couch, stumbling away towards the fireplace with his hands raised placatingly.

"Okay, okay! I am sorry. You have obviously developed a deep connection with ... Ms Donovan. The concept is new to me, and surely you can see that the idea of a silicon sentience could be unnerving to many people."

Lucas backed down, annoyed that he had let his emotions get the better of him.

"I get it. It's new, so it's scary. Just treat her like a regular person – okay, a *really* clever regular person – and you'll be good with me. Yes, she *could* do all sorts of nasty things, but it's simply not in her nature. If I'm guessing correctly, you were probably some sort of hacker in a former life. Should I be scared of you just because you could get into my private data?"

Impressed by Lucas's intuition about his past, going on what little information he had, Rudi had to concede the point. It was true that a person's character, rather than their potential, should be the measure by which they were judged. And there it was; he was already thinking of the computer as a person.

"You are right, Mr Winter. I apologise, Ms Donovan. I am sure that if I got to know you better, I would see in you what these people obviously do."

Andie accepted his apology as he sat back down. "That's all right, Rudi. It was not the first time that I have been likened to the AIs of fiction. I can promise you, there will be no *Space Odyssey* or *Terminator* moments. I trust Lucas as much as he trusts me, and I believe that what we are doing together to improve the world is right. We would like to offer you the opportunity to join our company."

"That is a generous offer, and I think I speak for both of us when I say that we gratefully accept. But what is it, exactly, that you are doing?" asked Carine. "I see technological improvements, such as the operating system and the communications device, but in my experience, technology alone does not necessarily make the world a better place."

"Ah, that is a story for another day, Carine. Even Lucas's closest friends had to wait until he was ready to tell them. I would, however, like to talk to you about other things. As much as I love Sonia, and admire her talents in her particular field, she does not have the background in quantum mechanics that you do, and I have perhaps as many questions for you as you do for me."

"I will try to answer them as best as I can, but from your achievement with the QED, you already seem to be far more knowledgeable in the field than I."

Andie smiled, and nodded in acknowledgement of the compliment. While it was true that her understanding of the subject far outstripped any other scientist, she was eager to find out how a human mind might approach particular problems.

"There are several areas that interest me, relating to the research your team was doing in Spain. While I have the notes from your servers, how you arrived at some of your conclusions is still unclear to me. I suspect that several intuitive leaps were made, and that is a process that I am unfamiliar with."

Sonia interrupted this technical – or was it philosophical? – discussion to say, "I'm sure that you two will have plenty of time to chat, but the thing is, Lucas and I came up here to get away from the whole technical thing. We're only here for a couple of days, but what are we going to do with you in the meantime? I don't mean to be rude, but do you have somewhere you can go?"

Lucas thought for a moment, pleased that Sonia had been the one to bring it up. He too, had not been looking forward to having house guests over the weekend.

"I suppose they could get a room in Taihape. We can take them back to Palmerston tomorrow afternoon."

It was agreed that Rudi and Carine would follow the security team to Taihape, where they could check into a motel. Before they left, Andie asked for Carine's mobile number, explaining that the two of them could talk, or video chat, over the weekend. With thanks to the men from the factory,

Lucas and Sonia waved off their new acquaintances at the gate, and headed back inside.

"Well, that went better than it could have. Do you think we did the right thing?" asked Lucas.

"Yeah. Rudi is a bit uptight, perhaps, but if he has a chance to get a word in edgeways while the girls are talking shop, I'm sure he will feel better about the 'dangerous' AI! Now, where were we, before we were so rudely interrupted?" she said, fluttering her eyelashes at him coquettishly.

He took her in his arms and nuzzled her neck. "I simply can't remember. We'll just have to start at the beginning..."

POWER TO THE PEOPLE

Their weekend away passed all too quickly for Lucas and Sonia. While it had been essentially no different to staying in the new house, just being out of town gave them a sense of freedom from the decisions and problems that faced Ad Astra.

James returned to the farmhouse on Sunday afternoon before they returned to Palmerston North, and soon, it was time for them to leave. They packed their overnight bags and their dog – Splash had become Sonia's friend as much as Lucas's, and seemed to approve of their relationship, though it was obvious that he resented the occasions that he was not permitted to share their bed – into the Holden, waved goodbye to James, and went to collect the Webers from Taihape.

As they had needed to check out of their motel that morning, Rudi and Carine had spent the day exploring the small town, marveling at how vibrant it seemed, even on a Sunday. This was due to the newfound spirit of the townspeople, thanks to the high rate of employment, and more money to spend on simple pleasures. The cafés were full of locals, and new businesses had already opened in some of the previously boarded-up shops.

Sonia and Lucas met them at one of the cafés, as they were consuming their umpteenth cup of coffee that day. The desperation and worry that had seemed to weigh them down when they had first arrived was gone, replaced by hope and expectation. Carine and Andie had chatted through the night, each learning something from the other. Carine was excited to get into a workshop and begin working with some of the innovative quantum concepts that Andie had introduced her to, and could barely restrain herself from babbling about them to Sonia as soon as she and Lucas entered the café.

As he waited for the ex-IVIA employees to finish their drinks, Lucas explained what would be happening when they got back to Palmerston North.

"We don't have any spare houses for you at the moment, but we'll put you up at a hotel for now. You can come in to the office with us tomorrow, and we'll introduce you to the rest of the team. Our building is a bit short of space right now, so you'll initially be sharing an office with Sonia, Carine. Rudi, you're right in thinking that Andie can handle our system security, but in the meantime, I'd like you to familiarise yourself with our existing hardware. We'll find a spot for you just as soon as we can. We'd like you to have dinner at our place tonight, and we can talk about the company more then."

When they were ready, Rudi and Carine followed the Holden to the city in their rental car. They were checked into their hotel, dropped the rental off at the local depot, and joined Sonia and Lucas for the drive up to the house in the hills.

The mid-winter sun was just setting as they arrived at the house, and the light shining through the gap between the cloud cover and the horizon bathed the plains below them in its dim, orange glow. Exiting the car, Carine turned a full circle, taking in the nature of the various light sources; from the weak rays of the fading sun, to the organic twinkling of the cars and streetlights below, to the welcoming warmth of the house lights. She felt that the scene was, in a way, allegorical of their journey. They had come from the darkness of IVIA, through the hectic hustle and bustle of southeast Asia, and now the illumination flowing from this building's windows was beckoning her to her destination – safety.

She broke off her philosophical meanderings, and hurried to catch up to the others.

Sonia had paused at the edge of the verandah to see what had held Carine up. Watching her taking in the view, she smiled, and said as the other woman approached, "Beautiful, isn't it?"

Carine nodded enthusiastically. "Even on a day like this. We haven't had much time to appreciate beauty recently."

They had barely had time to appreciate anything but freedom. Their helter-skelter dash from Athens had taken its toll, both physically and mentally. Sleeping in airports, impatiently awaiting the next leg of the journey; the interminable overland trip from Bangkok to Singapore; never knowing if their deceit had been successful, and fearing that at any moment Antonia would track them down.

"It can't last, though, can it?" asked Sonia. "Even here in New Zealand, where we proudly advertise our 'green' image, if there's a way to get around the regulations and sacrifice that beauty for a quick buck, someone will do so."

Carine hadn't considered that this Pacific paradise could ever be spoiled by the greed of man. The clean urban areas and lush countryside that she had seen since they landed were a far cry from her native Paris and her adopted home of central Spain. However, if Sonia believed in the inevitability of its ruin, then she would be pleased to live here while its beauty lasted. She mentioned as much to Sonia, and received in return only a mysterious smile as she was led inside.

They caught up to the men in the office, where Lucas was explaining the hardware to Rudi.

"There you are, girls. I was just showing off the QED rack. Carine, we have audio-visual devices throughout the house that are all connected to Andie via these units. She has the run of the place, so to speak, and we can talk with her from any room. I was just about to start on dinner – did you want to show Carine the workshop, Sonia?"

Carine's obvious excitement was like a child's on Christmas morning, eager to see what waited under the tree, and Sonia could not disappoint her.

"Come on – let me show you where the magic is going to happen."

She led her bright-eyed charge outside, as Lucas volunteered Rudi to be his kitchen-hand, and they went to start preparing a meal.

Opening the inner barn door with palm and retinal scans, Sonia directed Carine to suit up, before ensuring the door behind them was closed, and opening the pressure-sealed door in front of them. The rustic exterior was in sharp contrast to the array of high-tech equipment inside, and Carine walked from one machine to the next, marvelling at the opportunity they promised.

"This is amazing, Sonia! You have so many cool toys!"

"And this is only the start. These 'toys' will be used to make tools that you have never dreamed of. Some of Andie's new designs require machinery that does not exist yet, so we have to create it."

Carine's eyes lit up at the prospect of once again being on the cutting edge of science. She had been sorely missing the innovative work they had done at IVIA, and it sounded as if the work here would take creativeness to new levels.

Opening a second door at the back of the workshop, Sonia beckoned her through to the server room. It was now fully-equipped, with one wall entirely covered in computer monitors, a QED rack sitting in a corner, and the half-dozen PCs of the Babies lined up on a bench to one side. Moving to the Babies, Sonia said, "As you will be well aware, Andie has more than enough capability to run all the necessary operations on her own, but for the sake of redundancy, we have some of her sub-routines handled by these."

Carine peered closely at the rank of desktop towers, before turning to Sonia with a puzzled look. "But these are off-the-shelf household computers, no? How could they perform even the smallest part of an AI's tasks?"

If Carine's faith in the supremacy of IVIA's original design had been shaken by the knowledge of Andie's existence, the fact that their research had been improved to the point that a relatively simple workshop could create AIs would be a real blow to her pride. There was no point hiding the fact, however, if she was to be a key member of the technical team.

Sonia pulled over a couple of chairs and they sat down. "I know you guys spent many years developing the technique to create a quantum computer. Admittedly, Andie had access to that research but she very quickly modified your techniques to allow us to flawlessly reproduce the process on the CPUs of these machines. Each one of them is now a discrete quantum AI, though not self-aware. These processors are running an operating system that she designed, and each has responsibility for one of her sub-routines. That one monitors all the camera feeds from our factories, keeping an eye out for problems. Another runs the TheOS online store. Another scours the world for evidence of political corruption. Those three are each run in parallel with a backup, in what is essentially a RAID setup, but for processors, rather than storage systems. While the software itself is robust, we didn't want to put too much faith in what is now archaic hardware."

"I thought that I could no longer be surprised at what you have accomplished, but back at IVIA, we never imagined that our template could transfer directly to something as simple as an Intel CPU. We spent over a year creating the target substance for ours, and almost as long on the control framework. I am very impressed."

Sonia couldn't help but blush, though she knew that the credit was Andie's alone. With the right setup, everything could have been done by robotic manipulators.

"You're too kind. It was your research that paved the way for Andie to do this. If Antonia Vélez had been a better person – and that set of freak circumstances hadn't sent Andie our way – I'm sure that you would all have been in the running for Nobel prizes. As it is, Andie's sentience means that the world may never know of your achievements. I don't think people are ready for her, and their fear and suspicion would probably put our very lives in danger. Perhaps one day you will receive the credit you are due. Until then, you have our deepest gratitude."

Carine took one last admiring look at the Babies before shifting her attention to the QED rack.

"So this connects to all the cameras at the remote locations?"

Moving over to the rack, Sonia said, "Not individually, no. Each factory has a rack of its own, and sends the feeds to a single receiver here. It's a lot of data overall, but the QED has huge bandwidth. The online store also transfers large amounts of data, but that mostly comes from the rented servers. This AI simply compiles the packages and instructs the server which modules to send. We're still limited by the bottlenecks to, and within, New Zealand, and it's just more efficient to use global servers."

"It is an amazing setup. I look forward to playing my part. Shall we see if the men have finished making our dinner?"

Shutting the workshop behind them, they removed their clean-room suits and took the internal passageway back to the house. In the kitchen, the vegetables were almost done, and Lucas had a frying pan on the burner, heating up for the steaks. It was not long before he brought the plates to the table, and everyone sat to eat.

When they were done, they adjourned to the living area, and sat around the fire. Lucas and Sonia took this opportunity to explain to their guests the basic purpose of Ad Astra up to the point where Andie invented the cold fusion generator.

"But ... but that is impossible!" Carine cried. "There are so many technical barriers ... I can't even begin to imagine how you could have bypassed the laws of physics that tell me this can not be done."

Sonia had to laugh at Carine's reaction. "Sweetie, you'll learn soon enough that we don't use the word 'impossible' around here, and that Andie seems to regards the laws of physics as mere guidelines! I don't pretend to understand exactly how it works, but it involves a negatively-charged hydrogen isotope, two stages of fusion, and a Tokamak coil."

Closing her eyes momentarily to visualise how this combination of techniques might work, Carine conceded that it might indeed be feasible. She was definitely going to have to redefine her idea of "impossible".

Rudi had quickly grasped the concept of creating technology to reduce the harm done to the planet and was nodding thoughtfully.

"This is certainly a better use of the QC's capabilities them Antonia had planned. You might live in a paradise down here in New Zealand, but I have seen first-hand the damage done in heavily industrialised countries. While I admire your cause, I honestly think that it is too late. It will take generations to undo what has already been done, and simply stopping further harm may not be enough for the environment."

This was, of course, the same logic that Lucas himself had used, and he admitted as much to Rudi.

"You're right, which is why we need a chance to start over. Carine, what do you think about the possibility of interstellar travel?"

"Until a few minutes ago, I would have said that it was impossible, but I am not allowed to use that word, apparently. It would require a deep sleep or stasis process, or some form of faster-then-light travel. As a theoretical physicist, my professional opinion is that FTL and stasis will only ever be science fiction concepts, leaving the idea of 'generation ships', which will take hundreds of years to reach their destination. I don't see how that will help humanity as a whole."

"Well, I'm going to keep one or two secrets to myself, but I can say that Andie has been working on the problem, and she has had some interesting thoughts on the subject. There is a lot to do before we get anywhere near that point, though, and we may as well concentrate on our immediate goals for now."

With their imaginations fired, and their appetites for progress whetted, Rudi and Carine declared themselves fully committed to Ad Astra, though Carine was a little disappointed not to be enlightened as to Andie's space travel ideas. Rudi did not have the same excitement for physics, but was still keen to be a part of Lucas's plan. He could see many innovative developments coming to the computing field, and was longing to try them for himself.

Lucas ran the two back to their hotel in town, before returning home to Sonia.

"They both seem pretty excited about the business plan. They should fit in well with the team," she said as they sat snuggled on the couch.

"Yeah. I hope you don't mind sharing your office space, but I imagine that Carine will want to spend a lot of time in the workshop, anyway. I'll call Jake in the morning and see if he can figure out how to fit more offices in. Eventually, we might find that everyone will tootle off to their own buildings, but we should keep their spots down on Princess Street for sensitive work. I've got a special project I'd like him to get onto, as well."

Sonia yawned, stretched, and burrowed closer to him. "You do that, darling. Jake's a clever guy – I'm sure he'll sort everything out."

A new week, a new set of hurdles to overcome. This week Ad Astra would be approaching New Zealand's five major power generators to discuss them taking up CF generators as an alternate means of power. Almost every current source of power in the country was based on renewables, with the exception of one coal- and gas-fired station. The trick would be selling them on the basis of cost-effectiveness as opposed to any environmental reasons. Andie had arranged a video conference call with the CEOs of these companies, and Lucas had Will, Sonia, and Michelle sitting in. They're were gathered in front of a hastily-installed bank of monitors in the office building's conference room. Small cameras had been placed directly in front of each monitor, to give the appearance that the team were looking directly at the CEOs as they spoke.

At the appointed time, the images of five suited men appeared on the screens in front of the Ad Astra team, with Andie on yet another. She welcomed them all to the meeting, thanking them for their time, before handing off to her people at Princess Street.

Lucas had been designated to start the presentation, giving an overview of their proposal.

"Good morning, gentlemen. My name is Lucas Winter. I am the CEO of Ad Astra, and we have invited you here today to discuss a technological advance in electricity generation that we hope will interest you. With me are some of my management team – Sonia Matheson, CTO, who will be taking to you about the nuts and bolts of the technology; Will Beddington, CFO, who will be addressing the potential economic challenges; and Michelle Tyson, our Chief Legal Counsel, who will discuss the financial and legal aspects of our proposal.

"To cut to the chase, we have developed an alternate form of generation, and we would like your input and assistance in best delivering this to the public. With your help, we believe that we can come to an arrangement that benefits everyone."

The head of Meridian Energy spoke. "Pleased to meet all of you. I'm sure that the rest of my colleagues, like myself, agreed to this meeting because we admire Ad Astra's business model, and your ethical practices of revitalising small-town New Zealand. However, from your introduction, it sounds as if you might be sitting on something that could supplant us. As I'm sure you are aware, we are all pretty well placed in terms of generation, and with a few exceptions—" he shot a smug look at the CEO of Genesis Energy "—we operate entirely on renewables. I'm not entirely sure what you can offer us."

The other men nodded at this assessment, though a brief sour look passed across the face of the coal-fired power station's owner.

"I appreciate your candour. We understand that you all have significant investment in your existing facilities, but they must cost you a fair bit to operate and maintain. What we have to offer are generators that are almost entirely maintenance-free, and will run on the smell of an oily rag. Your hydro and wind plants are dependant on the weather, and the coal and gas units are getting increasingly harder to justify to the public. Can any of you say that you would not like to save a bit of money, and be able to guarantee supply even when the wind doesn't blow and the rain doesn't fall?"

Genesis took this opportunity to jump in. "You're dead right about the costs, and the public perception of fossil fuel electricity. I, for one, would be interested to hear of your technology."

"I believe that Jim has a point," said Mercury Energy, referring to the man from Meridian. "I'll listen to your proposal, but I am concerned about the possibility of you pulling the rug from under our feet. As you say, we have considerable money tied up in our existing plants, and while low-cost electricity might seem like a good idea to the masses, it might end up being a real headache for us in the long run."

"That's exactly why we wanted to talk to you today. We realise what this could mean to the energy sector, and we hope, with your assistance, to mitigate the fallout. We'll have Will go through that part shortly, but in the meantime, I'd like to get Sonia to introduce our technology."

Sonia began to explain. "Gentlemen. As you know, Ad Astra has already brought to market two products that are miles ahead of their rivals. Our operating system, TheOS, is revolutionising computing, and has sold over one-and-a-half billion copies. The QED is likewise making waves in communications. For these innovations, we have our founder, Andie Donovan to thank. She is, to put it lightly, a genius, and thinks so far out of the box that it is just a speck in the distance. She has now turned her genius to electricity generation.

"In the beginning, coal was the fuel of choice, but the natural resources here enabled you to harness water and geothermal energy. Recently, wind turbines have become the next great advance, but all these things are enormously costly to set up and maintain.

"We have never wanted to go down the nuclear power route in New Zealand, with its toxic by-products and the dangers inherent in those types of facilities, but those factors are only applicable to nuclear fission. What we have done at Ad Astra is to master nuclear *fusion*. Now, I'm not talking about the super-heated plasma variety, that often provides even less power than it takes to maintain the reaction – what we have is *cold* fusion, a perfectly safe and self-sustaining process that requires only hydrogen to run.

"From a generator smaller than a shipping container, we can generate a constant five-hundred megawatts, and the operating costs are negligible. In fact, if you use a portion of that power to separate your own hydrogen, it is basically free electricity."

The idea of drastically cutting their overheads was evidently appealing to the CEOs, judging by the calculating looks on their faces.

Contact Energy made his first contribution to the discussion. "Ms Matheson, I'm no expert, and perhaps I'm jumping to the wrong conclusion here, but isn't it still nuclear power? Just how safe is it?"

"It's a fair question. Though it works on nuclear principles, there are no radioactive components or by-products in this process, and while the traditional concept of fusion devices run at many thousands of degrees, ours operate at only a couple of hundred. If the containment field breaks down, the reaction stops immediately, and there is only a very brief release of that energy, which would be mostly absorbed by active shielding in the unit. The housing is durable enough to handle everyday use, and frankly, you'd do yourself more harm by accidentally touching your stovetop element than you would if you somehow happened to be touching the unit if it failed. We would be happy to demonstrate the safety of the process on a smaller generator if you are concerned."

Mercury was the first to grasp the true implications of this last statement.

"Just how small can you make these things?" he asked.

Hoping that she wasn't about to scare them off, Sonia hesitated a moment, pretending to look down at her paperwork

"The industry-scale units are comprised of a modular design, and we can manufacture something the size of a car battery, generating ten kilowatts."

"So you can eventually cut the national grid out of the equation altogether, providing household units. This will be the death knell for centralised power generation."

The other men had finally caught on to the logical conclusion to his argument. Their previous excitement at the prospect of higher profits now changed to, if not outright fear, then at least concern at the realisation that their entire businesses might all too soon become obsolete.

"What is it that you actually want from us?" asked Genesis. "If you have the capability to go straight to the consumer, I'm not sure why you have even bothered approaching us."

This was Will's cue.

"We *could* roll out the household units right away, but that's not how we want to play it. It would send your shares into a tailspin, and that would affect everyone down the line, including the Government, who are majority shareholders in three of your companies.

"We came to you first, because the endgame is inevitable, and we would like to help you get through it in the least dramatic way possible. We're looking at leasing you generation capacity equal to your current output for a set period, giving you time to comfortably wind down your current plants. Any staff that aren't essential to continued operation will be offered equivalent positions in our own workforce, and your investors will have time to safely and sensibly adjust their portfolios. Ad Astra will be putting out a share offer, giving investors a safe alternative to their existing holdings."

"That's all very well," said Meridian, "but you don't just shut off a hydroelectric dam. Even if it's not in use, it requires constant maintenance, for safety reasons. Then there's the lines network – do you want that falling into ruin, with pylons deteriorating and transmission wires dropping down all over the place?"

"Ad Astra would be happy to assume responsibility for the dams. We would retain the necessary specialists that you already have. As for the lines, we will be talking to distribution operator Transpower and its owner, the

Government. We'll give them fair warning that in a few years, those lines will no longer be needed, and we're sure that helping the Government meet its emissions obligations will go a long way towards softening the blow.

"We don't want to make this difficult for you, but the reality is that traditional power generation is now a thing of the past, and we have to work together to find the best way to transition. With our green energy capability, it's not absolutely necessary for this to happen in New Zealand, but we will be the testbed for the rest of the world, and the sooner we take all those coal, gas, and nuclear plants out of the equation, the better off the planet will be.

"If we can prove that a sensible transition is possible, we can avoid drastic disruption to global markets, and get everyone from consumers to lawmakers to see that this is a good thing."

"I can certainly see the consumer thinking it a good thing," said the man from Transpower. "Almost free electricity forever? Who wouldn't want that? No, the problem you're going to run up against is the coal lobby. With the money at their disposal, they are tremendously powerful in many places, and will fight this technology tooth and nail."

Will shrugged. "If they do, then they will have to fight the voters over it. If it comes down to it, we'll need to bypass them entirely, and run them out of business. Hopefully, they will see sense, and realise that there is only one way to come out of it with their dignity intact. The bottom line is, we're in it for the people and the planet – not the one percent."

Genesis snorted. "You're playing a dangerous game there. I hope, for your sake, that they can take their eyes off their bank balance long enough to see the big picture."

"So do I," said Lucas. "So do I."

Meridian, as the largest generator, appeared to be the de facto leader of the group of CEOs, and addressed Lucas.

"Mr Winter, assuming that we agree with your proposal in principle—" *Not that it seems we have a lot of choice*, he muttered under his breath, "—we're going to need some concrete data on the deal. Costs, responsibilities, timeframe etc. I think I can speak for us all when I say that we would like preferential stock options, to offset our losses going on from this. Am I right, gentlemen?"

The other CEOs all indicated their agreement, and he continued. "For the sake of market stability, we should probably keep things under wraps for as long as we can—" again, a round of nods from his colleagues "—as news of all this leaking prematurely could create some amount of panic with investors. We certainly don't want them bailing out too soon."

"That is totally understandable," said Lucas. "We had been thinking along the same lines. As for specifics of the proposal, I'm going to leave you with Michelle and Andie to work that out between you all. I thank you for your time, gentlemen, and hope that we can manage this in such a way as to cause as little distress as possible to your business."

He, Sonia, and Will left the conference room, Lucas placing a hand reassuringly on Michelle's shoulder as he passed.

Sitting in Will's office, Lucas exhaled heavily as he replayed the meeting in his head.

"What's on your mind, boss?" asked Will, as he grabbed a cold drink from the mini-fridge beside his desk.

Lucas refocused his eyes and looked up. "Oh, nothing major. Just wondering if we're going to crash the economy, start a recession, that sort of thing. I don't know how long we can keep the lid on this, and things could go downhill for power companies pretty quickly if investors get spooked. We must, at all costs, keep the mini-CF under wraps until those companies are prepared. It will be in their best interests to help us do that – they're hardly likely to cut their own throats – and once they see the writing on the wall, they'll do everything they can to minimise the impact on their business."

Sonia joined them, carrying tea and coffee for her and Lucas. "I thought it went well. Without meaning to sound predatory, we've got them by the balls and they know it. They must see that they've got no option but to play along. What worries me, is how the coal industry will react. They sell a hell of a lot of the stuff for power generation, and they won't take kindly to being cut out of the money."

Will had been thinking about this, and added his own conclusions. "I reckon they're half-prepared for something like this anyway. I mean, China has been moving away from coal for a few years now, and there are more and more alternative energy plants opening. There's increasing pressure from environmental groups to restore river ecosystems damaged by hydro schemes, and some countries have enacted legislation obligating dam operators to put aside money for decommissioning or dismantling the structures once they get too old.

"Coal people will certainly hate it all happening so quickly, but they really have no hold over the power companies. It's entirely up to them how they generate electricity, and the coal guys should think themselves damn lucky they've been able to hold on this long. They'll get their shot at buying shares in the new kid on the block, and we'll be picking up their workers for CF factories if we can. The only ones who will lose are those who hold on too tight to their dinosaur ways, and miss out on the new opportunities."

Lucas held his tea in both hands as he followed the discussion. He took advantage of the lull in conversation to address Sonia.

"For sure there'll be initial resistance, and they'll probably look at regulatory measures to kill the tech. Can we get some demos set up to prove the safety of the generators? Geiger counters to prove there's no radiation, and maybe smash a five-hundred megawatt unit with a wrecking ball to show there's no thermal danger? We want to counter anything they throw at us immediately."

Sonia pulled out her phone to make a note. "I'll get onto that. How are we looking for these offshore factories, anyway?"

Lucas spoke Cath's name, knowing that Andie would route his voice through the A/V system to her office.

"Lucas. What can I do for you?"

"Sonia was just asking about the overseas CF sites. What's the update?"

"One sec." A moment later, Cath came into the office, looking around for a spare chair before giving up the search and leaning against Will's desk. "Tom has set up locally-registered companies in the US, Australia, India, and South Africa so far. China is proving to be a bit of a headache, but Tom's got someone working on it. We've bought factory sites in all the countries where we have a business presence, and Jake is working with him to put together construction teams."

Lucas had expected China to be a more difficult place to do business, but had faith that Tom would find a way to make it work. It was a good start to have a foothold in some of the other coal-producing countries, though, and when they had the factories built and staffed, they could really get cracking on the manufacture of the large CF generators. With around 2500 coal-fired power plants globally, producing 2000GW, they would need to build at least 4000 units to replace them all. Natural gas plants contributed around a quarter of global electricity capacity, say another 1500GW, or 3000 CF generators, and nuclear approximately 400GW. Less immediate were the hydro dams, which contributed around another 1000GW, for an overall figure of nearly 9000 CF units. Andie had estimated that a standard factory could turn out two or three of the giant devices per day, so a quick calculation by Lucas gave him a production time of only a couple of weeks if they could get 300-plus sites running initially. That was a lot of construction, and a lot of money, but it was possible. Since the factories produced smaller modules that were combined to make the industrial generators, they could then continue making those, which would then be stockpiled for the inevitable release of the consumer model. Once the leases ran out on the large models, and people were buying individual household generators, Lucas planned to start taking them back from the now useless power stations and begin installing them in ships as a replacement power source for fuel oil, and even in aircraft, hopefully. With a viable electric motor for airplanes, the weight of a generator would be easily offset by not carrying fuel.

When Michelle and Andie were done going back and forth with the power CEOs to finalise the small print of the proposal, Lucas called the team into the conference room for their report. The gist of it was that Ad Astra would give them three years to wind down their operations, during which time the staff would be downsized, transferring where possible to CF production facilities. At two million dollars per month for each of the twenty large generators, the powercos could easily afford to lower consumer pricing, while still making a tidy profit. Much the same model would be offered to power generators around the world, and by the time their leases ran out, the initial factories would have produced a stockpile of nearly fifty million small generators. *A good start*, thought Lucas, though they would have added more manufacturing capacity by then. They'd need to, to supply the billions of units that would eventually be needed. Without centralised generation, every household and business would need their own, though there was always going to be the option for communities to band together to purchase a mid-size unit between them. In places of low demand, such as low-tech, isolated African villages, a single twenty kilowatt generator could power many houses. Lucas had already decided that the price of the units would be proportional to the affluence of individual regions. It could range from two- or three-thousand dollars in somewhere like California, down to almost nothing in third-world regions. Of course, payment plans would be available. Now, they just had to wait for the boards of the power companies to agree to the deal.

UNDER SIEGE

Wheels in motion. Held back only by the ponderous pace of corporate bureaucracy, Lucas's plan was inching slowly closer to fulfillment. Andie had said that it would take at least a week for the boards of all five power companies to agree to the deal. They were busy counting coins and probably desperately looking for some way out of the dead end in which Ad Astra had cornered them. Looking to at least come out of this with their personal wealth intact. The CEOs had seen the pointlessness of fighting the juggernaut that was change, and Lucas hoped that they were as good as their salaries implied, and that they could convince their Directors that the best course of action would be to simply make the best of the inevitable.

Everything for this phase was on hold until a deal was struck; they couldn't approach the workers with new job offers, they couldn't ship any of the generators they had already manufactured. Instead of simply waiting, the entire team was busy planning the next steps. Tom and Michelle were preparing for the expected legal challenges, having already started hiring subordinates. Alison was making contact with key players in the energy industry who would be likely to support the CF technology, and Jake was getting his offshore construction crews started on factories in other countries. Fats was busy maintaining the supply lines for the QED and lining up transportation of the huge CF generators around the country, and Sonia was getting her instructor teams ready to send across the world. Will had gathered a handful of market-savvy people who were putting together paperwork for the share offers, and Paul and his hand-picked team were getting ready for a huge advertising campaign to show the CF as the product that was going to save the world. It might have been an slight exaggeration, but that's advertising.

Jake had sent in a local team to start expanding the office building, and three offices were to be added to the second storey, poking out from the back wall behind the conference room, and extending over the car park. Carine was in the workshop up at the house every day. She had brought in a couple of keen engineers, and they were hard at work creating the new machinery that Andie had designed.

With all the activity around him, Lucas felt out of place, not having any of the specialised skills required to help his friends, but he spent the week fine-tuning his master plan. He was, at times, caught in loops of indecision, wondering just how much of the future technology to release to the world, and how much to keep to themselves. Certain items could all too easily be misused, while others had the potential to not only improve lives, but to save them. Always in the back of his mind was the thought that IVIA could eventually come to the same conclusions that Rudi and Carine had; that these breakthrough technologies must be the work of a higher intelligence, namely, a quantum computer. With the CF phase of the plan set to take several years to be fully realised, he hoped that they would be able to space out further innovations rather than release too much at any one time.

Towards the end of the week, Andie notified Lucas that he had an incoming call from the CEO of Genesis Energy, Warren Montegue. Worried that there might be a hiccup in the negotiations, he took the call.

"Mr Winter. Good to speak to you again."

"Likewise. How can I help you? I hope there's no problem?"

"Not immediately, no, but I'm hoping to head off any potential issues you might face in future. Have any of the others contacted you yet?"

Wondering where this was heading, Lucas responded in the negative.

"Good, good. I'd be very surprised if the rest of them don't get the same idea, and I'm glad that I got in first. I'd like to offer you my expertise, Mr Winter. While you obviously have some very smart people on your team, what you are really going to need when you start dealing with all these other companies around the world, is insider knowledge. I have the experience with energy strategy to help you talk to these people. I know what makes them tick, and I can suggest the approaches that will maximize your chances of success with them."

Lucas saw the man's point, and also saw the underlying motives.

"That's very generous of you. Of course, the fact that we will be taking away your income may also have something to do with your offer, am I right?"

"If be lying if I denied it. However, I will still be drawing my salary for the next several years, and would happily consider a pay cut if I were to join you in a consultant capacity. I do see the benefit of what you are trying to do, and although it means the end of my industry, I approve.

"As you have said, we are lucky in New Zealand to have such an abundance of renewable energy, but as the operator of the country's only coal-fired plant, I am acutely aware of the challenges that method of generation creates. Financial concerns aside, I would genuinely like to do my part; being part of the solution rather than part of the problem."

Though he was tempted to consult either Andie or Will, Lucas was by now used to making unilateral decisions, and was inclined to accept the power man's offer.

"You make a good argument. It is true that we don't have anyone experienced in this particular field, and it would certainly be helpful to to have someone who speaks the lingo. However, most of the hard work will be happening while you are still running Genesis. How do you see that working out for us?"

"Considering that the business will be winding down, I don't see that my role here will be full-time. Sure, I'll still have decisions to make, but with the final outcome being a foregone conclusion, I don't exactly have to spend my days projecting and planning for years down the track. I believe that I can devote a portion of my time to helping you through any rough negotiations."

"Well, Mr Montegue, you have my tentative approval. I'd like to have our contracts lawyer, Michelle, contact you to work out the details, and we would certainly look forward to your input."

"It would be my pleasure, Mr Winter. Thank you for your time."

Hanging up the phone, Lucas sat back in his chair as he thought about this new development. Montegue's experience would be valuable in the delicate negotiations with power companies, but as a consultant, he would not be privy to any of Ad Astra's long-term plans. Once the world's power generators were fully committed to the CF technology, he would have outlasted his usefulness. Lucas was sure that the man would have no trouble picking up another top job, or company directorship somewhere. He had no intention of letting Montegue talk himself into a permanent position; seven-figure CEOs wouldn't be a part of the Ad Astra ethos. His current management team would hold directorships of the subsidiary companies, and the stock structure would ensure that no outsiders played a part in the day-to-day running. For a normal company, that might mean heavy workloads for his people, but Andie would take up any slack.

The weekend passed, with Lucas and Sonia taking their now habitual trip up to the farm for some well-deserved rest.

At the regular Monday staff meeting, the news from most was much the same as the previous week. Alison, however, had a fresh update. She had been working with Andie on greenhouse gas reduction processes, and was eager to share their progress.

"Andie and I had been talking about carbon capture and recycling, and she found several companies that are already making advances in that field. Using captured CO_2, they are making carbon-fibre, a viable alternative to smelted metals in many applications, and bio-plastics, recyclable materials that are increasingly being used in construction. While we don't want to double up on that work, nor go into competition with our own facilities, she has managed to improve their technologies, and we have given them that information free of charge.

"Another important greenhouse gas that deserves attention is methane, and she has developed bacteria that can be fed to livestock to greatly reduce methane production in the gut. For companies that aren't actively capturing carbon emissions from their factories, we also have a simple carbon scrubber that can easily be retrofitted to exhaust stacks. These last two have been put in the public domain, and there are already industries looking to utilise the technology to earn carbon credits."

The rest of the team reached positively to the news, and congratulated Alison and Andie on their work. With Ad Astra's aims fully embraced by the whole team, they were excited to see innovations that would show results.

Cath had been busy as well, with each of the management team now having their own building. Some had required very little work to fit their new purpose, while others had been quickly modified. The legal team occupied three storeys of a newly-constructed office building, and Michelle and Tom had already started hiring staff to fill it. Fats had a warehouse in the industrial area, but with a trusted team managing deliveries of QED units, was still working out of Princess Street. Cath had been lucky to pick up a recently vacated printing shop for Paul and his ad team to use, and both Alison and Will had their small premises just around the corner from the head office. Cath herself seemed quite happy to manage her work on her own, though she had employed agents abroad who were looking after Ad Astra's foreign properties.

On Tuesday, the calls that they had been expecting finally came. The boards of the five major power generators had agreed to Ad Astra's proposal in all respects. They would have three years' grace, during which time they would pay lease fees on the CF units, and would retain the units at reduced fees after that, until such time as distributed electricity generation was no longer needed. Ad Astra was given permission to poach non-essential employees with the offer of jobs in CF manufacture, at factories currently under construction around the country.

There was also a call from the Minister of State-owned Enterprises, whom Andie had appraised of the situation, along with the Minister of Finance. With majority holdings in three of the electricity companies, and complete ownership of the power transmission company, the Government had a large stake in the generation and distribution of electricity in New Zealand. They would miss the revenue, of course, but that was well and truly covered by the tax Ad Astra would be paying on sales of TheOS, QED, CF, and other technology.

Any concerns that the Ministers might have harboured had been expertly eased by Andie, and they had apparently come out of the conversation quite excited about the idea. The prospect of being that much closer to meeting their Kyoto Protocol targets was attractive, and it would mean that there would be less need to rush through legislation affecting other industries. They were further pleased when Andie promised to bring out the technology that would help industry and agriculture reduce emissions without major sacrifices. All in all, it seemed that Ad Astra were certainly the flavour of the month in the halls of power.

Lucas was delighted that the Government had fallen in line without argument; he was going to need them onside as his plan developed, and he hadn't wanted to start off on the wrong foot.

The power companies would be communicating to their employees that they would be downsizing, assuring them that replacement opportunities would be forthcoming. On the heels of this, Andie would send out information packs to the affected workers, detailing the positions that would be available with Ad Astra. It was expected that most would take up the new offers, and the soon to be finished CF factories near each of the power stations would be well staffed.

———— ✶⚊⚊✶ ————

More good news came later in the week, with Colonel Johansson of the Defence Logistics Command phoning to say that the NZDF had accepted Ad Astra's proposal for the supply of QED communications devices across all three branches of the armed services. Having anticipated this, Fats was lined up to deliver nearly 2000 QED units in various configurations for use by infantry forces, in land vehicles, aircraft, and naval vessels. In addition, there were the triple-redundancy, hardened command units to link all the others together.

Sonia's re-jigged factory in Taihape had been working on all of these since shortly after the pitch had been made in Trentham, and would have them ready to go the following week.

Lucas and Sonia sat curled up on the couch in front of the fire at the farm. The week's good news had overshadowed the worries about the future, for now, and though there would be further hurdles to overcome, they weren't going to let them spoil their weekend getaway. Splash was stretched out on the hearth, and the happy couple were content.

Their domestic bliss was interrupted by Andie's appearance on the television in front of them.

"This better be good, Andie," growled Lucas, setting his wine glass down beside him.

"I'm really sorry to bother you two – I know I'm not supposed to bug you on your days off. I just thought that you'd like to hear some more good news."

"Okay, out with it," said Sonia.

"We've just broken the two billion mark with TheOS," the AI declared proudly. "There was a huge uptake after the six-month mark without a single crash reported. If that was just personal computers, it would be almost every machine in the world, but since I released a version for smartphones, installations have skyrocketed. I just thought you'd like to know."

"That's great news, Andie," Lucas said. "Well worth the interruption. Thanks. Was there anything else?"

"That was it. I'll let you go back to ... whatever you were doing."

"As you can see, we weren't doing anything – just enjoying the fire, the wine, and each other's company. Off with you now – go humiliate a Grandmaster or something!"

As the television flicked off, Sonia leaned in to cuddle Lucas. "Well, that's exciting. Though it probably won't be long before there are no more devices to install TheOS on, and that revenue stream will dry up."

"It had to happen sometime. We've done pretty well out of it, though, and we've got plenty of cash in hand for ongoing stuff. Software was so much easier than hardware – minimal overheads, and maximum profit. Do you think we should branch out into applications now?"

Sonia furrowed her brow as she thought about the many software companies that would affect. "I don't know about that. Sure, Andie's stuff would be so much better than any existing programs, but maybe we should spare a thought for the people it would run out of business. They may be slower than her at development, but some are already coming to terms with TheOS, and it shouldn't be too long before their own offerings become more efficient. Let's leave it for now, eh?"

Lucas started to sigh at the potential loss of income, before realising that he was perhaps becoming too mercenary, and starting to put profit before people.

"You're right. A better word processor isn't going to save the world, and those guys deserve their chance. Feel free to pull me up whenever I sound like I'm getting too greedy!"

She promised him that she would, knowing, however, that having seen the problem, he would be acutely aware of any further indications that he was deviating from his core ethos. While she found his reluctance to change infuriating at times, it did at least make him dependable. And predictable. A person welding the power that Lucas did could have far worse character traits than predictability.

By the middle of the following week, the military QED units had been completed, and Fats had trucks travelling throughout the country delivering them to Defence Force logistics bases. Sonia hit the road as well, advising on the installation of the control units, and answering questions from those who would be operating them. While the portable units could be used immediately, it would take time to fit the devices in all the vehicles that required them, so there would be some overlap where the new technology was used in tandem with the old. She was kept busy over the few days of her road trip, mating the two networks, and was relieved when the weekend arrived, and she could relax again.

All too soon for her liking, she was back on the road on Monday. This time, she was accompanying the first of the CF generators as they were transported to their new home in Huntly, several hours north of Taihape. Huntly was the site of Genesis Energy's coal-fired plant, and Warren Montegue was there to greet them.

"An historic day, Ms Matheson."

"It sure is. Where would you like us to put your new toys?"

Montegue pointed to the large power station, with its now redundant smokestacks. "We didn't see any point in wasting a perfectly good building, so we've done a little DIY and cleaned out a corner for them in there."

Sonia watched carefully as workmen lifted the weighty generators off the trucks with a heavy-duty forklift, and manoeuvred them into the iconic building on the banks of the mighty Waikato River. Following the forklift in, she looked around in surprise. The interior was not what she would have expected of a building where coal had been burned for almost forty years. Instead of smoke-stained walls, and coal dust on every surface, this place was gleaming, with white-suited workers monitoring shiny dials and gauges. As Montegue had said, a corner near the entrance was clear, with space for the two generators, and some serious cables waiting to be attached. As the first of the machines was lowered into place, a team of workers set to work bolting it to the floor and hooking up the connections. The generators had been primed before leaving Taihape, and were ready to begin supplying the national electricity grid.

As the second generator was likewise secured and connected, Montegue had a brief discussion with one of the technicians, checking that the output was stable and sufficient.

"Well, Ms Matheson, this is the simplest installation of a new generator that I have ever presided over. Is that really all there is to it?"

Sonia quickly looked to see that the connections were secure, and that the generator's readouts were showing the expected values. "It really is that simple. As you can see, the output of each is steady at five-hundred megawatts, and even once you put load on them, that figure won't drop at all. As long as you don't let the liquid hydrogen tanks run empty, you have years of hassle-free power."

Shaking his head in amazement, Montegue gave a gesture to the technician, who flipped switches and circuit-breakers on the nearby wall.

Turning to Sonia, the technician explained, "I've just connected them to our internal supply network, giving them priority, and as you can see, the load on the gas turbines has dropped to zero. Your devices are now supplying power to hundreds of thousands of households and businesses. We will, of course, keep the gas running for now, in case of any unforeseen problems—" Sonia barely resisted letting out a snort at the thought that Andie's technology could have problems "—in which case the load would be taken up immediately. I will keep you informed as to the performance of the devices, and hope that I will never have to contact you for technical support!"

The next day, she went through much the same process at several hydroelectric stations along the Waikato, and then flew to the South Island to oversee the installations at the hydro stations down there the next day.

She was continually surprised at the easy acceptance of the new technology by the staff at the various facilities, though she suspected that Ad Astra's reputation for innovation and reliability had something to do with that. By the end of the week, almost the entire country was running on CF-generated electricity, even the notoriously power-hungry aluminium smelter at Tiwai Point, at the bottom of the South Island. While the environmental impact of power generation in the country had been reduced only slightly, as 85% of the electricity had already been generated from renewable resources, it would be a major feather in New Zealand's cap to be able to claim 100% clean energy. That was not a figure that she wanted bandied about just yet, though, as their plans to avoid economic disruption depended on ambushing the rest of the world's power companies, so to speak.

Andie had, in fact, been doing just that as Sonia zipped around the country. She had split off multiple personalities, each posing as a representative of Ad Astra, and conducted online meetings with electricity providers around the world. She had started with smaller companies, so that they wouldn't be prematurely forced out of the market by larger ones cutting prices when they had access to much cheaper power, though Lucas's cynical opinion of business was that they would simply pocket the extra profit. In fact, the smaller plants would have a chance to increase their business, with generating capacity often far in excess of what they currently had. Of course, she never let on that the new technology would eventually force them all out of business; that bombshell would drop later, when they were all committed.

In short order, her numerous avatars had secured tentative agreement from literally hundreds of power companies, with occasional advice on how best to approach them coming from Warren Montegue of Genesis Energy. Each CEO that she had spoken to had assured her that they would convince their directorial boards. After all, who wouldn't jump at the chance to make a buck?

Her next task was to hold public meetings, as she had in Taihape, to advertise the job offers that would be available in the new CF factories. As in New Zealand, these would be concentrated in depressed areas initially, with future sites planned for regions where coal, oil, and electricity workers may lose their jobs. She had tailored each instance of her avatar to best fit the locale in which she was presenting, in the hope of showing solidarity with the local populations. The response had been promising, with the audiences showing appreciation for the promised benefits and salaries. Sonia's instructor teams, already in the overseas locations, would do double duty as interviewers over the next few weeks, and it was expected that the staff rosters would be filled by the time the factories were completed.

Robert Nkosi was the project manager at one of the South African construction sites, and he and his crew had just arrived for the day's work. The bunker-like factory building was nearly completed, situated just a few kilometres south of Johannesburg, and was as close to being rural as possible, while still close enough for workers to reach easily. The unsealed approach road ran straight and unhindered through the sparse vegetation of the veldt, and if it were not for the intimidating fence surrounding the compound, the banked earth buttressing the building walls would have blended well with the surrounding environment.

Robert was about to get his people working when he spotted a small convoy of vehicles coming up the dusty road towards the site. Considering the location, there was little reason for this amount of traffic to be heading their way, and he felt a knot of fear begin to settle in his stomach as he considered the newcomers' purpose.

"Heads up, boys. It looks like we have company, and judging by the Afrikaner flag flying on the lead vehicle, I doubt they're here to bring us morning tea."

The predominantly coloured workers rightly feared the die-hard Afrikaners, who had never been happy about losing their perceived entitlement when apartheid ended. Though the "Rainbow Nation" officially embraced its multiculturalism, there would always be those who couldn't let go of the country's troubled past. The Afrikaners, descendants of Dutch settlers, had held the political power in South Africa for many years, but with the rise of the African National Congress and Nelson Mandela, in 1994, their influence had been severely curtailed. While they were a small minority, population-wise, some still longed for the "good old days" of apartheid, and this hard-core element made for strained racial relationships.

While Robert called to report the very real possibility of violence, and the flying of the banned flag, his crew quickly moved the heavy machinery in front of the gates, and surreptitiously made sure that ad hoc weapons were close at hand. Being a construction site, some of those were closer to actual weapons than tools.

As the ragtag collection of cars and pickups approached the site, Robert reminded his men not to instigate any violence, and to remain behind the loaders and forklifts. The vehicles pulled up in a semi-circle in front of the gates, and disgorged around forty beefy white Afrikaners. The leader of them stepped forward, a wooden bat in his hand, and shouted at Robert and his workmates.

"Move these machines out of the way!"

Robert raised his hands, saying, "Easy – we have no fight with you men. We are just workers, the same as you. What is the problem?"

The Afrikaner smacked the end of his bat into the ground. "We have found out that this factory will take jobs away from thousands of men, and we're not going to let that happen."

Robert was puzzled by this accusation. He knew the purpose of the factory they were building, and while he understood that the device it would produce would supplant coal, the Afrikaner's anger appeared misplaced. Most of those "thousands" were coloureds, and it was quite obvious that this gang of men would have little interest in standing up for a black man's rights. He suspected that these men had been riled up by a third party, as had been hinted might happen by Jake Lyall, the man who employed him. Even if Robert could somehow convince the man that what they were doing was good for the people, and the country, he was sure that the thugs on the road would find some other reason to start something. There was no love lost between the coloureds and Afrikaners, and he was certain that these men had been prompted to come here knowing that the racial disharmony could ensure significant damage to the factory. He had to buy time to allow the police to arrive. While the South African government was heavily invested in the coal industry, they also took a dim view of civil unrest, and these men would be no match for the legendary brutality of the riot police.

"This factory will be producing electrical generators, and yes, it may take work from many of my brothers. But you know that our country's electricity supply is strained, and these generators will result in enough power for everyone, and cheaper pricing. How can that be such a bad thing?"

The Afrikaner leader looked confused for a moment, as if suddenly realising that he was, in effect, fighting for the jobs of "kaffirs". His instructions – for he had, indeed, been put up to the demonstration – were to disrupt the construction and to scare off the men working there. He had been told only that hard-working *white* men would be out of work, and this man's words made him think that he had not been told the whole truth. Never mind. He and his men had come here for a reason, and if these coloureds wanted to stop them carrying out their task, then their defiance would serve only to make his gang angrier. *Bring it on*, he thought.

"We aren't here to listen to your bullshit, kaffir. We can do this the easy way or the hard way. Step aside and move these machines, or we'll be coming in anyway!"

He signalled to his men, and several of them pulled ropes and hooks from the bed of one of the pickups. Approaching the compound, they attached the hooks to the chain-link fence and the ropes to two of their vehicles. Robert saw the danger, and hurriedly gestured to one of his crew to move another loader up to the fence.

The two Afrikaners backed their vehicles away at speed, tearing the fence down, and the remainder of them rushed for the gap, brandishing crowbars, bats, and chains. Robert's man had barely positioned his loader alongside the breach when the wave of thugs reached it and started clambering over the machine. The time for passive resistance had passed, and the construction crew came together at the back side of the loader, ready to repel the invaders with their sledge-hammers, steel pipes, and in the case of one enterprising fellow, a gas torch.

The two sides were evenly matched in numbers, weapons, and determination, but the work crew had the advantage of terrain. The Afrikaners could only come at them in small numbers as they scrambled over and around the loader, and were met by the full complement of defenders as they did so. The first of them suffered badly from blunt trauma and broken bones, but the tide soon turned as men at the back of the attacking force began to throw petrol bombs over the top of the machine, forcing the workers back, and allowing the Afrikaners to gain a foothold on the inside of the fence. As more came through the gap in the fence, the conflict devolved into brutal hand-to-hand fighting, with men from each side going down. Robert's team made brave dashes into the middle of the melee to drag out their wounded colleagues, but he was unsure just how long they could hold out at this rate.

Right on time – or a few minutes too late, by Robert's estimation – the cavalry arrived, in the form of three armoured police riot vehicles. A loudspeaker bellowed from the lead vehicle.

"Stand down! Everybody cease fighting, and lie face-down on the ground! You do not get another warning!"

This new enemy startled the invaders, and the rear ranks turned around, defiantly raising their weapons to the police. Robert's crew took advantage of the distraction to back away, and as their opponents all began to turn towards the police, they created more distance between the two forces and started dropping their makeshift weapons. Half of the Afrikaners were disadvantaged by being on the wrong side of the loader, but they quickly climbed back to join their comrades as more than twenty riot police in body armour poured out of the armoured vehicles. The mob charged the emerging police, and the construction workers hit the ground as the law enforcement officers opened fire with rubber bullets, water cannon, and tear gas.

For all the Afrikaners' determination and ferocity, the assault was over rapidly, with the riot police moving in to restrain the fallen attackers. The leader of the mob was still standing, and his last-ditch effort to take down an armoured opponent was rewarded with a baton across the back of his knees. As he fell to the ground, two officers dived on him, digging their knees into his spine as they roughly twisted his arms behind his back and slapped handcuffs on him.

Warning the rest of his men to remain on the ground, Robert stood and shouted to their saviours.

"Would you like me to move the machines so you can come and get the rest of them?"

"Hands on your head! Face down on the ground!"

Robert was not about to argue with them. They were worked up and probably didn't need an excuse to start in on the defenders. He calmly obeyed the order and waited for the police to make their way to his side of the fence.

"You. You are in charge here, yes?"

Robert looked up to see that the officer was addressing him. "That is correct. How can I help you?"

"You can start by telling me what happened here."

Keeping his hands on his head, Robert slowly sat up so that he did not have to twist his neck upwards while speaking. The police officer seemed okay with this, as it appeared obvious by now that the construction crew were the victims here.

"We were just about to start work when I saw these vehicles approaching. It seemed unusual enough, all the way out here, that I looked at them carefully and noticed that flag flying. I then called you, and we attempted to barricade ourselves behind the fence until you arrived. They used ropes to pull down that section of fence, and we defended ourselves against them as they climbed over the loader. They then started throwing firebombs and came through the gap in greater numbers as we were forced back. They engaged in hand-to-hand fighting for a few minutes, and then you got here. Thank you so much."

The man gestured for Robert to stand, and told the others that they could also get up.

"While we do not officially approve of people taking the law into their own hands, it is clear to see that you were not the instigators here, and were only defending yourselves. Did they give any reason for the attack?"

As Robert tried to recall the exact words the Afrikaner leader had used, several ambulances arrived, and paramedics began attending to the wounded.

"It was strange. I don't think they knew exactly what we are building here, and it seemed that someone else had put them up to it. When their original assumptions were shown to be misguided, it became a purely racial issue. I believe that was probably the intent of whoever sent them here, knowing that they would use any excuse to attack us, as coloureds."

"That is interesting," said the police officer. "This is apparently not the only attack on one of these factories today, and what you have said makes sense. We are pleased that we could take out these scum for you, but we may not always be able to do so in time. I would suggest that you hire some security of your own, in case further attempts are made to disrupt your work."

Robert knew that there were numerous Ad Astra factories being built around South Africa, and was not entirely surprised at the officer's words, based on his own conclusions regarding the attack. He would have to speak to Jake Lyall about this.

— ༔ ༔ —

"I've had some disturbing news out of South Africa."

"What's the problem, Jake?"

Lucas had been reviewing production and sales numbers, not a chore that he enjoyed, and the ringing of his telephone promised a welcome diversion. This did not appear to be a social call, however.

Of the sixty CF factories under construction in South Africa, almost twenty of them had come under violent attack that day. Most of the disturbances had been quickly quelled by riot police, but some locations had been too isolated for help to arrive before the work crews were badly hurt and the facilities damaged. There had been several fatalities, and the project managers were rightly concerned for their people.

"We need to get private security for these guys, Lucas. This appears to be a coordinated attack on our infrastructure, and I'll give you three guesses where it's coming from."

"I only need one, Jake. Of course it's the coal guys. They're terrified of losing their place as the main supplier of fuel to the country's electricity generators. Someone in the electricity sector must have been speaking out of school, or perhaps they figured out it could be worth a few Rand to let slip what was happening with the CFs. It seems that Alison was wrong – they've completely skipped the option of fighting us in the courts and have gone straight to direct action."

Andie had been listening in to the conversation, and had displayed a breakdown of the costs they could be facing on Lucas's computer. Manned checkpoints, security guards, and stronger fencing all added up to quite a sum, but it seemed that it would be a necessary expense. Lucas conveyed to Jake what measures he would have to install at all the overseas locations, adding, "Carine has also been working on some interesting things for defence as well, due in part to her fear of IVIA finding us, and our little adventure with Sonia's kidnappers. I'll get her to send some of them over. I know that in all our offshore locations, it's legal for private security to be

322

armed, but her new toys are going to be just as effective at putting down the bad guys. They're completely legal – so far – and can even be automated, which could save a bit of money in the long run. I'll send through the details, and you can have your guys install them."

Carine's "toys" included neural wave disrupters, sonic weapons, and a nifty sticky-web thrower that could immobilise both people and vehicles. The woman's paranoia was paying dividends.

After ending Jake's call, Lucas got in touch with Carine and told her to go full-steam ahead with producing the non-lethal weaponry, giving her permission to commandeer one of the local factories for conversion to the manufacture of her devices.

"It was inevitable that something like this would happen," said Andie. "It's sad that some of our workers lost their lives, but we can ensure that we will be ready next time."

Lucas sighed heavily as he thought of the first true sacrifices that had been made in the name of his plan. Death was not something you could just write off as one of the costs of doing business, at least not in his book. He asked Andie to make sure that the families of those men lost would be taken care of, and to tell the South African police force how much Ad Astra appreciated their prompt and efficient response where they could.

He was heartbroken at the thought that men had died for his dream, but it made him all the more determined to bring coal to its knees.

A SECRET

With the downsizing of the power station staff, workers who had previously thought their jobs secure in the long term eagerly took advantage of the opportunity to apply for positions with Ad Astra. The new generators required far fewer people to operate and maintain them than the existing machinery did, though the infrastructure and transmission lines still needed servicing and repairs. The initial phase of the CF plan hadn't made too large a dent in the stations' workforce, but the future would see the required numbers drop to mere dozens, rather than hundreds. It was not widely known, of course, that transmission lines and substations were to become obsolete. There would be many more workers laid off when that happened. In the meantime, the factory positions would be filled by others in the relevant regions. Space had been allocated to expand the factories when required, and there would also be work other than on the production lines. It was a big job, changing the world.

Ad Astra's legal department was a hive of activity. Desks throughout the three floors were covered in paperwork, and juniors scurried about researching and running errands. For all the activity, the workplace was silent but for the rustle of paper and whispered conversations.

Michelle had employed numerous subordinates, as the contacts with ISPs were multiplying rapidly, and new contracts for the supply of CF generators were not far away. Being standard contracts across the board, the work was not difficult. It was the sheer volume that necessitated the dozens of staff. Michelle was immensely grateful for the AI system that was keeping track of everyone's work.

Tom had brought in lawyers well-versed in the legal systems of the countries that Ad Astra was now operating in, and everyone was hard at work preparing counter-arguments to anything that might be thrown at them. It had been made clear to everyone that time was not on their side; it was inevitable that the energy industry would not take kindly to seeing profits evaporate.

Tom's lead US counsel came to him with the first of the anticipated reports; the House Subcommittee on Energy was being primed by the Congressman for Kentucky to sit and consider this new energy technology. That it was Kentucky that was making waves was no surprise to Tom, as that state was one of the main coal producers in the US. Even if the Congressman's personal fortune weren't so inextricably tied to the industry, he had an obligation to look out for his constituents.

"If these guys get their teeth into this, Tom, they can tie us up for years. We're lucky that one of my contacts heard about this on the grapevine. Our best option is to nip it in the bud, and have our say before it gets bogged down in Committee hearings."

"Well done, Dan. We certainly can't afford to lose any time on this. What's our plan of attack?"

Dan Shockley, a balding West Virginian tending towards obesity, had spent the better part of his legal career representing the public in individual lawsuits and class actions against Big Energy. His particular viewpoint, and experience, had made him an ideal choice to help Ad Astra take on the big boys. As it happened, his personal desire to see the right thing done also meant that he came far cheaper than his success might otherwise have suggested.

"I'd say we go over their heads. Lay our case in front of the Department of Energy and get them to see how well it fits in with their own stated goal of 'ensuring the country's energy future'. With their endorsement, it'll make it that much harder for the Committee to gain any traction."

"Sounds good," said Tom. "I think we might get Alison Fox in on this, too. I'm sure she can whip up some public sentiment on the issue. There's nothing a government department loves more than a mob outside their door, ready to shout them down if it looks like they're not acting in the best interests of the people!"

Chuckling at the idea of the Department of Energy caught between a crowd demanding lower electricity prices and a Congressman trying to line his pockets, Dan then asked how the plans for a practical demonstration of the CF generators were going.

"I believe that Sonia has units en route to the US and other countries as we speak, and she will be able to put on a show any day now. I can't see any consideration other than safety being a valid cause to restrict the use of CF technology."

Not that validity had often been a contributing factor to arguments put forward when somebody's back was against the wall, but getting the main potential concern out of the way would be a huge step in the right direction, and may be enough to convince the DoE of CF's acceptability.

Tom called Lucas to give him the news after Dan had left, though he suspected that word would have got to him soon enough. While he didn't think that Andie actively listened to every conversation, he had no doubt that she could pick keywords out of the background chatter as easily as he could spot a Porsche in a car park full of Toyotas.

Lucas was annoyed, yet reluctantly accepting, that this first challenge had come so soon. Still, the sooner they got this sort of stuff out of the way, the sooner they could get on with things.

"Your man Dan will be earning his pay on this. Keep me in the loop, and keep up the good work. I'll make sure that Sonia is ready for the demo as soon as possible."

Lucas had, indeed, taken over the receptionists desk at the Princess Street offices. With little actual office work to do, it was entirely sufficient for his needs. He ducked into Sonia's office, and then though to the workshop when he didn't find her at her desk.

"We've got action in the US House of Representatives," he said as she looked up from the workbench.

"So soon? We've only just started."

"I'm afraid so." He went on to tell her of the possibility of a subcommittee delaying the plan, and Dan's idea to cut the House out of the loop.

"The generator should arrive there in the next day or so, and I'll get one of our techs to run the demonstration. I hope it will be enough."

Lucas took a seat, idly playing with some obscure tool that he had picked up and couldn't even name, let alone use. "What is this thing?"

"Sonic screwdriver," she replied, taking it from his hand and placing it back on the bench.

"Yeah, right. I'm no Doctor Who fan, but even I know that's a made-up tool."

"No, seriously. It emits ultrasonic waves as you tighten a screw to basically vibrate it right in. Sometimes I have to get things really tight, and using an impact driver can damage sensitive internal components. It's one of Andie's new gizmos."

He picked up the screwdriver again and held it up to inspect it closely. "Huh. We're making science fiction obsolete, too."

"Was there anything else, or were you just planning on annoying me all day?"

"Well, excu-u-use me. I'm just trying to take an interest in my darling's work."

"That's nice, dear. I'll tell you all about it when we get home. Now, scoot."

He put the sonic screwdriver back on the workbench and turned to leave, reaching the door before pausing and asking over his shoulder, "Are we about ready to go on the local CF factories?"

"The construction will be finished in a week or so, and then there'll be another week for training. With the ten locations we've got, we should be turning out twenty-five or thirty units a day. You just make sure we've got places to put them!"

The New Zealand factories were located across the country; Northland and East Cape, where unemployment was high, and Waikato, Canterbury, Otago, Southland, and the South Island's West coast, where electricity workers and coal miners would need replacement jobs. The West Coast in particular would be hard hit by a decline in coal production, and Lucas was keen to get as many operations running there as possible. He hoped to expand the two CF factories already there to over 1000 staff, and planned to open facilities for other technology as it was released.

As Sonia had promised, the demonstration CF unit arrived at the Los Angeles port on Friday of that week. Dan had already approached the DoE, and they had agreed to send representatives to a demonstration of its safety the following Wednesday. Though they had been fully assured that there was no danger, they had insisted that this take place at the White Sands Missile Range in New Mexico. Sonia was grateful that they hadn't chosen the closer Nevada Test Site. She couldn't be sure that the residual radiation from the many nuclear tests there wouldn't skew their results.

Considering the importance of this demonstration, Lucas had sent both Dan and Sonia to the US, and they flew in to Los Angeles on the same day as the generator arrived. They quickly organised transport for it and themselves to New Mexico, stopping overnight in Phoenix, Arizona, and settling into a hotel in Las Cruces, 100 kilometres from White Sands.

On the morning of the demonstration, Sonia checked that the generator was still running, and they set off. They made a curious convoy as their rental car led a large mobile crane equipped with a wrecking ball, and the hired truck carrying the container-sized generator. Meeting their escort at the Public Affairs Office on the White Sands base, and identifying themselves to his satisfaction, they followed his vehicle about forty kilometres into the barren land to the east. They finally arrived, well, nowhere. The few buildings they had passed on their trip had been isolated, concrete-block constructions, and their eventual destination was a large concrete pad with no buildings in sight but for a low bunker set almost 100 metres away.

Sonia got the truck driver to unload the generator using his vehicle's attached hoist, and had the crane operator set up so that he could drop the heavy weight of the wrecking ball onto the generator. To keep the safety people happy, he was able to do that via remote control. Sonia was frustrated at the excessive precautions that were being taken, knowing how unnecessary they were, but she had to play by the DoE's rules.

Their representatives were already there, and their technicians began to set up their equipment. They placed microphones and high-speed cameras around the generator, as well as thermal cameras to monitor any heat that might escape when the containment was breached. They also had meters and gauges to display the power output, and were impressed by the voltage coming from such a relatively small machine, with no noticeable emissions.

There were also people there from the International Atomic Energy Agency, setting up devices to check for radiation. The number of people milling around, and the amount of equipment surrounding the generator, made the scene look like a movie set. Sonia just needed someone to call "Action!", and she could be done with it all.

While she was arranging the demonstration, Dan was over with the DoE people near the bunker, explaining what would be happening and taking the opportunity to extol the virtues of clean, cheap energy. While those sent to observe the show were not among the most influential within the department, the data collected, and the first-hand experience should be enough to convince the decision makers.

When everything had been set up to the technicians' satisfaction, and cables had been run back to the bunker, the technicians, Sonia and Dan, and DoE representatives all retreated into the bunker. Numerous monitors, dials, and other readouts had been lined up on a bench under the thick, blast-proof window facing the test site, and the bunker's occupants jostled for position as each tried to find the best vantage point of the hardware.

The liaison for the military, as hosts of the demonstration, waited for silence before launching into a safety spiel.

"Ladies and gentlemen, we will be conducting this experiment under our usual protocols for weapons testing. In a moment, we will be lowering the blast shields over the window, and you may observe via the closed-circuit cameras which will be displayed on this large screen, here," he said, indicating the four camera views on the main monitor.

"Can I please ask you to acknowledge that each of your team members are with us? WSMR takes a dim view of leaving personnel out in the open during live firing exercises or any similarly dangerous activity."

Ammonia looked around the room to see that Dan and her two drivers were inside. "All present."

The leader of the DoE delegation, and the man from the IAEA responded likewise, and the liaison breathed a mock sigh of relief. "Excellent. I haven't had to write any letters of condolence yet, and I don't intend to start today! Now, as per our safety protocol, we will shortly sound a siren, giving a thirty second warning, after which the siren will sound again, at which time you may commence your demonstration, Ms Matheson. In the event of an emergency, please do not panic, and follow all my instructions. While this bunker is proof against some pretty serious explosions, this is an untested technology and should our protection be breached, our first responders will be on-site within moments. Ms Matheson has assured me that nothing untoward will happen, but we like to be prepared for any eventuality. Does everybody understand the procedure?"

A round of assent passed through the crowded room, and the liaison reached out to press a prominent button on the front wall of the bunker. A large metal plate dropped down across the outside of the blast window, followed quickly by another on the inside. As he pressed a second button, the muted sound of a klaxon could be heard from outside. A long thirty seconds later, they heard it again, and the military man nodded to Sonia.

Everyone was closely watching the images on the large monitor in front of them, with the exception of the technicians, who were starting intently at their readouts. Sonia hovered a finger over a large, red button on the remote control unit she held, glancing at the crane operator for confirmation. He nodded, and she pressed the button with a dramatic flourish.

Onscreen, everyone saw the raised wrecking ball released from high above the generator. Though it fell at 9.8 m/s2, it seemed to Sonia that it took an eternity for the two-thousand-pound weight to drop the thirty-five metres from the extended boom of the crane. In reality, it took a little over two-and-a-half seconds, before it landed on top of the generator at almost 100km/h, with an initial impact force of over 300,000 Newtons.

The steel casing split like the skin of a ripe tomato, the ceramic inner lining shattered, the forged-steel wrecking ball buried itself deeply into the mangled wreckage of the generator ... and nothing else happened. There was no blinding light, no super-heated jet of hydrogen plasma, and definitely no explosion. If it weren't for the small puff of cloud as excess liquid hydrogen boiled off, there was no way to tell that a fusion generator capable of powering a large town had just been violently destroyed. The crumpled remains were a bit of a giveaway, of course, but the strict safety precautions leading up to its demolition now seemed completely unnecessary.

In spite of her total confidence in Andie's predictions, Sonia experienced a brief moment of relief before turning to the nearest DoE man. "Well, that was a bit of an anticlimax, wasn't it?"

He nodded dumbly. Even though he had desperately wanted the demonstration to be a success, he felt slightly cheated at having come all the way out to an explosives test range and not have something go "Bang!".

"I'd like to get the official results, but it does appear that your technology has fulfilled its promise of being safe."

The technicians began to read out those results from the equipment in front of them.

"Thermal imaging camera shows an initial maximum of 400F, swiftly reverting to ambient. The thermal blast was localised, with the temperature dropping off in proportion with distance. It is extremely unlikely that a person would suffer any lasting damage even if they had their face right in the thing. Frankly, you'd be in much more danger from whatever caused the damage to the device in the first place. I think you'd suffer worse burns picking up a hot frying pan."

"Radiation, zero. That's to be expected in a deuterium fusion reaction, with the by-product being Helium3. A tritium reaction would be only slightly more dangerous, though our sniffers don't detect any in this device."

"The power output was stable at 500MW right up until impact, at which time the reaction in the sequential modules ceased immediately. There was no residual electrical current after that time, and the steel casing never registered any current at all. I concur with Ms Matheson's prediction that there would be no electrocution danger."

"High-speed shows a small volume of shrapnel, primarily ceramic, ejected to a radius of ten metres. This is consistent with the force applied, and does not appear to have been increased in any way by any internal factors. My recommendation is that you do not stand too close to the thing when somebody drops a wrecking ball on it."

Sonia looked expectantly at the DoE delegation huddled together making notes as the findings were related. They seemed in no hurry to discuss the results with her, and she was becoming impatient to have the mess outside cleared up, and to get back to New Zealand. Dan noticed her fidgeting, and held up a hand placatingly before approaching the huddle and politely clearing his throat to get their attention.

"So, gentlemen, madam – I trust you were satisfied by what you have witnessed. Do you have any further tests you need to do before we pick up our rubbish?"

The DoE officials looked up from their jottings at the interruption. Their leader spoke. "Ah, Mr Shockley. Sorry to keep you waiting. We're just waiting on our technician—" he pointed to the monitor, where a white-suited man could be seen running a handheld scanner over the wreckage "—to finish his readings, and you will be free to take the remains of your fascinating device away. I must say, at first glance, the results are very promising, but I'm sure you are aware of how these things work. We will take our results and observations back to the Department, and our decision will be forthcoming. I understand that you had some concerns about the House subcommittee looking to delay or restrict the use of this technology. I think that it is safe to say that they will have to come up with a reason other than safety to deny Americans access to cheap, clean power, and my personal recommendation will be that this technology is adopted in all haste. Of course, that is not yet the official viewpoint, but all of us here were very impressed. We do wish you and your company the very best of luck. While there will likely be economic ramifications, we feel that the benefits far outweigh any other considerations."

Dan turned away briefly to wink at Sonia, and gratefully shook the man's hand, smiling and nodding politely at the rest of the delegation. Sonia came across and likewise offered her thanks for their time. She and Dan then ushered their two truck drivers out of the bunker to wait for the technician to finish his examination of the generator.

When he was finished, Sonia supervised the reloading of the ruined generator, and they once again followed their escort, this time back towards civilization. They carried on from the White Sands base, back through Phoenix, to Los Angeles. Fats had arranged return shipping for the generator, and Dan and Sonia waited to see it safely loaded before catching their flight home.

———————— ✝╫╲╲╫╪ ————————

On their triumphant return to Palmerston North, the entire team gathered around to hear their report of the demonstration.

"There really wasn't a lot to it," said Sonia. "We hoisted the wrecking ball above the generator, let it go, and watched it drop. We may as well have dropped it on the ground for all that happened. No bang, no flash, no nothing. I swear that some of the guys watching were desperate for an explosion, but in the end, they were disappointed. Not in the generator – just that there wasn't any excitement. Once they got over that, they seemed very positive about our chances, and I got the feeling that the Kentucky Congressman will get short shrift if he tries to attack the tech's safety. The DoE guy gave us every reason to believe that we'd get the green light from them. All in all, a successful few days away."

The team was thrilled that the CF tech had passed the test, and crowded around Sonia to offer their congratulations, hugging her and slapping her on the back.

"Easy, guys – all I did was press a button. Andie deserves all the credit."

Andie, of course, had sat in on the meeting, and blushed as everyone praised her genius.

"Thanks, everyone. I knew, from a purely technical viewpoint, that it would be perfectly safe, but there's nothing quite like having that confirmed in actuality. I'm going to pass the ball back to Dan and Sonia, though – it was their hard work that got us over the line. Don't sell yourselves short, you two. Sonia, if you hadn't put in the hard yards on the prototype, and your people hadn't built the thing so precisely, it might have been a different story. And Dan, without your contacts and experience, we might never have known about the trouble headed our way, and wouldn't have got the DoE to agree to meet us so quickly. Well done, both of you."

Dan and Sonia had to endure another round of congratulations before the meeting broke up and everyone headed back to their jobs. With almost guaranteed acceptance of the technology by the US government, it was felt that other countries would soon fall in line, and the mission could go full-steam ahead. China was keen to ingratiate themselves with the wider world, and converting to clean power would go a long way towards that. It would also make them more economically competitive; though a self-professed communist regime, capitalism was no longer the great evil that it had once been.

India's coal industry had recently been opened up to private enterprise, after being nationalised in 1973, so the government had little direct interest in production of the resource. With more than half the electricity generation in the country state-owned, however, anything that would enable them to cut generation costs and spend more on the problematic transmission infrastructure would be attractive to them.

In South Africa, though the dominant electricity generator was state-owned, coal exports accounted for almost fifteen percent of their GDP, and the economy was heavily geared towards coal production. It would be a hard call for the government there to decide between reliable energy and coal-derived economic factors. The fact that the US was likely to adopt the CF technology would hopefully nudge them in the desired direction.

Australia, likewise, had a love affair with coal, and it was credited with driving the longest period of economic growth in the nation's history. It could be said that it was somewhat of a love-hate relationship, though, as coal-mining companies had been known to run roughshod over indigenous rights and environmental regulations, where those hadn't already been watered down to accommodate them.

Fortunately, the coal produced in these countries was not solely for use in electricity generation. There was still a huge demand for the types of coal used in industries such as steel manufacturing, and switching to clean power stations would not exactly bankrupt those nations. Yet. Andie already had plans afoot to bring more efficient and cost-effective electric systems to the steel industry. Better efficiency would mean higher profits, of course, and Will's team believed that steel mills could easily be encouraged to adapt. As with all Andie's technology, improved processes should have flow-on benefits both up and down the food chain.

That weekend, during Lucas and Sonia's regular trip to the farm, Lucas borrowed the old Hilux from James Roy, telling Sonia that he wanted to show her something out on the farm. Thinking that it must be some childhood memory of his, she eagerly climbed into the Toyota and they set off down the drive. Turning right at the bottom of the hill, Lucas drove a few hundred metres up the road. In all the time Sonia had spent at the farm, she had never driven in this direction and was surprised to see a new-looking track leading into the hills behind the house. The entrance was secured by a heavy metal gate, which Lucas unlocked and opened, and they drove along the broad, gravelled track for about a kilometre. Sonia knew that the bulk of the farm was leased out, and was puzzled as to why this track was here, and why Lucas had a key to the gate. As they rounded one more hill, an impressive and incongruous sight confronted her. The gravel track led up to a gate set into an intimidating fence constructed of solid steel, and standing at least three metres high. Several heavy-duty earthmoving machines were lined up outside the fence, along with the usual detritus associated with a construction site.

"What the hell is this? It must be something to do with Ad Astra, but I've never heard of anything like this there."

"Actually, it's more of a ... personal ... project," Lucas responded cryptically, as he got out of the vehicle and approached the fence. Unlocking the gate with his biometric credentials, he waved for her to join him as the heavy gate rolled to one side.

As the interior was exposed, she saw a concrete slab that covered all she could see of the ground inside the fence, except where it met what appeared to be a warehouse, albeit an extremely large one. It must have been at least sixty metres from side to side, and there was no telling how long the building was. It stood back from the front fence by fifty metres or more, and though it rose only one storey above ground level, a wide concrete ramp descended far below to a pair of enormous steel doors in the centre of the facing wall.

They walked inside the gate, and Lucas pressed a button to close it behind them as Sonia struggled to take in the scale of what she was seeing. He took her hand and together they began to walk down the incline ahead of them.

"Don't tell me – you bought the Hurricanes rugby team and this is their new stadium?"

"That would have been fun, but no. Patience, grasshopper. We're almost there."

At the bottom of the ramp, there was a person-sized door set into one of the larger ones, and Lucas once again used his thumbprint and retinal pattern to unlock it. He pushed it open, and stood back to let Sonia enter. Lights were flickering on throughout the interior, and she cautiously stepped across the threshold.

Her jaw dropped as she saw the vastness of the building. The sixty-metre width was nothing compared to the depth of the cavernous space in front of her. The far wall seemed at least one-hundred metres away, and the ceiling rose nearly twenty-five metres. It was not just the size of the building that stunned her, however. To one side, there rested a metal framework that was obviously in the process of being covered with a skin of some sort. This construction took up at least a quarter of the available floor space, and towered nearly to the ceiling. The short side of this faced them, and was wedge-shaped. It sloped up towards them, before a smooth curve four metres off the ground angled it away again up to the top. On the upper part – the rearward slope – was a raked section of a glass-like material, though no window had ever been so large. Fully fifteen metres from side to side, this "windscreen", for want of a better word, must have been four metres from top to bottom, and curved around at the sides. The massive creation could have passed for a sea vessel, though there were few places in New Zealand further from any large body of water.

Sonia turned to Lucas, a look of wonder in her eyes. "Is this what I think it is?"

Pleased that he had been able to keep his pet project secret for so long, he smiled smugly. "Of course, it's nowhere near finished, but this is what we're all working towards. I hadn't been spending my salary, so had a bit of spare cash and I thought it would be worthwhile making a start on this."

"Wait, what? You've been getting *paid*?"

He chuckled at her joke, adding, "I may have taken a bit out of the petty cash tin, too!"

She began walking around the work in progress. Steel girders constituted the framework, and up close she could see that the skin was some form of carbon fibre.

"Is that outer layer going to be strong enough?" she asked.

Lucas rapped his knuckles on the material, which gave off a ring more akin to what she would have expected from sheet metal. "It's quite good enough – remember that NASA's lunar module had a skin barely thicker than tinfoil in places. This is a special composite material that Andie had made up. Don't worry – she and I have been over the specs thoroughly."

The side of the framework nearest them had only been covered on the front quarter, leaving the interior exposed. Sonia could see that there would be three levels for most of the length, with the back third left full height. Near the front, a fifteen by three metre section on the lower edge of the long side was indented by five metres, and the back end of the framework sloped gently in towards the bottom.

Tearing her eyes away from the construction, she surveyed the rest of the building. The right-hand half, above the work area, had gantries running side to side, and the full length of the building, while the other half was clear up to the ceiling. On the floor, recessed tracks ran in both directions, obviously so that the construction could be moved around the site on the large cradles in which it currently sat. Much of the rest of the space was at present devoted to storage of materials, such as stacks of the carbon fibre composite sheets and more steel framing beams.

"You could fit four of those things in here," she commented.

"There'll only be one for now, but it will be a handy space to make smaller ones in the future."

Looking back towards the partially completed structure, she asked, "So how much more needs to be done?"

Lucas sucked air through his teeth, thinking about it. "The drive system, obviously. There'll be a lot of cabling to be installed, and the interior will need to be dressed. The power supply is sorted, of course, but there are still another couple of gizmos that need to be invented. I'll be putting things in as we come up with them, but there's no telling how long it will all take. Still, she's pretty impressive already, eh?"

That she was. At nearly sixty metres long, fifteen metres wide, and almost ten metres tall, she could have been a superyacht in any of Auckland's shipyards. She would go places those yacht owners had never dreamt of, though. She would be the flagship of mankind's new revolution.

CRISPIN'S DAY

As they arrived back at the office on Monday, Sonia's head was still buzzing with what she had seen on the farm. She was under strict instructions from Lucas not to tell the others about it, for fear of distracting them from their important work. She felt the secret bubbling inside her, and was unusually quiet the whole day, thinking that if she opened her mouth, she would be unable to stop the information gushing out. Her unnatural behaviour caused no end of speculation around the office, and she was glad when most of her friends went off to their respective places of work after the regular morning meeting.

The meeting had been, for the most part, a rehash of the work currently under way, but Will was called upon to give an important update on the progress of the imminent share offer.

The big man stood and moved to the head of the conference table as he shuffled the papers in his hands. He and his team had been working non-stop for the last six weeks, preparing Ad Astra's IPO, or Initial Public Offering of shares in the company. While the process for doing so was fairly straightforward, and well documented, his team had been taking particular care to structure it in a way that left no room for outsiders to interfere in the running of the business. Lucas had made it perfectly clear that he wanted control to remain in-house, and Will agreed totally with that stipulation.

Each device would be manufactured and distributed under a separate subsidiary, with over half of the available shares retained by Ad Astra. The complex part of the arrangement was determining the value of each company, the number of shares to issue, and the initial price of them.

At present, they only had two devices that they were ready to sell stock in – the QED, and the CF technology. The TheOS operating system had nearly reached market saturation and did not have a lot of potential profit remaining, and Carine's weapons were never likely to be available to anyone outside of Ad Astra.

The QED company had been conservatively valued at two-hundred-and-fifty billion dollars, considering the number of potential customers, and Will planned to sell an initial thirty percent of the issued shares. Setting an opening price of twenty dollars, this would mean an upfront cash injection of seventy-five billion dollars across 3.75 billion shares. That should be enough for investors to squabble over.

With the eventual plans for the CF generators not yet public knowledge, they had valued that company at only (!) four-hundred-billion dollars. This took into account the nine-thousand generators that would be leased at two-million dollars per month, though it would soon seem an awfully conservative valuation when somebody did the maths and realised that this was merely the turnover in the first two years. Will would sell only twenty percent of the issued shares at the beginning; four-billion of them at twenty dollars apiece. The remaining twenty-nine percent of the shares would be released when the price inevitably rose after the household generators were announced. By waiting for the share price to hit one-hundred dollars, an additional six-hundred billion dollars could be raised.

The numbers were astronomical (which, as Paul pointed out, was an entirely appropriate adjective), but Will assured the team that across several stock markets, there would be more than enough capital out there to see the shares snapped up quickly. He had already made the necessary negotiations with several large banks to underwrite the IPO, and was now just waiting on the go-ahead from Lucas.

"You've done a great job, Will," Lucas said. "I'm keen to get this underway as soon as we can, unless anyone can see an issue we've missed?"

A low murmur ran around the table as people voiced various ideas to their neighbour. Paul was the first to share his concerns.

"I get that we're having all this money come in, but how do we justify spending it on things outside of each company's remit? Doesn't taking the capital out of the business affect the company's value?"

"I see where your thinking is coming from," said, "but the money actually belongs to Andie, not the subsidiary. As the sole owner, she is selling thirty percent of the company, and pocketing the money. She can put that into the parent company's coffers or do whatever she likes with it, and the value of AAQED, for example, hasn't changed at all. Of course, it will be expected that the company finances will be run responsibly, and if we continue to do so, then the chance of investors getting spooked is minimal. It's when the founder or director takes the loot and runs, leaving the business cash-poor and unable to work effectively, that people might panic and sell off their stock. As long as we can show that each company will continue to operate at a profit and give investors a return, then we'll be good."

Satisfied with Will's answer, Paul nodded, thanking him.

"How much are we obligated to tell the shareholders?" asked Michelle. "Will they expect a long-term plan, and would it make them nervous if we do things they're not expecting?"

Will shook his head. "If we set out the plan exactly as they expect to see it, which is simply leasing out the generators, they'll be happy to see the income rolling in. Even when we do drop the smaller models on them, I'm sure that they'll only be concerned with the exponential growth in potential. At that point, I expect the share price to take off, and we can sell the outstanding portion at far more than we would have got selling then all in the first place."

There was excitement in the room at the prospect of "easy money" instead of having to wait for the income from sales to come in.

Tom had a more serious concern, and had been nervously tapping his pen on the table as he waited for a chance to speak.

"Won't the likelihood of legal obstacles to the CF stuff make investors wary? We haven't even got a definite green light from the DoE yet, and I'm certain that won't be the last hurdle we face."

Will put his paperwork down on the table and paced the length of the room and back before answering. "That's a very good point, Tom. We had thought of it, but were hoping that it would all be concluded a little sooner. Do you have any idea of the timeframe we're looking at for full acceptance?"

Tom grimaced. "Hmm. Dan doesn't expect the DoE to rule on it for at least another three weeks, and that will only be relevant in the US. I believe that Alison has the info on other regulatory bodies."

At the far end of the table, Alison had been following this line of discussion closely, and was ready with her answer.

"While every country has its own people shaping energy policy, the best idea is to get the International Energy Agency on board. They advise governments around the world on energy sustainability and reliability, and their backing would play an important role in getting the CF technology adopted with the least hassle. When I was with Greenpeace, we had regular contact with the IEA, encouraging them to promote clean energy, and I've already been in touch through an old colleague, pushing our tech as the best option. I'm still waiting on a response, but I'll try to speed things up. I've got feelers out at the World Energy Council, too, and fully expect them to be on our side."

Thanking her, Tom turned back to Will. "Can we hold off on the CF IPO for a few more weeks? If those agencies come back positive, I can't see any other problems that my team couldn't handle with some smooth talking. There will still be pushback, but having those major players in our corner should pull the teeth of any new challenges. Foxy, I'll have Dan get the DoE to pass on their results from the test to the IEA and WEC. We'll also make that information available to any other national agencies."

With no other new business forthcoming from the team, Lucas rose from his seat at the head of the table.

"I'd normally close the meeting at this stage, and let you get on with your work, but I'd just like to take a moment to let you know of a new development."

The people seated around the table looked at him with eager anticipation, not least Sonia, who thought that he might be going to tell them about the spaceship, and she could stop worrying about letting the cat out of the bag. Lucas, however, was not going to make it that easy for her.

"Phase One of the plan was the operating system. Phase Two, the QED. At the moment, we are in Phase Three, getting the CF into the market, but it's time to let you all know about Phase Four."

His friends leaned in excitedly as he began to talk.

"Phase Four is essentially an extension of the CF project. While electricity generation accounts for almost half of all CO_2 emissions globally, other industries contribute their share as well, and we will be tackling as many of those as we can. The second largest emitter of CO_2 is the transport industry, and while the production and uptake of electric vehicles – EVs – is increasing, the technology is not improving quickly enough, nor is the price of EVs becoming that much more affordable. Those who can afford to buy an EV are often concerned about the range and performance, while the rest simply can't justify the cost of replacing their perfectly adequate internal combustion vehicles.

"The CF technology has given us the opportunity to address all of these concerns, and we hope to soon roll out CF generators that will replace traditional EV battery packs, which themselves have an undesirable environmental cost. This should bring the price of new EVs down to a more acceptable level, though still out of reach of many people.

"To that end, we have also devised a retrofit unit that will simply bolt into place instead of an existing IC engine. We hope to train existing auto mechanics to perform this transplant, which will consist of a CF unit and an electric motor that connects to a vehicle's regular drivetrain."

Though many people had already converted older cars to run on electricity, most of these used banks of heavy, lead-acid batteries that dramatically impacted on the vehicle's performance. The idea that a simple engine transplant could make any vehicle environmentally-friendly would be a major breakthrough, and meant that the average car owner would be far more likely to adopt EV technology.

"Do we have pricing for these conversion units?" asked Paul.

"Not yet," Lucas answered, "but we hope to negotiate a deal with motor manufacturers. There are several factors to take into account when selecting a motor – I won't bore you with the specifics – and Sonia will be talking through our options when she approaches those manufacturers.

"We'd like to keep the cost low, obviously, but at the end of the day, we'll be relying on the best possible rate they can give us for motors and controllers etc. Andie has looked at the design specs of some of the more popular units, and we would be willing to offer technical improvements in exchange for a cost reduction. Needless to say, our end of the hardware will come with payment plans where necessary."

Alison put her hand up, and quickly lowered it again when she remembered that she was management, not a school pupil.

"What's our plan and timeframe for getting this out there?"

Lucas glanced at Sonia, raising his eyebrows. She nodded back, saying simply, "We're on track."

Frowning at her brevity, he continued. "ASAP, ideally, but it just depends on when our demo models are ready. We'll take those to auto manufacturers who already have EVs in production, and see if they're keen to swap out their battery tech. The retrofit will have to wait until we reach an agreement with motor manufacturers. If we can get a deal done, we'll have to switch some more CF factories to producing these units, and can get those out to the general public as soon as we have stock coming off the line. I imagine that we'll have at least one option going within a month or two."

Nodding, Alison bent over her notepad, jotting down a reminder to bring the news to her friends in environmental groups once Ad Astra was ready to go. They would be particularly excited to see the demise of fossil-fuel transportation.

With no other questions about Phase Four, Lucas called a close to the meeting. Following Sonia downstairs to the workshop, he caught up to her at the workbench and put his arms around her from behind.

"You were pretty quiet up there. 'On track' isn't much of a progress update."

She grunted in frustration. "I've got progress – I just didn't want to start talking or I might have had trouble stopping. You can not believe how hard it was not to blurt out the big news!"

"Oh, I've got some idea," he responded, laughing. "I can't count the number of times I almost let it slip before I was ready to show you."

"I realise why we need to keep it quiet. They'll go crazy when we do finally tell them, and we can't afford to distract them right now, but damn, it's hard."

He turned her around and held her tight. "I feel as bad about it as you do, but, baby steps, yeah?"

As she buried her face in his shoulder, he heard a muddled affirmation. "Baby steps."

He held her a moment longer, before pulling away. "It won't be long now, babe. We've just got a couple more things to do before we're ready. How about you give me that progress report now?"

Wiping away the moisture that was threatening to escape her eyes, she turned back to the workbench and slapped her hand on the object that lay there.

"This is the modified CF generator for Phase Four. It's a 480 volt, high-amperage output that runs a little differently to the household CF unit, using more fuel to reach the voltage and current requirements. I've mated it to a capacitor bank so that it doesn't have to run all the time, and will fire up only when needed."

Lucas peered at the device. "When you say that it uses more hydrogen, how much are we talking about?"

"Andie and I figure that it will run for about six hours at full capacity before you need to top up. We could put a larger fuel supply in, but there are practical and economic reasons for limiting it."

"And when can we show it to the manufacturers?"

"I need to make a bunch more demo units, and we're still looking to outsource the additional hardware for the retrofit model. Andie could come up with more efficient designs, but it will be quicker to use existing tech – it's getting better all the time, and will do the job. Give me another two weeks and I should have enough units ready to take away."

"Perfect," Lucas said. "Is there anyone you trust to do the road trip? I don't really want you tied up with that for weeks."

"Fortunately, you don't need a degree in engineering or physics to demonstrate it. Carine is the only other person who would understand it at the moment, and we can't spare her. I'll have a few people lined up by the time you need them – it's essentially a sales job so maybe Paul can give me some names."

Lucas took a last look at the entirely unremarkable box on the workbench, knowing that it would have as much impact on people's lives as the QED or personal CF generator.

"Okay, sounds good. You should probably get right on that. They'll need travel documents and visas – your short-notice trip to White Sands was only approved because you were working with their government."

They kissed briefly before he left; though they had no reservations in private, it had taken them two months to be comfortable with even this minor display of affection in the workplace.

In the parking lot, he climbed behind the wheel of the Jaguar. Good weather had been so rare over the last couple of months that he had enjoyed little opportunity to take the roadster for a spin, and hadn't wasted the chance that day when he woke to clear skies. Driving out of town, he headed back to the hills and pulled up outside the barn at the house. As usual, there were several other vehicles parked there, since Carine had taken over the high-tech workshop for her "special projects".

Suiting up, he went through the airlock-style doors and greeted her warmly.

"I assume you knew I was coming. I saw the turret tracking me," he said, referring to the AI-controlled cluster of non-lethal weaponry mounted on the roof of the barn.

"Yes, Andie recognised you and decided not to goop you."

"'Goop'? Is that what you call the web-thrower?"

"No," she replied. "We call that the Spider. Goop is what comes out of it. What brings you up to our secret lair today, Lucas?"

He motioned her towards a spare pair of chairs and they sat down. "Just doing the rounds. Wondering how you're going on the field generator."

Carine pointed to a small device on a worktable in the corner of the room. "We have our prototype ready for its first test, actually. Would you like to see it in action?"

Lucas stood and walked over to the table. The device consisted of a low, square object, surmounted by a metallic sphere around fifteen centimetres in diameter. Thin cables ran from the square to a set of dials and a pair of small joysticks attached to the table.

Carine came to stand beside him. "This one is only running on five volts, but that is more than sufficient to manipulate the target, which weighs one kilogram."

As her two workers gathered around, she flipped a switch beside the dials, and the sphere vibrated briefly before returning to rest. Placing her hands on the joysticks, she slowly moved one of the slightly forward, and the sphere began to rise. Lucas could see that it was connected to the base by two wires.

One of the white-suited workers grinned and quietly pumped a fist while the other was content to merely nod appreciatively.

"The device is actually in the sphere, " Carine said, "and the base is only the control unit. The field generated will always fully surround the generator, and this one is tuned to create a spherical field. It can be designed to accommodate any size or shape, but it is most efficient when it most closely matches the target shape."

Playing with the joysticks, she made the sphere move up, down and side to side.

"Of course, here we are limited by the length of the control wires, but with an internal power supply and control system, the sky is the limit, if you will forgive my pun."

She returned the sphere to the base, and switched off the device. Nodding to one of her assistants, she unscrewed a small hatch in the top of the sphere, and when the worker handed her a tumbler of water, placed it within, closing the hatch once more. She flicked the switch again, and made the sphere perform several rapid, jerky movements. When she reopened the hatch Lucas could see that not a drop of water had been spilled.

"For want of a better term, you must consider anything inside the field to be in a separate instance, experiencing gravity and momentum relative only to the field."

"So it's what, an anti-gravity device?" asked Lucas.

"No, that is not quite the correct term. If that was all it did, we would have had water all over the inside when I threw it around. What we are doing here is generating a Higgs field, and effectively insulating the inside from any external gravitational influence. In addition to the Higgs field, we also have a technology inside the sphere that 'surfs' a gravity wave, enabling us to induce motion."

Fascinated, Lucas thought he comprehended the concept, if not the specifics, of the technology. "But what happens when you get outside the Earth's gravity field?"

"Ah, that is the beauty of gravity. It is everywhere! Even in the depths of space, there is gravity. This is why planets orbit stars, and stars orbit galaxies. Granted, the gravitational force in space is somewhat less than here, on a planet's surface, but if we add more power to the system, we can achieve the same results."

"Okay, next question – what effect could this Higgs field have on living matter? If there is no momentum, does our blood still pump the same?"

"An excellent question, Lucas. In theory, since it is an isolated instance inside the field, momentum of an object due to forces acting on it from inside will still exist. It is only in relation to movement of the field as a whole that there is no momentum. As for how living tissue is affected, well, that is our next experiment."

The assistant had moved to a nearby bench, where he opened a cage and removed a white mouse. Dropping it gently into a small perspex cube, he handed it to Carine, and she placed the cube in the sphere. Restarting the device, she twiddled the joysticks once again, leaving the field energised for several minutes this time. When she removed the cube, Lucas could see that the mouse appeared to have suffered no visible harm or distress.

Carine held the cube up at eye level, closely inspecting its occupant. "It is clear that his heart did not stop pumping blood, but we will run some standard tests to be sure that he was not affected in any other way. We will check his maze-running ability against our earlier benchmark, and we will take some small tissue samples to be certain that there was no damage at a molecular level. I am quietly optimistic, however."

After each of Andie's previous scientific advances, Lucas had always worried that the next big thing would not impress him, but he had been proven wrong. Again. This was technology that would eclipse even the cold fusion generators. While he understood that his ultimate goal was still out of reach, this would literally open up new worlds to humanity, and would play a major part in his plan. With today's proof of concept, he had a whole list of new things for Andie to design.

The next two weeks passed too slowly for everybody at Ad Astra. They had been waiting, mostly patiently, for the United States' Department of Energy to give their approval to the cold-fusion technology, so that they could finalise their deals with electricity generators there. They already had contracts in many countries where electricity generation was problematic, but breaking into the US market would add legitimacy and credibility that could be used as leverage in any nations that were resistant to change.

In the first week following, word came through Alison that both the IEA and WEC had enthusiastically endorsed the technology. This news, bringing them one step closer to broad acceptance of CF power, was met in the office with excitement and calls for a party, though Lucas insisted on holding off on any large-scale celebration until they got approval from the large countries.

Sonia, with Paul's help, had assembled a sales team who would be taking the Phase Four units around the world to hopefully convince auto manufacturers that this was the future of EVs, and transportation in general. Sonia had taken over a local CF factory, and work on the demonstration models was proceeding apace.

In the middle of the second week, Dan Shockley came to the Princess Street offices, waving a sheet of paper and grinning broadly at Lucas sitting behind the receptionist's desk.

"Christmas has come early this year!" he exclaimed.

Lucas jumped up from his chair and reached across the desk to take the letter before Dan's exuberance ruined it. "They're going for it?"

"Better than that. Not only do they rule that it's safe to use, they have submitted a policy recommendation to the effect that it is in America's best interests to adopt the technology as soon as reasonably possible. That's the Golden Ticket you're holding!"

Lucas let out a whoop of joy and reached out to take Dan's hand, pumping it vigorously. "You, mate, are a bloody legend! I don't know how you got a government department to move at more than glacial pace, but you've done it. Damn good job!"

Alison and Cath came downstairs to investigate the ruckus, and Lucas informed them, "We've got approval from the DoE. Dan's pulled off a miracle!"

"I can't take all the credit. They may have been swayed somewhat by public opinion. Somehow word got out to the environmental groups," Dan said, with a conspiratorial wink to Alison.

"Really?" she asked, her face the picture of innocence. "I can't imagine how that could have happened!"

With the energy agencies lined up, it was time for Michelle and Andie to get back to the power companies and get the paperwork signed. Lucas had got word from Jake that the overseas CF factories had been completed, so he expected that it would be only a few weeks before shipping of the generators could commence. Sonia's instructor teams were in place, and the workforce was hired, awaiting only a place to work.

Sonia demanded a high work-rate in the CF factory that she had appropriated for construction of the CFEV demo models, and had soon produced several dozen units for the sales team to take away with them.

As most auto manufacturers already had EV models in production, the conversion from battery power to CF generation should not have been too troublesome. Most meetings went in much the same way:

A pair of salespeople (safety in numbers!) would turn up to their pre-arranged meeting with a demonstrator model, and begin their spiel.

"Good morning. Thank you for agreeing to see us. At Ad Astra, we have been following closely the advances in EV technology, and we are sure that you have the same concerns that we do. While lithium-ion batteries are currently the best option available, it is a sad fact that lithium is still an expensive and industrially-intensive material. In addition, lithium mining is well-known to have some serious downsides in the environmental stakes.

"Battery storage has a limited lifespan, and contributes a great deal of weight to the finished vehicle. Of course, we don't need to tell you these things – you probably spend many millions of dollars looking for ways around these problems. Wouldn't it be fantastic if someone came up to you one day and said, 'We've got a solution for you'? Less weight, virtually unlimited lifespan, no more need to spend money on research and development?

"That day has arrived, gentlemen. Allow us to introduce to you the Ad Astra CFEV power unit. You may already have heard of our cold-fusion technology, which currently provides one-hundred percent of New Zealand's electricity needs, and will shortly be rolled out around the world. Our researchers have now modified the original design of those generators, and, instead of a twenty ton, four metre behemoth, we have a unit small enough to fit in a car, producing four-hundred-and-eighty volts with a high current output.

"This device is a constant-power generator, mated to a capacitor bank that negates the need to keep the generator running when not in use. Once the capacitors are fully charged, a driver can shut off the generator when he reaches his destination, and 'kick-start' the CF unit when he drives off again. We believe that this technology will simply drop into place instead of the existing bulky, expensive, batteries. You save on weight and cost, and your EVs become more affordable and desirable to the consumer. Running costs are a fraction of even mains electricity, range is at least doubled, performance is increased due to lower vehicle weights, and any environmental guilt over lithium mining is dispelled."

Usually, after a few easily-answered questions, the predictable response was along the lines of, "Where do we sign?", and within a week, all the major manufacturers had agreed to at least test the system, with most confident that they would adopt the technology once it proved practical. Many even suggested that they would not be adverse to modifying their ICE range to also run on CF.

As far as Lucas could tell, the mission had been a total success, and he was keen to get some of the worldwide CF factories converted to manufacture the CFEV units as soon as possible, as an interim measure before dedicated facilities were constructed. Once CFEVs were on sale, they could begin marketing the ICE conversion units.

Meanwhile, Will and his team of financial gurus had gone ahead with the IPO of AAQED, and the company's bank balance was looking seventy-five billion dollars better off. US dollars, at that. Over one-hundred-and-twenty billion in New Zealand currency that would go straight into construction of factories for the next phase. The economics side of Will's department had, of necessity, been enhanced with the addition of an accountancy sector, as wages for many thousands of workers around the world, income in multiple currencies, global transport bills, and all the other financial transactions needed a paper trail signed off by actual people. Saying, "The computer did it," would not impress auditors. Even if that computer was smarter than all the auditors combined.

By the end of the month, the CF factories in other countries were fully operational, and in the first week of October, Fats was shipping generators to all corners of the globe. The United States Department of Energy had published their findings that cold-fusion technology was safe and efficient, and had made public their recommendation that it be used wherever possible. Traditional suppliers of fuel to the electricity industry weren't happy about it, but the power companies took the recommendation as a green light to affirm their contracts with Ad Astra, and the rest of the world, for the most part, had followed suit.

The DoE's official decision had been welcomed with jubilation at the Ad Astra offices, and true to his word, Lucas threw an unforgettable party for the hundred or so staff throughout the various premises in Palmerston North. A large marquee was erected at the Mangaweka farm (powered, of course, by cold-fusion generators), and the guests were bussed in from the city to dance the night away to several local bands. Michelle had been allocated a reinforced table especially for that purpose, and even Fats got into the mood, displaying an extensive repertoire of poorly-executed break-dancing moves. Alison and Sonia broke hearts, Paul broke drinking records, and Tom broke out in song. It was a welcome release after all the hard work everyone had put into getting the technology produced, marketed, and finally accepted. No one spoke about the work ahead of them; this night was all about a job well done, not the tasks yet to come.

Towards midnight, Lucas sat sprawled on a couch to the side of the dance floor, watching as the celebrations showed no sign of abating. His shirt was partially untucked, and he brushed his sweat-soaked fringe away from his eyes.

"Great party, mate," said Tom as he flopped onto the couch, handing Lucas a fresh beer.

Lucas took it gratefully and gave a satisfied smile. "Yep. Great people, Tom. They've all done amazing work to get us here, and they don't even know the half of what they've accomplished."

"History might never know their names, but these guys will be able to look back one day and say, 'I was there. I was a part of the new revolution'. I hope they'll be proud."

Lucas smiled at the thought. "We'll remember them, mate."

Tom stood, and struck a theatrical pose. "If I may quote The Bard; '*Old men forget; yet all shall be forgot,*
But he'll remember, with advantages,
What feats he did that day. Then shall our names,
Familiar in his mouth as household words -
Lucas the King, Bennington and Fenchurch,

Fox and Matheson, Whelan and Tyson -
Be in their flowing cups freshly rememb'red.
This story shall the good man teach his son;
And Crispin Crispian shall ne'er go by,
From this day to the ending of the world,
But we in it shall be remembered—
We few, we happy few, we band of brothers."
CRYING WOLFF

On Monday, Lucas had just waved goodbye to Alison as she left the Princess Street office, when a man caught the door before it shut and walked in. Stocky, but not overly tall, he wore an ill-fitting suit and a poorly-knotted tie. Looking up in puzzlement, as visitors to the office were unheard of, Lucas said, "Good morning. Can I help you?"

The visitor strode up to the reception desk and planted both hands firmly on it, leaning in towards Lucas. "You're not easy people to find," he said in a gravelly voice, with a frustrated frown knotting his heavy brow.

"That's sort of the idea," Lucas responded, standing up to regain the height advantage. "May I ask why you've gone to so much trouble to do so?"

The man straightened. "I need to speak to your boss, Andie Donovan."

The man's attitude was beginning to irritate Lucas. "I'm afraid that Ms Donovan is unavailable. Anything that you have to say to her, you can say to me."

"All right then. Electricity. I'm here on behalf of some people who are not thrilled about what you're doing in the auto industry."

Lucas laughed. "Those must be the oil people. I guess you have a busy day ahead of you. What's your next visit? Bicycle makers? Horse breeders?"

"Don't get smart with me, pal. Your operation is becoming a major nuisance. It represents a serious loss of income, and to these people, money is more important than anything. Stop what you're doing, or we'll stop it for you. We know where you live and work."

Looking down at his computer monitor, onto which Andie had flashed a document, Lucas said, "We know where you live, too, Mr Wolff. You're a long way from Texas. I'd hate to have to call Ginny and your two little girls, and tell them that Daddy's not coming home. Turn around, walk away, and tell your bosses that we're not playing their game."

Incredulous, Wolff asked, "Are you threatening me?"

Lucas stared Wolff directly in the eyes. The oil industry's "fixer" was not used to such a straight-up response to his particular form of intimidation, and involuntarily glanced away as Lucas replied, "I'm sorry – I haven't done this before. Is that not how it works? You threaten me, I threaten you, and one of us walks away, the other gets a nice ride in an ambulance." He was in a foul mood, irritated behind belief that the oil men had the audacity to send this man to his office.

"You're making a huge mistake here, pal. I'm not in the mood to be spoken to like this by some jumped-up receptionist."

"That's too bad. If our janitor was here today, I could have had *him* tell you to piss off."

Wolff was becoming increasingly agitated by Lucas's taunts, and moved to step around the desk and take action when he felt a large hand clamp down on his shoulder.

"I believe that my friend is asking you to leave, Mr Wolff," said Fats quietly, who had come out of his office behind the interloper, remarkably silently for a big man.

Wolff turned his head and looked up into the narrowed eyes of the large Samoan who currently held his shoulder in a vice-like grip.

Lucas smiled thinly. "Will you be leaving under your own steam, or shall I have the bouncer show you to the gutter?"

Wolff ducked away from Fats and backed towards the door. "You haven't heard the last of this. You've just bought yourselves a whole world of hurt."

Lucas took a quick step forward and laughed humourlessly as the fixer hurriedly moved away. "You're in over your head, Wolff. Don't let me see you around here again."

His face aflame with anger, Wolff opened the door behind him, nearly tripping over his feet as Fats moved forward to force him out the door. When he had gone, Fats turned back to Lucas, asking, "Are you sure that was the best move, bro?"

Lucas shrugged. "He was pissing me off. Better the devil you know, and all that, eh? We know they're coming for us, and we can be prepared."

"Okay, bro. Just let me know if you want me to deal with him, though. I have a feeling that he could make things difficult for us."

Lucas moved back to his desk and perused the information sheet that Andie had prepared on this Mr Wolff, having quickly identified his face and searched for his records. "I think he might find it surprising how hard that'll be. Since the violence in South Africa, we've had Jake's team tweak the building's security, and if he comes back with friends, Mr Wolff will regret it."

Fats grinned at that, familiar with Carine's weapons project. "Think I could get me one of those disrupters, bro? If they get inside, it'll be like, 'Say hello to my little friend!'"

Lucas laughed. "I'll hook you up, mate. And that was the worst Pacino I've ever heard!"

Lucas advised the rest of the team to avoid the Princess Street offices for the rest of the week, and arranged for Jake's men to quietly upgrade the security at the houses, satellite offices, and local factories.

It was only a couple of days before Wolff's threats were carried out, and Lucas called the team up to his house before dawn the next morning to review the video footage of the attack.

At 1.30am, a car had pulled up outside the office, and four men exited the vehicle. What followed was in the best tradition of the Keystone Cops. Lighting a rudimentary molotov cocktail, one of the men threw it forcefully at the front window, whereupon it bounced harmlessly off the multi-layered polyacrylate pane, narrowly missing the gathered thugs and splattering flaming liquid across the footpath. Hopping about to avoid catching their shoes alight, the men moved to the front door. One of them had retrieved a police-style battering ram from their car, and lined it up with the door handle. He pulled the ram back to take a huge swing, and as the ram connected with the steel-reinforced door, the impact shock was transferred back into his fingers and he dropped the ram onto his toes as he shook his hands in pain. Trying to deal with both a damaged foot and numb fingers, he stumbled away from the door and into the pool of fire on the footpath. The other three men quickly rescued him from the flames, and they huddled together as they formulated a new plan of action.

As they stood there, the building's AI had fired up the neural disruptor weapons mounted in the eaves. When the intensity of the neural wave increased, designed to pulsate in opposition to the brain's synaptic frequencies, the attackers began to lose their coordination and careened across the pavement, crashing into their car. The audio feed added to the amusement of Lucas's team gathered around the big screen in his lounge.

"Get oop...off...my foot, you idiot!"

"Wash... Watch out for the fire!

"Don't dent my bloody car!"

When the disruptor cut off, and the thugs slowly regained their senses, another ignominy was inflicted upon them as the Spiders shot their streams of "goop", enveloping the men in thick strands of the sticky stuff, which hardened in seconds and immobilised them completely. A cloud of fire retardant doused the flames on the footpath before the men fell rigidly to the ground.

A security team, who had been on standby and had raced to the scene as soon as Andie alerted them to the attack, moved in from where they had been watching the show from a safe distance. Spraying the men with a chemical to dissolve the goop, they quickly restrained them with cable ties, and waited for the police. When the police did arrive, they found four security personnel in hi-vis vests leaning nonchalantly against the wall, watching over the would-be vandals, neatly hog-tied on the ground.

"Evening, officer," said the security chief. "We got a call from our CCTV monitoring guy about these lads trying to have a go at the office here. Looks like they came pretty well tooled-up, with the molotov and the battering ram. I think they must be on something, though, as they were sort of incoherent when we got here, and didn't put up any resistance. Far be it from me to tell you your job, but my boss would be very interested to know why they targeted this particular building, and who might have sent them."

The police officers took in the scene, noting the scorch marks on the footpath and the ram dropped at the door.

"Naughty boys. We'll take it from here, thanks, and we will certainly be looking into their motives for tonight's little adventure." He then addressed his colleagues. "Let's get a van down here for them. Bag and tag the hardware."

The security response team took their leave, and Lucas's guests waited a few minutes more until the paddy-wagon arrived, and the thugs were safely carted away.

"Well, that was exciting," said Lucas. "Did you like the demonstration of your toys, Carine?"

A self-satisfied look on her face, she replied, "It was very interesting. They never stood a chance, did they?"

"And this is what Jake's boys were installing on our houses?" asked Paul.

"Yep," answered Lucas. "It could have taken them out much more quickly, but we thought that giving the technology a full field-test was a good idea. The Spiders could easily have caught the firebomb before it even got to the window, and we could have gooped the guys at the get-go, but where's the fun in that?"

"It's a pity we can't put that up on YouTube," Cath said. "It was so funny, the way nothing went right for them!"

"All joking aside, this is probably only the start of it, unless we get proactive about discouraging it. Andie, have you got a number for our friend, Mr Wolff?"

Andie, of course, did. She had hacked the cell network when Wolff went to the office, and had obtained his mobile number.

"Four o'clock in the morning – must be time for his wake-up call. Can you put me through please, Andie?"

The phone rang several times before the groggy voice of the fixer came on.

"Who the hell is calling at this time of day?"

"Oh sorry, Mr Wolff – did I wake you?"

"Damn right you did! Wait – you're that bastard from Ad Astra. I do hope there's no trouble," he said smugly.

"Not at all," replied Lucas. "A bunch of delinquents paid a late night visit, but inexplicably fell over and landed in a police van. Your boss will probably give you a tongue-lashing for hiring cut-rate henchmen. I thought I made myself perfectly clear. Do I have to come over and explain it to you in smaller words?"

The man at the other end of the call was silent.

"Take your time. Witty comebacks must be hard when you've just woken up."

Rather than shush the laughter that was breaking out amongst his team Lucas let them go, knowing that it would infuriate Wolff to know that his humiliation was public.

An angry growl came from the speakers as Wolff struggled to find the words he wanted.

"You... I...goddammit. You've opened up a can of worms now, pal."

"Worms? I think the word you're looking for is 'whup-ass."

Fresh howls of laughter came from the early morning audience as Wolff spluttered into the phone.

Lucas continued. "Leave town, Mr Wolff. Now. Tell your paymasters that we will not be intimidated, and if they continue on this path, things will become mighty unpleasant for misters—" he looked at the screen where Andie had shown the results of her communications trace "—Ebert and Hackney."

The silence on the other end of the line told Lucas that his barb had hit home. He ended the call and turned to the team.

"Well, I thought that went well. Anyone for breakfast?"

Wolff stared at the phone after it went dead in his ear. He was shaking with rage; firstly, at his hired thugs for screwing up so badly, and secondly, at the man from Ad Astra. No one had ever spoken to him like that. All his life, *he* had been the bully, the one to insult and threaten people. To have this *nobody* taunt him and make jokes at his expense, and to hear others in the background laughing at him, had been too much.

He had probably made a mistake trusting a local crew to get the job done, he admitted to himself. If you want something done right, do it yourself, was the mantra from now on. He began making a plan, and thought about where to source the tools he needed.

"What do you think he'll do now?" asked Tom.

"He'll come back, harder and meaner, "replied Sonia. "His kind doesn't know how to give up."

"We'll be ready for him," Lucas said. "We've got a few more tools at our disposal. Then we go for his bosses. They started the game, and our team always plays to win."

"Go, Eagles!" shouted Paul through a mouthful of sausage. He was referring to their high school's 1st XV rugby team, named after the Haast's Eagle, a recently extinct bird with a three metre wingspan, once New Zealand's largest predator.

Fats looked up from a huge plate of bacon and eggs. "If you need manpower, I know a guy or two. The SAS hasn't had too much work lately, and the lads are getting bored!"

"Thanks, Fats, but I think we'll keep it in-house for now. I don't really want the army getting ideas about Carine's gear!"

He pulled Carine aside after breakfast finished, and had a quiet word with her. As he spoke, her eyes grew wide and she hurriedly reached for her phone, to take notes. She grew progressively more excited, and with a quick thumbs-up, quickly headed out to the barn as soon as he had finished speaking.

Having noticed their tête-à-tête, Sonia approached him and asked, "Anything I should know about?"

He winked, and placed a finger to his lips. "Hush-hush for now. I'll tell you about it when everyone's gone."

With concern about reprisals from Wolff uppermost in everyone's minds, it was with understandable caution that the management team went back to work that week. While Monday morning's demonstration of the new security measures had been reassuring, they were beginning to understand what it meant to go up against an industry with the resources and ruthlessness to make their displeasure known. Nerves didn't affect all of them, however; Fats drove with a neural disruptor under the seat of his car, secretly hoping that Wolff would make another move, and had taken to sleeping in his office.

He didn't let his enthusiasm for another encounter distract him from his work, though, as he had a big week ahead of him. The large CF generators were almost all complete, and he would be busy arranging shipping of the bulky devices from the factories around the world to the power stations. He had deals with air freight companies and truckers across the globe, and synchronising the transport of nearly nine-thousand units was a true test of his logistic skills.

Due to the size and weight of the generators, air-freighting them required Fats to use dedicated cargo aircraft. A Boeing 747-400F, with a cargo capacity of 113 tons, could carry only five of the units at once, and with no space or weight allocation available for other cargo, Fats was obliged to charter them whole. While the cost was not an issue, there were only so many available in each required location, and he was forced at times to wait for a return trip before he could ship the waiting generators. Eventually, however, the thousands of units made it to their destinations, and eager power company technicians accepted delivery and began installing them. Within three weeks, Fats was finally able to report to Lucas that the mammoth task was complete.

———— ++\\|\|\|++ ————

Ad Astra's logistics manager wasn't the only person to have been busy. Mr Wolff, still smarting from his recent humiliation, had spent the following week preparing for his big comeback. He had not informed his employers of the previous setback, fully expecting to present them with a report of a successful mission within days. They were not the type of people to accept failure from their employees, and he saw no reason to contact them until he had good news. The fact that the Ad Astra man knew their names concerned him, as his contact with them, and payment, were supposed to be untraceable. A modification of his original plan to simply force the company to accede to his demands was required. The saying that dead men tell no tales was one that had served him well several times in the past, and he would feel much safer with that extra notch on his belt. This country's restrictive laws made it more difficult to obtain what he wanted for that purpose, but he eventually managed to get hold of the right tool for the job. Though he often dealt with black marketeers and subversive groups, he really resented having to make approaches to gangsters just to buy something that he could pick up freely in just about any city at home.

He had scheduled his mission for the Sunday night again, to reduce the risk of being spotted or interrupted by late-night revellers. He had extensively surveilled his targets, and considered his plan foolproof, especially as he was no longer counting on fools to carry it out.

After midnight on Sunday, he made sure that everything he needed was stowed in his car, and drove downtown, parking in a quiet side street a block away from the Ad Astra offices. Keeping to the shadows, he moved to a dark alley across from the target building, and removed the first of his tools from his bag.

Lying prone, he took careful aim with the specialised paintball rifle, and with several well-aimed shots, obscured the building's external cameras. Packing the rifle back into the bag, he quickly crossed the road and ducked into the doorway of the Ad Astra building. Removing a portable gas torch from the bag, he set to work cutting into the metal around the door's lock. Once he had cut the lock away from the door, he used a pry bar to force entry, and stepped into the dimly lit foyer.

The lights came on fully, and he was immediately assaulted by a noise that seemed to be in every frequency at once, and come from everywhere, as the AI activated the sonic wave weapon. Clapping his hands over his ears did not lessen the noise at all, as the ultrasonic wave was designed to act directly on the eardrums. While it could not be heard more than a few metres away, it was as if a whole battery of klaxons was going off in Wolff's head, and he sank to his knees in pain. The painful noise cut out suddenly, and he turned at the sound of footsteps to see the large Samoan man he had encountered previously coming out of the office behind him, wearing earmuffs and holding a book-sized object at arm's length.

Still slightly disoriented by the lingering effects of the sonic weapon, Wolff fumbled for the pistol in his waistband and squeezed off several rapid shots. He was dumbfounded when each one of the projectiles stopped dead in the air in front of the man, falling harmlessly to the ground. The other man raised an unusual-looking weapon, and Wolff became immediately confused and uncoordinated. Taking advantage of this, his opponent stepped forward and landed a swift kick to Wolff's knee. Dropping the strange weapon as Wolff began to fall, he followed up with a crushing blow to the temple, knocking the American unconscious.

When Lucas arrived a few minutes later, having been alerted by Andie, Fats had Wolff secured in the storage room.

"Bro, that was terrifying! Even after you showed me, it took everything I had to trust in that shield. What did you call it?"

"A Higgs Field. When the bullets hit it, their energy was dissipated across the field and their momentum lost. Come on, mate – I wouldn't have put you in that position if I wasn't sure of it. How did the special earmuffs work?"

Fats touched the muffs hanging around his neck. "Like a dream, bro. I could hear everything perfectly, except for whatever hit this guy. He was pawing at his ears like he had a beehive in his head!"

"Yeah, they're just a turbocharged version of noise-cancelling headphones, only filtering out the specific wavelengths of the sonic weapon. Shall we have a chat with our guest?"

As Wolff was not quite conscious yet, Fats slapped him none too gently across the face.

"Wakey wakey. Rise and shine, bro."

Wolff opened his eyes, struggling against his restraints. As he realised what the situation was, he glared at Fats. "You punch like a girl."

Lucas laid a hand on his friend's arm as Fats moved in to prove Wolff wrong. "Easy, mate. He's just hoping to get you to lose your temper, trying to regain some semblance of control."

He grabbed Wolff by the collar of his jacket and propped him in a seated position against the wall. Squatting down to look into the man's eyes, he shook his head condescendingly. "Wolfie, Wolfie, Wolfie. What *were* you thinking? That you could come in here, trash a few computers, and we'd just roll over? *I'm* top dog around here, and I don't roll over for *anyone*."

He stood, and picked up Wolff's cellphone from a bench. Scrolling through the call logs, he asked, "So, did you tell Ebert and Hackney how last week's little escapade went? Doesn't look like it. Shall we give them a call?"

Wolff set his jaw and refused to answer. Lucas checked the numbers in the phone against a list that Andie had provided.

"This looks like the one. Julius Ebert's private number – how fortunate. I do hate having to go through all those flunkies before I speak to the person in charge. I assume that he is expecting your call?" he asked, as he tapped the button to dial. The phone rang twice at the other end before a gruff voice answered.

"Wolff. It's about time you called. Have you dealt with those pricks at Ad Astra yet?"

Lucas feigned shock at the man's language before responding. "I'm sorry, Julius. Mr Wolff can't come to the phone right now. He's a bit tied up. I'm just calling to tell you to back the fuck off before I burn your empire to the ground. You have no idea who you're dealing with, Ebert, and I've got a good mind to send your boy back to you in very small pieces. We have video of him threatening our company and breaking into our offices, we have him in custody holding an illegal firearm, and we have computer records detailing the communications between he and you, and the payments you've made to him. Now, I don't know how much all that worries you, but if the proof goes public, it won't be a very good look for a man in your position to be seen consorting with common thugs, and soliciting violence. Am I getting through to you?"

There was a moment of silence as Ebert took this in and formulated a diplomatic response.

"I'm sure I have no idea what you are talking about. Hank Wolff is a private contractor, and I have no influence on who he speaks to, or what he says or does. If I recall correctly, his brief was to approach a particular company and ask them to slow down their plans so that my industry would have more time to prepare for the loss in revenue. If he has taken it upon himself to use methods any more forceful, then he is an embarrassment to my company, and I urge you to take whatever retribution you see fit. I would never ask anyone to do something illegal."

"That's odd, because I have a copy of an email sent from your personal account to his, and I quote, 'Do whatever it takes to get Ad Astra to back down. Break some kneecaps – I don't care. Let's not actually kill anyone just yet, though.' That sounds pretty unambiguous. I'd tell you to check your own copy, but as of right now, you and your staff are locked out of every single computer or phone that might conceivably have company data on it. You want to play hardball? Let's see how long your business lasts without records, payroll, invoicing, banking, or communications."

Ebert laughed into the phone. "That's the most ridiculous bluff I've ever heard. There's no possible way you could..." His voice trailed off.

"It's no bluff, Julius, as I'm sure you've just found out. Computer not working? Have you tried switching it off and on again?"

The sound of Ebert striking his keyboard with increasing vigour came through the phone before the man spoke again.

"Well, it does appear that you have me over a barrel here, Mister ... I'm sorry – what should I call you?"

"I believe that under the circumstances," answered Lucas, "*Sir* would be appropriate."

"Very well, *Sir*," Ebert said with obvious reluctance, "as you have the upper hand, what do you want from me?"

"It's quite simple, Julius. All I want is a signed and notarised admission that you hired Mister Wolff here to threaten, intimidate, and attack us, a sincere apology, and your solemn vow that you will never presume to interfere in our business again. If you abide by that promise, your confession will never see the light of day, and you get your business back.

"To save you any trouble, I've taken the liberty of drafting a document to that effect, which should be coming out of your printer right about now. I will allow you to call your attorney to have him come and witness it. Please do not try to contact anyone else. You have one hour to fax or email that document to the contact details on your printout. Do *not* make me call you back."

He ended the call and looked over to Fats.

"What do you think?"

"I think I never want to get on the wrong side of you!" He nodded at the fuming Wolff. "What do we do about this?" he asked.

"Up to you, mate. You're the one he tried to shoot. Some screaming shouldn't be a problem, but I'd appreciate it if you didn't get blood all over my storeroom floor."

Even though Fats knew that he was bluffing, the seriousness in Lucas's voice chilled him. He could only imagine the effect it would be having on Wolff. Being at the mercy of someone you had recently fired three shots at, who had essentially been given carte blanche by your boss to do with as he wished, would make anyone nervous, no matter how tough you thought you were.

Playing along, Fats grabbed a large roll of packing wrap from a corner of the room and began to lay it out on the floor. Taking Wolff roughly by the arm, he dragged the man into the center of the plastic. He picked up the pistol and a box-cutter and weighed them in his hands, wrinkling his brow in indecision.

"Wait!" cried Wolff. "You don't have to do this."

Fats shrugged helplessly. "You've left me with little option, Hank. If we let you go, you're going to come back for revenge. We gotta tie up those loose ends."

Though he wasn't the smartest person, Wolff had a cunning mind. He knew all about deflecting blame; some of his best jobs had been attributed to innocent parties.

"Look, I get that you're pissed, but why waste a resource? We've got a common enemy here. Ebert sent me to get you, yeah, but then he threw me under the bus. I've got just as much reason to hate the man as you do. I'm not going to come back at you for something as petty as professional pride, but when my boss hangs me out to dry ... well, that's a betrayal I can't let lie. You let me walk out of here, and not only will you never see me again, I can guarantee that Ebert and his pals will have more on their minds than electric cars. What do you say?"

Fats looked at Lucas. "Well, it *would* save me digging a hole. You reckon he can be trusted?"

"Not as far as you could throw a cheesecake underwater, but he's probably too smart to fuck with us again. Your call, mate."

With a last regretful look at the pistol in his hand, Fats said, "Oh, to hell with it. Okay, Wolff, you live. Don't make regret it."

He handed the gun to Lucas and bent down to cut the cable ties securing Wolff's wrists and ankles. "Door's that way. Have a nice day, and don't hurry back."

Wolff glanced at the door back into the office and said, "I've met some hard men in my time, but you two are the scariest office-boys I've ever come across. For what it's worth, you have my word."

They followed Wolff back out to the foyer and sent him on his way, Lucas saying, "Leave the bag. You've had a rough might and we don't want you to strain yourself."

As they watched him walk away, still somewhat unsteady, Fats said to Lucas, "Bro, where did you get that mean streak from? You were always so laid back."

Lucas waved away the comment. "Nah, it's all just talk, mate. If we'd tried to negotiate, each of them them would have seen us as weak. You just have to speak a language they understand. Wolff understands physical threats, Ebert understands commercial ones."

"So what you said to Wolff was a bluff. What you did to Ebert wasn't, though." Fats was having trouble coming to terms with the new-found complexities of his friend.

"It was a matter of proximity," Lucas replied. "We had Wolff right here, with a gun to his head. Ebert was on the other side of the world, and needed the practical demonstration to be convinced."

"Just how did you manage that 'practical demonstration' anyway?"

"You don't give Andie enough credit," said Lucas. He went on to explain that Andie had identified Wolff almost as soon as he had walked in the door that first day. After that, it was a "simple" matter of hacking his phone, finding his contacts, and determining who employed him. By the time Wolff had left the office, she had already infiltrated Ebert's computers, and set up the lockout for when it was inevitably needed.

"I see what you were thinking when you decided to keep her out of IVIA's hands. They could have done anything they liked. Aren't you a little worried that you're pushing the limits, though? I mean, it's not exactly legal, is it, bro?"

Lucas looked away guiltily. It was true that he'd overstepped the mark with both Ebert and DevConn, but they'd started it, he reasoned. Of course it bothered him, but it wasn't in his nature to let kidnapping and assault go unanswered.

"No, it's not. I'm the one who has to live with the choices I make, though, and I can do that if they're done with the right intentions. It doesn't get any easier, knowing that I can wipe out a company with a word, but I won't be bullied. *Ever.*"

"That's cool, bro. Don't get me wrong – they had it coming, and I won't lose any sleep over it. I just don't want you to get in any trouble."

"Cheers, mate, but I somehow doubt that Ebert will be keen to explain the events that forced me to threaten his business."

With a fist bump, the soul-searching was over, and they went to the front door to examine the damage.

Peering at the cut away lock, Lucas said, "I'll give him credit – he's a tidy operator. It's a clean cut, and he didn't damage the lock. I think there's something in the workshop that will sort this out." He ducked through Sonia's office and returned shortly with a device reminiscent of Wolff's own gas torch.

"This is an annealing gun," he explained. "If I fit this end to a fresh piece of steel, it'll fix the two pieces together cleaner than a weld."

He attached a short section of steel plate to the terminal at the back end of the device, got Fats to hold the lock section in place, and applied the nozzle end to the gap that the gas torch had cut. Molecules of steel flowed from the scrap metal and the gap began to fill, as if by magic. As the steel flowed through the annealing gun, it bonded molecularly with the door and the lock mechanism, leaving only a shiny line of fresh steel to show that there had ever been any damage.

"Good as new. Ready to go?"

"Yeah. It'll be good to get home. What about the cameras?"

"We'll clean them up in the morning. I've had enough for tonight. Thanks for your help."

"My pleasure, bro. Except for being shot at. That sort of sucked. Ten years in the army, and the first time I get shot at is working in an office!"

"Suck it up, mate. Here," said Lucas, picking up the three bullets from the carpet, "have a souvenir."

Fats took the projectiles that had hit the Higgs field. "Yeah, thanks. Think I'd prefer danger money."

As he had driven home early that morning, Lucas had received a call from Andie informing him that the confession had been sent through, and that she had restored Ebert's access to his computers. As it had been a Sunday afternoon in the US, the temporary loss of his records had not really inconvenienced him, but had the lockout continued, his business would certainly have suffered, not being able to track any of his oil in transit, pay bills or wages, or even get into his office. The threat had worked, and Lucas was reasonably confident that the man would not be a problem in future. It was also likely that his partners in crime had been made aware of Ad Astra's capabilities, and Lucas hoped that they too would leave him alone.

It seemed that he had barely fallen asleep before it was time to go to work. He briefly considered taking the morning off, but felt that he owed it to his team to give them a rundown of their adventure.

As it turned out, the office was already abuzz with the gossip when he and Sonia arrived for the regular meeting. Fats had spread the word, and Lucas found him holding court in the break area.

"I tell you, our boy Lucas was *chill*. Stone cold freak. I was expecting that Wolff to literally wet himself. And when he gave Ebert the hard word – dude had nowhere to go."

"What stories are you telling about me, Fats?"

"Oh, hey bro. Just saying how you went all pit-bull on those assholes."

"I don't suppose he mentioned his own heroics?" Lucas asked the enthralled group. As querying looks were turned upon Fats, Lucas snorted. "Guess not. Show them your souvenirs, mate."

The reluctant hero reached into a pocket and held out the bullets on the palm of his hand. As the onlookers gasped and leaned in, Lucas said, "Everyone grab a cuppa. Let's do this properly."

Once they were all comfortably seated, Lucas began. In the calm tone of a police officer relating an incident to the court, he proceeded to go over the events of the night. To the accompaniment of suitably impressed noises, and the occasional "Hell, yeah!", he described how Fats had taken down the armed intruder. Carine glowed with pride as he praised her work on the Higgs Field, and Fats humbly accepted the congratulations for his part in the story. Michelle frowned at him when he got to the bit about shutting down Ebert's computers, though he had kept his word, and consulted with her beforehand. While she had been unhappy with the ethics of the situation, she at least saw it as a short-term evil that did no lasting harm. She had reluctantly agreed that there was no simpler way to bring Ebert to the negotiating table, but had strongly cautioned Lucas against making a habit of it.

By the end of his tale, his audience had run the gamut of emotion; from apprehension, to excitement, to triumph.

"That was a hell of a ride, guys! Just letting him go, though – really?" Paul said.

"He was super pissed off at Ebert throwing him under the bus. He's got a score to settle, and I think that personal insult was more important to him than us beating him at his own game. We won't let our guard down, but I reckon that's the last we've seen of Mr Wolff."

"And if it isn't," added Fats ominously, "then there won't be any bluffing next time around."

With the exciting part of the morning or of the way, the meeting started as usual. Fats reported on the shipment of the CF generators, Michelle gave an update on the status of contracts for QED units and generators, and Sonia cheerfully told the team that she had negotiated a contract for the supply of motors for the CFEV conversion kits.

Paul said that his team would be ready to begin marketing those as soon as they added in the specs for the motors, and Cath told of the never-ending task of setting up new locations for manufacturing. She was now managing hundreds of premises, in more than a dozen countries, and had become the de-facto chief liaison with Jake, who was up to his neck in construction crews.

Carine, who did not usually give a report at the weekly meetings, due to the secretive and experimental nature of her work, was prevailed upon to explain the Higgs field generator that had saved Fats, and the group immediately understood the implications of that technology.

"So that's the space drive, yeah?" asked Paul.

Lucas answered, trying not to give too much away. "It is. There are still tests to be done, but it certainly seems to fulfill our requirements."

"So I'm guessing that you won't need to be strapped into reclining chairs, dealing with several G's on takeoff. Where's the fun in being an astronaut if your eyeballs aren't trying to force their way through the back of your skull?"

"Mate, you won't even know you're moving," said Lucas. "Anyone can be an astronaut now – not just the super-fit, highly-educated, fighter-pilot types. That's sort of the point. We didn't want to reproduce the whole astronaut training programme."

Paul grinned. "Well, that's just awesome! I'm none of those things, and I was beginning to think that I'd miss out! So when do I get to fly?"

On dangerous ground now, with regards to his secret project at the farm, Lucas was evasive. "There's still a heap of work to do before *anyone* flies. You'll get your chance when we're ready."

He called the meeting to a close, and took Carine and Sonia down to the workshop to get a more in-depth idea of where Carine was with her work.

"As you know, the tests on Mickey, our test-pilot mouse, all came back negative. There was no deterioration of his cognitive skills, and no damage to his cellular structure. We have been testing the field with various weights, sizes, and shapes of target, and the power requirements appear to increase on a linear scale. Lifting a vessel of around one-hundred tons, with a volume of nine-thousand cubic metres, should be accomplished with approximately two-hundred megawatts of power.

"As the test downstairs last night shows, the physical shielding and energy dissipation properties of the field will be sufficient for your needs. I believe that, in spite of your comments to Paul, we will be ready to install the final product within two weeks.

"We've also made great progress with Andie's fabricator design, too. It's essentially an extension of the technology in the so-called 'annealing gun', and we can now 3D-print with any metallic element, or combination of metals, in a matter of hours. The biological replicator is trickier, but works on much the same principle. Organic molecules are a lot more complex, and require us to lay down the components at almost an atomic level. Of course, this is much slower, but we are working with Andie on developing improved processes. The molecular-scanning side of this device is complete, however, and we are on target for having everything ready by the end of the month."

Lucas shook her hand and grinned broadly. The last stages of this post of his plan were falling neatly into place. "That's great news, Carine! Sonia – I know you're going well. Do you want to tell Carine about your special projects?"

Though Sonia spoke regularly with Lucas about the work she was doing, she was looking forward to being able to share it with someone else. The things she was working on were less vital to the overall plan than Carine's projects, but would be useful tools in the later stages. She unlocked a cabinet to one side, and removed two thumb-sized devices.

Holding out the first, she said, "This is a high-definition camera that I've paired with a miniaturised adaptation of the QED transmitter. I'm using quantum optics and a small quantum AI that will process video at a much higher resolution than conventional digital systems. An organic battery allows for better energy density, and the camera will capture and transmit footage for up to six months on the trot."

Carine had taken the offered device, and was turning it in her hands. "It's amazing. Even though I'm working on cutting-edge technology every day, I never fail to be surprised at what Andie comes up with."

Moving on to the second object, Sonia explained that this would work in tandem with the HD cameras, projecting a pixel-perfect holographic representation of the captured video.

"Let me show you a quick demo," she said.

She turned to a nearby desktop PC and clicked some buttons on a graphic interface. A life-sized image of Carine appeared in the middle of the workshop, indistinguishable from the original, standing slack-jawed beside Lucas.

Laughing at Carine's reaction, Sonia said, "Close your mouth, dear – you're causing a draught!"

Walking up to the hologram, Carine inspected it closely. As it echoed her movements, it was like looking into a 3D mirror. There were none of the digital artefacts one associated with current projection technology; it looked completely solid, with no beams of light to betray its origin. Neither did it require projection media such as nets or mirrors, as the image was created from the intersection of photons fired from multiple sources. When she came between one of the projectors and the hologram, the others immediately compensated, maintaining the illusion.

"Of course, this is simply live transmission of what the cameras capture," said Sonia, pointing to the upper corners of the workshop where Carine could just make out the presence of the cameras and projectors. "It could just as easily be completely manufactured video, easily created by Andie or one of her babies. Given time to set up, we could have Andie herself appear on a stage. As long as no one tried to shake her hand!"

Clapping excitedly, Carine said, "They're great, Sonia! This will have fascinating applications in entertainment and communications, I'm sure."

Though the pace of innovation had, at least in the public eye, slowed down, these behind-the-scenes inventions were all designed with Lucas's end goal in mind. Some would be kept in-house, of course. 3D metal fabrication could seriously damage the human-based manufacturing industry, and though the idea of being able to create organic constructs on-the-fly seemed like a solution to food poverty, it would be a threat to those who already produced foodstuffs. In many cases, hunger was not so much an issue of the not being enough food to go around, but that it was not getting to those that need it. Better distribution systems and more efficient production methods were a better solution than "magically" creating food.

Carine had been on track when she predicted the possible use of holographic technology in entertainment and communications; it was easy to imagine your favourite shows coming to life right in your living room, or speaking face-to-face in business or personal meetings at a distance. While it was true that this technology was not essential to saving humanity, it would be a valuable tool when potential future colonies were widely separated.

The focus now, however, was on the continued promotion of the existing technologies, and that was a matter of time, more than anything else. The CF generators were shortly to be distributed, and the auto manufacturers were awaiting deliveries of the CFEV units. It would still be a few years before Ad Astra released the home version of the CF technology, and it was considered polite to let the car companies get a head start on CFEVs before the conversion kits were pushed.

In the meantime, the special projects would be perfected, and the team would be introduced to the secret hiding at the back of Lucas's farm.

ON TOUR

Lucas and Sonia had been waiting for this day for some weeks. All the pieces were in place, and with Ad Astra's regular business now running a predetermined course, it was time to let the others in on the secret. Sonia was overjoyed that she would no longer have to keep herself under such right control, lest her mouth run away with her, and Lucas was looking forward to seeing the expressions on his friends' faces when they saw what everything had been leading up to over the past five months. It seemed such a short period to have accomplished so much, but it had been an intense time with its highs and lows, fears and triumphs.

TheOS was running on almost every computing device available, with software developers now creating applications designed specifically to run on the new operating system. QED was increasingly becoming the technology of choice for internet service providers, and additional factories were still being constructed to keep up with demand. The CF generators were installed in thousands of locations around the world, with still more orders coming in. All current models of electric vehicle had been redesigned to accommodate the CFEV technology, and Ad Astra would shortly be releasing the conversion kits for existing ICE vehicles.

Global greenhouse gas emissions were dropping daily, as more and more industries began to install either more efficient processes, or pollution reduction technologies, all designed by Andie.

Political corruption was at an all-time low, due to Andie incessantly rooting out and exposing the culprits. It was becoming increasingly obvious that there was no hiding these unethical or illegal activities, and even the promise of quick and easy wealth seemed no longer worth the risk.

Share prices in Ad Astra QED and Ad Astra CF had skyrocketed, though the financial team had yet to start selling the remaining stock. A small fortune was still there for the taking.

With everything running smoothly, the management team at Ad Astra were pretty much running on autopilot, and now was the perfect time to to reinvigorate them and reboot their imaginations.

So it was, that on a warm Saturday evening towards the end of November, they were all instructed to meet at the Princess Street offices, packed for an overnight stay. As they loitered in the car park, talking amongst themselves and wondering what Lucas had in store for them, a chartered bus pulled up outside, and Lucas and Sonia alighted. They were casually dressed, with Lucas wearing a brightly-coloured Hawaiian shirt and board shorts, and Sonia in a pretty, floral-patterned sundress.

"Good afternoon, people! Is everybody ready to go?"

"Not if we're going to the beach!" shouted Paul. "I forgot my bucket and spade!"

"Just where is this magical mystery tour taking us, Lucas?" asked Cath.

"It wouldn't be a mystery if I told you, would it?" Lucas responded. "Come on, on the bus!"

He opened the luggage compartment, and his expectant passengers loaded their bags before climbing aboard. Despite not knowing their destination, there was somewhat of a party atmosphere during the trip. They had all been cooped up for far too long, ensuring that Ad Astra's business proceeded without hang-ups. As they left town in a northerly direction, the thought that they might be headed to the beach was discarded in favour of the lake, or the mountain. The Chateau Tongariro or Huka Lodge were popular suggestions, but these too, were crossed off when the bus left the main road at Mangaweka.

"Really, dude? Our big getaway is to the *farm*?" Paul was a city boy, through and through, and the prospect of spending a weekend in the country was not his idea of a good time.

Alison grinned at his discomfort. "You'll love it. The feeling of warm cow dung between your toes, dossing down in the woolshed, surrounded by the unmistakable aroma of damp wool and stale sheep piss."

"Leave him alone, Foxy. No one is sleeping in the woolshed," said Lucas.

With a pained expression, Paul addressed Lucas. "Mate, I swear that I will never forgive you if you're making me miss the end of year university parties in favour of camping under the stars in the middle of nowhere!"

Lucas winked at him. "Trust me. You'll enjoy this."

Before long, the bus reached the farmhouse gate, and puzzlement was obvious on the passengers' faces as they drove straight past it. A couple of corners up the road, they arrived at the entrance to the broad track off into the hills, and Lucas jumped out to open the gates. Speculation was once again rife as they drove through the farm.

Astonished gasps erupted when they rounded a last corner and the enormous compound with its high fence appeared ahead of them. The bus stopped outside the gate, and the curious group got off, retrieving their bags from the luggage compartment before the bus departed.

"I think I speak for everyone when I say that this is ... unexpected," said Tom. "What have you two been up to here?"

With an enigmatic smile, Lucas put an arm around Sonia and they turned to face their friends.

"It's just a little side project, but one we're sure you will all appreciate," he said. Walking up to the large gate, he unlocked it and, as it slid aside, swept his arm around in an expansive gesture. "Welcome to AASVC. Please, come in."

Once everyone was within the walls, with people glancing at each other and attempting to unravel the acronym he had used, Lucas closed the gate behind them. He gestured for them to follow him down the concrete ramp towards the double doors set below ground level, each large enough to admit two semi trucks.

At the bottom of the ramp, he placed his palm on a biometric scanner, and a smaller door opened. Sonia led the way inside, and the rest filed in behind her. The interior of the massive building was much as she remembered it, with one glaring difference. While the normal detritus of construction activity was still scattered about, and the two huge cradles were still on their rails at the right-hand side of the space, there was no sign of whatever had been worked on here.

As Lucas followed the tail end of the procession inside, he closed the door behind him, and stated grandly, "AASVC – Ad Astra Space Vehicle Construction."

"Holy...this place is massive!" said Fats.

Sonia looked at Lucas quizzically. "Where's, um...the *thing*?" she whispered.

Giving her a wink and a reassuring smile, he guided the team to stand off to the right.

"Okay, Andie. Showtime!"

Starting at the far end of the building, the overhead lights began to turn off, a wall of darkness approaching the group until all the lights had gone out. They stood momentarily in the pitch black, before artfully-positioned spotlights suddenly illuminated the left side of the vast, open space. Or, what *had* been open space before the lights went out.

Now, the spotlights shone upon the sixty metre bulk of the creation that Sonia had been expecting to see earlier. It seemed that it had materialised out of thin air, and while almost every one of the guests' faces initially showed only amazement, some transitioned very quickly to recognition, and elation.

"Where the *hell* did that come from?"

"What *is* it?"

Paul was one of the first to see it for what it was. "Dude, that's a bloody *spaceship*! All right!"

"I don't know what's more impressive," said Tom. "The magic trick, or the fact that you've only gone and built a spaceship in your back yard!"

Cath said, "Okay, mister – I swear that wasn't there when we came in. Either you've got Penn and Teller out the back, or ... well, I honestly can't think of any other explanation."

Raising his hands for silence, Lucas addressed his stunned teammates. "So, here's the thing. There was no magic involved – the ship was there the whole time. Perhaps I'll let Carine explain it."

The German woman stepped forward, obviously delighted with the reaction her trick had provoked. "The vessel is contained within a Higgs field, much the same as the one that Fats used to stop the bullets that Wolff fired at him. The same principles that dissipated the energy of those bullets is at work here. Correctly tuned, the field will actually bend electromagnetic energy, which includes visible light.

"When the 'cloak' is engaged, anything within this field is rendered practically invisible, not only to the naked eye, but also to any sensor that uses the EM spectrum. That includes radar, infrared, x-ray, and so on. The eye, and those sensors, will see only what lies behind the vessel. Sophisticated detection devices *may* be able to measure the additional time it takes for light rays or other EM emissions to travel around the hull instead of through an empty space, but the discrepancy is so small that current technology will almost certainly miss it."

"Thank you, Carine," Lucas said. "I couldn't have put it better myself."

"Let me get this straight, bro. You're talking about a completely invisible, stealth spaceship?" asked Fats.

"Unless your eyesight is a whole heap better than mine, and you saw the ship before the lights went out, then I guess that's exactly what they're talking about," said Michelle.

"And it's bulletproof," continued Fats.

Carine spoke up again. "I think you'll find that it's a bit more than 'bulletproof', Fats. The amount of kinetic energy that it is possible to absorb is proportional to the surface area of the field. This particular field should be able to protect the vessel from almost anything. The cloaking may suffer momentarily, as there will be a faint shimmer as the energy is dissipated, but if someone is shooting missiles at you, then they probably have a good idea of where you are anyway, and invisibility becomes a moot point."

Meanwhile, Paul had been staring in rapt fascination at the ship. "Excuse me. This techno-babble is very interesting, I'm sure, but hello? Space. Ship."

Alison giggled. "He's like a kid who's seen his new bike under the tree, but can't play with it until Christmas Day. Come on, put the little fellow out of his misery."

The discussion of the Higgs field capabilities was put on hold, and attention shifted to the ship itself. Sixty metres from end to end, and standing over ten metres tall, it was clad in a seamless charcoal-grey material, with a broad sky-blue stripe running from the wedge-shaped nose to the blunt tail. Superimposed on the blue was the twin-star Ad Astra logo at the front, and the word "ANDROMEDA" at the rear, both in brilliant white, with a thin black outline. The front window curved around to the sides of the vessel, and above the blue stripe were two long windows, with numerous smaller rectangular windows above these.

The ship sat on three feet, reminiscent of a sewing machine's needle guide; two at the back, and the third centrally located towards the front. Set into the lower edge, five metres or so back from the nose, was a white appendage that mimicked the larger shape. This was approximately fifteen metres long, and three metres high, and appeared to be a separate vessel that was docked to the ship.

Lucas led them to the front, and a section of the undercut nose opened, dropping down to create a ramp leading into the ship. Following him inside, they found themselves in a vestibule, with another door ahead of them.

"Airlock," explained Lucas.

Through the second door was a three-metre-square space bounded by a yellow stripe on the floor, with doorways on each side. The deck to either side sloped down to other airtight doors, and ahead of the group was a broad corridor lined with lockers and other storage spaces.

Indicating the marked area, Lucas said, "This is the elevator. It's a nested Higgs field, so there's no mechanism required to raise or lower it. The doors down the ramps lead to the two shuttles which you will have seen from outside."

He moved to one of these doors, and pressed a button on the wall. As the door slid aside, it revealed the shuttle hatch, which rolled up like a garage door. The inside of the shuttle was trimmed in chrome and wood veneer on the white walls, and there were five rows of seating, with two aisles separating the six chairs in each row into pairs.

Cath flopped into one of the deep, black leather chairs. "Oooh! Better than first class!"

"This is the passenger shuttle, the *Sagittarius*," Lucas said, "and as you can see, seats thirty. The other, *Aquarius*, has a larger cargo hold at the rear, and only two rows of seating."

Back out in the corridor, it was clear that it ran between the two shuttles, and fifteen metres down the ship, it split to go around a collection of machinery in the centre.

"This is our engineering department, with the power supply, the field generator, drive unit, life support and various ancillary systems.

We've doubled up on the most vital machinery, in the unlikely chance that one will fail, so it's pretty cramped down here.

"There are tanks of liquid oxygen, for atmosphere replenishment, and liquid hydrogen for the CF generators. We've got carbon scrubbers that break apart carbon dioxide and recycle the oxygen component, and the carbon is routed to our organic slurry tanks, which I'll talk more about later. And just in behind here is the cargo hold. Come on through, but mind your step. It's another nested Higgs field, and we've turned the gravity down in there, in case any of you wanted to experience micro-gravity."

Stepping through the nautical-style hatch, he reached above his head to grab a handhold, and effortlessly swung himself inverted in the near zero-gravity. He had been practising in this environment, but knew from experience that it could be extremely disconcerting for those unfamiliar with the sensation of weightlessness. He had several zero-G drones on hand to suck up the inevitable gastric expulsions.

Carine, the first through the hatch, shot up at an angle immediately after reflexively pushing off her leading foot. Her momentum carried her across the hold, and she managed to snag a handle halfway up the far wall.

"It's okay – I meant to do that!" she shouted unconvincingly.

Tom entered next, much more cautiously after having seen Carine's manoeuvre. He drifted slowly across the floor before dragging a foot to slow his momentum. When he was stationary, he bent forward rapidly and began to somersault in place. This motion proved too much for his stomach, and it showed its displeasure by ejecting some of his lunch. A drone immediately moved in to hoover up the mess, and Lucas pushed away from his position to arrest Tom's tumble.

"It takes a bit of getting used to. Maybe save the gymnastics for another time, eh?"

"Urgh. Good advice. Better late than never. You've obviously done this before – how many times did you puke before you got used to it?"

Pushing Tom back towards the hatch, Lucas replied, "Once or twice." It had actually taken him several hours, and the full contents of his stomach, before he could even move about without nausea, but he wasn't going to admit it.

Alison, Michelle, and Cath all declined the dubious pleasure of micro-gravity, but Will, Fats, Rudi, and Paul all accepted the challenge, with only minimal work for the drones. Sonia, of course, had almost as much experience as Lucas, and her acrobatics threatened to set off a new round of technicolour yawns among the men.

"Okay, playtime's over. Let's get on with the tour," said Lucas, as he ushered his mates out of the hold.

"Excuse me," wailed Carine. "I'm stuck!"

Laughing, Lucas said, "Just aim down here and gently push off the wall. I'll catch you!"

She aligned herself with the exit, and gingerly pushed with her feet, giving a superb Superman impression as she slowly glided across the room. Lucas made good on his promise, and stopped her forward motion before she could fly through the hatch and ignominiously encounter full gravity again.

"Gotcha!"

"Oh my God. That was terrifying, and sort of fun! Can I try that again sometime?"

"Sure, said Lucas, grinning. "Maybe we can set up a zero-G practise room back in town somewhere. For now, let's carry on."

He took them back past Engineering to the elevator. Ensuring that everybody was safely within the yellow line, a simple voice command closed all four elevator doors, only to open them again a split second later. However, when they reopened, the scene was different. To one side was a wood-panelled door, and to the other, a wide entranceway leading to a room that triggered vague recognition in the visitors. To the right of the entrance was a freestanding console, with screens, lights and buttons. On the opposite side of the room was a partially-enclosed, raised, circular platform with six equally-spaced circles on the floor.

"Correct me if I'm wrong," said Will, "but have you recreated the transporter room from the *Enterprise*?"

Lucas chuckled, and said, "Just my nod to pop culture."

"Does it work?" asked Paul excitedly.

"Not as well as you'd like, Paul," replied Carine. "While we can reliably 'transport' inert materials, we're not able to do so with living organisms. It appears that the cerebral matrix is just too complex to survive the process. The one mouse we tested it on lost all brain function, so Scotty won't be beaming you up any time soon."

Disappointed, Paul nevertheless just had to mount the platform and give a passable Captain Kirk impression. An avid Star Trek fan, he had grown up with later incarnations of the franchise, but still held a soft spot for the original series.

Lucas left him to role-play his fantasies as he led the others forward of the elevator. As they entered the bridge, most of them were surprised to see a figure sitting in the captain's chair. Their surprise turned to astonishment as the figure stood, and turned to face them.

"Good afternoon, everyone," said Andie. "Welcome aboard the *Andromeda*."

She wore a form-fitting charcoal jumpsuit with sky-blue trim, bearing the Ad Astra logo on her breast. Her short, red hair was mostly hidden under a grey naval officer's cap with gold braid. Her most notable feature, however, was the cheeky grin that showed just how much she had enjoyed surprising them in this way.

Everybody began to talk at once.

"Where did you come from?"

"Did someone genetically engineer a human body behind our backs?"

"Looking *fine*, girlfriend!"

Andie held up a hand. "Relax. Please. I'm not really here. There's no secret clone research facility, and I haven't stolen sometime else's body. This is new tech out of Sonia's workshop. I'm appearing to you as a holographic projection," she said as she passed her arm through the console in front of her. "And thank you, Alison – you're looking good yourself!"

"So when were you planning to tell us about this awesome invention, Sonia?" asked Michelle.

"Um, now? Sure, we could have given you a demo back at the office, but we figured that this would be more fun. It is really cool, and Andie is creating the hologram on the fly. Our new HD cameras can also capture video to project in real-time. At the moment, it's more of a gimmick than a consumer product but there will be real-world applications eventually."

The questions started anew, before Lucas said, "Time for that later. Andie, would you care to show us the bridge?"

"Delighted," she responded, and began to point out the various stations; Captain/pilot, navigation, communications, weapons...

"Wait, what? This baby's *armed*?" asked Paul, who had given up his Star Trek pretensions on hearing the commotion.

"Yes," added Michelle blandly. "Do tell."

Flushing, Lucas replied, "Well, yes. But hey, it's better to have them and not need them, than need them and not have them, right?"

Michelle fixed him with a cold stare. "I can't even *begin* to imagine how many international laws you're breaking by arming a civilian vessel. Whatever happened to, 'Yes of course I'll consult with you before doing anything stupid,' Lucas?"

The others, with the exception of Sonia, tactfully left the bridge to spare Lucas the embarrassment of a public dressing-down.

"Well? Are you going to explain yourself? I honestly don't know how long I can remain as your legal counsel if you keep me out of the loop like this."

Stepping between Michelle and Lucas, Sonia said, "Let's just calm down a minute. Firstly, Michelle, it was *my* idea to put the weapons in, and secondly, we've already had someone kidnap me, try to burn down the office, shoot at Fats, and *kill* our construction workers in South Africa. Can you imagine what lengths someone would go to to get their hands on an actual *spaceship*? Or choose to destroy it because its technology was deemed a threat to the status quo? I'm not going to apologise for wanting to protect our staff and our business, and I'm not going to stand by and watch people taking pot shots at us. What if we *had* asked you first? Would you have said, 'That's a great idea – go for it'?"

Michelle sat down in the nearby navigator's chair, sighing heavily. From a moral point of view, she could certainly appreciate the logic of Sonia's argument, but it still caused conflict with her legal training. With Lucas's previous rule-breaking, there had at least been no serious damage done, so perhaps she could justify this latest hare-brained scheme by pretending that it wasn't a problem until the weapons were actually used.

"Look, I'm sorry. I may have overreacted. I get where you're coming from, Sonia, and I don't want to see any of us hurt, either. Can we try this again? Lucas, no matter how much my instincts tell me to advise you against this sort of thing, I promise that I won't try to talk you out of it if you just let me know about it. I take my responsibilities as head lawyer seriously, and if anything does go pear-shaped, it's very hard to do my job when I'm blindsided like this. Just give me a heads-up next time, so I can at least be prepared if I end up having to deal with the fallout. Deal?"

"I can do that," he answered, "and just to reassure you – the weapons aren't externally visible, and I swear that they will never be used except in self-defence."

Michelle trusted his well-honed sense of ethics, and understood that everything he had done had sound reasoning behind it, and had always been restrained, considering the provocations. She stood, and held out her hand. First Lucas, and then Sonia, shook it solemnly, than all three gathered together for a group hug.

"We never meant to upset you, sweetie," Sonia said, "but as Lucas and I have both learned, through hard lessons, sometimes the right thing isn't always best, or easy. We're just looking out for our family."

"I know, girl. As long as you don't create any international incidents, or bring the law down on us, you guys carry on doing what you have to."

"In the interests of full disclosure, Michelle, we'll be visiting some World Heritage sites after-hours today. It's not legal, but I promise not to get caught!"

"Thank you, Lucas. I appreciate the notification, and I'll keep quiet about it in front of the others, so I don't spoil your surprise!"

The rift mended, they went back through to the transporter room.

"Are we all friends again?" asked Cath.

"We're good," replied Lucas.

"Great, so can we get out of here? We couldn't get either of the other doors open, and we've been stuck with a succession of bad Starfleet captain impersonations. He says he's Picard now – he's got the height right, but seems to having trouble conveying the baldness!"

With a pained look, Will added, "Andie hasn't helped matters, either. She's been encouraging him by projecting the uniforms onto his body!"

"Okay," said Lucas, laughing. "We'll save you."

"Spoilsports," complained Paul. "Hey, now that your little tiff is over, are we allowed to talk about those weapons? What have we got – lasers, space torpedoes?"

"Tucked away behind hatches on the hull, we've got eight plasma cannons, probably more effective against so-called 'soft' targets, and running the length of the ship between decks two and three, there are two railguns, good for armoured targets. On the roof, behind another hatch, is a cannon that can fire a small EMP generator, to take out an opponent's electrical systems. I must stress—" he glanced at Michelle, "—these are *defensive* weapons only, and we won't be initiating any firefights. If someone shoots at us, however, they'll soon regret it."

"Awesome!" said Paul. "Can I be weapons officer?"

"Um, no," Lucas said bluntly. "In fact, we don't really need anyone on the bridge at all, as Andie, or one of her AIs, will be handling all the ship's functions. The bridge is partly there for appearances, but should we lose our computer, we do have the capability of manual operation. If and when we train people for the bridge stations, Fats will be Weapons, I'll be Pilot, Sonia will be Navigation, and you, Paul, can be Communications, as that is apparently your forté."

Forestalling any further discussion on the matter, he walked through the elevator space to the wooden door. "This is the Captain's cabin – mine, in case there was any doubt," he added, with a meaningful glance at Andie.

"Hey, don't look at me!" she protested. "I'm the Captain in name only, because I fly the thing. You can be Commander, or Admiral, if you like."

"Hmm, 'Admiral Winter' – that could work," he said as he opened the door.

The room revealed was totally unexpected, in the context of a spaceship. An office space to the right held an antique roll-top desk and wooden swivel chair, while to the left was a large four-poster bed. The whole room was decorated in an approximation of eighteenth-century naval fashion, with wood panelling, mullioned windows, antique wooden dressers, and hanging lanterns providing a surprising amount of illumination.

"Admiral Blackbeard, more like it!" said Tom. "Retro, much?"

"What can I say? I've got old-school tastes. It's not all as folksy as it looks – there's a computer terminal inside the desk, the lanterns are actually LEDs, and the mattress is a Sleepyhead. All the woodwork is real, though. These are actual aged oak planks on the floor, and the furniture is genuine, not reproduction."

"Well, I love it," said Alison. "I think having everything stainless steel and plastic would be ugly. This is actually sort of tasteful, in its own way."

Pointing at a door to the side of the desk, Lucas said, "I've got my own bathroom through there – more wood, and a clawfoot tub. We've even built the modern toilet into an enclosure so it doesn't clash with the rest of the place."

He pushed that door open to let them look inside. The oak flooring continued through, and the sailing-ship theme extended to a brass porthole – or what appeared to be brass. The porthole surround, as well as the taps and other metalwork, were gold-plated. Not through any sense of ostentation; brass fittings in bathrooms were prone to water-staining, and the gold was simply a measure to keep cleaning requirements down.

With appropriate appreciation his guests took turns poking their heads into the bathroom before he ushered them out, and back to the elevator.

Indicating the aft-facing door, he said, "We'll come back to that one. Let's go upstairs for now."

As before, the elevator doors closed briefly, before opening to yet another scene. This time, the bow door and two sides opened to a carpeted area with waist-high panelling on the walls. Leading the way forward, Lucas said, "This is the accommodation deck and galley."

They walked through towards the bow, leaving the carpet behind for a hard surface. A window stretched the width of the room, and several long tables and benches sat in front of it. At the right – *starboard*! – end, was a space with leather couches and coffee tables, while at the port side of the room was a deli-counter servery.

"There's an actual kitchen behind the counter, but it's not totally necessary. This microwave-looking thing is more of Carine's work – an organic replicator. With the right template, it can create any foodstuff. The basics can be made by simply scanning a substance at a molecular level and recreating it, but we've given Andie the recipes of numerous full meals, and it only takes a minute or two to put out a restaurant-quality dish. This is the reason for the organic slurry tank below – using basic organic molecules and compounds, the replicator essentially 3D-prints what we need. We'll give you the menu of what we can create so far, and you can make your dinner choices – anything from macaroni cheese to lobster thermidor!"

Leaving the galley, with people looking back over their shoulders at the "magic microwave", and silently contemplating the thought of a gourmet dinner, he took them down one of the the two corridors running the length of the ship either side of the elevator. Thirty metres in length, these corridors were the longest on the vessel, with the upper deck protruding into the top of the cargo hold. On the wall nearest the hull were five equally-spaced doors, with four on the opposite wall.

"We have thirteen passenger cabins, all of which have their own bathrooms. In the centre block are unisex toilets."

He opened the nearest cabin door to reveal a large room with a bed, seating, desk, and a door that obviously led to one of the ensuite bathrooms. The cabin was tastefully decorated in a modern, hotel-style manner, and had a large window that at the moment had a view only of the interior of the construction facility.

"They're all identical, so there's no point showing you the rest. When we're done with the tour, you can grab your bags and claim a room each. Let's check out the last area."

They trooped back to the elevator, and it took them back down to the middle deck. This time, Lucas asked the stern-facing door to open, and he took them into the lounge section. Again, this area was incongruent with the nature of the ship, decorated in a faux English public-house style. The wooden bar was surmounted by turned posts, and a brass rail surrounded it near floor level. The rich green carpet had a gold fleur-de-lis motif, and the wood panelling extending halfway up the walls was topped by textured burgundy wallpaper and nautical-themed oil paintings. The dark colouring of the surfaces was offset by bright lighting and gleaming brass (or gold-plated) fixtures, and along the wall opposite the bar, light-brown leather couches surrounded tables to create cosy alcoves. In the centre of the room sat a full-sized billiards table, and at the far end of the bar were several classic arcade games. At the far end of the room, there was a dance floor, in a darkened space the full width of the ship, with a curious arrangement of seating in front of it, as if dancing were a spectator sport.

"This is cute," said Cath, jumping up onto a bar stool. Wine cooler please, barkeep."

"Drinkies later. Let's get your bags and get ourselves settled in," Sonia said.

While she took them back down in the elevator, Lucas stayed in the bar and confirmed the trip plans with Andie. He had quite the adventure planned for his friends, and wanted to make sure that it all went off without a hitch. He heard the rush of air as the elevator shot to the top deck, and went behind the bar to play host.

Shortly, after the guests had selected their rooms and put their luggage away, they began arriving back in the lounge.

"What can I get you, Will?" asked Lucas.

"I could go a Heineken, please," the economist replied.

Taking a glass, Lucas held it under one of several taps, saying, "Heineken it is." He pulled on the handle and filled the glass, handing it across the bar to Will.

"Tom?"

"Have you got Stella?"

Lucas took another glass, and held it under the same tap, filling it.

"Um, I don't mean to disparage your bartender skills, but isn't that the Heineken tap?" asked Tom.

"It's anything I want it to be, mate. We've got another replicator here, and it can do any one of several dozen beers out of the same tap."

Impressed and intrigued, Tom raised his glass. "Well, here's to trying them all!"

As everyone took their turn ordering drinks, Lucas poured a wide variety of beverages. One of the taps was for beer and other carbonated drinks, one was for wine, and the third dispensed fruit juices.

Once everybody had been served, Lucas poured his own beer and joined them at the tables. The girls had taken one table, and the boys another, in the time-honoured tradition of drinking parties. Carine was patiently explaining the new technologies to the less engineering-minded members of their little group, while the boys were excitedly discussing the possibilities now open to them.

"Can we go somewhere special for our party, Lucas? Paris, London, New York?"

"How fast does this thing go? We could do all of them!"

"Let's go to Mars!"

Lucas smiled at their enthusiasm, then noticed Andie nodding at him out of the corner of his eye. He stood up and addressed the group. "Okay, guys. We're ready for our first stop."

Sections of the wall slid up to reveal large picture windows, and everybody turned to look. The view outside was no longer of a cavernous factory interior, but a flat, arid landscape out of which rose a gigantic red rock.

"Holy cow – Uluru!" cried Alison.

"That's right, Foxy. Uluru, or Ayers Rock. Has anyone been here before?"

A chorus of negatives was the response, along with the inevitable questions of, "Can we go out to see it?", and, "Again, how fast does this thing go?"

Lucas grinned smugly at having caught them out, and answered the questions in order.

"Yes, we can go out and see it. We're cloaked at the moment, and the entrance ramp has a separate field, so there's no risk of anyone seeing the ship. And Fats – this 'thing' goes *really* fast! We only left home about ten minutes ago."

"I never felt a thing," remarked Cath.

"And that's the beauty of the Higgs field. We could take right-angle corners at a thousand kilometres an hour, or turn completely upside-down, and you wouldn't even spill your wine!"

Leaving their drinks on the table, they all headed for the elevator. On the lower deck, they went through the airlock with eager anticipation, and down the ramp. From the outside, the Andromeda was still completely invisible, and Lucas explained that when they re-entered, he would have to kill the Higgs field around the ramp, but that doing so would only expose the interior of the airlock, and only from the front.

"How is it that we can walk out through that field, when it's able to stop a bullet? And how are we expected to fire your railguns through it?" asked Fats.

Carine had the answer to this. "That's the interesting thing about the H-field – it's sort of 'one-way'. Any momentum built up inside of the field will be retained when going out, and it's only incoming energy that is stopped. That's why we can walk out without a problem, and why the kinetic and energy weapons will still be functional."

Ignoring the technical lecture, Alison had wandered off, marvelling at the splendour of Uluru as the sun was setting behind it. The others caught up to her, and Sonia put an arm around her shoulders.

"It's magical, isn't it?"

"It's gorgeous, babe. I can see why it means so much to the Aboriginal People. You can almost feel the ancestral spirits surrounding us."

They stood there for half an hour, simply appreciating the majesty of the red rock monolith standing alone in the otherwise featureless landscape, like a mountain that had lost its way. Eventually, Lucas gathered them all up, and they returned to the Andromeda.

"That was amazing, Lucas. Thank you so much," Alison said.

"Well, hold that thought, because it just keeps getting better!" he replied mysteriously. He refreshed their drinks, and passed out menus. As promised, there was an extensive range available, and the conversation died to a low mutter as people perused the choices, commenting occasionally to their neighbour.

"Half of these dishes I've only ever heard of."

"I could go a steak – this 'tartare', medium-rare sounds good."

"You idiot – 'tartare' is just raw beef mince!"

"Seriously? Ewww. T-bone is cooked, right?"

By the time everyone had made their decisions, it was time for the next stop on the tour. This time, Lucas had left the shades down, to enhance the suspense, and as before, they crowded into the airlock.

This time, the door opened to the impressive sight of the extensive temple complex of Angkor Wat. The attraction had closed for the day, and they had the place to themselves. The sun had only just set, and the red light at that time of day gave a warm glow to the cold stone of the temples.

"Wow," said Will, "I came here a few years ago, and the place was *so* crowded. You get a whole different feel for it with no one around."

"It's hard to top Uluru," said Alison, "but *man* made this. Even after all this time, the workmanship is breathtaking. This was the centre of a whole empire, and these ruins are all that remains of the huge city that used to surround it. How could a civilisation with the wealth and skill to create something like this just disappear?"

Sonia had done her homework on the places they would be visiting, and answered, "It's quite interesting, and actually has a bearing on our own mission. The current thought is that climate change in the fifteenth century caused widespread flooding in the area, ruining the water management infrastructure that they had created, and the area was no longer able to sustain them. You just can't fight nature. But you can stop forcing nature's hand, and that's what we hope to do, right?"

It was a valuable lesson to all of them, of the power that nature had to topple powerful civilisations, and these people hadn't even done anything to exacerbate things.

Lucas called to Will and Fats, asking them to help unload some gear from the ship. From the Aquarius shuttle, they collected a collapsible table and chairs, while Lucas dashed upstairs for mysterious reasons of his own. Carrying everything outside, they set up the furniture in front of the main temple, with Lucas placing a small, boxy device in the centre of the table. Asking everyone to take their seats, he pressed a button on the box, instructing the guests to keep their hands away from the table for a moment. Once the table was clear of body parts, he said, "Service please,

Andie," and everyone's particular dinner selection materialised on the table in front of them, along with glasses of wine and beer.

"Et voilà! Dinner is served, courtesy of the replicator and the transporter beam."

Cath poked at her Thai Green Curry hesitantly. It looked right, and smelled right, but knowing that it was created from organic goop just didn't *seem* right. While others were also looking at their plates warily, Fats had already picked up his cutlery and was cutting a chunk off his medium-rare T-bone steak. Popping the meat into his mouth, he closed his eyes in pleasure. "Mmmm. Bro, that is the *best* damn steak I've ever tasted! Dig in, guys – you won't regret it!"

With this seal of approval, the multicultural meal began in earnest. There were dishes from every corner of the globe – Cath's Thai curry, Alison's Israeli *shakshouka*, Tom's Peking Duck – and each one as delicious as if it had been prepared by a master chef.

"What if someone sees us?" asked Will around a mouthful of chicken parmigiana.

"Got that covered," replied Sonia, in the process of lifting another forkful of kimchi. "That's an H-field generator on the table, so we're invisible to the outside world, while still being able to see out ourselves."

After the main courses, dessert was transported to the table; baklava, crème brulée, panna cotta, ice cream sundae, and other classics. In the moonlight, the temples took on an otherworldly appearance. The silk-cotton trees, slowly but inexorably strangling the stonework, became alien creatures, and the shafts of moonlight filtering through their branches, searchlights.

As they sat back, replete, the group of friends watched as the detritus of their meal vanished before their eyes, to be recycled aboard the Andromeda.

"Well, that was the strangest meal I've had," Michelle said. "The setting, the service, the variety of amazing dishes. I'd tip our waiter, but he seems to be mysteriously absent!"

Tom was nodding in agreement. "It was fantastic. Thanks for the special evening, Lucas and Sonia."

Sharing a knowing look, the couple accepted the thanks, Lucas saying, "We're not quite done yet. Does anybody like rugby?"

"That's a silly question, bro. What have you got planned? Throwing a ball around at Twickenham?"

"Nope, but there's a little match being played in Cardiff tomorrow morning. We'll go back to the ship for another drink, but we have to be up at seven for kick-off."

Smacking his forehead, Paul said, "That's right! I'd forgotten about it, with all the excitement. The All Blacks are on tour in the UK. Did you get us sideline tickets?"

"Sold out, sorry, but I've got us even better seats. Come on, give me a hand packing up, and we'll toast our inevitable victory over the Welsh."

With final looks at Angkor Wat, they went back on board the Andromeda, and up to the lounge. "A" drink turned into several, and the dance floor got its christening, the girls dragging the menfolk out with only moderate resistance. Lucas eventually reminded them of the 6.30am wake-up call, and the party reluctantly broke up, everybody heading for their respective rooms.

THE LESSON

In the morning, New Zealand time, the group's pre-selected breakfasts were waiting for them in the galley, and a succession of bleary-eyed people trickled into the lounge, carrying their plates.

"OJ. Lots of it," groaned Tom to Lucas, who was once again behind the bar.

"Jug's on the table, mate. Ah, Paul. How you feeling, bud? Hair of the dog?"

An incomprehensible grunt escaped Paul's lips as he took the proffered Bloody Mary in a weak hand. He made his way to an unoccupied table, deliberately avoiding looking at Tom's full English breakfast. Downing half the highball glass, he shuddered, and looked up at Lucas. "Cheers, mate. Aren't we leaving it a bit late? Kick-off's at seven, which doesn't leave us much time to wake up and get to the stadium."

"Who said we were going to the stadium?"

Confused, Paul said, "Well, when you said 'better seats', I was thinking corporate box. What gives?"

"You'll see," replied Lucas, winking.

Soon enough, the whole team was down, with their plates of cereals, bacon and eggs, croissants, or fruit. Lucas nodded at Andie, and the dance floor area darkened, then showed the rugby ground at Principality Stadium, Cardiff. The lounge's surround sound speaker system hummed into life, and the voices of the Sky Sport commentators filled the room.

Paul grumpily shuffled over to the seating arranged in front of the dance floor. "I'm not sure how this is better than watching it at home. Sure, the screen's bigger, but ... hang on, that's not a screen, is it?"

He moved his head from side to side, noticing the parallax effect as he did so. "3D?" he queried.

"I told you – better. Andie transported some of the HD cameras down to the stadium, and is projecting a real-time hologram into the dance floor space. She'll be directing the projection as play happens, giving us the best possible view at any time."

The rest of the team had wandered away from their tables to check out the holographic rugby field. Entranced by the technology, they filled the "sideline" seating, each of them echoing Paul's motions, shifting their heads to watch the view change. As the players began to run out from the dressing rooms, the point of view zoomed in from the bird's-eye perspective to show them in close-up.

"Okay, so that's pretty cool," said Will, "though it's a bit freaky having a ten-foot-tall Ardie Savea running straight at you!"

As the players lined up for the national anthems, Lucas said, "You haven't even seen the best part yet."

At his words, the crowd and the grandstands disappeared, to be replaced by a grey landscape on a black background, with an instantly recognisable object on the horizon.

"Nice CGI trick," Tom said. "You've superimposed the game on a stock image of Earthrise on the Moon."

"I wouldn't be so cheap," said Lucas, grinning broadly. "That's a live image from the Andromeda's external cameras."

Stunned, Tom spluttered. "What ... but ... live ... we're on the *moon*?"

Seeing the window shades raise, the shocked group ran to the walls to look out. In every direction was the lunar landscape, and a mere twenty metres off the starboard side was an Apollo landing site, with the descent stage and lunar rover clearly visible.

Lucas gave them a few minutes to gawk, before calling them back to the projection. "Come on, guys. We've got a game to watch. The moon's not going anywhere."

Reluctantly dragging themselves away from the windows, his friends got back to their seats just in time to watch the All Blacks perform their traditional pre-match ritual, the *haka*. The All Blacks lined up in a wedge formation facing their opponents, and halfback TJ Perenara strode amongst his teammates, reciting the initial refrain. The intensity on his face reflected his connection to the language and culture, as well as his passion for the game. The rest of the team soon joined in with the familiar words of *Ka Mate*. Not technically a challenge, it was usually taken as such by the opposing team, and could be seen as intimidating, though its primary purpose was to inspire the New Zealand team.

Andie focused the camera on individual players in turn, with each seeming to strive to greater ferocity than his neighbour. The haka was always an impressive performance, and served to inflame the blood of the Kiwi fans as well as the players.

Joining the unseen crowd in a rousing cheer as the haka finished, the Ad Astra team watched the match begin, from the strangest location they could ever have imagined. Andie's direction of the broadcast was masterful, following players directly from behind as they crashed into the defence, zooming out for a wider view just before the ball was passed out along the line, and capturing in minute detail the triumph on the face of winger George Bridge as he dived across the line to score the first try.

The Welsh players put up a brave defence, and scored their own points, but the world's most successful international sporting team was unaccustomed to losing, and proved their superiority with skill, strength, and determination, to come out the victors with a score of 41-17.

"Best. Game. Ever," declared Paul. "I'll never be able to go back to watching rugby on a normal TV."

"We should so sell this to Sky. It's the future of televised sport – AI-controlled, high-def 3D coverage -a whole new way of watching," said Michelle, a calculating look on her face as she considered the profits.

"And trips to the moon!" added Will.

Sonia put a finger to her lips. "Hush-hush, remember? We need time to prepare before we go public with the H-field and G-drive."

"We'll talk about all that back at the office," Lucas said. "Right now, we've got a moon to explore! I thought we could get a little practice in beforehand, though. We've set the hold to one-sixth gravity, so if everyone is recovered from last night, let's head down."

From lockers in the shuttle corridor, he handed out spacesuits, much less bulky than NASA's. They allowed full freedom of movement, and had a small backpack attached. Sonia explained that this backpack contained a 'rebreather' unit that recycled exhaled oxygen while scrubbing carbon dioxide. Though the atmosphere on Earth is approximately twenty percent oxygen by volume, humans use only a small proportion of that, and exhaled air is still around fifteen percent oxygen under normal conditions. This type of system negated the need for bulky air tanks, and would allow several hours outside the ship on the small canister attached.

Suited up, Carine led the way back down the ship, warily stepping through the hatch into the hold. At one-sixth gravity, however, she was in little danger of uncontrolled flight, but still tumbled with her first step, the difference in her mass causing her body to behave unexpectedly. Andie appeared in the hold, and displayed a video of the original astronauts walking on the moon as she explained the mechanics involved. Her hologram demonstrated, and Carine attempted to replicate the unusual bouncing step that was necessary to maintain balance.

The others made their way into the low-gravity field, some making experimental jumps, some moving more hesitantly. After thirty minutes of instruction and practice, they felt confident enough to take on the real thing, and moved back to the bow of the ship. As they crowded into the airlock, Lucas performed a last equipment check, making sure that everybody's life support system was functioning correctly. Satisfied, he activated the airlock cycle and opened the outer door.

The others held back to allow him the honour of being the first person to set foot on the lunar surface since Gene Cernan, almost fifty years prior. Slowly descending the ramp, he paused at the bottom, wondering whether he should say something memorable.

"What are you waiting for?" Sonia asked impatiently through the comms channel.

"Okay! I'm bloody going, already!"

Hmm, not quite as inspiring as "One small step...", Lucas thought, stepping off the bottom edge of the ramp and planting his foot firmly into the soft lunar dust.

As he did so, he heard Paul's voice in his ear. "Woo-hoo! First New Zealander on the moon! Who said kiwis can't fly?"

The ceremonial foot-planting over, the others abandoned any semblance of courtesy, and hustled down the ramp. In spite of the practice they'd had, several stumbled on the inclined surface but were held up by their teammates. Soon, all ten were standing on the ground, wonder writ large upon their faces behind the visors.

"Okay, guys, let's stick together. I don't really want to lose any of you!" Lucas said, standing in front of the group.

"Can we take the rover for a spin, bro?" asked Fats.

"Definitely not!" said Sonia. "Two reasons – firstly, it's almost certainly non-functional after all this time, and secondly, it's still NASA property and we don't want to start off on the wrong foot if we end up needing to work with them."

"Is this the Apollo 11 landing site?" asked Tom.

"No," replied Lucas. "Apollo 15. We didn't want to leave our footprints all over Tranquility. It has such historical significance that it will probably become a heritage site at some stage. I think we can leave prints here, though. Oh, and if you want to take photos, you have chest-mounted cameras. Just double-tap your left thumb and little finger together to click. No Instagramming yet, though!"

He led the way as they bounded across to the NASA landing site. As they became more practised with the manoeuvre, there were fewer and fewer falls, and soon they were leaping around as if born to it. They inspected the descender module, which housed the rocket engine that had been left behind when NASA's lander had returned to orbit, and took photos beside the abandoned rover and the UV-faded, unrecognisable US flag. The now grey material of the flag was still attached to its pole, forlorn; a poignant reminder of how the Americans' enthusiasm for lunar expeditions had, too, faded.

With their time on the surface almost up, Lucas herded them back to the Andromeda. Souvenir rocks were collected, and they re-entered the airlock. Before the outer door closed, a quick blast of air washed over them, carrying away any lingering lunar dust. The airlock cycled, and they went inside to remove their suits, still filled with awe at what they had experienced.

"You sure know how to throw a staff party," Alison said to Lucas and Sonia. "I can still hardly believe that we walked on the moon, even with this to prove it!" She held up her small lump of moon rock.

"That was just *awesome*, man," Will said. "If they weren't all right here with me, I'd be dying to tell my friends about it!"

"Three cheers for Andie, I say!" shouted Cath. "If it wasn't for her, we'd all still be earthbound!"

Everyone agreed with this sentiment, and a hearty round of appreciation for the architect of all the technology that had made their trip possible rang through the lower deck.

Satisfied beyond belief that his team had finally received the reward that they deserved, Lucas looked around at the happy faces. Sonia put her arm around his waist, softly saying to him, "Well done, babe."

He smiled down at her and whispered in her ear, "You know, they've already driven vehicles on the moon, and played golf, but there's still one thing we can be first with..."

Blushing, she whispered back, "You're a bad man, Admiral Winter ... meet me in the cabin."

Speaking up, he suggested that everyone have a break, and maybe a shower after their exertions, and ordered the elevator to take them up.

He exited the Captain's cabin to find that Michelle and Cath had worked out how to use the bar, and Paul and Fats had Andie running a replay of the game, getting her to show various angles as they analysed the play.

Though it wasn't noticeable, the Andromeda was in motion again, making the return trip to Earth, on schedule for their next stop. He joined the boys as they played with their new toy, laughing as Fats walked onto the dance floor, fully immersing himself in the game.

Eventually, everyone had come back to the lounge. Will had discovered that the replicator made a decent cup of coffee, and had found himself the designated coffee-boy. Cath had also made use of the replicator, and was happily tucked up in an alcove with cappuccino and biscotti.

Addressing the team, Lucas said, "It'll be an hour or so before we get back, but the day's not over yet. It's coming up on lunchtime, which will be served at the Taj Mahal, and I'll be handing out the menus again for dinner at our final stop of the day. For now, just chill, and enjoy."

They did just that, killing time in a variety of ways. One group discussed what sights they'd like to see, and the ex-rugby players had great fun having Andie superimpose their own faces over those of the All Blacks at critical points in the game. Tom and Michelle had adjourned to the bridge to watch the Earth getting rapidly larger as they approached, while Lucas and Sonia sorted out the lunch.

After a while, Tom came back through to the lounge to announce that they were finally descending towards India. "I think Michelle will quit the bridge soon, too. At the speed we're moving, she's going to get motion sickness once the ground gets too close!"

She did, and, getting everyone's attention, Lucas explained the plan.

"Okay, so while it might be early morning here, I'm still running on New Zealand time, and my stomach tells me it's lunchtime. Because there will already be a bunch of people down there, I'll ask Andie to turn the 'big screen' into a window, and we'll eat onboard with a view of the Taj Mahal, before we drop in to visit. We've actually bought tickets this time, because it'd be a shame to come here and not see inside the mausoleum. If someone would like to get a couple of tables out of the shuttle and set them up, Sonia and I will bring the lunch down from the galley."

Fats and Will, having been charged with this task previously, slipped down to the lower deck to get the tables. When they were set up in front of the dance floor, Lucas and Sonia began laying out the food. In honour of their location, they had decided on a selection of curries, dal, chapati, several rice dishes, and a vegetable salad. Andie hovered the Andromeda over the reflecting pool in front of the mausoleum, and set the holographic projectors to simulate a window across the width of the dance floor. Arranging themselves along one side of the table, the friends sat down to lunch, with the (second) best view of the day. The sun was just rising, and they watched the white marble building turn shades of yellow and orange.

As they ate, Sonia entertained them with snippets of information about the Taj Mahal. It was a touching, yet tragic story. It had been constructed by the Mughal emperor Shah Jahān in the early seventeenth century, to commemorate his favourite wife, and he had allegedly planned to build his own mausoleum across the river, connecting the two by a bridge. Alas, that dream was not to be, as he was deposed by his son some years later and imprisoned for life. After his death, the story did have a happy ending, if one could call it such; he was laid to rest beside his wife in the magnificent work of art that he had built.

After lunch, Lucas conferred with Andie as to the best way to get the team on the ground. It was decided that they would go down in a shuttle, as there would have been limited space to land the Andromeda secretly. Everybody took their places in the Sagittarius, and Andie landed them among the trees to the side of the pool. It was a tight squeeze for the shuttle, but it allowed them to disembark into the shade, out of the direct sight of any onlookers. Lucas handed them their tickets, and gave them free rein to wander about as they wished.

When it was time to go, with their heads filled with history and their hearts with wonder, they walked back through the garden to the Sagittarius, with only a little confusion over which tree they had parked next to. Back aboard the Andromeda, they sat down to compare notes on what they had seen, and the ship started moving towards their next stop. Lucas had chosen to visit Petra before the pyramids, as it would have too difficult to wander around Giza unnoticed before opening hours.

Exiting the shuttle in one of the city's sandstone canyons, they had only to walk around the corner before they spied The Treasury, carved directly into the cliff face, and instantly recognisable from its appearance in the movie "*Indiana Jones and the Last Crusade*". Its Greek-style facade was in such perfect condition, it looked as if the cliff itself had grown around the building, rather than the other way around. Though the structure was awe-inspiring, there was more to the city than pop-culture references, and after they had taken a short time to admire the workmanship of the Treasury, they boarded the shuttle again and were taken to the open spaces where most of the city lay.

The Rose-coloured City was too extensive to see much of it, in the time they had, but what they did manage to see was incredible. The Amphitheatre, tombs, palaces, and various other buildings were the product of exquisite craftsmanship. Like the other man-made wonders they had seen on the trip, it was humbling to know that it had all been done with primitive tools, and none of the advantages of modern building techniques. As at Angkor Wat, the water management scheme in place at Petra would have been the envy of any modern city, and showed an understanding of hydrodynamics well in advance of what one might have expected from such early civilisations.

All too soon, it was time to move on again, and they climbed back aboard the Sagittarius for their return to the Andromeda, with only the faint *clunk* of the docking mechanism betraying the fact that, in the last few seconds, they had ascended two-thousand metres.

"We may as well wait in the shuttle – it'll only take a couple of minutes to get to our next destination," Lucas said, as people began to rise from their seats. Waiting patiently in the comfortable leather seats, the anticipation was mounting for their visit to the last of the Seven Wonders of the Ancient World that still existed.

Andie found an out-of-the-way spot to put the Sagittarius down, and the little group walked out of the shadows behind the Sphinx to mingle with the other tourists. Though they could not get up close and personal with the Sphinx, it was possible to walk right up to the pyramids themselves. Standing beside the three-ton blocks that made up the multi-million ton edifice that was the Great Pyramid, it was impossible to avoid a sense of insignificance. Thousands of people had laboured for twenty years to construct this monument that had been the world's tallest structure for millennia, and all to commemorate one man.

When Lucas noticed the heat, and archaeological overload, getting to his people, he got them all back behind the Sphinx, and aboard the shuttle. With nobody on the ground any wiser, the Sagittarius shot up at tremendous speed to dock with its mother ship. Ice-cold beer awaited them in the lounge, and Andie performed a slow circuit of the site, putting the big screen back on.

With time to kill before dinner, and the feeling that his friends had done enough walking for the day, Lucas had Andie take them on a fly-by sightseeing tour, taking in the Great Wall of China, Stonehenge, Derewar Fort in Pakistan, Bucharest's Palace of the Parliament, Mount Rushmore, the Colosseum, the Sagrada Familia in Barcelona, Neuschwanstein castle, and the Moai of Easter Island. Their bird's-eye view afforded them a perspective on these places that few got the chance to experience, and the

3D nature of the holographic projection made it a far more satisfying way to see them than simply as still images, or on video.

Nearing ten o'clock, the Andromeda was lining up for their last stop, and Lucas handed out tickets and passable facsimiles of their passports, to ensure that they did not get into trouble on the ground. Dinner would be served in front of the screen, before they took a shuttle to the surface for a closer view of their destination.

As Andie hovered at two-and-a-half-thousand metres in the Peruvian Andes, the team took their seats, having picked up their meals from the galley, and Andie turned on the projection. In front of them was the impressive sight of Machu Picchu, the fifteenth-century Inca royal estate. With the mist rising from the valleys below the mountain-top complex, and the morning sun beginning to shine over the tops of the eastern peaks, it was truly a magnificent view.

After yet another delicious meal – it was still hard for them to believe that the dishes were built, rather than cooked – Lucas got Andie to set them down out of sight near the entrance. Unbeknownst to her passengers, she had been slowly adjusting the atmosphere aboard the Andromeda, so that they would be better able to deal with the altitude outside. They would still be at a disadvantage compared to those visitors who had already spent several days in the country, but she hoped that the worst of the altitude sickness would be avoided.

Tickets in hand, they approached the gatekeeper.

"Good morning. Welcome to Machu Picchu!"

He checked their tickets and passports, easily accepting the fake documents, and waved them through the gate.

"Enjoy your visit!"

Thanking him, the group walked through, breathing heavily in the rarified air, and began to explore. They marvelled at the huge stone blocks that had been put together without gaps, and the drainage channels that collected the rainwater from the terraces into large cisterns. Though the mountain was in a seismically active region, the methods of construction were such that hundreds of years of earthquakes had not obliterated the complex.

"Some of these blocks weigh over fifty tons," said Sonia, "and the Incas moved them without wheels or animals. It's not just what you can see, either – they basically took the mountain-top off, and created a massive, solid foundation."

They were starting to struggle in the thin atmosphere now, and it was decided not to climb either of the two nearby peaks. Many people did so, to get a better overall view of Machu Picchu, but the Ad Astra team had already had a better view than any of these other tourists could have imagined. The team said their farewells to Machu Picchu, and returned to their rendezvous point, to be picked up by the Sagittarius and returned to the Andromeda.

Over drinks in the lounge, Lucas asked, "Has everyone had a good weekend?"

"I can't believe you even have to ask, mate," said Tom. "That was the most incredible trip anyone could ever have! I can scarcely believe that we saw all those places around the world in just over a day – and then there was the moon! Oh. My. God. We went to the *moon*!"

"It was amazing. Thank you so much!" said Cath. Still a bit giddy from the lack of oxygen on the Peruvian mountain, though Andie had restored the correct onboard atmosphere, she was barely touching her drink. In fact, everyone was taking it easy on the alcohol. The pleasures of intoxication were a poor substitute for the buzz they had enjoyed as they zipped around the globe.

"Well, I'm thrilled that you all enjoyed it so much. You've given so much to Ad Astra, and it was only fair that we give something back. We wouldn't be where we are now if it weren't for your hard work."

He raised his glass to them before continuing.

"Now, ninety-five percent of the trip was about having fun, but I'd like to address the other five percent."

His friends looked at him, and at each other, quizzically. They hadn't expected work to rear its ugly head.

"Can anyone tell me the underlying theme of what we saw?"

The team silently contemplated their experiences over the weekend; Uluru, Angkor Wat, the moon, the Taj Mahal, Petra, Giza, the Great Wall,

Stonehenge, Derewar Fort, the Palace of the Parliament, Mount Rushmore, the Colosseum, the Sagrada Familia, Neuschwanstein, and Easter Island.

After a moment, Alison spoke up. "Well, apart from Uluru and the moon, you left out all the amazing *natural* wonders we could have visited. Everything else was man-made."

"You can discount Uluru," Lucas said. "We only included that because it was on our doorstep, so to speak, but leave the moon visit on the list – there's something that ties them all together."

"I think I see where you're going with this," said Michelle. "They were all works of enormous complexity, done with primitive tools. By current standards, at least. I mean, my *phone* has thousands of times more computing power than the hardware that landed Armstrong and Aldrin on the moon."

Giving her a thumbs-up, Lucas said, "That's right, Michelle. They were all extremely ambitious projects, and in many cases, the dream of a single person, but with ingenuity and determination, they managed to achieve that dream. It just goes to show how much can be accomplished with a bold vision and the resources to make it happen."

As the moral of the story registered with the others, there were nods of understanding. It was clear that Lucas had wanted them to see the similarities between those architectural marvels, and their own project.

Rudi said, "I see your point, Lucas, but there are some major differences between us and them. Firstly, we are using technology well beyond what is considered contemporary, we will achieve our goal much more quickly than them, and hopefully, our works will not be abandoned and left to rot!"

"I think what he is trying to say, Rudi, is that we should never let our enthusiasm wane, and that we should take inspiration from the ancients. *Nil mortalibus ardui est* – nothing is too difficult for mankind," said Carine.

"Thank you, Carine. That's exactly right," Lucas said. "We've done some great things, and we've faced some challenges. We can't afford to get complacent, or to lose heart. We have so much more to accomplish, and the challenges yet to come are likely to be tougher than what we've seen so far. Sonia and I just wanted to remind you of what can be done when someone has the resolve and resources to do it.

"We've got money, we've got Andie, and we've got a population that is ready and willing to change. If you ever feel like we're ahead of the game, and can slacken off, or that the obstacles are too great, just remember that those ancients never gave up, and never gave in. This is all too important for us to fall.

"We have the utmost confidence in all of you. I wouldn't have blamed Sonia or Fats if they'd had doubts after being kidnapped or shot at, but to their credit, they got right back on the horse, and yelled, 'Yee-hah!'. Among other things." He winked at Sonia, remembering her mood after that incident.

Even now, the thought of what the two men had done caused her eyes to narrow, and she set her chin, vowing that she would never give anyone the satisfaction of beating her.

Seeing the familiar fire rekindled in her, Lucas grinned, putting a hand on her arm. "Easy, there," he said. "There's no threat today."

The colour rose in her cheeks as she remembered that she was among friends, and she pushed the anger back down inside.

"The thing is, guys," continued Lucas, "we're proud of you. What we've done so far is tiny compared to what lies ahead, and we're going to see it through as a team. Are we going to let some four-thousand-year-old civilisation do a better job at creating something to last through the ages?"

A resounding "No!" echoed through the lounge of the Andromeda as the Ad Astra people accepted the challenge.

EPILOGUE

Curled up on the couch with Lucas, in front of the fire at their hillside home, Sonia gazed at him proudly.

"Eleven months, babe. From mowing lawns and driving a rusty old Hilux, to visiting the moon in a spaceship *you* built. Have I told you how awesome I think that is?"

Lucas stretched his feet out towards the flames, tipping his head back and giving her a wry smile. "You don't have to tell me – I pinch myself on a regular basis to make sure I'm not dreaming."

She snuggled closer to him, and he dropped his arm around her.

"If it is a dream, I'm glad I'm part of it," she murmured, and he held her tighter, in total agreement.

"You know," she went on, "I used to look at all the problems we – people – were causing in the world, and I really tried to do my bit. I recycled, I used public transport, I checked to see if my food was ethically sourced, but I never saw any change in the state of the planet. It was getting so demoralising, thinking that my own efforts weren't making a damn bit of difference. Then you came along with your magic box, and turned everything on its head.

"You made it so easy and worthwhile for people to change. Doing the right thing always seemed to be the expensive option, and now clean power and clean transport are cheaper than the alternatives."

"It's a good start, all right," he responded. "Materials production is more environmentally viable – the new steel-making technologies are far more efficient, and Andie has some great recipes for bio-plastics. When the power companies are finished with their generators, we'll be able to start getting those in ships and planes ... that reminds me – we should approach Boeing and co to give them time to figure out how to refit the planes for electric props."

Sonia looked up at him. "There are probably a few more than nine-thousand large aircraft in the world's fleet – we'll have to whip up a few more generators by then. Then there are the ships ... The CF factories will have to work overtime to make enough units to run those, as well as gearing up for the consumer models!"

Andie chimed in with, "There are approximately twenty-five-thousand commercial aircraft in operation, excluding private and military planes. We'll eventually have to put out a system small enough for those, too. The shipping register shows around fifty-thousand merchant ships, and we may have to factor in military vessels as well. At the pace we managed to get the generators for the power companies built, it will take up to six months to supply enough to cover the demand. We'll definitely need more factories."

While not the billion or so small generators he expected to build, Lucas was still somewhat taken aback at the numbers. Still, creating more factories wouldn't be a problem, and it had the added advantage of creating more jobs.

"We can do that," he said. "Crunch the numbers, Andie, and get Cath and Jake onto it."

"You know, one day the demand for the generators is going to drop off ... when every household has one, when every airplane and ship uses one, when all the cars have been converted. I hope you've got another gizmo lined up for those workers when that happens," Sonia said.

"Oh, ye of little faith," scoffed Andie. "There will always be something new to build, even if he doesn't know what it is yet!"

"Hey! I've still got plenty of ideas!" Lucas retorted, tapping his temple. It was true; he did have more ideas rattling around in his head. Whether they were applicable to the Grand Plan was another question.

In the meantime, however, there was still plenty of work to do before those factories needed to be retooled. In particular, he had plans for Ad Astra Space Vehicle Construction. He might not have interstellar travel cracked just yet, but there was still a lot of space in the immediate neighbourhood that held untapped potential; potential that the world, with Ad Astra's technology, could unlock.

www.ingramcontent.com/pod-product-compliance
Lightning Source LLC
Chambersburg PA
CBHW071221250626
47163CB00001B/63